HERITAGE OF SHAME

MEG HUTCHINSON

Heritage of Shame

Hodder & Stoughton

First published in Great Britain in 2003 by Hodder & Stoughton
A division of Hodder Headline

2 4 6 8 10 9 7 5 3 1

A CIP catalogue record for this title is
available from the British Library

ISBN 0 340 82484 0

Typeset by Palimpsest Book Production Limited,
Polmont, Stirlingshire

Printed and bound in Great Britain by
Clays Ltd, St Ives plc
Mackays of Chatham plc, Chatham, Kent

Hodder & Stoughton
A division of Hodder Headline
338 Euston Road
London NW1 3BH

My grateful thanks to David Mills and the staff of Walsall Leather Museum for their kind help and advice. Any mistake in my attempt to portray the very highly skilled work of saddle-making is, I assure the reader, very much my own.

Meg Hutchinson

Output of the leather industry during World War One was prodigious, with saddles numbering in excess of half a million. A hint of the efforts of the saddler can be detected in an extract from a speech quoted in *Saddlery and Harness*, 18 March 1916. The chairman of Messrs D. Mason and Sons Ltd of Walsall reported that in the two years (1914–15) 'since the outbreak of war, in addition to many thousands of sets of gun harness and infantry equipment they [this firm] had supplied over 100,000 military saddles'.

I

'I want nothing of Jacob Corby . . . and that includes you!'

Eyes, dark-ringed and bright with fever, played over a gaunt hard-faced woman.

'I came to this house for one reason only, that being to give you the benefit of a doubt I never truly held, a doubt which said you could not possibly be the same spiteful, selfish, cold-hearted woman a child of six years was so afraid of. I see that memory was not false, you have not changed . . . but then neither did your brother.'

'My brother was a fool!' Eyes glittering like ice-bound stones Clara Mather glared at the thin young woman who held one hand protectively across a swollen stomach. 'Jacob was a fool!' she repeated scathingly. 'But you are a bigger one if you think to come marching back laying claim to what I have worked to keep alive; you will never have the Glebe Works, I will see you beg in the streets—'

'No, Aunt, that you will never see.' Anne Corby's quiet interruption rang with contempt.

Harsh with scorn the older woman laughed, her cold eyes sweeping the swollen stomach. 'No? Then how else do you expect to keep your bastard?'

'I will keep it.' The young head lifted proudly. 'How need not concern you. Be assured I will never look to you for help though every stick and stone, every penny of what you claim to be yours is rightfully mine. As the daughter and only child of Jacob Corby, everything he owned is mine.'

Quick as it was, Anne Corby caught the flash of fear leap in those hostile eyes and at the same moment she realised she had been wrong in one thing: she was no longer that frightened child going in fear of her father's sister, rather the woman was afraid of *her*, of her taking away all she rejoiced in. But in that there had been no change – Jacob Corby's daughter wanted nothing of him!

'I see you recognise the truth of what I say,' Anne continued, ignoring the twitch of pain beneath her hand, 'that the Glebe Works and all that goes with it is my inheritance. But keep it, Aunt, and every night before you sleep thank your brother, thank Jacob Corby for leading his wife and daughter into hell, thank God for the delusion that took him half across the world and left you sole mistress in his stead.'

She had never thought to speak that way. She stood outside the house that had held her childhood and her dreams, as well as the fears she had remembered during the long days and longer nights of bone-racking journeys her father had insisted on making while living out the mission he believed had been given him from heaven. Anne only now realised she was trembling. Wasn't it true she had hoped for some sign of welcome, for the offer of a home? But one look at her father's sister, one glance at those remorseless eyes had told her she was as unwelcome here as she and her parents had been in so many places. She had seen and understood her reception today but, unlike her mother, she had been able to turn her back and leave.

Yes, she had turned her back, left the house which was truly hers . . . to go where? The question left her empty, draining the last of her anger. Without money, with nothing to sell which would raise enough for a night's lodging there would be nothing but the hedgerow. Anne Corby was used to that, but the child? She drew in a breath against a further twinge of pain; what if her baby should come during the night?

Was it time, had it been nine months since . . . ? A sharper twinge sent her stumbling against the wall surrounding the house though it was not pain in her stomach had her cry out but the wave of horror which filled her mind, blotting out all but the memory of that day. She had called at a tiny wood-built house asking for a glass of water. The man who answered had smiled and though his curious form of language had been unintelligible to her he had understood her request and, pointing across the yard, had led her to the well. She had taken the ladle he filled from the rope-strung bucket, drinking her fill and smiling her gratitude as she handed back the crudely carved instrument.

But her thanks had not been enough, he had caught her wrist, sending the ladle spinning from her hand, and at the same moment brought his bearded mouth hard on hers, his free hand pawing at her breasts. She had screamed when his mouth lifted, tried to twist away from him but his strength had been too much, and laughing he had thrown her to ground still firm with the last traces of winter. She had begged him to let her go, her terrified eyes asking what her foreign tongue could not; but though he could not have failed to know the revulsion coursing through her he had freed his body from heavy peasant trousers then snatched at her own clothing, and with a grunt had forced himself into her. How long she had screamed, how long he had pushed into her she could never fathom, she could only remember the shout as he rolled off her, the shout followed by a bucket of water thrown over her, and the man's wife driving a heavy boot against her ribs. And the man had laughed! His clothing still open he had stood over her and laughed!

'Be you unwell, wench?'

With her breath riding terrified cries, the nightmare of

memory drowned the voice beneath the coarse laughter filling her mind, until a rough shake had her sag heavily against the wall.

'Lord, wench, be you alright? You look as if it's the devil himself you've seen.'

The devil might have been more merciful, he might have taken her down into the fiery pit her father had been so fond of preaching about; instead she was left to endure the hell her life had become. It had been hard before the child had begun to grow in her womb, but once it could no longer be disguised . . .

'Be you alright? Can I take you inside?'

Swallowing the nausea that memory always brought, Anne shook her head. 'No, no thank you.'

'I thinks as you should go in. Judging by the looks of you it seem you be close upon your time. Come, I'll help you to the door.'

'No!' Brushing the hand extended towards her, Anne straightened then swayed as a sudden rush of blood had her brain swimming.

'That be it!' The voice was suddenly sharp. 'There be no two ways of playing . . . you needs be inside.'

There was concern beneath the brusque tone, but as her arm was taken Anne pulled back. 'Not – not in there. I – I am not welcome in that house.'

'Not welcome!' A face came closer to her own, eyes set in a thousand tiny lines looking deep into hers. 'You be her . . . that babby. You be Jacob Corby's little wench – Anne.' The lined eyes smiled. 'You be Anne Corby, least that was your name when your father took you from here but I see it is you'll have a different one now.'

Pain, sharp in its warning, had her hand go to her swollen abdomen. If she said nothing of the truth maybe . . . but lies, whether the self-believed kind her father had told or the sort of blatant one hovering so close to her tongue, neither could mask the truth for ever.

'No.' She gathered her courage as the face pulled away. 'No, my name is not different. Now you see why those doors are closed to me.'

The fingers grasping Anne's arm lessened their strength but did not withdraw. 'That's a reason and though I don't be in agreement with it I can't deny another's rights to follow their own judgement; but I'll lay a pound to any man's penny it don't be the only reason you've been turned from that door, nor be it the true one neither. It's my thinking the Glebe Works be at back of it. But where's your father, wench? He'll soon put paid to his sister's high-handed ways.'

With a cry she could not hold back breaking from her, Anne clutched her stomach, and the hand holding her arm went swiftly about her waist, its strength supporting her. The voice was brusque once more: 'That business can best be left to Jacob Corby but you, wench, you need a bed and a woman's hand.'

So her brother's child had returned! Clara Mather paced restlessly about the sitting room of Butcroft House. Jacob had fathered no more children, certainly no son or the girl would not have referred to the property as being hers . . . her inheritance. Clara's fingers clasped painfully together. The inheritance was Quenton's – her son would be master of the Glebe Works, her son and no other!

Was it not Clara herself who had worked on Jacob, fed his fantasy of bringing the Lord to the heathen masses, encouraged his delusions of a God-ordained mission to carry his message to the darkest corners of the world by always finishing every family prayer with one of her own, speaking the words aloud while pretending they existed only in the privacy of her heart, murmuring a prayer for someone to

be sent, one who would be brave enough to carry on the
work of the first evangelists, to follow in the footsteps of
Peter and of Paul and carry the Word to foreign lands.
Maybe the Lord had not heard her plea but her brother
had. Jacob Corby had gathered his wife and daughter and
followed a dream she had so fervently hoped would carry
them into oblivion. But the child had returned. Except the
child was no longer a child, Jacob's daughter was nigh full
grown, in a year she would be twenty-one – an age when,
if she wished, she could marry freely. With a husband at her
side she could have everything! Clara's eyes narrowed, their
gleam one of pure venom. If Jacob's daughter married, then
all of her own hopes for Quenton, her dreams of her own
son becoming master of Glebe Works would be ashes in the
wind. But would a man take a woman who had a child born
out of wedlock? The hope died as it came. There was many a
man would be willing enough even though he took a bastard
as well as a bride when that bride brought with her a dowry
of Jacob Corby's property. Twenty-one – an age when she
could take everything into her own hands.

Oh yes, she had said she wanted nothing of Jacob, nothing
of what had been his, but how long before that tune changed,
how long before she was back in this house, a lawyer at her
side? But she would not have it, she would not take what
belonged to Quenton, what she, his mother, had kept for
him. He was the rightful inheritor, he the one her brother
had seen as following after himself as master of those works,
acknowledged him in all but the written word. Then had come
along Viola Bedworth with her pretty curls and wide eyes full
of innocence, and within three months Jacob had a wife and in
due course he had a daughter . . . an heir of his own body.

But marriage had not turned her brother from his path,
more the opposite. A heart trusting in the Lord and a life
led according to the teaching of Chapel had rewarded him

with a loving dutiful wife here on earth; carry that teaching to the foreigner and what rewards would be his in heaven? His sister had agreed. She too would dearly love to carry the Word of the Lord to non-believers, to spread the wonderful message as those first disciples had spread it but the Lord's hand rested on her brother, he and not she had been chosen for the work. Those had been the words so often murmured with a tearful sniff and they had not been lost. He must go the way the Lord pointed, Jacob had said; he could not deny the call.

The call! Clara Mather's face twisted disparagingly. Even as a child her brother had been a fool. With his eyes closed to reality he had only ever seen what he wanted to see and in the call he saw a halo sitting on his own head but none of the hardship which must rest on the shoulders of his wife.

You must not worry over what you leave behind, Clara had encouraged. God goes with you, brother, but He will not desert me, He will give me the strength to safeguard your interest here and keep it against your return . . . only keep it in hope you will never return had been what was behind that encouragement. Yet in spite of hope, despite her dreams, her brother's daughter had returned and with her a child in the womb; a bastard? That was probably the truth of it but the father did not matter, it was still Anne Corby's child and Jacob Corby's grandchild . . . another claimant to the business Jacob had never shown real interest in. It should have been left to her but their father thought as most men of his time and many yet still thought, a woman did not have the brain for business, and so the whole inheritance had been Jacob's. Teeth clenched behind thin lips, both hands pressed tight against her dark skirts, Clara Mather's eyes were iron hard. She had run the business, kept it flourishing for fourteen years and she would not see her son robbed of it now, robbed of what was his, what *must* be his. No, neither Anne Corby

nor the fruit of her whoring would take from Quenton . . . his
mother would make certain of that.

'Mother . . . Mother, help me . . . please!' Trapped in a world
of pain Anne cried to the figure that watched but made no
move to come to her. 'Mother, I asked for water. Believe me,
I did no more . . .' It ended in a cry, her whole body contorting
in a spasm of all-consuming agony but still the figure shrouded
in black remained still. 'The man . . . he . . . he seemed . . . he
smiled as he handed me water and then . . . Mother, I speak
the truth . . . please! Oh please, I need you . . .'

Wave after wave of searing pain dissecting her words Anne
reached a hand to the figure but it turned and walked away,
leaving her to fall into a pit of shadows, shadows which came
and went until out of them stepped her father, his gaunt face
twisted with disgust, a hand raised in condemnation.

Harlot! Child of Satan! Deceiver of men!

Eyes brilliant in their anger stared at her.

*You will burn in the fires of hell! The Lord has turned His face
from you, whore and Jezebel!*

'No!' Anne's head twisted from each invective, the words an
almost physical blow. 'Father, please . . . you must listen . . .
it . . . it was rape . . .'

Bent over the perspiring girl, Unity Hurley's mouth clamped
in a firm line. Stood on her own two feet a wench could deny
the truth but laid on the childbed, racked with agony, that
truth would reveal itself. Pain such as this young woman
was suffering was a broom which swept the mind clean of
lies, it left no corner in which they could hide. Rape – that
most vile of crimes a man could commit against a woman –
rape had seen the beginning of a life now struggling to enter
the world.

'Not much longer,' she murmured pityingly, 'just a little
while and you can rest. It will soon be over.'

But that was a lie no broom could sweep away. The pain of this night might be soon over but the real agony, did this girl but know it, was just beginning for her. The birth pangs would bring her a child but they would also bring a life of misery. The man had taken his sport; the woman would pay the price! Supporting the tiny head as it emerged, Unity glanced as the ashen-faced girl slumped against the pillows, dark-ringed eyes closed with fatigue. For Jacob Corby's girl the price would be high.

Lost in her shadowed world Anne heard none of the woman's words, only the pain was real, the pain and the odium blazing in her father's eyes.

'Father!' It was a helpless whisper, a cry for understanding and forgiveness but as her own hand reached towards the one raised in censure the tall figure merged into shadows which swirled and receded then swirled again, each time filled with faces – a bearded, grease-marked face which laughed as it lifted from her body, the angry face of a woman who threw a bucket of icy water, her mother, tears streaming down her sunken cheeks, and behind them all her father . . . but now he lay peacefully asleep.

'Father.' She whispered again but the murmur was caught by a sudden cold breeze which carried it to merge with a louder, stronger voice.

'. . . *in the true and certain knowledge* . . .'

Beneath closed eyes Anne Corby stared at the rough wooden box, crudely cut corners no proof against the icy blasts slowly hardening freshly excavated mounds of black earth to stone. The touch of winter gripped more tightly by the day. Soon it would be too late . . .

'. . . *ashes to ashes* . . .'

At her shoulder, huddled in her thin coat, her mother's sob was snatched by the wind.

'. . . *ashes to ashes* . . .'

The hard voice strafed against her half-frozen ears but was lost against the voice of her thoughts. Did it matter the box was no protection against the wind, could it make the body inside it more stiff than it had been when living, was the blood more cold now than when it had coursed its wasted journeys through the veins of the man lying inside it? A man as devoid of feeling in life as he was now, a dead empty shell.

Turning her shoulder, seeking some protection from the nerve-deadening gusts screaming in from the steppes, she fought the rising urge to walk away, to ignore what was happening to the remains of the man she had so very long ago grown to hate, to leave this cemetery now, to ignore the man who had so often ignored her. But she would stay, stay for her mother's sake, stay while her father was lowered to his grave. But she could pretend no pity, no love.

Closed eyes were no barrier against the pictures playing in her mind as she watched herself standing at the open grave, heard her own thoughts as she stared at the plain box, no flower alleviating its severity. But then there had never been any alleviation of her father's severity so it was a perfect match. A hard, self-opinionated man, he had driven his wife and daughter as hard as he had driven himself, giving very little time or thought to either of them; Jacob Corby had had little time for anything but his God.

And now you will meet Him, Father. Anne watched the priest raise his hand over the coffin. May He reward you as you deserve, give you the crown you strove for by dragging my mother, half-starved, across the world.

'It be all done, wench, the child be 'ere.'

Unity Hurley gathered the tiny living bundle into her arms as she looked at the young woman she had helped give birth. Seeing the rapid movement behind the mauve-shadowed lids she shook her head. The wench was suffering still, but from a pain no midwife could heal. Wrapping the infant in a piece of white cloth she laid it aside and covered its heat-soaked mother with a blanket.

But Anne heard no word of sympathy, felt no touch of comfort. In that strange netherworld, held in its greyness, she felt only the rush of air, bone-cracking in its coldness, as it swept across a tiny churchyard whistling through trees stripped of every leaf, moaning as it whirled about headstones in its unseen search.

In the bed Unity had laid her on, Anne Corby shivered as the freezing fingers of that wind seemed to wrap about the thin figure she was watching – a figure she knew was her own – and seemed to clutch at ragged skirts, pulling with breath-snatching gusts to the very edge of that open pit, dragging her even now as her father had dragged her in life, forcing her to follow his footsteps into death itself.

Trembling as from intense cold, she did not hear Unity call for the bricks left heating in the oven or feel their warmth as they were laid beside her; her closed eyes saw only the glittering drops of holy water, her ears heard only their tinkling when they fell like tiny frozen tears on that wooden box, and her heart said they were the only tears Jacob Corby deserved.

Watching the shadows of semi-consciousness she saw herself dig the heels of worn-out boots into the hard ground then lower her eyes, not wanting to see more. She could not remember a time when she had truly felt love for the man who had fathered her and she could shed no tears for him now, but her being ached for the frail woman sobbing quietly beside her, the one person in her whole life who had shown her any love, her mother, Viola.

'*Whither thou goest I will go.*'

The umbilical cord severed, Unity Hurley paused in her washing of the girl's bloodstained legs as the words whispered into the now quiet bedroom. What horror had this wench suffered? One thing was clear, rape was not the all of it.

'*Whither thou goest . . .*'

The familiar words repeating in her shadow-misted mind, Anne saw herself reach for the slight, black-draped figure, drawing it close against her.

'*. . . I will go.*'

That Viola Corby had done: true to her Old Testament namesake, she had followed the journeyings of her loved one. But, unlike the Biblical Ruth, her journeying had not ended in happiness, she had been trawled from country to country, following without complaint, trying only to protect her child, to give her the love her father never gave. Convinced he held a mission from God Jacob Corby had marched his pathetic family across the continent of Africa and on into Europe.

Coughing, Anne had no knowledge of the gentle hand which wiped her mouth or felt her hot forehead. She felt only the acid gall rise in her throat, glad it prevented her joining in the prayer fighting its losing battle against a screaming wind. May Jacob Corby's God show him forgiveness, for his daughter never would!

2

'The child be a scrap but all things considered that's no surprise. But the wench, it be her I feel sorry for. She was all but done for when you fetched her here, and the birthing of that babby, well –' Unity Hurley shook her grey head as she looked at the man sat finishing his evening meal '– the girl is going to need the help of heaven to get over that; days and nights of pain teks its toll of healthy women but when one be underfed as that one . . . all I can say is God help her!'

Turning to the fireplace gleaming silver-black from the hours of her life given to polishing it, Unity busied herself with a large black-bottomed kettle, hiding the concern she could not dismiss. Laban had always had a soft heart, he would give help to any who needed it and she would not deny him that, but to bring home a girl already in the throes of labour, a girl whose own family had turned her away . . . and that family supplying Laban with lorinery. Clara Mather would not take kindly to that.

Like many another in Darlaston she knew the vindictive strike of that woman's hand, had seen her father destroyed by it when it took away his job. Being given the sack had robbed his family of food but it had robbed him of more, he had lost his dignity, the pride a man felt in keeping his family, and he had died a broken man. That was the action of a grasping woman, so what action would her vengeance take – and she would be certain to visit vengeance on Laban once news of the delivery of that child reached her ears – would it be the same spite which could cause them to suffer as her father had suffered?

'I couldn't leave the wench, couldn't turn me back on her.' As though reading his wife's thoughts, Laban Hurley rose quietly from the table.

'I know you couldn't and neither should you,' Unity answered quickly, masking the guilt of her own thoughts.

'But . . . ?'

Turning to face him, all of Unity's dread showed on her face. 'But,' she said, 'you asks me "but" when you knows yourself the nature of her who lives along of Butcroft House, knows the spite of her. Clara Mather wants none of that niece of hers, you said that yourself, told it as that wench upstairs told it to you, and what Clara Mather don't want don't find no place in Darlaston and for sure not here in Blockall.'

'So what do we do?' Laban smiled at the woman he had married forty years before. 'Would you have me lift the girl from that bed, carry her and her newborn to the workhouse?'

'No!' Unity's head shook rapidly. 'You know I wouldn't want that, Laban Hurley, but – but are you not feared of what might happen?'

Taking her in his arms the love that had endured from his years as a lad surged fresh in Laban's heart. 'I don't be feared of nothing so long as you be with me,' he said, kissing the lined cheek, 'and the day don't be yet dawned when I be feared of Clara Mather.'

He was not feared. Unity rested her head against her husband's chest. But maybe he should be, maybe they all should be. Jacob Corby's sister had been resentful all her life and with the return of that man's daughter, and now a grandson to challenge her, who could tell what resentment and spite might turn to . . . or upon whom its shadow would fall?

★　　★　　★

'I tell you it was her!'

Across the small town, in the house her father had built then bequeathed to her brother, Clara Mather glared at her son.

'She came to this house, stood in this very room. Do you think I don't recognise my own niece!'

She should recognise her. Quenton Mather moved to a chair and dropped into it. No doubt his mother had dreamed of that child and its parents for fourteen years, dreaded the day when one or all of them would return, and now it had happened.

'Then if it was Anne Corby where is she now, why is she not here?'

'Like father like son!' Clara spat. 'He thought things just took care of themselves but they don't. Jacob's daughter is not here because I sent her packing.'

'You sent her packing.' Quenton sounded amused. 'And what of your brother, did you pack him off also?'

'Jacob is dead.'

'And his wife?'

What of his wife? Clara's fingers tightened. There had been no mention of her. If she still lived she was Jacob's next of kin, his legal beneficiary. But if Viola were alive would she not be with her daughter, the child she had doted on? Of course there was the possibility she had been left to rest somewhere, had let the girl come to Butcroft House in her place . . . There were many possibilities but none that could not be taken care of, and her sister-in-law when found would receive all of that care, just as would her child and her offspring!

'Your aunt was not spoken of,' Clara answered, feeling her son's eyes on her. 'Seeing the state of the daughter, how exhausted she looked, then I supposed her to have remained behind to rest.'

'So when next our relatives pay us a visit there will most likely be two of them?'

'Three!' Clara replied bluntly. 'Jacob's daughter was carrying a child.'

A child! Quenton's eyes narrowed. One more contender in the game. No wonder his mother was agitated, she could see the fruit of her malice being snatched from beneath her nose; but if she lost the race then he lost the trophy, Butcroft House together with the Glebe Works would belong to the cousin he detested.

'That puts a new aspect on things,' he said, rising to his feet. 'A daughter and soon a grandchild; I would say Uncle Jacob has left his affairs nicely worked out.'

Watching him walk from the room Clara felt her anger flare. His father had much the same thought. Married to the daughter of the owner of the Glebe Works he had imagined his own affairs nicely worked out, but she had had other ideas. Clara Mather had no intention of being the docile little wife, grateful to be married, content to follow a man in all things and have a say in nothing, acquiescent and malleable. No, that had not been suitable to her, so she had changed it. Slowly . . . so slowly! She had taken her time, always appearing so devoted, so caring of the husband who became gradually more and more ill, experiencing breathing difficulties and increasing tiredness.

'*You must be prepared.*'

Clara smiled as the often remembered words crept again into her mind. The doctor had murmured them on one of his visits, visits she timed to fall well between those bouts. Her husband, he had said, was suffering a disease of the heart, one which could end his life quite suddenly. And so it had, except the real cause of death was a little extra dose of the poison she had been adding to the prescribed medicine. Aconite, the common Monkshood also known as Wolfsbane was a very useful plant . . . and it still grew in a corner of the garden!

Unity Hurley touched the brow of the girl lying half conscious in the narrow iron-framed bed and felt the heat of fever. The girl had given her all in bringing her child into the world, now only heaven could help her. Laying a cool wet cloth where her hand had been she collected bowl and towel then, before leaving the bedroom, murmured a prayer to ask heaven's help, but Anne Corby neither heard nor felt. Cocooned in her grey world she watched those terrible yesterdays, stared across the black hole which waited to close over the remains of her father. Through the dark mist of semi-consciousness a priest dressed in long black robe and high black hat of the Russian Orthodox Church lifted a hand, tracing the sign of the cross while intoning his final invocation to the Almighty, asking His blessing on the soul of the man who had sacrificed a wife and daughter on the altar of self-righteousness.

Behind their fragile shield her eyes followed the movement of icy air weaving the breath of the priest into delicate lacy patterns of white hoar frost before laying them reverently across his dark, bush-like beard.

His duty done the priest snapped his prayer book closed. It was too cold to be outdoors, too cold to be at the task of burying a foreigner; one more week and the ground would have been frozen solid, too hard for a grave to be dug and the body would have been stored in the waiting house on the outskirts of the village until spring, and he would have been in Roskoyeva's Inn with his feet on the stove and a pot of hot wine in his hand.

Without a word to either of the two women standing opposite him at the graveside he turned, thick fur-lined boots crunching his farewell on the ice-filmed snow as he hurried towards the huddle of houses grouped close around the tiny, spire-topped church as if they sought divine protection from the horrors of a fast-approaching winter.

Placing an arm about her mother's shoulders Anne held her against the drag of the wind. They were alone, there was no one in this whole vast continent who might help them or give them comfort, no other single human being stood with them in the bitterly cold cemetery; even the carter who had transported the rough coffin up the hill from the village had departed the exact moment his cart had been relieved of its burden.

In her trance-like state Anne watched herself gently turning her mother away from the black gash in the ground that would hold no headstone to tell of who lay buried there, her dreaming eyes following the marks of the cart's wheels, black serpentine lines creeping across the virgin whiteness of freshly fallen snow. She could not really blame the carter for leaving them, he need hold no loyalty towards perfect strangers, and she had long since forgone expecting sympathy. They were foreigners here, she and her mother, and until yesterday her father also, strangers in a strange land. Jacob Corby had dragged his family across the face of Africa, Europe and into Russia, month after long month in a lifetime of searching, and for what? With her free hand she pulled her shabby brown cloak from the clutch of wind which increased its fury, holding the thin cloth tight against her. What had Jacob Corby searched for except his own selfish salvation!

The picture real in her fevered mind, the thoughts returning as if new, Anne seemed to feel that same anger hard and chilling as the wind trying its damnedest to rip them apart while she held her mother close, the bones of her wasted body biting through the layers of their clothing.

Waste! That was the legacy Jacob Corby had bequeathed his wife, waste both of her body and of her life, and she, his daughter, hated him for it. She was glad he was dead, glad that the monotonous sermonising, which dismissed and denied every comfort to his own life and to theirs in the name of a God he preached as love, was silent for ever. Her father had looked for salvation but nowhere in her soul could she hope he had found it. Holding her mother as they stumbled together against the biting wind, she hoped only that he had found damnation.

Bending her head before the invisible screaming spiral that sought to hold them in that ice-bound cemetery, sought to force them back towards the open grave, to reunite the living with the dead, Anne Corby walked away from the remains of a father who had given her nothing but a lifetime of misery.

'Do you take me for a fool, Fanny Simkin? If I believe you then I believe in the Christmas fairy!'

'Then you best hang up your stocking, Polly wench, for this year it'll be filled to the top.'

As she pored over a fillet of steak Clara Mather's ear caught the talk of two women stood at the counter of the butcher's shop.

'Unity 'Urley buying teats . . . you'll tell me next her give birth to a babby and we both know that can't never happen for her be past childbearing long gone, same as we does, thank God! And Laban keeps no livestock that might need hand rearing so I reckon whoever told you that story were pulling your leg.'

'I'd have held to that belief meself if it weren't for what me own eyes seen. I'll take two of them but you trim the fat afore you weighs 'em, I can get fat for free along of the slaughter house!' Her attention temporarily transferred to the butcher, the woman pointed to a tray set with mutton chops then turned again to her friend, resuming their conversation.

'So what did them eyes o' yourn see?'

'They sees fat where there ain't none!' The butcher's remark was quick as he placed the chops on the scale.

'They sees plenty as some folk thinks they don't.' Her tone holding a hint of caution, the wax cherries on her bonnet nodding, the woman turned her face to his. 'Like where a certain somebody went after a certain shop closed last Saturday night . . . and who that somebody went with.'

Whipping the chops from the scale the butcher turned to a table holding sheets of brown paper, the two women sharing a smile as they saw his colour deepen behind the generous whiskers.

'You can weigh me a pound of sausages,' the woman said as the brown-wrapped parcel was handed across the counter, 'and make sure it *be* a pound, these eyes be sharp to see weights and measures as they be to see faces!'

'So who said Unity 'Urley were buying teats?' The amusement afforded by the butcher's embarrassment fading against this newer gossip, the shorter woman pressed for its sharing.

Her keen look not straying for a second from the scales, her companion answered enthusiastically, ''Tweren't nobody had to tell me, I seen it for meself in the chemist shop along of Church Street, Unity 'Urley buying teats and one of them boat-shaped glass bottles for feeding of babbies whose mother's br—' She paused as the butcher looked up. 'Well, them as can't be fed natural, like.'

'But what would Unity be buying such for? Ain't as if her had any daughter, no nor any daughter-in-law come to that.'

The sausages now wrapped, the butcher took a silver coin from an outstretched hand, dropping it into a drawer set beneath the counter.

'That were what struck me.' The bringer of gossip waited while several copper coins were counted into her palm. 'Unity 'Urley don't 'ave no wench so who was it her were buying teats and bottles for? Ain't nobody I've heard of being delivered this last couple of weeks and when I asked old Doughty who it was they was fetched for he said as he d'ain't know.'

'Ar, well he would!' The second woman sniffed. 'He be so tight-mouthed he makes a mute look like a preacher!'

Having given the change the butcher rubbed both hands across his long apron. 'That be a good policy when some folk be around – listen but don't speak.'

'That be summat you should pay mind to then!' Red cherries bounced rapid as the answer their movement accompanied. 'One man's faults should be another man's lessons. You should learn more'n the butcher's trade – like keeping your nose out when it ain't invited!'

Pointing out her own selection of meat, Clara merely nodded at the man's remark that 'when arguing with them that be stoopid let 'em know they don't be doin' the same,' as both customers stepped beyond hearing.

Her own change carefully re-checked before being counted into a leather purse she placed her purchase in her basket, leaving the shop with a brief 'Good morning.' Out in the street she breathed deeply. No woman had been recently delivered of a child, Unity Hurley was past the age and she had no female kin. It could only point to one thing!

'*What difference does it make! What difference?*' Clara's grey-pebble eyes had glared across the dining table. '*It is another to lay claim upon the Glebe Works, another to stand between you and the business my father built, that is the difference.*'

'*You are only supposing a child has been born, and you are only supposing it is Anne Corby's child.*'

It might have been the father speaking and not the son. Anger cold inside her, Clara laid knife and fork on her plate.

But she would not let one be as mindless as the other had been, she would not allow her dream to be lost.

'*As you say, I am simply supposing.*' She spoke quietly but ice crackled in each word. '*Now you suppose for a moment, Quenton. Suppose your cousin, who will be of age in a short while, takes her inheritance, and not only that but makes an immediate Will naming her child after her. Where will you be then? I can tell you where you will not be. You will no longer be here enjoying the comforts of this house, nor will you be driving a carriage, much less one of those dreadful horseless ones I know you moon over. And while you are supposing on that think on this also, it will not be you who will be master of those works, it is not your voice will be listened to, not even by an apprentice, for you will be gone, dismissed, sacked like any common labourer. Once her hands prise yours loose then all you have, all you can ever hope to have, will be lost. How will it feel, Quenton, how will it feel to go cap in hand to any who might be disposed to give you employment? And what employment would they give? No, my dear son,*' she smiled scathingly, '*not one with a large desk and little work upon it, they would not sit you in a director's chair. Own to it or not, there are precious few in this town would not rejoice to see things take exactly that path I have just outlined to you.*'

She had seen her words drive home.

Dressed in plain cotton nightgown Clara plaited her faded hair, tying each braid with a white ribbon.

She had watched her son's eyes, seen the realisation dawn as each point drove like a nail. He wanted no poverty-ridden life, the sort lived by so many of the men who laboured beneath his hand. He had been brought up with all the comforts her brother's money could pay for, comforts he would want to keep.

Climbing into bed she turned off the lamp. Quenton was

like his father in some respects but he had enough sense to know which side of his bread was buttered.

Closing her eyes, Clara's thin-lipped mouth smiled in the darkness. Her son would not ask again what difference did it make!

3

What would she tell this child when he was grown? How would she tell him of his beginnings? Anne looked at the tiny blanket-wrapped bundle lying beside her. Could she tell him he was the result of rape, that he had been conceived out of violence by a man whose name she did not know and whose language she could not speak, that she had prayed God so many times to cleanse her womb, to carry away the evidence of the abuse she had suffered? But her prayers had gone unanswered and now a child was born, a child she must rear alone. But how did you rear a child you had no money to feed or clothe, how long would it survive sleeping under hedges open to every aspect of weather? Truth was it would not. She must take the baby to the workhouse, give him to the care of the Parish. That might not afford him love but it would afford him life.

'There, you look a lot better.' Unity Hurley placed a tray on a bedside table. 'You'll soon have a bloom on that pretty face. I must admit, though, I had me doubts the first few days but that be all over now, we'll soon have you right as ninepence.'

'Mrs Hurley –' Anne paused, feeling for the words that would say what must be said '– Mrs Hurley, I am very grateful for what you have done—'

'Hush your words, wench,' Unity flicked a hand, 'I done no more than any woman would have done.'

Any woman! Anne remembered the meeting at Butcroft House. Clara Mather could not be reckoned among them.

'Please,' she watched the nimble fingers pour tea from a small cream teapot, its fat belly garlanded with pale pink roses, 'I – I have to tell you, the child's father . . . I have no—'

'There be no need to go on.' Setting the pot down, Unity glanced at the pale, drawn features. She had lied saying the bloom would soon be returned to those waxen cheeks; given what had been cried out during the long hours of labour it would be a miracle should it ever return. 'There's no need of telling of the fathering of that child for I've heard it already.'

'You – you know!'

'Ar, wench, I knows though it don't be only the absence of a ring told me.'

'Told you the child is a bastard!'

Sympathy welled inside her but Unity pushed it aside, taking instead a firm, no-nonsense tone as she poured milk into the cup set on the tray.

'That is no fault of his and none of yours neither. He don't be the first as were got by the forcing of a woman and I hold no doubt he won't be the last, but a life allowed must be a life lived. It will be hard for both of you, wench, but there is no avoiding of that.'

No avoiding! Two simple words but they sat like rocks in Anne's heart. Life had been given, allowed by heaven to happen, but why, why condemn an innocent babe to a life that would forever carry the stigma of illegitimacy?

Question not the Lord. One of her father's favourite sayings. But, though Jacob Corby may not have known it, those words were used only when in his deepest, most secret soul he did question, when he asked for reasons, as she had asked during that last terrible journey and so many times since. But heaven had not answered, she was alone as she had been in those vast snow-covered wastes; but not as helpless. Her mother could do nothing to relieve the suffering imposed on a child by a father who saw only the glory of his own delusion, but she could help the son born to her. Throwing back the bedcovers she stood up, swaying when her senses reeled.

'What in the name of all that be holy do you think you be doing!'

Concern honing her tone, Unity loosed the spoon and somewhere in her whirling world Anne heard it clatter against the prettily painted crockery.

'You don't be ready to go getting out of bed yet, the child be but a week old. Lord, whatever next!'

'Mrs Hurley,' Anne caught the hand settling her back onto the pillows, 'the baby, I – I have to take it—'

'You'll be taking it nowhere, my girl!' Unity answered firmly. 'Least not for some while yet. You need to rest and get your strength back, time then to do whatever be in your mind.'

Reaching the cup from the tray she held it towards Anne. 'Now you drink that while I take the child downstairs, it's time he were bathed and set to sleep in his own bed.'

She had not touched the child. Unity picked up the small bundle from where she had laid it on the bed an hour before. The girl had not once held him in her arms, not once smiled as the infant was brought to her, not once referred to him as her son. Curling a tiny finger about one of her own, Unity glanced at the young woman whose eyelids lowered to shut out sight of the child. Defence against a love which might have stirred in spite of herself – or was it rejection? She had spoken of him only as 'the child,' or 'the baby', never calling him 'my son'. She did not ask that he be brought to her, made no comment when told of his well-being. It was as if for Anne Corby he did not exist. Had the hurt been so terrible, the shame gone so deep she could not face it? But turning her back would not erase any of it. Unity looked again at the tiny face nestled in the blanket. Anne Corby must follow her own path but, try as ever she might, the shadow of an innocent child would be forever at her shoulder.

Carrying the child against her breast, Unity crossed the room to the door then looked back at the face white almost as the pillows.

'Drink the tea while it be hot, girl, then settle yourself to sleep.' She spoke softly, no trace of censure marring her words and only pity behind her gentle smile.

Drink the tea while it be hot! As the door closed Anne lifted a glance drowned with tears. She had used almost the same phrase to her mother, but that tea had not been given to them out of kindness. Her head falling backward onto the pillows, her blurred vision watched the evening shadows come together, forming and grouping at the foot of the bed, becoming misty figures, figures which so often peopled her nightmares.

'You will feel better after some hot tea.'

Watching through the eyes of memory Anne saw herself holding the weeping figure of her mother, helping her from that bleak snow-swept graveyard, following in the footsteps of the priest who had turned from them without a word and was now a small black mark against the whiteness.

Stumbling together, flakes of snow clinging to black veils hindering their sight, they made their slow way towards the low-slung inn that was the heart of Radiyeska village. Anne watched her hand push open the heavy wooden door, a hand frozen beneath its thin cover of a cotton glove. The place had felt warm after the bone-splintering cold of the cemetery but there had been no welcome in the faces which turned towards them, only a visible, almost tactile animosity; animosity oozing now from the shadowy figures playing about her bed. Men, each bearded and heavily clothed, each with a hat of dark Astrakhan fur seeming to grow upwards from unkempt whiskers, sat in a group around the huge iron stove, a haze of evil-smelling steam rising from coats and breeches drying in the heat, their eyes like black beetles, hostile and furtive, watching every move. Yet none moved, none offered a place against the stove.

But why had she expected them to? The cup forgotten at her side, Anne's mental eyes followed the scene built out of shadows, her brain recalling the thoughts it had harboured as she had helped her mother out of her damp cloak. Why should these men be any different to the hundreds of others they had met while tramping across God-forsaken wilderness where a pale skin had been seen as a visitation of some devil, or through towns where they had been laughed at, villages where they had been stoned?

Settling her mother at the one unoccupied table, unoccupied because it was so far from the stove as to feel none of its direct heat, the spectre of herself glanced about the room. Apart from tables and benches it held nothing, its one attempt at decoration a wooden icon of the Virgin and Child. Everything they had seen since coming to this limitless land had been made of wood – churches, houses, the inns in which her father had sometimes allowed them to rest – and to her it seemed its people too were of the same unfeeling substance; but no, the people of Russia were not made of wood, stone was a better description.

'*Could we have some tea, please.*' Locked in the phantom world of memory, Anne saw her lips move, heard the words reality could not hear.

Months of trudging from village to village had helped her acquire a smattering of the language, but it seemed the dialect spoken in one area differed from that in the next so she could never truly learn in any depth. Now she smiled at the frowning, heavy-faced woman dressed in rough clothing, a shawl wrapping her head and hiding all but a small greasy patch of mouse-coloured hair which dribbled onto her forehead. Her reply was incomprehensible, muttered while one hand lifted towards the icon then swiftly marked the sign of the cross over her large bosom.

From the circle about the stove a wave of sniggers spread and Anne saw herself swallowing hard before her lips repeated their request. They were unwelcome here, she and her mother, yet they might afford a few minutes of sport.

'*We would like some tea, please!*' It held an edge crisp as the snow outside that inn but she saw they had understood, both the woman and her foul-smelling clientele, that much was obvious from the smirks and nudges passing between them, so whatever the reason the request was being ignored it could not be put down to lack of understanding.

'*It doesn't matter, dear.*' The shadowy image of Viola Corby touched a hand to her daughter's arm. '*I really do not want any tea, let us go to our room.*'

'*No, Mother!*' Determination pulled her own mouth to a straight line and her haze-compiled face stared ignoring the dumpy woman's fresh torrent of angry words. This time there would be no Jacob Corby to forbid her into silence, this time her mother's needs would be met, that and nothing but that would be Anne Corby's creed in life, and no one would forbid that creed ever again.

Her retort, a demand and not a request, exploded a further burst of abuse but the woman went towards the rear of the room. Behind Anne, her mother coughed into a delicate scrap of cloth, her thin shoulders folding inwards against the sting of pain.

'*I really do not want any tea, Anne.*' The shadow-created figure wiped its mouth with a self-conscious move designed to hide phlegm spotted with blood.

'*It is warmer here, Mother.*' Anne turned to her, bending to rub the cold hands between her own. '*You do need some hot tea.*'

The pillows at her back, that small unheard voice somewhere in her mind trying to tell her it was no more than
memory, Anne felt only the shudder as her mother coughed
again, heard only the racking sounds bubbling in her mother's
tortured lungs, saw only the fear in her own face as she turned
to face those watching men.

'*Please,*' she said, '*if you moved just a little there would be room
for my mother beside the stove; we have just come from seeing my
father to his grave and*—'

'*You should have stayed there with him!*' A bear of a man,
stink rising from him, waved a deprecating hand. '*That be the
best place for all bloody foreigners, though I begrudge them a place
in the beloved soil of Russia!*'

Loud shouts of approval closed off the rest and she turned
back to her mother as the mistress of the tavern came in with
a brass samovar, its elegant, high-curved spout glinting in the
dim light, two handleless pottery cups beside it on a wooden
tray. Giving Anne a look carrying such a volume of dislike her
tongue might have found difficulty in expressing it, she set the
tray on a plain-topped table then turned to her more preferred
customers, her opinions of foreigners besmirching the country
with their fouling presence meeting with loud agreement.

Pouring tea into each cup, Anne handed one to her mother,
seeing the fingers which took it tremble from more than
physical coldness. Sipping the hot liquid Viola Corby looked
at her daughter. Patting the hard bench she murmured, '*Sit
down, Anne, there is something I have to say.*'

At the foot of the bed the unreal figures moved close
together, one coughing again into the handkerchief while the
other looked anxiously at the twin spots of colour burning
high on the sunken cheeks, at the unnatural brilliance flaming
in faded blue eyes, and the bitter resentment she had felt then
curdled afresh. For weeks she had watched her mother grow
steadily weaker, watched and wept at her own inability to do

anything to change the indomitable attitude of the man who placed the responsibility for all things at the feet of his God, making a sacrifice of all that was his.

It was then her mother told her they were to come home to England. She sat for a moment, the coarse voices talking so loudly now forgotten. Home to England! But how could they? It was so far and the harsh breath of winter was already sweeping the land. Her mother mistook her silence for fear yet it was not fear that coursed in her but the sharp, almost painful tug of premonition low in her stomach.

'*I want you safe at Butcroft House before*—' She was taken then with a spate of coughing which left her breathless but determined to go on. '*There is nothing here for us now that your father is – is no longer with us. We have no reason to remain. We – we will go home, Anne, home where you should have been long ago among – among your own people.*'

The twin patches of colour darkened to carmine and tiny beads of perspiration spotted her mother's forehead even though she shivered.

'*We will talk about it tomorrow.*'

Anne remembered the icy fingers that had touched her heart with terror as she had helped her mother to her feet, a terror so strong it had her teeth clenched hard together, a terror which had proved well founded.

With her heart pounding in her chest she turned her face to the window. No more! She did not want to remember any more! Outside the night was turning silver as a high moon rose, and though she shut her eyes tight the pictures played on across inner eyes, each movement clear and defined, every silent word loud in the ears of her mind.

The tiny room below the eaves of the inn was freezing cold. Taking a cover from the bed she wrapped it about her mother's shoulders then set her gently on a wooden stool, the only other article of furniture the room possessed. They needed a fire. Telling her mother as much she walked back down the stairs.

Even now, her waking mind telling her it was all in the past, that the nightmare was ended, Anne's body trembled.

The men had still been seated about the stove, their clothing sending silent misty tributes towards the low ceiling, and in every eye she could see derision.

'*Madame Roskoyeva?*'

At the outer edge of the circle, a man with a flat-topped Astrakhan hat low over bushy eyebrows swilled beer from a pot before rising from his seat.

'*What do you want her for? Tell Peter Ilyovitch what you need . . . as if he didn't know.*'

She had felt the threat of him but stood her ground . . . her mother had to be kept warm through the night.

At the foot of her bed the shadow-formed face laughed at hearing the request for a fire.

'*It's not fire you want.*' He moved more quickly than she could have thought, grabbing her and pulling her down onto his knee while one hand ripped open her blouse.

'*Hey, Ilyovitch,*' one of his companions called, '*it will be your arse gets warmed should your wife get to know what you're doing!*'

His beer-soaked beard pressed against her throat, a thick-fingered hand squeezed her breast as the man who held her laughed thickly. '*She won't know unless you tell her and I doubt you'll be doing that once you've had a turn.*'

The other man shook his head. '*I shan't be wanting a turn, Ilyovitch. I'm particular about who I stick mine into and it certainly won't be no foreigner!*'

With her eyes still pressed shut Anne winced, seeming to feel again the sharp slap to her face as she tried to struggle free.

'*Oh,*' her attacker had roared the answer, '*then the bit you shagged senseless on the Finn border was no foreigner, nor the daughter of that German family you spent the night with when we passed through Riga, huh! You passed through that one alright and her no more than twelve years old and I'm going to do the same to this one!'* Laughing he had clamped his greasy mouth to hers, his hand releasing her breast to push her skirts up over her thighs, then, releasing her mouth roared again. *'If they don't want Russian prick they shouldn't come here and this one needs a dose so let's see her don't leave disappointed.'*

From the rear of the stove a man heavy with sheepskins called above the laughter. *'Leave the wench. Just today the priest laid her father in his grave.'*

'Then he won't be giving me any trouble, will he?' It was growled, lust thickening his words. *'And neither will you, little foreigner. Once Ilyovitch has parted your legs you'll be no trouble to any man. Foreigners are no different, they have nothing a Russian woman don't have.'*

'Then why bother, Peter Ilyovitch?'

The shadowed forms became suddenly still, her own terrified breathing the only sound.

'Why have you come back down here?'

A sob trembling on her lips Anne watched the ghostly scene come again to life.

'It's bad enough having you in my house without you flaunting yourself.'

The presence of the tavern owner's wife had restored a little of the sanity to Anne's brain, the same sanity which told her now that what she watched was illusion, a figment, but it was a figment she could not dismiss. Lying against her pillows she watched the scene play about the bed.

'I came to ask for a fire to be lit in our room, this man attacked me.'

Disbelief blatant in her small eyes the woman almost spat

accusingly, '*Had you stayed in that room he couldn't have
touched you.*'

'*I wouldn't bet a wooden rouble on that, Ilyovitch would get
his hands on a woman no matter where she was.*'

Hands on broad hips, the woman glanced to where the
voice had come from, her voice riding the laughter of the men.
'*Not in this inn!*' She raked a withering glance over each face.
'*And if Ilyovitch or any other of you can't control what's in your
trousers then you can leave right now . . . and you –*' she turned
the angry stare on Anne '*– get yourself back to that room before
I pitch you and the other one out.*'

She had not even listened, she wanted only to condemn. It
was a trembling breath she drew as the woman stomped from
the room. The man who had grabbed her, his hot stare had
not left her. He was a danger, yet she could not give up now.
The nights here were long and very cold, her mother must be
protected.

Praying he would not seize her again she had run, following
the woman into the rear of the house. But it was not the
woman who waited for her there.

'She must have been near asleep for when I walked to the
bedside her cried out.'

'The girl were probably startled.' Laban smiled, lighting a
long-stemmed clay pipe.

'That wench were more than startled, you asks me I'd say
it seemed her were fair terrified.'

'Nightmares do that to folk.' Laban puffed steadily, returning a waxed spill to a pot stood in the hearth.

That was right enough. Unity Hurley carried the tray into
the scullery, emptying the untouched tea into a pail set
beneath a shallow brownstone sink. But a body were not
plagued by the same dream day and night, yet each time of
her going into Anne Corby's room the girl had jumped fit

to burst her skin. It weren't natural. Pouring hot water over the crockery, Unity refilled the kettle from the pump in the yard. Indoors again she washed cups mechanically, her mind wandering.

The girl Laban had brought to the house showed a gratitude for each thing done for her, politely thanking for the bringing of water for washing, for food or a drink, but behind the civility lurked a fear. It showed in the girl's quick cry whenever she was taken unaware and blazed in the depths of sad eyes. Was that not to be expected? The wench had been raped, that was enough to put fear into any woman.

Rape, yes, that was terrible. Unity answered herself as she flipped the huckaback drying cloth over the rope line stretched just below the scullery ceiling. But even that horror could not account for what she saw in that girl's eyes, a repugnance nothing short of loathing, an abomination which gleamed dark and odious, yet it was more than that; beneath the repulsion was an agony, unhappiness so deep and wounding that eternity itself may never heal the scars.

And the child which had been born to her? Picking up the kettle, Unity stood for a moment. What was to become of him? So far the girl had not attempted to hold him, had turned her face away whenever he was brought to her. Was another life to be ruined by a man's lust, would the child pay as well as the girl, pay for a sin he had no part in committing?

4

Anne watched the woman laying the warmly wrapped child in a large drawer set on top of a chest stood on one side of the bedroom.

'You've no need to get up should he wake for I'll hear 'im. I sleeps light.' Unity tucked the covers around the baby then turned to smile at Anne. 'I would take the drawer into our room but Laban is always up with the birds and I wouldn't want this little 'un disturbed; but like I says I'll know when he wakes and I'll see to the feeding of him so you just close your eyes and sleep.'

A fresh candle set beside her, Anne murmured her thanks. Sleep . . . the chance to forget, to be free of the memories that tormented her hours, the phantoms which plagued her every moment; but as the door closed behind Unity they rushed from every shadowed corner, grey ghosts relentlessly playing out her past.

The kitchen of the inn formed behind her closed eyes. Heavy, smoke-blackened pans clinging like dark scabbed sores hung on walls unrelieved by dim light emanating from a fireplace.

Trembling as much in reality as in that unreality Anne saw herself searching for something in which to carry wood to build a fire. She would have to go back through that room, past those leering men whose tongues were as vicious as their faces and that would be torment enough without going empty handed.

'*What are you looking for?*'

Behind her the voice was low and Anne's flesh, already creeping from the touch of Ilyovitch, crawled afresh. Turning, she faced its owner. Standing six feet in heavy fur boots, thick, grease-stained clothing adding to his bulk and increasing the threatening power of him, a man she had not seen before ran small ferret eyes the length of her.

Her heart beginning to thud, she watched him position himself between her and the door leading to the room with the stove.

Trying to sound calm though a pulse in her throat threatened to choke her, Anne replied, '*I was looking for Mrs – for Madame Roskoyeva.*'

Barricaded behind fleshy mounds ferret eyes narrowed. '*But she is not here.*'

With an impatience almost as strong as her fear Anne clicked her tongue.

'*I can see that Mr . . .*'

'*Roskoyev.*' The eyes flicked to her breasts then back to her face. '*I am Madame's husband.*'

'*Then perhaps you can tell me where I may find her.*'

'*My wife is tired, she has gone to bed.*' The eyes once more flicked to her breasts, lingering longer this time.

Anne felt the roof of her mouth dry with a new fear. He was standing in front of the door that led to the stove room. Glancing to her left she saw the only other door, one that was also closed. Heaven alone knew where that might lead and instinct warned her not to stray further from the public room of this awful place.

Swallowing hard she forced herself to look at him. '*Then maybe you will tell me where I can find wood for a fire and something to carry it in.*'

'*Maybe I will, maybe I won't.*' He passed his tongue over his lips, taking with it grease-laden hairs from his beard. '*Wood for fires have to be paid for.*'

'*Of course.*' The fear she had swallowed regurgitated in her throat as Anne answered, '*Put it on our bill and it will be settled when we leave.*'

He took a step towards her, his thick, fur-lined boots making no sound on the earth-packed floor.

'*The payment I require doesn't get put on a bill.*' He smiled showing yellow teeth pock-marked with decay.

Anne glanced again at the door trying to judge in her mind whether it would be better to go through the one that could lead to anywhere or whether to try to push past the man barring her way to the room serving as the bar of the inn.

'*My wife is not here,*' Roskoyev smirked, misinterpreting her glance, '*but I am here. Whatever she could do for you I can do . . . perhaps even more,*' he took another step towards her, his jowled face spreading with a leer, '*and certainly more interestingly.*'

Warning pricking along her veins, Anne clasped her hands tightly at her sides in an effort to control the trembling threatening to overwhelm her. If she could sound matter of fact despite the solid fear blocking her throat, and if she could ignore the innuendo of his words and the flare that had leapt to his ferret eyes, he might step out of her way.

'*I wanted to ask Madame if we might have a fire in my mother's room, I fear she is not well. Probably she has taken a chill, it was so terribly cold in the churchyard.*'

'*A fire in your mother's room.*' The guttural tone thickened noticeably as he stepped near, his massive frame closing her against the cold wooden wall. His little eyes reflected the anaemic yellow light filtering beneath the door, lending his face an even more animalistic appearance. '*Now that, my pretty miss, is a thing we do not allow, the risk of fire is too great.*'

'*But my mother must be kept warm.*' Anne turned her head from the stink of the man's breath, she wanted to scream at him to move away but didn't dare, it would do no good to cause yet another scene.

Eyes closing even further the keeper of Radiyeska's only inn stroked his greasy beard and Anne winced against his beer-soaked whisper. '*A service that is not often performed must be paid for, little foreigner.*'

Her stomach churning at the sourness of his breath she tried to answer without breathing in the air he fouled. '*Of course, I expect it to be put on our bill—*'

'*Oh no, Ninotchka,*' he interrupted quickly, '*a service of such a special kind must be paid for by a service equally special.*'

Rancid odour rose from the body he pressed hard against her, a hand grabbing at her breast and kneading the soft flesh beneath her dress. '*You want a fire for your mother then you pay, you pay the price I ask.*'

'*No!*' The cry wrenched from her as she fought to push her way free. Not again, oh God, not again. Twisting to avoid the wet fleshy mouth she heard the grunt of pleasure as he pulled her to him, forcing her closer against the throbbing flesh at the base of his stomach.

'*No . . . please, no!*' She was crying openly now, disgust and fear too strong for her to hold. How could men so vile be allowed to live, why for once could not the God to whom her father had sacrificed each of their lives protect her, why could He not strike this loathsome creature dead?

The hand left her breast to fumble with the buckle of the belt that held up the grease-marked trousers. '*Sshh, Ninotchka,*' he breathed against her face, '*you will like what Boris has for you, see how strong it is.*' He grabbed her hand, pushing it hard into his crotch. '*See, see how it dances for you—*'

'*Roskoyev!*'

It was not the voice of the Almighty but Anne thanked Him for it and for the effect it had on the man forcing himself upon her. Twisting away as his hands dropped from her she leaned heavily upon a pot-strewn table, tremors of relief competing with the dry, racking sobs shaking her body.

'*Roskoyev, you child of a pig!*'

Her hand already fastening on a heavy iron pot the man's wife glared as a broad leather belt fell about his feet.

'*What is this foreign filth doing in my kitchen, and what the hell do you think you are doing mauling her all over?*'

The fire doused in his loins, the man looked warily at his wife. '*I was trying to help this little foreigner.*'

'*I've no doubt.*' The tight mouth parted grudgingly but the words were shot out. '*Helping her to your prick. And you –*' she directed a lethal glance at the girl holding on to the table '*– I interrupted the same game you were playing with Ilyovitch, you are so much the bitch in heat you turn from one man to another, any man, every man, it doesn't matter to you who it is so long as the itch between your legs is scratched.*'

'*Please, I came only to ask a fire be lit, my mother is not well, she – she has suffered so much already today and she is so cold.*'

Watching tears glint on that face of shadow, Anne did not feel the real ones now coursing down her cheeks.

Turning a withering glance on her husband the woman's eyes gleamed their anger. '*Get out!*' she screeched at him. '*Get out, you whoremonger, and get a fire bucket burning. I will take it upstairs.*' The furious glare swivelled to Anne. '*And you . . . tomorrow you go!*'

In the shrouded darkness of her room in the Hurleys' house the slight snuffling sounds of the sleeping infant brushed against the silence, while in a room only she could see, Anne heard nothing but her mother's choked cough. It had been less than twenty hours since the black-robed priest had lifted the crucifix commending a dead man's soul to its maker, hours in which she had not missed her father at all. Dropping the last of their pathetically few belongings into the valise she snapped the catch. Jacob Corby had given her nothing but life, a life which must be lived to his pattern; but his death gave her and her mother freedom, freedom to abandon their eternal wandering.

From the downstairs room of the inn voices of departing men floated up to her. Brushing a stray curl beneath her bonnet she gave a final straightening to her skirts; dull and brown they seemed to symbolise the life she had been allowed to lead, but soon that life would be over and they would be in England, the land which glistened in her mind like some beautiful green jewel.

Picking up the valise she made her way downstairs, her stomach churning at the memory of last night. She knew her mother needed rest and warmth but fear of what could happen if they stayed here had stilled the protests in her mind. Had her mother guessed what had happened? Anne closed tight fingers about the handle of the valise. It had been dark in their room and she had grabbed her cloak, fastening it against the cold as soon as she had entered; she had hidden the torn bodice of her dress and yet her mother's eyes told her she had hidden nothing.

At the foot of the stairs Viola Corby was settling her account and Anne felt her skin prickle as small intense eyes swept her.

'*Let me take that.*' Boris Roskoyev reached for the valise.

'*It's not heavy.*' Anne moved quickly to her mother's side. She hated the man, hated the way his look devoured her, his hands so ready to paw at her. '*I can manage. Are you ready, Mother?*'

'*Quite ready, Anne.*' Viola pulled on her gloves. '*Mr Roskoyev has been kind enough to supply a horse and troika, we can leave them at the railway station at Plivna where he will collect them later.*'

So he had organised transport to the station – Anne gave the man the faintest of nods – but at what cost? The man wouldn't do God a service unless payment were of the highest.

'*We can leave at once then.*' She looked at the twin spots of colour in her mother's pale cheeks, at eyes too bright, and felt guilt sting inside. Her mother ought not to be travelling especially with winter settling in, but they could not stay in this village.

'*In a little while, Anne,*' Viola Corby faltered, guessing at the fear in her daughter's eyes. '*Unfortunately Mr Roskoyev has not the time at the moment to harness the horse.*'

What was it the odious creature hoped for this time? All of Anne's loathing was in the look she threw at the tavern owner. Was it more money or was there some more devious idea behind the delay?

'*Of course, Mr Roskoyev must be very busy.*' Trying to keep the distaste from her voice Anne deposited the valise at her mother's feet. '*But I can harness the horse perfectly well myself, I've done it often enough in the past. You wait here, I'll pick you up at the door in a few minutes.*'

Outside she lifted her skirts free of the frozen mud and made her way to the rear of the wooden buildings which seemed to huddle together against the cold. The stable proved no difficulty in finding, the stench of uncleaned stalls reached out, drawing her towards it. Lifting her skirts higher against the filth on the floor she crossed to the one stall housing a horse.

'*You are to pull a loaded troika?*' she murmured, stroking the thin animal. '*You don't look strong enough but I must take you, my mother could never make the walk into Plivna.*'

Clenching her teeth against the strong odour she clucked softly, calming the nervous animal backing against the side of its stall. Still murmuring she reached for the padded collar, lifting it to the animal's neck.

'*I could do that for you, Ninotchka.*'

The voice whispered through the half light and Anne swallowed her scream. Even in the gloom of the stable she recognised the glitter of those strangely mottled little eyes and the huge frame filling the opening to the stall.

'*I can manage, thank you.*' Her reply was strained and her hand trembled where it rested on the rusty tackle.

'*But why should you when I can do it for you?*' A leer spread across the unwashed face as he moved towards her. '*Payment will be pleasant for both of us, I promise you.*'

All the fear of the night before rose sickeningly as Anne realised she was trapped, the bulk of him blocked the doorway to the stall and there was no other way out. '*I – I don't need any help.*' She settled the collar more firmly across the animal's neck, hating the way her voice trembled. The last thing she wanted was for this man to know how much she feared him.

'*Come, little English girl.*' He was behind her, his hands on her waist.

As she watched the drama unfold behind her closed eyes the fear that had risen in her then seemed to clutch at her now, holding breath prisoner in her throat.

'*Boris knows how to take care of you, Boris knows how to bring you much pleasure.*'

Breath escaping with the same rush as it had in that stable, Anne saw herself kick backwards but he was already twisting her around, one arm circling her hard and preventing any move. The rancid smell of him filled her nostrils and she felt she would suffocate as she tried not to breathe the stale air gushing from his open mouth.

'*There is your mother's fire still to pay for . . . and now is the time!*' His mouth was pressed to her neck, a thick-fingered hand clutching at her breast and all the time his hated voice, thick with the intent of his body, muttered in her ears.

'*Such little breasts . . . Boris likes little breasts and he will like what you have between your legs . . . yes, little English girl, you will give Boris what he likes.*'

His mouth pressed hard on hers. Fighting him would be useless. This man was not above beating her to get what he wanted, and injured she could not take care of her mother. Yet she could not let this man abuse her. There might be one way . . . one way to escape. Forcing herself to relax against the foul-smelling body she moaned softly . . . if he thought she were ill . . . !

But he did not think her ill. He took her soft cry as one of pleasure. Releasing her, he dropped both hands to the broad leather belt about his waist, swift expert movements undoing the huge metal buckle, leaving it to fall about his feet. Gripping the waistband of his trousers he snatched them open, revealing a column of flesh sprouting from a bush of dark hair.

'*Now, Ninotchka,*' he breathed. '*Now you and Boris will pleasure each other, eh?*'

If she were to do anything at all it had to be now! Anne felt the breath catch in her throat. It had to be now while she was free of the grip of those arms. Lifting both hands she clawed at the lust-lit face, dragging her fingernails savagely down each cheek and leaving scarlet trails among the grease-matted beard. Feeling him draw back, his gasp of pain filling her nostrils with the stench of his hot breath, she placed both hands flat against the barrel of his chest and pushed with all the strength left in her.

The unexpectedness of what she did catching him unawares, Boris Roskoyev reeled backwards, his feet scrabbling for a hold on the muck-strewn floor, but his heel landed in a pot of manure and he slid further out of the stall, his back coming up heavily against a thick wooden roof support.

Trembling, her own lungs squeezed dry of air, Anne

watched the man sprawled at her feet. He was winded but not unconscious and his eyes had never left hers. A leer twisting what she could see of his mouth above the great bush of his beard, he began to scramble to his feet. Afraid to pass him in case he caught at her and dragged her to the floor beside him, Anne waited for the onslaught she knew would come, knowing also with terrifying certainty that it would not end short of rape.

Seconds followed on seconds. Behind her the stamp of the startled horse disturbed an eerie silence. Gaining his feet he stared at her but did not move.

How long? Her blood surging with fear Anne watched the man intent on raping her. How long would he wait before striking? Would there be time? She glanced at the door of the stall. Perhaps she had winded him enough to slip past him.

Gingerly she stepped forward then stopped as he too moved, completely blocking her way.

Her mouth opening in a scream she could not produce Anne shrank against the partitioning wall of the stall.

Just feet away from her the bear of a man grinned again. '*See, my little foreigner, was Boris not right? Now you would shout your delight at what he brings you.*'

His small ferret eyes gleaming, his hands freeing flesh enveloped in matted dark hair, he came towards her. Frozen with fear Anne watched him.

'*Come, little one, come let Boris give you pleasure.*'

Again he was so close her throat filled with the stink of him and her blood curdled as he reached for her.

A silent scream filling her head, Anne gripped the halter she had not even realised she had taken from a peg inside the stall and lashed it towards that leering face, bringing the metal bit hard across the side of his head.

Twice in rapid succession the metal found its mark, the

third time slicing empty air as he staggered backwards, hitting against the post he had sprawled in front of moments before.

It was the dark stain released Anne's brain from its prison of fear. Darker than the grease that already stained his clothing it spread like a shadowed pool just below his throat, bathing the collar of his lambswool jacket, seeping downwards across his chest.

Eyes still glittering, mouth stretched in the same leer, he stood unmoving . . . watching but unmoving.

Now, Anne told herself; she must try to get past him now or be released only when he had used her to satisfy himself. Her eyes holding to his face she stepped forward then stifled a scream as she saw, at the centre of the spreading stain, where the lump of his throat showed below the bush of his beard, a small black hole. Its edges perfectly neat as if carefully cut with scissors, the flesh folded back on itself, folded away from the thick metal spike that protruded several inches from his neck, a spike that had taken his throat with it.

He was dead! She had killed him!

Anne's hand rose in the candlelight, pressing against her mouth as it had pressed then, holding back the nervous vomit that spewed against her lips, but still her inner eyes remained glued to the horror.

She had killed him!

'I didn't mean . . . I didn't want . . .' Spoken aloud the words hung on the stillness of the small bedroom. Every nerve trembling, as in that stable, she stared at the shadow-made picture, stared at the man who it seemed at any moment would reach for her. She had not meant to harm him, she wanted only that he leave her alone. Then, the clarity of it almost blinding, came the thought: who in Radiyeska would believe her? Who would believe a foreigner? And what of her mother? She, Anne, would be made to pay but what might these people do to her mother?

Her mind hardly registering the movement of her hands she lifted the bridle she still held, passing it over the horse's head. Trying to keep her glance from straying to the man suspended from the spike that had penetrated the base of his skull to emerge from his throat, Anne finished the task of harnessing the animal; now it remained to lead it out of the stall and couple it to the troika. She must do it, she had to if she were to get her mother away from this place.

Her brain still numb with fear she moved forward then hesitated, her stomach knotting at the soft swish of sound from the wooden pillar. Forcing herself to look at the man still standing there, Anne's fingers gripped hard on the bridle.

He was moving! A whispered sob echoed like thunder in her ears. Oh God, he was moving!

Her grip on the bridle dragging at the horse's mouth caused it to pull away, the jerk of its head snatching Anne from the brink of unconsciousness, forcing her to watch the trousers slide down the thick legs.

5

Dishes rattling as they were placed on the table registered Unity's anger and disbelief. 'That woman had the cheek to come herself to your workshop? Huh! I hope you set her on her way summat sharp!'

'I offered her a chair.' Laban Hurley hid his smile. Unity was not particularly good at hiding displeasure and though he knew it was unfair on his part to provoke her he could not resist.

'You offered her a chair! You surprise me, Laban Hurley, you really does. It ain't no chair I'll be offering that one should she bring her sharp nose to poke along of my house, it will be more like a broom laid to her backside! If ever a woman were tainted with the devil's touch it be Clara Mather! So what was she wanting? Weren't no leather purse I'll be bound.'

'No, it was no purse.' Taking the unlit pipe from his mouth Laban laid it on the mantel then seated himself at the table, waiting for the mild explosion he knew would come.

'Then if it were no purse what were it?'

Unity's tone said more than her words. Patience had been strained to its limit. Wanting to smile, Laban thought better of it; Unity would stand so much teasing and no more.

'Said she had come to discuss the making of a saddle . . . a present for her son's birthday.'

'Sounds like you had no belief in that.'

'No more than you yourself would have.' Laban watched

the delicious-smelling mutton broth being ladled into his bowl. He was hungry as a hunter.

'That's true enough.' Unity sliced fresh-baked bread into thick chunks, setting a plate of them nearer to her husband. 'I don't judge a bull terrier by its collar and I don't judge a woman by the cut of her clothes. Clara Mather be sly and won't never be no other. Son's birthday! I wonder how long it took her to think that one up.'

Dipping a chunk of bread into his broth, Laban chewed before answering. 'We did discuss a saddle.'

Her own spoon halfway to her mouth, Unity paused then set it back into her bowl. 'Discussed,' she said irately. 'Oh yes, Clara Mather would discuss all right, but tell me she placed a definite order, tell me discussion went so far as that!'

His head shaking briefly Laban soaked another chunk of bread. 'Clara placed no order, but then I had no expectation her would. It were no saddle she come to find out about, it were the wench lying up in that bedroom.'

Taking a square of bread Unity broke it into smaller pieces, dropping each to float like minuscule white islands in her broth before submerging them with the back of her spoon, triumph in every move.

'I guessed as much.' She pressed harder. 'Same as I guessed she would soon make a move to find out for sure it be Jacob Corby's girl been delivered of a child, but to go speaking to a man, well *that* I never did expect; but then a woman afeared as Clara Mather don't pay no mind to niceties.'

'Afeared.' Laban glanced at his wife. 'Would the woman be feared for the girl and the child? If so, why turn her away from Butcroft House?'

'Laban Hurley, sometimes I think there be naught in your head save leather!' Unity sighed, exasperated. 'It's Butcroft House Clara Mather fears for, that and the lorinery business she has had the running of all these years. She knows Jacob's wench can claim what belongs to her by right of birth and after her then any child born to her; when that happens Clara and that lad of her'n will have nothing more than Anne Corby has a mind to give them. And if the wench has any sense at all the only thing she will give that aunt of hers will be the time of day!'

The same thinking had occurred to him but Laban had needed to hear it said. Always a man to give another the benefit of doubt he had tried to apply the same to Clara Mather but it hadn't worked out very well. The woman had attempted to mask the real purpose of her coming to his workshop, taking the longest route to say anything, not once being direct. That method never did sit well with him.

His meal done, Laban expressed his enjoyment of it as he always did. Unity worked hard, doing all the chores required of running a home as well as helping with the stitching of bridles and saddles, a job she did better than any man, and a word of appreciation went a long way.

'Did Clara ask was the girl with us?' Unity watched him settle to his pipe.

'Not as such.' He tapped the spill against a fireplace brilliant from the black leading Unity gave it every week. 'Said as Jacob's daughter had appeared one day out of the blue then left again as quick; that Quenton and herself were worried as to where the girl could be.'

'Worried, yes, but for themselves. That lad be no better than his mother. He'd be only too pleased to hear that Anne Corby and her babby be gone from the world!' Unity banged the used dishes onto the tray, the sounds of her washing them coming clearly to where Laban sat.

Quenton Mather had learned as he had been taught. Having reached an age where other lads were apprenticed to the lorinery, learning the trade of metal-working, the fashioning of horse brasses, the making of steel accoutrements necessary

for bridles, harness, stirrups and many other pieces for coach
and carriage, he had not been placed at the foot of the ladder.
The nephew had acted as master, except the true master of
the Glebe Works had never behaved that way. Jacob Corby
might not have held a deep interest in the business his
father had bequeathed him but neither had he sacked men
with families to support then loaded their work on top of
that the few kept on were already hard put to finish in a
week. That had been Quenton Mather as a lad, and as a
man he was no different. Laban tapped tobacco from the
pipe. Taking the Glebe Works from the control of him
and his mother would prove a difficult task . . . difficult and
dangerous.

Keep it, she had told her aunt. Keep all that was once your
brother's. She had meant it. Her father had given her nothing
whilst he lived and she wanted nothing from him now he
was dead. But that was not wholly true. Anne felt a twinge
of guilt. During those early years of her childhood, the few
years before the bug of evangelism had bitten so deeply that
he was lost to its virus, he had provided the comfort of a good
home; yes, she and her mother had had that, but where had
been the love?

Across the room a soft whimper sounded from the makeshift cot.

Where had been the love?

Like an accusation the words hurled back at her. Guilt
which had been a twinge a moment before seemed suddenly
to lie like a great weight on her shoulders. The whimper came
again and, without knowing, Anne had moved to stand beside
the drawer. Her father had denied his child the greatest of
gifts . . . love; she was doing the same.

'But I dare not,' she whispered as the whimper became a
cry. 'I dare not love you, that would mean a life of misery for

you, always going from place to place knowing no real home. I can't do that to you, it wouldn't be fair . . .'

She had heard the baby cry before. Stood where she could see the tiny face, the miniature hands so perfectly formed, she felt the same sweep of emotion which seemed to shake her whenever she watched Unity feed him, an emotion so strong it had her heart racing and tears flowing as she murmured on.

'That is why I have to leave you, why I dare not let myself love you.'

As if in answer the child's eyes opened, seeming to say what the tiny tongue could not. Her heart exploding with its own reply she caught the warm bundle in her arms, her lips against the tiny questing mouth. Holding him, the warm softness of him resting on her breast, she felt her soul sing. He had not been born of love, he could know no father. Life would be hard . . . but it would be harder without love. Holding him for the first time, the tiny, dark-fuzzed head nuzzling her face, a great swelling surge rose from the deepest parts of her, carrying her on a huge invisible tide. She had tried so hard not to love him, to cut him from her; but the child in her arms was more than just the product of her body, more than her heart, he was her soul . . . he was her son.

'I can't give you riches.' She smiled through her tears. 'You will never know the comfort of a fine house, you will have only what I had, a mother's love. But it is yours wholeheartedly. I will never let you go . . . never leave you.'

Standing unheard in the doorway of the bedroom Unity Hurley felt the stab of old anguish. She had once whispered those very same words.

There had been no joy from Laban Hurley. Clara Mather slammed the pen she had been holding hard down on the desk. He had not owned to Jacob's daughter being in his house, not owned to a child having been born there, but why else would that wife of his be buying feeding bottle and teats, and for whose child if not that of Anne Corby?

She should have kept the girl here, let the child be born at Butcroft House, she herself handling the delivery. It would have been so easy, a hand over the mouth and the child would never have taken a breath. It would not have been thought strange, so many infants died at birth. If only she had thought – Clara's fingers tightened angrily – if only she had held her temper there would be one less, one less to claim what she intended to be Quenton's. But it would still be his; one or two, no number of lives would stand in the way of that, nor any business either!

She too had been careful of what she said but her meaning had been clear. Clara's mind switched to the office of Regency Leather works. It had been strewn with papers. But she was not duped by the seeming carelessness, no such carried over into the work of Laban Hurley, he was acknowledged the finest saddler in all of the Black Country if not all of England; even royalty came to Laban Hurley for saddles and bridles . . . but Laban Hurley came to her, to the Glebe Works for his lorinery! She had reminded him of the fact that, important as the leather-working was, it needed the addition of metal pieces, not simply those of decoration such as the horse brasses so beloved of firms delivering any manner of goods and wishing their teams to be seen as the best, but bridle bits, stirrups, frames for courier and Gladstone bags and the thousand and one other things the loriner supplied . . . supplies which she might, unfortunately, be forced to discontinue.

She had thought her veiled threat to have brought results, for Laban Hurley to own to having her niece in his house. She could have gone on from there to openly threaten, to tell him the girl must go or his living would go. She would make no more pieces for Regency Leather and Laban Hurley would

be forced from business. That had been her one weapon but
Hurley had countered its strike before she had hurled it.

'*It does a man good to hear another's trade be flourishing.*' He
had smiled at her when saying it. '*As for your being perturbed
by being unable to accept my own orders for the lorinery then
rest your mind easy for it causes no problem. You be the only
foundry of that sort in Darlaston and I be the only saddler, but in
Walsall town there be several, every one of which knows the name
of Laban Hurley and the quality of his work. I thinks there'll be
none not proud to link their trade to his.*' He had opened the
door of the office and the sounds of tools against leather had
rushed in but they had not drowned the last of his words, or
the warning contained in them.

'*Ar, Walsall has many a loriner a man can buy from, and each
saddler his supplier . . . I hopes you finds your business continues
to flourish.*'

They had not been empty words nor had their meaning
gone unrecognised. He could buy anywhere, but where outside of Darlaston could she sell? No, what she had thought a
threat to Regency Leather had been a threat against herself.
But where one door closed another opened. She had failed
in that venture but there would be no failing in the next. Her
niece must be gotten rid of once and for all . . . and so must
her bastard child!

'I have been a burden on you long enough, I – I just wish there
was a way of repaying your kindness other than returning to
Butcroft House and claiming my father's property.'

'There be no need of you thinking of repayment, the good
Lord seen fit to entrust us with the caring of you and your
little lad, it don't be our way to seek to throw that trust back
in His face.' Unity did not glance up from stitching a bridle.
'Would do no good to go see Clara Mather, she were left in
charge 'til her brother returned and that will be her stand; she

will release the reins only when Jacob Corby hisself stands afore 'er.'

'Then she will never release them,' Anne answered quietly. 'Jacob Corby is dead . . . we buried him in a Russian cemetery.'

With the first words spoken, the rest followed. Like waters breaking free of a dam they poured in an unrelenting stream until the whole story was told of their endless trekking, of the hostile glares and often physical blows followed by threats to their lives driving them from country to country, from the continent and deserts of Africa to the cold plains of Russia. Perhaps it was there in that country her father's proselytising had been most resented. The people had their religion and their churches, their belief in the one true God had been as strong as Jacob's, only the form of their services were different. But for her father those services had held the overtones of idol worship, they needed to be cleansed of the rituals he saw as belonging to the worship of Baal and Ashtoreth, to the stone idols of heathenism.

'It grew worse as we went from village to village, my father ever condemning the people, telling them heaven closed its eyes to their worship, that the mother of God wept at their failure to follow the true path. But a path which varied from his only in its use of icons and incense, one in which every heart loved and revered its saviour as did his own could not be disowned of heaven. My mother saw that clearly but as clear to her eyes was her duty, she was Jacob Corby's wife and as such it was her duty to follow wherever he led. I think that even in their anger those people saw that and it was their reason for not letting us starve.'

Unity had not spoken. Listening in silence, her hands manipulating two needles, one threaded at each end of the same length of twine, she stitched with the surety the years of working with her husband had given her. Now she said quietly, 'God rest his soul. He were wrong in what he done but the good Lord has a knowing heart and ever-open arms, may the soul of Jacob Corby find peace in them.'

Anne watched the dexterity of the other woman's hands, the left pushing its needle through the small hole the diamond-shaped blade of the awl had made in the leather, her right hand sending its needle through the same hole then both pulling the thread tight.

'So Jacob Corby died following his star.' Unity's hands moved rhythmically. 'That must have been hard for your mother to bear, but a grandchild will help ease the burden of sorrow. Will her be following after you or do you go to her?'

In the short silence which followed the question Anne fought to retain the nausea spilling up into her throat. Sat close to the light of the window, Unity felt the tension. The wench had other sorrows yet to bring from the dark regions, other wounds which would not begin to heal until they were laid bare.

'My – my mother will not be following after me and – and I cannot go to her. I wanted to stay with her . . . I wanted—'

Sobs took the place of words, thickening and choking in Anne's throat and though Unity's heart twisted, though she ached to comfort, to say no more needed to be told, she stayed firmly on her stool, her eyes on her stitching. Comfort of that sort was the wrong balm, whatever the stuff of Anne Corby's nightmare, as with a boil, it needed to be drawn, to have the poison extracted from it, only then would it begin to fade and allow the wench peace.

'I tried to fight them off.' Her voice almost a whisper, each syllable trembling like breeze-caught leaves, it seemed Anne watched a scene within herself. 'I tried to keep them away but it was no use . . . they were so many . . . they were so cruel!'

6

'I – I watched the trousers . . . saw them lower to the man's feet . . . I thought . . . I thought—' The tortured whispers emptied into the silence of Unity's kitchen.

'But he did not move. Then I saw, spreading from the base of his throat, covering his jacket in bright glistening red, a glitter which matched that in his eyes. I thought then he would come at me, finish the evil he was intent upon, but the seconds passed and still he did not move.'

Breathing tight and shallow as she must have breathed then Anne talked on, a commentator describing some invisible picture.

'Then I saw it, in the centre of the scarlet circle, saw the iron spike protruding from his throat. I knew no one would believe the truth; I was a foreigner . . . he was one of their own. But I had to get my mother to some place where she would be looked after. I harnessed the horse and all the time those eyes were fixed on me.'

In its cot the infant stirred but neither of the women moved. 'I put my mother in the sleigh, making sure the blanket covered the rifle I had found in the stable. Mother knew the owner had said to drive myself and he would collect the sleigh later from the station. The sky was leaden and the weather showed every sign of deterioration but I knew we had to leave before the man I had killed was discovered. We had not been driving long before darkness almost as deep as night settled over the land and flurries of snow whipped our faces. I had no idea how far it was to the station or even which direction it lay and I sensed the horse was tiring. The snow flurries became more regular and a biting wind screeched across the sweep of desolately empty land, partnering the huge flakes as if in some dance which circled around us, blinding in its movement. It was then I heard a new sound, one the horse also heard. It came from the timber line away to the left, a long high-pitched howl like a soul in torment.'

Words dying away, Unity stole a quick glance at the young woman sat opposite. The small face was white with remembered terror, the fingers twisting in and out of each other in horror at what it was played in her mind.

'Wolves!' The word was pushed between clenched teeth. 'The horse had scented them, its fear causing it to stumble. I looked round at my mother. Her head was lying forward on her chest and I thanked God she was asleep, that she was spared more worry. Through the swirling flakes I could see the expanse of snow unmarked by the lines of any sleigh and no hoof print marred its smoothness. The world was new and empty, devoid of any living thing other than us and the moving, indistinct blur of grey shapes keeping pace along the tree line. I had heard the talk in villages we passed through, talk of wolves driven by hunger stalking sledges and knew the danger we were in. I plied the whip but the horse could go no faster; even when the howl came again and was answered by short snapping barks it could only stumble on. We were being stalked!'

It was said quiet as a breath of summer air, the essence of fear flavouring every word. Lost now in the nightmare Anne Corby spoke only to Anne Corby. Needles plying the leather, Unity steeled herself to remain silent. Sharing the horror was the only medicine likely to heal the wounds in this girl's heart.

'Another howl sliced the silence, answered again by short

snapping barks. As if acting upon a given signal the shapes separated, positioning themselves in the pattern of a hunting pack. I'm afraid . . . I am so afraid!' The words became silent in Anne's mind. 'The whip cracks, the sound smashing across the stillness like a pistol shot. The sleigh has become a competitor in a race, a race that means life for the winners.

'The snow is deepening, it sucks at the horse's hooves with every step, slowing its headlong flight, giving an added advantage to the highly skilled killers beginning to close in. The whip . . . lay it across the horse's flank. Crystals of ice are spreading like diamonds in a setting of jet lacing its mane, flecks of foam spinning back from nostrils flared wide with terror the tired animal plunges forward. "Pull!" Anne screamed aloud into the lacerating wind. "Pull . . . pull!" Then she reeled as though a terrific gust snatched at her, ripping at her clothes, wanting to tear away her head as a tribute to its strength.'

Remaining silent Unity worked on. She could only guess at the trauma in the girl's mind.

'Afraid to loose the rein . . . I have to blink rapidly to clear the blinding flakes from my eyes. To the front of the pack the lead wolf lifts its head to howl like a minion of hell . . . it has made its move! Swift and silent as a shadow it has darted forward, snapping at the horse's front legs. "The rifle, Mother!"' Anne's head turned to look across her shoulder, her wild shout causing the baby to whimper but Unity made no move. 'A few shots might cause the wolves to drop back, give the horse enough leeway to outrun them into the town.

"The rifle," I shout again, "for God's sake, Mother, use the rifle." The wind laughs, snatching the words, tossing them into infinity.

'Hair threaded with crystals of ice whip across my face cutting into my skin like claws while fresh flakes of snow

drive blindingly. "The rifle!"' Part sobbing and part screaming she called to the phantoms in her mind. '"Use the
rifle!"'

But there had been no answering shots, only the screaming
of the wind as it snatched the cries, whisking them into the
obscurity of a white hell. Anne's one hope lay with the horse
but she knew the pathetically thin creature was waging a lost
battle. The effort of lifting itself clear of deep snow was rapidly
draining its strength and, almost as if it knew this, the lead
wolf repeatedly darted forward, causing the horse to falter and
scream in fear, snapping jaws grazing its fetlocks.

As if the memories governed the move Anne touched her
left wrist. The reins looped about her hand strained into her
flesh as she fought to hold the sleigh steady, while with her
right hand she raised the whip, snaking it along the grey back,
and momentarily the wolf gave ground.

Using the moment she slewed in her seat, half turning to
call again to her mother to use the rifle. But the wolf seized the
same moment. Changing tactics, its weight jolting the speed-
ing sleigh, it leapt, bared yellow fangs snapping at her mother's face. Too terrified to shout Anne slashed with the whip.

Snarling and slavering, venom-filled eyes closing with hers,
the wolf slid from the sleigh and rolled into the soft snow.

Again she laid the whip along the horse's quivering flanks.
The animal, half crazed with fear, was near to breaking but she
had to drive it on, they had to reach Plivna, the alternative . . .
but there was no alternative!

'Our Father—' The whispered prayer began then stopped,
Unity shivering against the bitterness of Anne's next words.
'What use is there in prayer? There is no God . . . no caring
Almighty! How could there be, how could a God of love take
and take and give nothing but fear and pain in return? You
were wrong, Jacob Corby!'

Laughing and sobbing at the same time she seemed to lift a glance to leaden skies.

'You were wrong! There is no God, you wasted your life, you took your miserable little existence and laid it on the altar of Mammon, it wasn't any God you worshipped, Jacob Corby, it was yourself!' Drawn so deeply into the past Anne did not realise she spoke the words aloud, only that she cracked the whip, the wind filling her mouth and driving down into lungs aching and burning from breathing ice-packed air. Beside the sleigh the grey terror shadowed the struggling horse, grabbing at its legs, snarling and snapping at the snaking whip.

Again and again the offensive was launched, the pack acting in organised concert to besiege the flagging horse on both sides.

Flicking the whip at the nearest of them she did not shout. She needed to conserve every breath, every ounce of energy. If her mother would only shoot, she must be awake now, must know the danger they were in.

In the closed world that was her mind, Anne saw herself half turn, saw her mother, the thin figure leaning far over the edge of the sleigh, one gloved hand trailing the ground; saw the several lean grey bodies loping an easy guard on both sides and her own mouth open; but the cry was lost in the searing howl which rose above the wind. As if in obedience to it a wolf darted inward, grabbing the trailing hand while a second sank yellowed fangs into her mother's arm, tipping the sledge sideways in a combined pull. At the exact same moment two wolves attacked the horse from each side and sank teeth into its hind quarters, bringing a frenzied scream ripping from the terrified animal. Nostrils quivering, glazed eyes rolling, it reared, its front legs kicking at the icy air, its paralysing fear snatching its balance and leaving it to fall. As it did, the rest of the pack closed to the kill.

Absorbed in the shadows of memory, Anne did not hear herself call for the rifle, sensed only the crack of the whip and the wind driving against her face.

Watching the drama of it play across drawn features, Unity Hurley felt her own heart quicken. What hell had this wench lived through, what black pit did she stare into now?

Tentacles of memory binding her to itself, holding her fast in that white world of terror, it seemed to Anne the nightmare lived again. Skirts wrapped about her legs, the wind screamed its mockery as she clambered over the driving seat into the body of the sleigh, trying to drag her mother from those snarling, slavering jaws. Why had she not fired the rifle? Then, the thin figure a weight in her arms, she knew why . . . her mother was dead!

Close to her skirts powerful jaws snapped. She whipped away the rugs which had covered her mother, throwing them on the snow where they fell like small brown oases on the pristine whiteness. The death screams of the horse had died into silence when Anne began to laugh; the sound reaching back from that far yesterday, filling her brain with wild hysterical peals reaching to the horizon, bouncing back in rippling crazy waves. Among the wolf pack feeding in the crimson snow one tapering head lifted and turned, its blood-soaked muzzle drawing back in a low snarl.

'You are wrong, Father!'

It seemed to Anne she still laughed down into those slavering jaws.

'You were wrong about your God.'

'Hush, wench, it be all over now.'

Dropping her needles, Unity moved quickly, folding the trembling girl in her arms.

'You be safe now, it be all over.'

But as the shaking figure sobbed against her breast, Unity Hurley knew the trauma of Anne Corby's past was not yet all told. And that of her future was just beginning.

His wife's retelling of what had been told that afternoon now finished, Laban Hurley took the clay pipe from his mouth gently tapping the small white bowl into his palm to clear the remnants of tobacco. 'So Jacob Corby and his wife are both dead. Do you reckon her over at Butcroft House has the knowing of it?'

'They'll have the guessing of it, her and that son of hers!' Unity sorted the leather strips Laban had brought home for stitching into 'Sam Browne's'. It seemed she stitched more and more of these cross belts for army officers.

'Ar.' Laban nodded, shaving paper-thin slices from a stick of Shag tobacco. 'That lad'll have guessed, they be two for a pair, what one knows t'other knows.'

'Don't take a power of guessing . . . when the wench showed up at the house, neither of her folk with her . . . well, it don't need no hammer to drive that nail in. Clara Mather p'raps hadn't had the telling of how that brother and his wife died, God rest them, but Clara will have no fears they do be dead and that'll be a part answer to her prayers.'

Pressing the shavings into the pipe, Laban lit a spill at the fire, holding the flame to the bowl. 'Part answer . . . what . . .' he spoke and sucked alternately, '. . . what mean you by that?'

'Mean!' Leaving leather belts to fall across the kitchen table Unity crossed to the door giving on to the stairs, listening for fully thirty seconds before closing it firmly, then, keeping her voice low, she turned to her husband. 'You know nicely what I mean, Laban Hurley, it's been Clara Mather's dream that Jacob and each of his family be dead, that way the Glebe Works along of all 'er brother owned would go lock, stock an' barrel to her. That be the prayer that woman wanted granting!'

'Now you can't be speaking of what you don't know.'

A remonstrative frown backing the sentence had no effect upon Unity. Quick as summer lightning her reply flashed back.

'I know one thing, that being you wouldn't lay a year's takings to my being wrong! You might not be as free with your tongue as I am but your mind carries the same thoughts . . . now you tell me that don't be so!'

Returning the spill to its pot in the hearth, Laban knew himself defeated. He would not lie, not that it would have served any purpose, after so many years of marriage Unity knew the inside of him as well as she knew the outside.

Back at the table Unity selected a strip of leather and threaded a length of twine each end through a separate needle. 'They don't all be dead though do they?'

Through a haze of lavender-grey tobacco smoke Laban watched the deft movements. Placing the leather strip into the jaws of a metal clamp he himself had made to hold the material firmly, Unity set her left foot into a stirrup, the pressure of it pulling down on a leather strap to close the jaws.

'The daughter is still alive, and now there is another, a grandchild to stand in the way.'

'Then that be an end to Clara Mather's dream.' Laban's eyes followed the quick in and out of the stitching needles.

Unity pulled sharply at the thread, double-locking each stitch. 'I think not. Jacob's daughter might not want what her father left but one day the child lying in that drawer will be grown and who is to say he will follow his mother's choosing, who is to say he won't claim that inheritance? Clara Mather be shrewd enough to know that and so does her son . . . and ain't neither of them will go handing it over quiet.'

Chewing the slender stem of the pipe, Laban stared into

the fire, his wife's words rattling like pebbles in his mind. Clara Mather had become used to being the main voice at Glebe metal works . . . very used! Unity was not misled in her thinking nor was she mistaken in her words; Jacob Corby's sister would not relinquish what she held, not happily or otherwise, nor would her world lie peaceful so long as the girl and her child lived.

So long as the girl and her child lived!

The words echoed, stunning his mind with their implication. Clara Mather had always been a vindictive woman, heartless in her dealings with those employed in the metal foundry, ruthless with any buyer who crossed her, and she would be no different with her niece. As his gaze locked on flames darting like blood-tipped spears, Laban admitted what his thoughts had been leading to: Darlaston was no safe place for Anne Corby and her son. Given what Unity had told him of the girl's past, given it was true – and there was no reason for believing otherwise – then that girl had already trodden the paths of hell, but here she must walk an even more dangerous road, one which the devil's own advocate walked. And that particular disciple would not hesitate to push her off.

7

'Why do you have to go? At least give yourself a few days more of rest. It drains the strength birthing a child and you hadn't much of that to begin with.'

Glancing at Unity's lined face creased now with a frown, Anne shook her head. 'I promised I would do as I had been asked as soon as I reached England.'

'Well, it were no fault of yours that you couldn't, a babby don't wait on nothing nor nobody to be born; when the apple be ripe it falls from the tree and ain't nothing can go a stopping of it, but nature makes sure the tree be rested after fruiting and you should do the same.'

They had followed this line before. Each time she spoke of leaving, Unity had found some reason why she should not. The last one had been the matter of churching, a service whereby she had to ask forgiveness of God for her sin of conceiving a child . . . *her* sin! She had wanted to scream at that, scream it was she had been sinned against, that rape was a crime not a choice, a torment not a pleasure. But she had not voiced her protest, she had gone to the church of St Lawrence and asked that forgiveness as a gesture to Unity and her husband; the only recognition of their kindness she was able to pay. But this time she could not concede.

'Please.' She tried a smile but tears welling in her eyes washed it away. 'Please understand, I have to go—'

'You have to go to that house, that I understands!' Unity's reply was sharp. 'But what happens after that? Your breasts have no milk so how do you feed that little 'un when he cries with hunger . . . where do you leave him if you find work? You need to give thought to all of them things and more, like what if either of you takes sick or has a fall . . . what if it be that happens crossing of a heath where no soul walks from one week's end to another, what of the child then, who will be there to care for him?'

Her lips trembling, Anne lifted the child from the drawer which served as a crib and held the tiny body close against her own. She had thought of all of those reasons and a thousand more besides, each one telling her the baby would be better cared for in a home for foundlings, the workhouse would see he was placed there. But each time her mind reached that conclusion her heart had withered, curling and crumpling like a dead leaf. But was it fair to set her own feelings above the welfare of her son? *Her son* . . . Anne felt the whole of her being sink beneath a deluge of love and pain. That was the very crux of the matter, the child she held was her son, in the weeks since his birth he had become the breath in her lungs, the blood in her veins, he was the beat of her heart, the substance of her soul; to part with him, to tear all of that from her would leave her a hollow shell.

'I have thought of little else.' She looked at Unity. 'That is why I must take my baby and give him to the care of the Parish.'

She had known it would be difficult, the pain of parting would go deep, but she had not reckoned on this. Teeth clenched against a searing emptiness, Anne forced herself to walk on. Her son would be cared for, it was better for him he be left behind. Better for him, yes, but for her . . . ? The shawl Unity had lent her was pulled low over her head, hiding the worn patches of a coat which had been shabby when her mother gave some of their last few kopecks for it in the market place in Zovskoye.

Anne fought tears rising from a bitterness she covered but could not bury. Her mother had been ill for months, each day seeing her grow a little weaker, and what had Jacob done? He had prayed! '*The Lord will provide,*' he had said. '*He will not abandon His children.*' And the Lord had provided, He had provided a meal for timber wolves by allowing them to snatch her mother from that sleigh. Breath locked in her throat as the vision of those grey snarling shapes, yellow fangs sinking into her mother's body, flashed into her mind. That had been the provision heaven had made for Viola Corby; and for Viola Corby's daughter it had provided rape and abuse.

She had trusted the man when he had said she was welcome to water from his well, no thought of the evil lurking in his mind had entered her own; it had been so easy for him . . . so easy! He had laughed as his wife had thrown the contents of a wooden bucket, soaking her to the skin, then kicked her with heavy clog-like boots as she chased her from the yard. That was her son's father. That loutish, grease-stained pig of a man was the father of her child. How could she tell a child that? How could she tell him he was the result of rape, the memory of which even now terrified her? And if he ever found out would he see it as rape or would he judge her a willing partner, a whore happy to give herself to any with the means to pay? She had faced many terrors, known a thousand heartbreaks but that would be one she could not face . . . nor would she have to: her child would be left where no one knew the facts of his conception, no one knew he was a bastard, no one save Unity and Laban Hurley and they had given their word.

Trust! It rang like a bell in her brain. She had trusted before, trusted her father to do what was best for his family, trusted until it had dried in the arid deserts of the Sahara, withered

in the savage heat of Arabia and in the vast frozen plains
of the Russian Steppes before dying completely beside that
well . . . trust! It was so easy to give and so easily broken,
but this time . . . this time her heart told her, Unity Hurley
would not break that trust nor would she herself go back on
the word she had given Mikhail Yusupov.

Suddenly she was back in Russia. Flashes, each more vivid
than the last, showed a crazed horse running for its life . . .
snarling wolves snapping at its fetlocks . . . a thin figure
dragged from a sleigh by yellow fangs red with blood . . .
a girl laughing hysterically – then something those phantoms
had not disclosed before: the crack of a single shot, the noise
reverberating across the wastes of snow, drumming fingers of
sound along the tree line, smashing deafeningly against her
ears and folding the laughter back into her throat . . . then
the figure standing on the sleigh jerking spasmodically before
falling backwards across the wolf-ravaged body.

The coach had come upon them too late to save her mother
and too soon for Anne, for she had wanted to die too, to end
a life that was nothing but misery. But heaven had denied
that also. They had taken her with them, she had been told
later, taken to their home at Krymsk near to the sea of Azov.
She remembered little of the days and nights of that long
journey, only that she was as unwelcome among the servants
into whose care she had been given as her family had been
elsewhere in that country.

Deaf to the sounds of the road she walked, blind to the
people around her, Anne heard only one voice, a voice which
spoke softly behind her.

'*I would not tell her your secrets.*'

In her mind she watched as her hand dropped from the
muzzle of the horse she visited whenever she could escape
the watchful eye of the cook; she turned, all the fears from that
other stable rushing chokingly into her throat. Tall enough to

fill the doorway, broad shoulders tapering to slim hips, riding breeches tucked into black knee-length boots and held at the waist by a broad leather belt, a man stood, one hand raised to the lintel, the other grasping a short-handled riding crop.

'*Who are you?*'

The voice had been quiet and well modulated with no trace of the coarse tongue of the kitchens, but it was the belt held her attention. Staring at it she was instantly back in the inn at Radiyeska facing the threatening figure of its landlord.

'*Answer me, girl. Who are you?*'

Among the shadows of her mind, the man dropped his hand from the lintel.

'*Have you no tongue!*'

He had taken several steps before a smothered scream escaped clenched lips, bringing an instant frown with the next question.

'*Why are you so afraid? You will come to no harm from me.*'

Seeing the conflict in her face the man had come no closer. His tone had remained level but in the shadowed stable Anne had caught the whiff of irritation as he spoke.

'*If you will not tell me who you are then maybe you will tell me what you are doing here in the stables?*'

The memory of that inn alive in her mind, Anne had struggled to answer.

'*I – I came to see Lady.*'

'*Ah yes.*' The irritation faded as he glanced towards the horse. '*You were telling her your secrets, but that is not wise. She is fickle, that one; is that not so, Lady?*'

The horse snickered softly and the man's eyes asked Anne if he might step closer, and when she did not cry out he stretched a hand to stroke the animal's nose.

'*Do not lie to me, my beautiful one,*' he stroked gently, '*you would be any man's mistress for a carrot . . . but for an apple –*' he had glanced at the fruit in Anne's hand

and sighed '– *oh Lady, you would break my heart for an apple.*'

'*I'm sorry, I will leave.*' Anne saw the shadow that was herself step towards the doorway of the stable and the man's quick smile.

'*And deprive my fickle love of her apple! You would not be so cruel.*'

'*It is not allowed for me to visit the stables.*'

'*Who told you it is not allowed?*'

The question was sharp but the hand fondling the horse remained gentle.

'*I was told so when I was brought to this house.*' She answered, not realising her fear had vanished. '*The cook said every part of the house and grounds except for the scullery is barred to me because I am a foreigner.*'

Time and memory had not faded the look which had marred that handsome face, a look of anger she had glimpsed before it was hidden.

'*I see.*' Strong fingers had stroked the velvet muzzle. '*Unfortunately many of my countrymen still have a mistrust of those not born in Russia, but, God willing, they will one day learn that beyond our borders all is not governed by the devil.*'

'*My parents were English.*' She had volunteered the information, evading the need to speak of the attitude of people she had met while tramping through this man's country. '*I don't remember very much of it, we left when I was still very young.*'

'*So you are English, then that is the language in which we will converse, but it would feel more friendly if you told me your name.*'

Anne's eyes travelled past him to the groom who had entered the stables and now stood staring at them. Following the gaze he spoke rapidly to the man who turned back towards the cobbled yard but not before Anne had seen the look of contempt in his eyes. He would tell the cook where she had been and that would bring the thin cane stinging across her shoulders.

'*I beg your pardon for being here,*' she made to move past him, '*I must go, I shall be needed in the kitchen.*'

'*You may go presently.*' He moved just one foot but it was enough to effectively bar her way. '*But first, your name.*'

Wanting to be away she answered abruptly, '*My name is Anne Corby.*'

'*Anne.*' The smile returned to his mouth, lifting the corners slightly. '*To me it carries the sound of England.*'

'*Do you know England?*' Momentarily forgetting the threat of another beating she had looked eagerly at the tall man, his dark hair falling loosely to his brow. '*Have you been there?*'

'*So, our new servant has not forgotten her homeland.*'

Lifting her head she had stared, her fear of the cook's impending punishment forgotten as she answered with cold pride, '*I am not a servant. I was brought to this house by Mikhail Yusupov but that does not make me one of his servants.*'

'*Neither does it.*' He inclined his head, his smile leaving his mouth. '*My apologies, I was wrong to call you that. So, you were brought here by Mikhail Yusupov.*'

There had been no sense of awe in his voice, awe which coloured the servants' tone whenever they spoke of that man.

'*But why did he leave you here?*'

'*I do not know, unless it was because I was ill.*' She turned a nervous glance towards the stables' entrance. '*Excuse me, I must go, the servants will have finished their meal and I will be needed to wash the dishes.*'

'*You were ill, you say?*'

He either had not heard what she said or did not care.

'*Are you the girl rescued from the wolves?*'

Anne remembered her surprise. '*Yes,*' she had answered, again looking towards the entrance to the stables.

'*Who set you to washing dishes?*' This time there was no gentleness in his voice only a crisp anger.

She did not want to answer. The longer she stayed there talking the more trouble there would be when she returned to the scullery; whoever this man might be it was best their conversation ended now.

'*I asked who set you to washing dishes?*' He had caught at her or she would have moved, his hand fastening on her arm, dark, angered eyes looking into hers.

'*That is what I was supposed to do, I have to earn my keep while I am in this house.*'

'*Who told you that?*'

It was turning into an interrogation. Anne watched herself pull her arm free. Who was this man asking so many questions and why was he suddenly so angry?

'*You have no need to answer,*' he said as her glance again shot towards the doorway, '*you have told me already.*'

Allowing her to pass he followed as she left the stables, his brows falling sharply together as the strong light fell on Anne's face showing the blood congealing around the fresh cut on her temple.

'*And did the same one do that to you?*' His eyes touched the wound, his mouth taut with anger.

Her hand going to the cut she felt suddenly self-conscious. Why should a man she had never met before be so angry on her behalf?

'*It does not matter,*' she had answered.

'*Do not tell me what matters!*' Taking her chin in his hand he turned her head, examining the bruises on her cheek. '*From the look of these it would seem you have been struck before, many times.*'

'*Please, I must go, when she finds out I was here—*'

'*The same thing will happen again!*'

Even in her reverie, Anne heard the snap in that voice, the razor edge of anger.

She had looked at him a new worry clouding her eyes. She was dependent on the cook, it rested with her whether or not help was requested of the man who had brought her here, the help which would get her home to England; if the cook were alienated by questions concerning those bruises then she would refuse to give any kind of assistance.

'*Please,*' she had pleaded, '*please don't say anything . . . promise you won't.*'

Pictures flashing through her mind showed the man drop his hand from her face, the other tapping the riding crop against a boot with short angry movements, Anne drew close to the hedge as a wagon loaded with threshed corn turned through an opening leading to Bentley Mill.

'*That I will not promise,*' he said tersely, '*but this I do. Never again will you receive a blow in this house, nor in any place where I am present.*'

He kept that promise. A week later she was taken to a room dark with wood, beams and panels accentuating heavy furniture, and there she met the man whose rifle shot had saved her life, Mikhail Yusupov, the father of the man who had spoken so kindly to her. There were explanations on both sides, and at the end of them the older man advised she return to England; Russia, he said, was in turmoil, there was a threat of war with Germany, the army was not only ill-equipped for such an event but it was led by incompetents, yet the Tsar refused to accept any such advice. Then Mikhail muttered something about Bolsheviks but his son had swiftly interrupted and the older man had become silent. But only for a few moments.

The wagon having passed, Anne walked on, her mind filled with the past.

Mikhail Yusupov had waited a few moments, then, ignoring

his son's quick words of caution, withdrew a prettily inlaid box from a drawer of a tall cabinet.

'*You have expressed a desire to return to England.*'

The words rang so clearly in her brain that Anne halted abruptly, the shuffle of her feet sending a browsing rabbit scampering across a newly mown wheat field.

'*Father*—'

The son had tried again but the father answered, '*This must be, Andrei, let it reach once more the hands of the vile Rasputin then Russia and maybe the whole world will be*—'

He had stopped there, his blue eyes sharp beneath darkly winged brows. '*Anne Corby,*' he had spoken calmly though long fingers moved restlessly over the lid of the box, '*I will pay your passage to England if you will take this box*—'

'*Mikhail Mikhailovitch,*' Andrei had stepped forward, '*since when have the Yusupov demanded remuneration for a kindness?*'

The fingers moving agitatedly about the box stilled and the face, handsome behind an elegantly trimmed and pointed beard showing only the faintest streaks of grey, smiled its apology.

'*My son is right and I am shamed, forgive a man anxious for his country, Miss Corby, you will be given passage home.*'

It seemed the end of the matter, Andrei touching her arm as his father returned the box to the cabinet, but Anne had brushed the touch aside, addressing the older man in the fashion of his country.

She walked on following a narrow track running between fields of yellow corn.

It had taken every ounce of her courage but she lifted her head to stare into those ice-blue eyes.

'*Mikhail Mikhailovitch Yusupov.*' He had turned quickly at that, a hint of appreciation shadowing his mouth. '*I thank you for your further offer of assistance and I gladly accept, but only on the condition that I carry that box with me.*'

'*You would make conditions, little English girl!*'

The brows had fallen together. Anne seemed to feel again the tremor which had trickled along her spine. The man had absolute power in his own house, he could have her disposed of and who would there be to think anything of it, except perhaps Andrei.

Swallowing hard she faced the older man, her reply firm as the stone foundation of the house. '*Sir, even a little English girl has her pride.*'

What did the box contain? To this day she had not seen. Pausing beside tall stone pillars, Anne glanced at a mellow red-brick house visible at the end of a long drive. She knew only that Mikhail Yusupov had implored she take extreme care of whatever was wrapped in black velvet and given into her keeping the day of her departure. Andrei had insisted he be the one to accompany her to the harbour at Anapa, several times impressing upon her the need to speak to no one of what she carried with her. He had seemed afraid – if that strong face could show fear – afraid of whatever nestled in that small piece of velvet even being exposed to the light of day.

'*Anne,*' he had whispered as she stepped onto the gang-plank. '*It is not too late . . . my father should never have asked you to carry so terrible a responsibility. Return the package to me and I—*'

'*No!*' she answered quickly. '*I gave my word and I will keep it.*'

Features drawn with anxiety he had raked the bustling dock with a keen glance before taking her hands in his. '*Then hide it well, Anne,*' he said hurriedly, '*for with that package goes the peace of nations.*'

Walking towards the house Laban Hurley had given direction to, Anne watched the anxious face of Andrei Yusupov slip slowly from her mind's eye.

'*Hide it well.*'

She had done as asked. In the tiny cabin assigned to her she had removed one shoulder pad of her jacket. Carefully cutting it across she had placed the small velvet-covered object between the two halves before sewing them together and stitching the pad back inside the jacket, replacing the lining with tiny, almost invisible stitches. She had reasoned that neither passenger nor crew of the ship would see anything strange in her wearing a coat while on deck and when not on deck she kept strictly to her cabin. In that way the package entrusted to her had been always with her. Even Unity and Laban had not been told of it. Unhappy as it made her to keep anything hidden from them she had felt bound by her promise to the Yusupovs. The Hurleys knew only that in the past the Russians had known the owner of Bentley Grange and had asked Anne to deliver to him a message of friendship.

. . . the peace of nations . . .

Her steps on the drive the only sound, Anne shivered.

Whatever lay still hidden in her jacket, it was far more than a message of friendship.

8

Anne Corby had given birth to a son! Clara Mather's pinched mouth tightened. There had been no name spoken, no word of just who it was had given birth but the talk of a child having been delivered in the Hurley household was all over the town and she didn't need more than one guess as to the identity of the mother; and that guess wouldn't be Unity Hurley!

Setting her basket on a well-scrubbed table she marched from the kitchen without a word to the daily woman. Clara could afford a live-in servant, perhaps two or three but who could say where inquisitive noses were poked when a body's back was turned.

A son! She stalked about the gleaming sitting room, a finger tracing every surface, hard, bead-like eyes searching each corner for the faintest smear of dust. Clara Mather did not pay four shillings a week to be left with dust! Jacob's girl had a son . . . It had been bad enough to be faced with her return, but now . . . Quick sharp movements, not unusual with Clara, were accentuated by the agitation bubbling inside her. There had been the possibility of stillbirth, of the child being born dead . . . but fate had not been so kind, it was alive and that meant Quenton could lose everything. A child, even a bastard child, could inherit if a Will so decreed.

Had Jacob's daughter written a Will? It stopped Clara in mid-step her dust-searching stare hanging in space. Had she drawn up a document claiming her rights and would that document have been written so that those same rights would be passed to her child? The girl was bound to have papers, her own certificate of birth, her parents' marriage lines. Viola Bedworth had always been most conscientious, and more so after marrying Jacob; that being so she had taken all things of that nature with her when he had dragged them off on his own fool's errand.

Papers! Clara's hands snapped to her side. They were of great importance in the eyes of the law, they could prove many things and accomplish many acts, such as taking away what she had spent years in building up, or giving Butcroft House and Glebe Metalworks to a wench or her son. Yes, papers were of vital importance, they carried a deal of power.

Fingers folding into her skirts, her tight mouth screwed against her teeth, Clara made for the privacy of her bed-room.

Papers carried a deal of power, but not the power to restore life to the dead!

She would wait. Clara walked across a bedroom which echoed her no-nonsense way of life. She had changed this room almost immediately her brother had left Butcroft House, throwing out pretty lace-edged bedcovers and wide-frilled pillowcases. Fol-de-rols were for the empty headed and no one could label Clara Mather empty headed.

Pulling aside a plain, beige-coloured drape she stared down the length of the wide garden, her eye resting on a blaze of tall, brilliant-blue flowers. Yes, she would wait. What she had to do must have no observer and she herself must do all things as normal. She ought not to have stormed to this room as she had, that in itself was liable to raise questions in that woman's mind, and questions – of any sort – were the last thing she wanted. She must think of a reason, a logical cause of sweeping out of the kitchen. Releasing the curtain she let it fall into place. As she turned a smile touched her tight mouth when her eye caught the one picture she allowed to adorn the empty walls; the gleaming crimson of a painted sunset seemed to speak to her. Of course. The smile remaining, she crossed to the bed and sat on its edge. It was the perfect solution!

'I med the tea as usual, mum.' The daily help looked up as Clara re-entered the kitchen. 'Will you be wantin' that there basket emptied?'

Though it was usual for her to refuse, Clara nodded assent as she poured tea into a plain white china cup. Let the woman empty the basket, let her see it contained nothing but meat and vegetables.

Waiting until the foodstuffs had been placed in their various places, Clara let a short breath labour in her throat and one hand touch her corseted stomach.

'Be you alright, mum? You don't seem yourself.'

It had worked! Clara kept her elation well hidden beneath a frown of pain.

'Coming from the Bull Stake –' her hand moved soothingly over her stomach '– I was taken with a monthly. I thought to have finished with the wretched business. I had to go straight upstairs to wash and put on some protection—'

'Oh you don't have to tell me . . . be a curse to women, be that. Every month the same and when it be over you finds yourself like as not to have summat worse to cope with.' The woman shook her head dolefully. 'It be a woman's lot . . . half a dozen monthly showings and then another babby in the belly! But at least you ain't got that to worry over, not with you being a widder woman.'

'That is the one mercy of widowhood.' Clara spooned honey into her tea.

'And these be a mercy when a body be in pain.' Delving into a drab cloth bag always placed within sight whenever she came to the house the cleaning woman produced a slim rectangular packet of thin white paper, its black lettering forming the logo 'Seidlitz Powder'. Handing it to Clara she nodded encouragingly. 'They be right good, swallow that then get yourself a lie on the bed for half an hour and you'll feel a ton better.'

Insisting the woman take the one penny cost of the medicine, Clara waited until she had left then flung the packet into the fire. The woman had swallowed the reason for that earlier slip of behaviour and the inevitable gossip of 'her up at Butcroft still seeing her monthlies' would do no harm.

Working quickly she washed teacup and pot, returning each to its place, then glanced at the clock ticking quietly on the mantel. It wanted several hours before Quenton would return.

Her glance travelling beyond the window caught the brilliance of the tall blue flower. Wolfsbane. It had served once before, now it would serve again, but not fresh gathered.

Moving quickly she almost ran to her room, there collecting the flowers and leaves she had dried and hidden; the packet which held them was glued to the underside of the lowest drawer of a tall chest compiled of six. Placing it in her pocket she turned next to the wardrobe. The mourning suit she had worn at her husband's funeral, and which had ever since been covered by a linen clothes bag, hung at the back behind the few gowns she had allowed herself to buy over the years. Taking it out she lay it across the bed. If her plan was successful she would be wearing the suit again . . . quite soon.

Reaching beneath the linen cover, her fingers quickly found the ruched satin muff and in its secret inner pocket the tiny bottle. Holding it in her hand she stared at the dark green reeded glass, watching the light gleam from it in a hundred glistening emerald points. It might be called beautiful . . . but it would hold death!

Having put the suit back in the wardrobe, she returned

to the kitchen. Taking a ceramic basin from the dresser and setting it on the table she placed the bottle beside it, then emptied the packet of dried leaves and flowers into the basin. The use of dried leaf and flower produced a potion many times stronger than was made using the fresh variety, and she wanted a lethal concoction.

Reaching for the kettle simmering on the hob of the shining black-leaded grate, she paused. There may be no second chance, this might prove a case of win or lose . . . and she would not lose!

Snatching up the basin, she carried it to the dining room. Quenton had acquired the habit of a glass of brandy after his evening meal, and easing the stopper from the square-cut crystal decanter she poured a little of the golden liquid over the dried flowers. Alcohol dissolved all the chemical properties of the plant rendering a solution far more effective than water alone. Back in the kitchen she bruised the plant material allowing the brandy to soak well into it. When she was sure every drop had been absorbed she tipped the sodden mixture into a sieve, using the back of a wooden spoon to press every drop of liquid from it. But that was not enough; the tiniest bit of leaf or petal left in the juice was a risk she could not take.

Taking a fine linen bag from a drawer of the dresser, she strained the liquid through it into a glass jug. Again and again she repeated the process until the liquid was clear as the glass itself. Clara lifted the jug, holding it at eye level as she inspected the crystal-clear contents. There was such a small amount, but a few drops were all it would take!

And the colour and taste of the tincture . . . but what about the smell of alcohol? A brief smile touched the hard mouth. Most of the alcohol was held in the mass of leaves and flowers which had absorbed it, that would be thrown away; she needed only the few drops of extract whose colour would dissipate completely when added to other drinks. Stirring a spoonful of honey into the liquid Clara watched them combine; honey and a few hours' exposure to the air would eliminate the faint odour of alcohol, then added to milk or tea it would not be detected at all.

The jug, now covered with a crotcheted cloth, glass beads tinkling against its sides, caught the crimson rays of the setting sun; so like the picture on her bedroom wall. Red as the blood she had pretended was leaving her body. Flinging the empty packet and wooden spoon into the fire she took the basin into the yard smashing it against the cobbles, throwing the pieces into the rubbish heap. It would seem she had dropped it while cooking and cleared the remains from the kitchen. The jug would follow once the contents had been transferred to the bottle.

That tiny bottle – Clara allowed herself the rare luxury of yet one more smile – that beautiful, deadly little bottle.

'You!'

Glancing at the wisp of a girl, her chestnut hair drawn back from a small heart-shaped face, the pale skin emphasising eyes which seemed too big for it, Sir Corbett Foley could not empty his voice of disbelief.

'You have a message for me?'

Fingers pressed together, Anne tried to still nerves stretched to breaking point. She had been tempted to turn away, to run back along that corn-edged track, disappear into the emptiness of heath. But she had persevered, coming nearer and nearer this large, two-storey building with its brick chimneys and tall, wide-arched windows, coming nearer the spectres of the past. The servants had been pleasant enough, the cook inviting her to a chair in the kitchen while the butler had taken her request to the master, yet in their eyes she had seen the tell-tale traces. Like the owner of Bentley Grange they too did not believe she could be the conveyor of any message, much less one to no less a dignitary than Sir Corbett Foley.

'Yes.' She swallowed hard but the 'sir' remained stuck in her throat.

'And who are you?' Eyebrows like silver caterpillars crept closer together.

Memory's gates flung suddenly wide, disclosing a small girl dressed in pale lemon organdie trimmed with yellow sash and bows, ribbons of the same colour scooping up shining chestnut-coloured ringlets, her green eyes wide with alarm as she ran to hide her face in her mother's skirts while a tall man with a dark goatee beard and metal-grey eyes smiled an apology for startling her. He could be startling still. Anne jumped as a silver-topped Malacca cane thumped the floor of the book-lined library.

'Answer me, girl. I don't have all day to waste!'

Clearly as impatient as she remembered him he rang the small silver bell set near his high, winged leather chair.

'My – my name—' She coughed, forcing the obstruction that was sheer nerves to leave her throat. She had faced much more daunting situations in her short life and she would face this one. 'My name is Anne Corby.'

'Am I supposed to know you?'

It was sharp, rattling like rifle shots over snow-bound steppes and Anne's fingers tightened.

'No.' She lifted her head, her gaze steady on one which did not flicker. 'No, Sir Corbett, I do not expect you to remember me but my parents often enjoyed the pleasure of your company both in their own home and here at Bentley Grange.'

'Parents?' The silver caterpillars moved to join, the eyes beneath them narrowing to a concentrated stare.

'Jacob Corby and his wife, Viola.'

'Corby!' The cane thudded again, the silver brows rising.

'Jacob Corby . . . that would be Butcroft House, would it not? Viola . . . beautiful woman . . . beautiful . . . get out, man . . . get out!' he barked impatiently at the butler who had answered the summons of the bell. 'Yes, Viola . . . a wife for any man to be proud of . . . and you,' he peered closer, 'are you the tot I frightened with my loud voice – are you Corby's daughter?'

'Yes,' Anne answered quietly, 'Jacob Corby was my father.'

'Was?' The owner of Bentley Grange leaned forward, the leather of the chair creaking with the movement.

'My parents are dead.' Keeping her explanation as brief as facts would allow, Anne told her story, told of the years of endless trekking, the travels that had ended so tragically; but of her rape and the birth of her son she said nothing.

'It was wrong.' Silver hair glinted in the light streaming through tall, multi-paned windows as the man's head swung slowly from side to side. 'It was wrong to take a woman and child, expose them to God knows what hardship and danger. Corby was ever a stubborn man but a dedicated one and there can be no combination more impenetrable to common sense. You have my deepest sympathies, child . . . a pity, a great, great pity; but we have to thank heaven you were saved.'

He had listened yet somehow she felt this distinguished-looking man did not believe all she said. Could it be he thought her here to beg his charity? The thought irking her pride Anne felt her jaw tighten.

'Heaven is thanked daily,' she clipped her words, 'it is my regret I could do no more than thank Mikhail Mikhailovitch Yusupov and his son, Andrei, but sometimes even heaven smiles twice, I may yet be given the opportunity to express my gratitude in differed terms.'

'That would never do.' Anne watched the autocratic features dissolve into a smile. 'These Russians are proud beggars.'

'We all have our pride, Sir Corbett.'

'I see I have injured yours.' The man's hand moved once more to the small bell. 'For the sake of the friendship I had with your parents I ask your pardon; I'm afraid the long years of being without my own dear wife have blunted my good manners, as for the social graces –' he swung his head gently but his grey eyes twinkled '– she said I never did have an abundance of those. But I can see why Mikhail chose to ask you to be his courier.' He broke off to order the butler to bring tea, waiting for the library door to close before continuing. 'He was ever the perceptive one among our group at Cambridge, he could smell a fraud at a hundred paces. He will be happy to hear you are not dead after all.'

'Dead?' Anne frowned. 'Why would he think me dead?'

'I am afraid we both thought the same thing. You see, my dear, Mikhail wrote to me saying his niece was paying a visit to England and that she would pay a call on her uncle's old friend. It's a ruse we often used as young men when the other's . . . er . . . female acquaintance . . . was about to call. I knew he had no niece and that, like myself, old tricks had been left behind once he married, so when I read his letter I knew there was something he wished me to know yet was too important to set down on paper.'

His hand lifting as the tap of the returning servant sounded at the door, Anne kept her silence. The whole thing was beginning to sound like some adventure story.

Setting the cane aside and inviting her to serve the tea he gave the departing servant several seconds before furthering his explanation.

'It was a week or so after his letter that I read in the newspaper an account of a ship being damaged during a storm in the Bosphorus and when, months later, you still had not arrived we both had to assume you had not survived.'

'The ship I sailed on was damaged in a storm,' Anne said, fighting memories suddenly swirling in her brain. 'I – I was fortunate enough to be taken to shore in a lifeboat. The ship, it seemed, would be quite some time in repair. For reasons of my own I could not wait and having insufficient money to take passage on another ship I had to make my way overland. It took longer than I had supposed.'

And it had been as difficult a journey as any she had taken with her father. With her teeth pressed together she struggled to dismiss the visions rising like dark spectres from the caverns of memory.

Sir Corbett Foley's astute gaze caught the tremble of fingers before they locked together. This girl had suffered more than a storm-blown ship. Had it been to do with the message Mikhail Mikhailovitch had given her to bring? God damn the man! Why could he not have given it to a fellah? A man was more suitable every time, no woman knew how to handle danger!

'I am sorry to have given rise to concern, the Yusupovs might think I took their help while having no intention of fulfilling their request; please explain—'

'I told you, old Yusupov can smell fraud, he would have sniffed you out had you any such intent; but put any qualms aside, I will write to him this evening. But now you must give me his message, tell me exactly what it was he said to tell me.'

The tea untouched beside her, Anne saw again the room heavy with dark wood and a man whose eyes became sharp and intense as she spoke of the home her mother had kept alive in her stories, of the little town of Darlaston set in the heart of England, heard the hiss of an indrawn breath marking the answer, yes; she had also spoken of a Bentley Grange and the man who had lived there at the time they had left England, a man by the name of Sir Corbett Foley.

'It was no spoken message.' Anne forced her mind to clear. 'He asked only that I bring a box, that I take every care it should not be discovered.'

'A box.' Corbett Foley glanced at the tight knit fingers pressed into Anne's lap. 'No doubt that went down in the Bosphorus.'

'Yes,' Anne nodded. 'But not due to any storm.' Speaking quietly she outlined her reason for removing the contents then dropping the box itself overboard.

The wench had more sense than he had given her credit for, but sense and courage were two entirely different fish, Mikhail should still have sent a man; faced with any kind of threat a woman was bound to give way. Walking miles across country with her parents was all very well; but alone . . . ? For once Mikhail Mikhailovitch had erred in his judgement, the girl had obviously been threatened and had given the cloth-bound object in order to secure her own safety; well, she could not be blamed, he would say as much in his letter.

'If I may borrow a pair of scissors.' Anne had watched the nuance of thought chase across the man's face, now she rose to her feet. 'The object given me by your friend is still sewn in the shoulder pad of my jacket.'

9

Unity Hurley bent over the work Laban had brought home for her to do. He still trusted her to help in the making of a saddle saying she had skills it took men years to learn. But then Laban forgot how many years she had worked beside him, the hours she had laboured while the business found its feet. She had watched every stage, followed the deft moves of his hands, listened to his explanation of every aspect of the industry, learned the quality of leather and the method of preparing and dyeing, become familiar with buffing and burnishing, carving, channelling, moulding and skiving, in fact all that the strength of her hands could do, and she had done it well enough to be given tasks he trusted no other to do; and this was one of them.

The saddle had been ordered from Bentley Grange but Unity knew that had it been a collar for a wagoner's horse the quality would have been the same, Laban Hurley allowed only the finest to carry his name. He had prepared the piece himself. Her fingers touching the soft pigskin she followed the stages mentally; the alignment of flap and panel, pressing the softer lining leather into the gullet or body to get the shape of the inside of the saddle, the rubbing with the masher, a tool which helped obtain a deeper imprint of that shape, the marking of a centre line which she had stitched to hold the two parts together. Now she would attach the pigskin facings already cut out by Laban. Placing the grain side of the facing to the grain side of the panel she selected a sharp-pointed harness number two needle, its slight thickness rendering it more suitable for stitching linings to saddle panels, then threaded it with a length of number twenty-five thread, this Laban also favoured for the job in hand. The thread doubled in the single needle she would need to use, she slipped a thimble onto one finger, glancing once at the drawer which had held the child. She had argued against it. Unity bent her head over the leather and began the process of back stitching. She had argued so fiercely, but like her father before her, Anne Corby had a mind of her own.

The girl had suffered hardship, there were no denying that. Unity pushed the needle through the places already indicated by a pricker, a toothed punch which had marked and partly penetrated the leather in order to guide and ease the path of the needle. But through the years of her growing that hardship had been offset by the presence and love of parents. True, Jacob Corby had displayed little of that, but love for his daughter had been in his heart, else why would he have taken her with him, why hadn't he left her behind where she would have the comfort of a home? He surely would have given mind to the extra burden traipsing a child along would bring, but take her he had; that said something in his favour. The comfort of a home but one empty of love, that could have been the childhood of Anne Corby. Unity pushed the needle with her thimble. But for Anne Corby's son there would be neither love nor comfort. He would never know his father and the chance to know his mother was being snatched away.

The foundling hospital or the workhouse! She pulled the thread tight. One were as soul-destroying as the other. Anne Corby could have no idea of the life she was condemning her child to, no knowledge of what she was truly parting with.

The needle becoming still in her hand she glanced again at the drawer. It had served as a bed twice before . . . each of her sons had lain in it. Matthew and Luke, both the centre of her world. The silence of the kitchen was suddenly invaded by laughter and the calls of children's voices, her eyes seeing two tumbling figures as her mind recreated the past. One older by a year and a half, taller by half a head. Matthew, who had grown so quickly he was a man before she had known it, Matthew of the dark hair and deep brown eyes, Matthew as skilled in the leather as his father. Watching them with the eyes of memory Unity smiled as the younger one tangled his lithe body about his brother, wrestling him to the floor. Luke the madcap, Luke with the laughing face. Lost to the yearning of her heart, Unity's hand moved to stroke the tousled brown hair and, as he had on that awful day, her younger son stood to face her. He was no longer a child, no longer the boy she had sung to sleep after some nightmare or who had held back the tears of a scraped knee; he was seventeen and a man.

'*Don't deny me, Mother.*'

Unity gazed into eyes that pleaded while her own brimmed with hot tears.

'*This be my chance to see summat of the world . . . please.*'

'*I'll look to him, Mother, I'll keep him close.*'

Out of the shadows her elder son came to his brother's side. The two of them tall and grown, filling her heart with pride while they broke it.

So she and Laban had agreed. Together they had watched their sons leave to join the army. That was the last time she had kissed their faces, held their strong young bodies in her arms, the last time she had heard their voices speak their love for her. They had been sent to fight a Boer invasion in Africa. The letter had come with a photograph showing them in uniform, Matthew's eyes solemn and thoughtful, Luke's with the echo of a laugh.

. . . I'll keep him close . . .

The words echoed in her heart, re-echoed against the pain in her soul.

Matthew had done that. In a place called Natal he had stepped in front of Luke; the Boer knife was meant for his brother. It had hit him full in the chest. It was an act of bravery. A survivor of that battle had told her.

An act of bravery! Unity stared at the illusory faces in her mind. That she would never doubt, but it had not saved Luke, he had died beside his brother and her world had fallen apart. She and Laban had lost their sons. A sob escaping her throat, she tried to hold the fading faces a little longer in her mind, to see the smiles, to hear the voices, but like mist in the sun of morning they melted away.

Yes, they had lost their sons. Her fingers trembling, her whole body throbbing with the ache she would never fully lose, Unity's tear-shrouded gaze rested again on the drawer. But the love they had shared in the years of their growing, the memories . . . they would be with her always, the treasures a mother locks away in her heart, treasures which could never be taken from her. And what would Anne Corby have? All of the pain but none of the pleasure. And the child?

Blinking her vision clear she ran a finger over her stitches, eight to the inch and neat as Laban was sure they would be. This was to have been Laban's legacy to his sons. They would return from the war to take over Regency Leather; but fate had decreed otherwise, it had snatched the dream away. Yet it was not fate decreeing Jacob Corby's legacy be denied his grandson, not fate snatching that dream away but Jacob's daughter!

The needle dug into the soft pigskin facing, biting savagely at the thicker leather of the saddle panel. Was there any difference? Her sons had been sacrificed for the sake of Empire, Anne Corby's would be sacrificed for the sake of pride.

★   ★   ★

That unexpected return of a monthly still had her feeling nauseated, she would prefer the house quiet and to herself today.

Clara Mather's cleaning woman slipped the shawl about her shoulders. Not allowing herself time enough to knot the ends together beneath her drooping breasts, she clattered quickly from the kitchen and along the back path, crossing open land which led on to Hill Street. It was the first time Clara Mather had given summat for nothin'. The woman grasped her four shillings tightly in the palm of her hand. Four shilling! You could have set a Christmas turkey in her mouth when Clara Mather had handed over six days pay for five worked . . . a turkey ar, the woman grinned, and still found room for the plum pudding! She hurried on towards the Bull Stake. The Lord was good, and her wouldn't say the devil were all bad, not if what had 'appened were anything to go by. Monthlies were the curse of the devil, was what her mother had moaned when the pains took her; well, let him visit it on Clara as often as he liked, for one woman's suffering were another's pleasure.

Having watched the woman down the path and allowed several minutes against a possible return, Clara slipped the bolt of the kitchen door. She did not want to be disturbed, she wanted the house to herself but not because of any monthly, real or otherwise. Her steps quick and loud on the green-and-cream-tiled floor of the corridor leading from kitchen to the front door she hesitated at the foot of the stairs listening for any sound. Satisfied she was alone she went rapidly up the stairs to her bedroom. This was the one room of the house the cleaning woman did not clean. Clara glanced around at the plain austereness. This room, like the shopping and cooking, she took care of herself. She had watched the woman closely the few minutes it had taken to tell her she would not be needed today, watched as she replaced her shawl, seen the eagerness to be gone. An eagerness not exceeding her own.

Clara took up a small bottle hidden behind the curtain. Her eyes had stayed on the woman's face, searching for any sign she had detected a whiff of this. Clara eased the cork free and sniffed at the contents before holding the bottle to the light of the window. Such a small amount. A smile cold as a viper's kiss touched her mouth. Barely covering the bottom of the bottle the tincture showed through the green reeded glass. There was enough. She had left the extracted juice of wolfsbane overnight, allowing the fumes to evaporate before pouring it into the tiny bottle. Then she had brought it here to her own room. Holding it now beneath her nose she sniffed again. There was no trace of brandy . . . either in the kitchen or in this bottle. In fact it gave off no odour other than a slight sweetness of honey.

Unity Hurley had bought bottles and rubber teats. That could only mean that the child could not be fed with the breast, it would have to be fed cow's milk, cow's milk sweetened with honey!

Replacing the cork she looked at the bottle fitting easily into her palm. Here was Quenton's future, a future secured for him by his mother.

Sir Corbett Foley looked up from the object he had unwrapped. Even from where she stood several yards across the room Anne saw spears of light dancing from the bed of dark velvet, a myriad starbursts seeming to leap from his hand. He had stared at it so long, the nuances of expression on his face changing from surprise as he had peeled away the layers of cloth to . . . what? Anne kept her glance on the bearded face; was it accusation, did he think there should be more to what he held, that Mikhail Mikhailovitch had entrusted her with something which was no longer there? No. She met the keen eyes. It was not accusation played in them; anxiety, then? No, it was more than that . . . those eyes held fear!

'Did you look at this, examine it before sewing it into your jacket?'

'Had Andrei or his father wished me to see the contents of the box they would have shown it to me. They did not. Nor did I take it from its cover. They gave me their trust and I would not break it.'

There was an honesty in those eyes he could not question. Sir Corbett Foley glanced again at the object in his hand. The girl had shown tenacity, a strength of spirit. He closed the velvet wrapping. Mikhail Mikhailovitch, the old dog, had not lost the knack of recognising the best.

Opening a door set so unobtrusively into a large book-filled cabinet that, had he not touched it, Anne would not have realised it was there, he set the object carefully inside, then closed the beaded glass doors.

'You have displayed an integrity of which your parents would have been proud.' He returned to his chair. 'But did Mikhail tell you nothing of what you carried?'

Anne shook her head. 'At first he spoke of a possible war with Germany and how ill-equipped the country was to meet such an event, that the army was led by incompetents and the Tsar refused to recognise the fact. He also said something about the Bolsheviks. Then he took the box from a cabinet and when Andrei tried to interrupt he said, "This must be . . . let it reach once more the hands of the vile Rasputin then Russia and maybe the whole world will be—"'

'Rasputin! I might have known. That man is evil personified, the devil incarnate!' The lids closing momentarily over brilliant eyes, Sir Corbett Foley breathed deeply before raising them, then asked, 'Whilst in Russia did you hear of that man?'

'Not in the villages, but at the house in Krymsk among the servants. I often heard the name whispered. It seemed everyone was almost too afraid to speak it.'

Unconsciously reaching for the Malacca cane he rested a forefinger on the silver knob. 'As well they might,' he said quietly, 'that man's evil told him many things.'

She could understand the servants being superstitious, that was a trait she had met wherever her father had taken them; but Mikhail and his son . . . ?

'Mikhail said nothing more?'

Her thoughts interrupted, Anne paused. Why so many questions? Why was this man as agitated as his Russian friend had been? What was so important about that package?

'Only that I take extreme care,' she answered. 'Andrei too, at the harbour in Anapa, he repeated the instruction several times and then as I stepped onto the gangplank he said something very strange. He said, "Hide it well for with that package goes the peace of nations."'

'Ahhh.' As his fingers tightened about the cane he breathed expressively. 'Andrei knew well the man Rasputin. He holds the poor Tsarina in his grasp. She believes he can cure her son of the haemophilia which plagues him, so Rasputin manipulates her and through her the Tsar. Mikhail told me in his letters of how the man had demanded the piece now in that drawer. It had been kept locked away during much of the reign of Nicholas's father who was convinced that its having some sort of special power was not all legend. Then with his sudden and unexpected death following its exhibition in the Winter Palace others had felt the same way. But Nicholas and Alexandra were not given to superstition, so the piece remained on public view and one disaster followed another. The day of their coronation fourteen hundred peasants were trampled to death in the rush to see the royal pair, a few years later hundreds more were gunned down outside the Winter Palace as starving people demanded food; the air of Russia became tainted with revolution and Bolshevism, which was submerged only when war broke out with Japan. Yet, after all of that, Rasputin was allowed to wear that – that thing and God alone knows what mischief he has worked with it.'

How could people believe a piece of jewellery – for that is what it had to be – could be responsible in any way for the things just spoken of? Anne watched the man opposite glance at the cabinet with its inconspicuous drawer. This was 1914 not the Middle Ages, people just did not believe such things any more; yet Mikhail Yusupov had and so it seemed had Andrei, now it was obvious Sir Corbett Foley held that same belief.

'But surely all of those happenings can be no more than coincidence.' Anne put the thought into words.

Switching his glance back to a face which still showed traces of all that the girl had suffered, he smiled regretfully. 'War is never a product of coincidence, Miss Corby; always behind it is a devious hand and a mind controlled by a lust for power; like my friend Yusupov I believe Rasputin is that mind and there are men only too ready to be influenced.'

'But he no longer has that—'

'Amulet.' He supplied the word. 'No, Rasputin no longer has that. Though, like a flood, once evil begins it cannot be stopped but must run its course. The hounds of war are straining at the leash. I fear time is running out for the peace of nations!'

It was incredible, too unreal to be believed. Yet it had happened. Anne walked slowly along darkening streets, her mind going over the hour spent at Bentley Grange. She had not looked at that amulet, had not touched it yet had seen the effect of it. Three sensible, down-to-earth men, none, so far as she could tell, given to flights of fancy yet each held that amulet to possess an unnatural power; but how could it? It was only stone and metal, the work of some jeweller.

Satan works in many ways.

A phrase her father had often used returned to her mind. Maybe that could not be disputed, but a piece of metal set with stones . . . that was carrying belief too far! But that need not concern her, she had kept her word and given the amulet into the keeping of Sir Corbett Foley, now she could forget the past altogether.

Nearby a handbell sounded its authoritative ring, snapping her back to the moment. Across the narrow road a woman dressed in dun-coloured dress and calico bonnet tied beneath her chin stared for a long moment then was gone, the heavy door of a low-roofed building thudding closed behind her, the scrape of bolts telling it was locked for the night.

Her throat tightening, Anne continued to stare at the jumble of several buildings abutting each other in a medley of shapes and size. The workhouse! A shudder worked along her spine as she looked at the small-paned windows, one tiny line of glass showing between heavy, cotton-crocheted curtains, giving them the appearance of half-closed eyes. A ray of the dying sun glinted through the smoke-blackened air which was a perpetual shroud hanging over the town and for a moment the glass of one window gleamed dully then it was empty and dead. Like that woman's eyes! Anne touched a hand to her mouth. They had been empty, staring at her with a hopelessness which screamed; a soul-destroyed, God-forgotten hopelessness!

It had shown on the tired face. Weariness of life no longer wanting to be lived. This was the life her son would know. A sob rising in her throat she pressed her hand harder against her mouth. That first time of holding the tiny body in her arms she had been filled with such sweet pain, a feeling so intense she had almost cried out. She would never leave him, those had been the words whispered against the tiny nuzzling head, words of love and longing, words which in the fierceness of emotion she had meant then in the dark hours of night had realised she could not. It had lain like lead in her heart, the weight of it stifling her soul, but with the coming of dawn she had known it had to be. Unity had tried to argue otherwise, but Unity Hurley had not been a small child holding on to her mother's skirts as they tramped endlessly, exchanging desert and wilderness for jungle and fever; true, the terrain of England did not hold such terrors but the hardship of sleeping under hedges, of never being sure of finding something to eat . . . that was a life no newly born child could survive. She was his mother, she had the right to love . . . but her son had the right to live.

Sobs stifled behind her hand she began to run. Her steps echoing, she turned along Church Street, her breath grabbed in painful snatches as she reached the darkness surrounding St Lawrence church. She had to rest, get her breath. Leaning against the ancient lych gate, its carved wood catching the first beams of a rising moon, she dragged several long, smoke-tasting draughts of air deep into her lungs.

It was for the best – best for her son! Looking back the way she had come she saw the tall chimneys of that awful building rising black and dominant against the slate-grey sky of evening. She must always remember that, but memory would not ease the guilt of leaving him . . . nor would it mend the heartbreak. Tears blurring the chimneys she straightened.

'What's your hurry, girl? Stay with me a while.'

It whispered low and threatening from the shadows cast by the lych gate. Her hands automatically grasping her skirts, Anne lifted them to run but too late. Her cries were stopped by the gag of a strong hand and she felt herself snatched back on her heels, being dragged deeper into the all-concealing darkness that was the shadow of the church.

10

'I knew if I waited long enough . . .'

Soft as the hiss of a poised snake the words penetrated the chaos of Anne's screaming senses.

'Now be a sensible girl, don't struggle 'cos it will only cause you hurt, and don't cry out for if you do it will only make things worse for yourself.'

It was a warning, simple but blinding in its clarity. She had been grabbed and dragged into the darkness of the churchyard, hidden from sight of passers-by on the street and it could only be for one reason . . . to satisfy a man's lust.

'I mean what I say . . . stay quiet or it'll be the worse for you.'

The hand covering her mouth slid away and as it did a scream of sheer terror was already tearing from Anne's throat.

'I said not to cry out!'

A slap so hard it jerked her head sidewards on her neck emphasised the words as Anne was swung forward then slammed hard back against the stone wall of the church.

'Please!' The word jerked out on the breath knocked from her. 'Please . . . I – I have no money.'

'Money!' A laugh low and hoarse touched the quiet of the evening. 'Who said anything about money . . . it's not your purse I'm after. I plucked you off the street for a different purpose altogether.'

Visions of a heavily built, thick-bearded man bearing her to the ground rose before Anne's eyes and despite herself she screamed again.

'I warned you—'

'Fair's fair.' Harsh and angry the voice whipped the darkness and Anne felt her attacker snatched away from her. 'You warned the girl now let me warn you, we see men like you as vermin in this town and they find themselves treated as such, so it would be suitable to your health if –'

Beyond the tall yew trees standing sentinel-like about the darkened churchyard the moon sprinkled a drift of pale light through the branches.

'– You!'

Anne's rescuer broke his warning as the face of the man he had grasped was illuminated as if by a myriad tiny flickering candles.

'Up to your old tricks again, eh Mather!'

She wanted to run, to get away from this place, but rigid with shock Anne's limbs refused to move. Trembling, she listened to the rage throbbing like quiet thunder in the voice of the man throwing the object of his anger against the wall as if it were a rag doll.

'Such a brave man –' the voice thickened with disgust '– take on any man, won't you, Mather . . . so long as he be more than sixty and less than sixteen . . . and women! They hold no problems for you, since to tell who it is waylays them in the dark means fathers and brothers most like lose their livelihood. Well, I carry no fear of you or of anything your mother can do, so run off home and tell her it was Abel Preston kicked your dirty arse!'

'You . . . you'll . . . regret this.'

Shook from him by the bounce of his body against the wall, the sentence was fragmented but the threat running through it was unbroken.

'No.' It came on a laugh of pure contempt. 'I'll regret this if I don't give it to you.'

As if loath to witness the act the moon hid behind a gauzy veil of cloud but even in the ensuing shadow Anne was aware of an arm drawing backwards, heard the strike of a fist on flesh, saw the figure of a man sprawl his length on the ground, and as he scrambled to regain his feet a boot kicked at his backside sending him, still half bent, scuttling into the darkness.

'He won't bother you again, miss, not unless he wants every bone in his worthless body broken, and Quenton Mather's not a man to take risks . . . of any sort!'

'Quenton!' Anne felt her insides tremble with old fear. 'Are you saying the man who – who – are you saying he was Quenton Mather?'

'No other, though I doubt you'll get very far should you lay a complaint against him. Money talks as loud in Darlaston as it does anywhere and Clara Mather has enough to smooth her son's path, she has done it time and enough before tonight. But I suggest you get along home, a churchyard isn't the happiest place to be even in daytime.'

But Anne had not heard for the drums beating in her head. Her own cousin! The son of her father's sister . . . 'Quenton!'

The name, though trembling almost inaudibly on her lips, was caught by the figure beginning to walk away. 'You know him?' Abel Preston turned.

Memories she had thought long dead surged into Anne's mind and the old fear grew, grasping her throat. She knew him, knew the cruelties he was capable of, the spite he had so often vented on a young child.

'Has he done this before . . . has he? By Christ, I should have killed the reptile and to hell with what his mother could do!'

'He – he has not attacked me before.' At least not with the

intention he seemed to hold tonight. Anne kept the last to herself.

'But you know him . . . you spoke his name.'

To deny it would lead to altercation and that might well prove the key which would release the tears locked in her throat.

'Yes,' she whispered. 'I know him, Quenton Mather is my cousin.'

For a moment it seemed the man had not heard for he simply stood staring at her in the uncertain light. Then with the tone of someone presented with a thing he thought gone for ever, his answer rocked by the blow of complete and total surprise, he faltered, 'Anne . . . you are Anne Corby?'

She nodded at the boy smiling from the past and to the man stood watching now.

'Yes, Abel,' she replied quietly, 'I am Anne Corby.'

'You fool!' Clara Mather's voice throbbed with anger. 'Why did you have to play your game here in Darlaston, you have the money to follow it in any town.'

'I didn't expect . . . I didn't think—'

Clara's usually cold eyes blazed the fire of wrath. 'No, you didn't think, but then you never do. You are like your father, incapable of thinking of anything other than getting the bloomers off a woman . . . any woman!'

Poor father. Quenton hid his own anger. To think you were the woman he got to shed her bloomers, what a tragedy for him. No wonder he died young, killed by regret no doubt.

Making no attempt to hide the disparagement of his thoughts Quenton answered snidely, 'Such accusations show your true mind, Mother. You are full of ill nature . . . and you profess so often to do only what is best for me. How wrong you are on both counts, you do what is best for Clara Mather . . . and I am no rapist.'

'Then why force a girl into the churchyard?'

'To do what you have tried to do and failed. Ever since you told me Anne Corby had returned I have watched for her and tonight I saw her standing outside the workhouse in Victoria Road.'

The workhouse! Clara's nerves jarred. The girl was young and able bodied so they would not take her in, but the child . . . ? She had not seen into that drawer clearly but there had been no sound; could it already have been disposed of, placed like many another on the doorstep of that institution and left? Was that the reason the girl was standing there? If so, the chance of getting to it was as good as gone.

'When she walked towards Church Street I followed,' Quenton went on. 'I jumped over the wall and ran to the lych gate, waiting for her to pass. I was going to warn her not to remain in Darlaston.'

'And now Abel Preston is witness to what you have done!' Clara scorched. 'He saw you with her and has brain enough to guess what you were about should she go missing, and he is one who won't hesitate to shout it out loud. To get rid of the girl now will be like announcing it from a platform!'

'Get rid of her!' Quenton winced but pain from his bleeding mouth was the only cause.

'You want the Glebe Works, don't you!' Clara's rage flared again. 'You want to be its owner? Well, you won't be, not truly, not so long as Jacob Corby's daughter or Jacob Corby's grandchild is alive to claim it.'

'And you, Mother, don't let's forget you!' Quenton stared at the waspish face. 'Yes, I would like to become master of Glebe Metalworks but that will not happen whether your brother's heirs live or not, you enjoy that position far too much to give it up even for me; but so long as I continue to live as I do then I have no quarrel with that, you can be iron master for as long as it pleases you and I will play along. As for murder?' He paused. 'Agreed, so long as I am not called upon to do the deed.'

Like father like son! Virulent and wild as heath fire, Clara's thoughts blazed unchecked as she watched him go from the room. Content to sit back while she did all the work.

As for murder? Agreed, so long as I am not called upon to do the deed.

The words stilled the fever of her brain. The son would not kill . . . but the mother would!

'I saw that woman's face outside the workhouse, saw the despair, the hopeless empty look in her eyes . . . I can't do it, I can't leave him there.'

A prayer of thanks swelling her heart Unity Hurley watched the young woman scoop her child from the drawer and hold him against her breast, tears streaming down her face.

'She had looked so desolate, so empty, it seemed her very soul was dead. I can't let that happen to him!' Anne kissed the tiny face.

'Thank God you've realised afore it were too late.' Busying herself with the covered milk jug the older woman hid the mist that had risen in her eyes. 'Children belong of their mother no matter what, your own parents had sense enough to know that and took you along of them, hard though it were for you.'

'But I was not an infant and neither were my parents totally destitute. They could feed and clothe me for the first years of our travelling. I haven't the means to do that for my baby . . . Oh Unity, what do I do? Leaving him will break my heart but keeping him means he is likely to starve.'

'You don't need to leave him nor be he like to starve.' Unity looked up from stirring a spoonful of honey into the warm milk. 'Laban and me, we've talked of this, we want you to live here in this house. It won't be no charity,' she said seeing the quick look dart from the girl's eyes, 'not if you take a share of the work of the place and p'raps take and fetch stitching Laban sets for me, for the time saved means another piece stitched to say nothing of the walk saved my legs.'

To live in this house, with the couple who had been so kind to her, a place where her child would be cared for. Anne's hand trembled against the downy cheek. He would be cared for, this woman had already demonstrated the fact, but would he be safe? Her aunt must by now know of his birth, and Quenton . . . he knew she was still in Darlaston and both of them wanted her father's legacy . . . But would they harm an innocent child in order to keep it? The vicious malignancy she had seen that day so clearly displayed in Clara's eyes returned vividly to Anne's mind and with it the answer to the question: yes, they would.

'He were fractious after her left.' Unity poured the milk into the bottle, securing a thick rubber teat at each end.

'Her?'

'Oh, I forgot to mention, Clara Mather called not an hour after you were gone, said her wanted to talk with you but it were my guess she'd got word of that babby being born and come to see for herself.'

Her aunt had been to this house! Anne's arms tightened convulsively about the whimpering bundle in her arms.

'But her got short shrift!' Unity sprinkled a few drops of the milk on the inside of one wrist before handing the bottle to Anne. 'I told her, there were no welcome for her in Unity Hurley's house.'

'The baby –' her eyes wide with anxiety Anne forced the question past lips stiff with fear '– did she touch him?'

Unity's grey-streaked head swung with definite rhythm. 'Not as I saw and I took my eyes from her no longer than it took to lift the kettle from the fire and set it on the hob.'

No longer than it took to lift the kettle from the fire and set it on the hob! The anxiety in her eyes shivered an icy frisson along Anne's every nerve. Ten seconds ... twenty? She remembered the rapid darting movements of those hands, the speed with which they could deliver a slap or snatch from a child; those seconds could prove enough to a determined Clara Mather. But what might she have done, in what way might she have harmed, was she in some way responsible for the fractiousness Unity spoke of?

'The woman were here no more than a few minutes; left with her tail atwixt her legs, you need have no worries of her coming again, for Clara Mather be smart enough to know not to try the patience of Unity Hurley.'

No, her aunt would not come to this house again but that did not mean she would not strike at the child should the opportunity present itself. Anne watched the tiny mouth suck hungrily at the teat. It had seemed, when Unity offered a home, that heaven had offered a gift, only to snatch it away at the moment she reached for it ... just as her aunt had so often done to a child years before, grabbing away the proffered sweet or treat and always with that cold viper smile Anne had not forgotten.

Bending to the small head nestled in her arms she rested her lips against it, smelling the sweet warmth of him. It would not be fair to him, having him here where her aunt was a constant threat, nor was the worry of that a way to repay the kindness of the Hurleys.

'Is it be any fairer to take him on the road, lay him open to Lord knows what hazards?' Unity snapped on hearing the same. 'You no longer have just yourself to think of, my wench, you have a child and though it ain't always easy his needs must be put afore your own. The child needs food and he needs warm shelter and if you won't let it be found in Laban Hurley's home then it needs be one for foundlings.'

'No!' Anne's quick cry startled the baby feeding in her arms and he rejected the thick, dark-coloured teat, his blue eyes opening as he cried his own fear.

Crooning with soft hushing sounds she soothed him, the whole of her swelling with love as a tiny hand fastened onto her finger. She had not asked for this child, had prayed heaven on her knees to take it from her body before it could be born, had worked herself 'til she dropped from fatigue on that long slow journey back to England yet still the child had clung to her womb; and now he was in her arms and she knew nothing would ever break the bond of her love for this tiny scrap of humanity.

Watching closely Unity felt a sympathy her sharp words had hidden. It was a miracle only the Lord Himself had understanding of, the love that sprang so quickly in a mother's heart, a tender yet soul-tearing emotion which increased with every day she held her child in her arms, growing as she watched with anxious eyes while it grew to take its own path in the world.

When they be young they makes your arms ache but when they be growed they makes your heart ache. The saying which had been her mother's echoed softly in her mind whilst inner vision showed two young men smile and wave as they left to join the army.

'You leave that child at the foundling hospital and I'll offer a home to him. I'll rear him as my own and God help Clara Mather if she so much as looks in his direction; so whatever you decides . . . go or stay . . . that little lad will live in Laban Hurley's house.'

Maybe . . . if she signed papers . . . gave Glebe Metalworks legally to her aunt then her son would no longer be any threat, and they could . . . The thought broke off as the infant turned away from the bottle once more, his legs drawing to his stomach and a wail of pain screwing his tiny face.

Almost feeling his pain as her own Anne looked with

worry-dark eyes at the child writhing in her arms. Was this how he had been earlier, this afternoon . . . in pain? Guilt at having left him rose in brilliant tears hovering at the line of her lashes.

'Seems he has a bit of wind.' Unity reached for the kettle poured a little warm water into a shallow dish then fished a cinder from the ashes of the fire and added it to the water. 'A drop of glede water will soon bring that up. Give him here to me . . . we'll soon have him right as ninepence.'

Taking the baby she sat with him cradled in one arm then, first testing the temperature of the contents of the dish against her own lips, fed him several teaspoonfuls of the water.

'There,' she crooned, lifting him to lie across her shoulder, 'old Unity knows how to make that nasty old pain go away.'

How could it? Anne glanced at the dish, a film of fine grey ash covering its cooled surface, and felt her insides quicken. She had seen the results of dirty water in so many places . . .

'There, me little man, that be better . . . all that wind be gone.'

Unity's lined face creased in a smile as the child burped noisily. One hand marking light circles across the tiny back she nursed him a little longer before laying him in the drawer.

'You can push them fears from your mind.' Straightening, she turned to Anne. ''Twere nothing more than a touch of wind, babbies fed on a bottle are often subject to it; it gives 'em bellyache but don't be serious, a drop of glede water cures that more often than not.'

If this was one of the times it did not? Anxiety still strong in her chest Anne dropped to her knees beside the drawer, taking a tiny closed fist between her fingers . . . what if the cause of her son's stomach pain proved not to be that of wind? Her aunt had been to this house and Clara Mather was not a woman given to social visits . . . Her glance following Unity's gathering of feeding bottle and dish she felt her anxiety close like an iron band cutting off the breath to her lungs. There could be only one reason for her father's sister to call here: to harm the child she saw as a threat to her own lifestyle and to that of her son. Had she already done that? Had Clara Mather already struck?

11

The fear of that thought weighing like stone Anne rose from her knees as Unity returned with bottle, dish and spoon carefully washed, placing them on the dresser ready for further use.

'There be time to do a bit o' stitchin' yet.' Unity glanced at the clock, its tick loud in the quiet kitchen. Laban would not be home before nine, she thought, selecting a piece from the several articles he had brought for her to work. Like herself he used labour as a means of forgetting but, as with her, it proved no palliative, no lasting balm which eased the pain, no cure for the grief she knew gnawed deep in his heart, the sorrow which brought the stifled sobs that even now she sometimes heard in her own sleepless hours of night. Laban crying for his dead sons.

The pain of her thoughts sharp as a surgeon's knife she picked up a bridle carrying it together with a lamp to her chosen workspot, a table drawn close beneath the window. Seeing the sudden droop of her shoulders Anne pushed her own thoughts away, but they were not gone for ever, they were merely hidden in the pockets of her mind, waiting their chance to emerge as hurting and worrying as before. Glancing now at Unity she asked, 'Can I help? I'm no stranger to a needle.'

It would do no hurt to include the wench in more than the cooking and preparing of meals. Unity nodded, refusing to admit to herself this was a ruse, a way of getting Anne Corby to see this house as more her home.

'There be a saddle cloth to be stitched,' she answered, pointing to a piece of fawn-coloured cloth laid to one side, 'it be felt cloth so the needle will pass through easy enough, t'ain't tough like leather.'

It was cut in the same shape as a saddle but slightly larger, and Unity placed together two matching pieces of the soft material. 'They needs be joined with a whip stitch first then a binding strip stitched along the joint, once that be done the edges then needs be bound with a strip of yonder red cloth, Sir Corbett Foley still has a preference for the red for that were the colour of his regiment of Guards.'

'He looked so different in uniform as I remember, very different from the way he looked today—'

Handing her needle and thread Unity did not look up as Anne broke off, but returned to her own stitching of a bridle.

'I – I did not tell you this before because of the vow I made to Mikhail and Andrei Yusupov, a vow never to speak of that which had been entrusted to me to deliver to Sir Corbett at Bentley Grange, but now my promise has been kept and the amulet safe in his keeping I would like you to hear everything.'

Catching the older woman's nod she spoke on softly, her fingers plying the needle skilfully as her story was told.

'. . . then the ship foundered and one of the crew bundled me into a lifeboat. I remember looking back at people left behind because of too few boats, of others calling out from the water all around us. I don't think I will ever forget those cries.'

Unity kept to her stitching, holding her own silence as Anne paused then went on.

'I thought to be placed aboard another boat, several put out of Istanbul bound for England that first week but none would give passage without being paid and I had no money, what had been given to me by the Yusupovs had been left behind in the tumult of being shipwrecked. I was at my wit's end when a woman I met near the Grand Bazaar said she would help me. She called a carriage, telling the driver to take us to Üksüdar, which proved to be a very old district of the city with a warren of narrow streets and four-storey, ancient-looking timber houses all crowded together and backed by slopes covered with tall cypress trees. We entered one of the houses, it was so different on the inside. The floor was covered with thick, beautifully woven carpets and cushions were scattered like brilliant flowers, each one catching beams of light which danced through the carved latice screens. It was all so peaceful and lovely. First I must be allowed to wash and then perhaps some tea followed by a long rest. I was so very grateful.

'It was later, in a room whose walls were inlaid with marquetry depicting beautiful gardens, and which had in the centre a large cushion-strewn divan, that I heard voices coming from another room. They were just loud enough for me to hear. I suppose that conversing in English with the woman she thought that to be the only language I understood, but the years of travelling had afforded me a smattering of many others. I recognised the words "hashish", and "cariye" then a name, Mehmet Pasha, followed by "seraglio". I had no time to dwell on what I had heard for a young girl entered the room bringing a large brass bowl of warm scented water, rose petals floating on the surface. She returned moments later with an exquisitely embroidered robe indicating she would take my own clothes, probably to wash them; but I refused, I could not risk what I carried being found. It was a temptation to bathe the whole of my body but somehow I felt I had to remain not only clothed but alert.

'Then the woman I had met earlier came back. The man who would help me was unable to come to the house tomorrow for not only was it Friday, the day of rest and worship, but also the feast day of the local saint. He sent his apologies and asked that I stay and rest until we could meet. Then she excused herself saying she had an engagement; she would not return until the next day but in the meantime I was to make myself comfortable.

'I had been alone for some while when the younger woman brought a tray of mint tea. Placing it on an ornately carved table she touched a finger to her lips then closed the door. My frown must have told her I could not understand her babbled whispers so she executed a series of slow movements. Pointing to the steaming silver pot she shook her head vehemently, in what obviously seemed a warning, then supplemented it by pretending to fall asleep, lifting her eyelids with her fingers and letting them close, her head lolling on her chest. Then, whispering one word, "serare", she left.'

'So what were all that about?' Unity asked, her eyes not leaving her stitching.

'I wondered that myself.' Anne paused in her own sewing, her glance fixed on a room visible only in her mind. 'The girl's eyes had been so full of – of pity. She had tried to tell me something which was for my own good, then the words I had heard from beyond the thin wooden walls returned and I realised what she had tried to indicate was that I was in danger; hashish was a drug and it must be in the tea, Pasha was the title given to a high official, seraglio meant harem and cariye a concubine. The whole thing fitted together like a jigsaw puzzle. I was a stranger to Istanbul, I had no family and therefore no one to wonder what had happened to me. The woman had taken me to that house not as an act of charity, not to help me get to England, but to pass me to some man as an addition to his harem.'

'And the other word . . . the one the young woman whispered . . . what were the meaning of that?'

'I could not fathom that . . . not until I followed each of

her actions precisely.' Anne's eyes moved, following some phantom. 'She was already at the door, she looked at me with that intense look and pointed at the handle then shook her head with two or three jerky movements before whispering "serare". The word had to mean lock, and the shake of her head meant no . . . the two together must surely be she would not lock the door. I waited for what seemed an eternity then opened the latice screen covering the window. The room was several feet from the level of an empty street, but injury was better than what was in store if I stayed in that house and it could be someone other than the girl who came to my room, so I jumped. The breath was knocked out of me but my limbs were sound and knowing I could not risk making my way through the streets I ran up the slopes and into the cypress woods. I had no idea of which way to go but I had to get to the dock, try to get passage home to England. I waited until almost sunset before venturing to the edge of the treeline.

'Stretched out along the shoreline the city looked like the enchanted land of fairytales. Bathed in the lowering sun numerous cupolas gleamed like great golden balls resting on white marble, the minarets rising beside the domed mosques were graceful and slender as gold needles and the chant of the muezzins calling the people to prayer gave the whole a feeling of peace, a sense that nothing so evil as abduction could ever take place there; but I knew the fear inside me was not groundless, that what the young girl had tried to warn me of was only too real, and to avoid it I had to get away before my escape was discovered. I could not tell what lay the other side of the forest but that was the only way open to me. It was so dark among the trees, I – I kept remembering the wolves attacking the horse . . . snatching my mother . . .'

It took all Unity's strength of will to prevent herself going to the girl, telling her there were no need to say more; for there was every need, if the nightmare was ever to fade it needed bringing out into the open. Closing her lips against words still fighting to be said she stitched on, leaving space for the runner loop needed where the rein crossed the cheek of the horse.

'Then I heard a call.' No more than a whisper now Anne's account of what had happened so many months before went on. 'It was just a sound on the breeze, almost a rustling of the leaves but I knew it was a call, the sound of one human to another. My escape must have been found out. I panicked then, running blindly, hitting against the trunks of trees, their branches clawing at my face and then I was being thrown to the ground.'

Dear God, no! Unity's swift horror checked the rhythm of her needle. Not raped twice . . . surely heaven would not allow a woman to suffer that!

'It was a man.' Anne continued with her own stitching of the saddle cloth. 'I could only just make out the shape of him in the darkness, he pulled me to my feet then passed me to his companion, a girl who signalled me to stay quiet. They obviously knew the woods well for they moved quickly, the girl holding my hand, urging me to keep up with them. They turned out to be members of a band of gypsies and next morning when they broke camp they took me with them. In the days that followed I was given a share of their food and at night the men constructed a bender tent, a half circle of rods, hazel or willow, covered with a canvas and a blanket to cover me. Sometimes I had a mattress of bracken but most often it was bare earth; I could not be taken into a wagon for I was a gaujo . . . a non-gypsy. Their words were not all strange to me, it seems they speak a universal language for my parents and I had often heard it among the different groups we met. From the start I was kept an outsider; the juvals, the women, turned their heads from me and the chavvies did not treat me as other children had but ran from me whenever I tried to speak to them. Often from the edge of the campfire I would catch the words "kalo", and "mullo", they meant black ghost, and people would cross themselves as they looked at me, while even the jukels, the dogs, slunk away when I went near. People were afraid . . . but of what? They did not say but when their path led in a different direction and I was given into the care of another lovari, as gypsy groups term themselves, they would talk quietly and I would again be treated as before, fairly yet always with that same sense of fear. With the passing weeks my pregnancy became pronounced and firewood began to be left near my tent but still no one entered it. I was fearful of the child being born before we got to England, of there being no woman willing to help. Then, when I joined yet another group travelling through France an old woman came one night to sit at my fire. She stared at me for a long time her eyes sharp and brittle as coals.

'"*You speak pogadijib, the language of the Romany?*" She spoke softly so no other could hear and when I nodded she looked at my stomach. "*You carry the fruit of a mellalo, a filthy diddikai . . . a man not of your own country . . . the child in your womb was planted by no Romany.*"

'"*No.*" It was all I answered but it was enough for she nodded again, satisfied by the reply. I thought she would leave me and go to her place among the others but instead she drew tobacco and a clay pipe from the pocket of her skirt. Having lit it she sucked on it for several moments, then eyes half closed peered at me through the veil of tobacco smoke.

'"*A chavvie in your womb don't be all you were given the carryin' of . . . there be something else . . .*"'

Anne's fingers paused in their task as she watched the scene playing in her mind.

'"*There be what my people call a black ghost, a dark evil that walks with you, don't deny it for naught be hid from them with the power to see and old Beshlie has the sight. A jewelled piece*

were given into your keeping across the water, given by a Rai,
a great lord who fears for one greater still."

'I thought she had finished speaking and in the silence I
saw the faces of the others illuminated by the flames of their
fire, faces drawn with more than a passing anxiety; it was
clear in the way they clutched the younger children to them,
hiding their heads with shawls and scarves . . . it was as if the
dark ghost they feared stared at them from the surrounding
shadows.'

Pulling her linen thread tight with each stitch Unity listened
without interruption as the quiet flow continued.

'The woman called Beshlie stared straight at the spot where
the amulet was hidden, I thought she would tear it free, take it
from me, but even as the thought ran in my mind the pipe fell
from her mouth and onto her skirts and though I wanted to lift
it away I could not move, it was as if the woman's stare had
become a net imprisoning me with invisible strands I could
not break.

'"*The Rai thinks to save his king.*" The voice seemed no
longer her own, it had become deep and hollow while her
eyes . . . her eyes had widened, each pupil extended until the
whole was one circle which glittered like jet in the firelight,
and though she spoke there was no movement of her lips.
"*But it be too late,*" she went on, "*the great one be already*
marked for death, marked by that he scoffed as superstition.
Three times more the earth will journey around the sun then
in the seventh month of its fourth circle the kalo evil will strike,
its foul black fingers will fasten about the Rai, his juval and his
chavvies, the great lord and all of his family . . . for them it be
already too late, they have looked on the devil's trinket, touched
its evil and though they be innocent of guilt they will be sucked
into his maw."'

Across the streets the clock of St Lawrence church struck
the half hour, its sound echoing like a mourning cry in the

silence and Unity shivered, touching her breast with the sign of the cross.

'Lord save us,' she breathed, 'to think you carried that – that thing 'alf across the world. If that gypsy woman knowed what 'er 'peared to know why let you keep that trinket . . . why not destroy it there an' then?'

Seeming to wake from a dream Anne blinked several times in rapid succession before replying, 'The restriction which had held my limbs fell away and the woman picked up her pipe. Everything was normal yet her eyes still cut deep into me.

'"*You have not uncovered the amulet,*" she said, "*you have not gazed upon it yet still its malignance has reached out for you. The shipwreck which almost took your life, the woman who would give you into the service of a man whose slave you would be . . . think you they be coincidence, the whims of fate? No child they be the workings of the Dark One, it was his hand reached to you and it will reach again . . . destroy the piece now while there be yet time.*"'

'So why didn't you?' Exasperation throbbed in Unity's question.

'Because I had given my promise to deliver it to Bentley Grange,' Anne answered simply. 'I told the gypsy this and she nodded as if it were already known to her. "*The way is set,*" she murmured, "*heaven has placed its counterweight in the balance scale, an honest hand and a truthful heart be the measure of its choosing but treachery and malevolence weigh heavy against it. Remember, little gaujo, reveal your secret to none but him to whom that piece be intended for the hand of evil be ever ready to snatch it. Heed the warning of old Beshlie, treachery and malevolence be waiting.*" She left me then and I retired into my tent but long after I could still hear the soft murmurs of men and women and knew they talked of me, and the next morning I was taken to the port of Cherbourg, my passage to Dover paid and a sovereign pressed into my hand. It was the gift of the Romany, Beshlie said, it could not be returned without slight to them. There was so much I wanted to say, to ask how I could show my gratitude for their help but she and the women with her moved away into the crowd lining the quay and I lost sight of them.

'The ship was a postal packet operating between the two ports and though a chair was placed on the deck I stood the whole time clutching the rail, memories of the shipwreck refusing to leave my mind. But finally it was over and I was ashore in Dover. I had thought I would remember the town for it was from there I had sailed with my parents but I could recall nothing. I must have looked confused because a man excused himself then asked might he be of service. I said I was looking for the railway station and he replied he was on his way there, and if I wished we could go together. He was so well dressed I was afraid my shabby clothes would be an embarrassment to him but he laughed that off.

'I remember we had walked no more than a minute or so when he said we must cross to the other side of the street. I stood beside him at the edge of the footpath waiting for a wagon to pass when two dogs hurtled around the corner snarling and barking at each other. They came so close . . . I heard the snap of their jaws as they brushed against me and the memories of – of—' The words choking in her throat Anne sucked in a long trembling breath, waiting a moment before proceeding. 'Panic took hold of me, I stepped backwards away from the dogs and my foot caught in a drain. There was a hand against my arm, it felt like I was being pushed though it must have been someone grabbing to save me from falling beneath the wagon.'

The bridle stitched, Unity let it rest in her lap. 'Someone! You mean the man going along with you to the station?'

'No.' Anne's shake of the head was brief. 'It was a lad, he caught the skirt of my coat, pulling me from the road. I toppled backwards and he covered me with his own body, protecting me as several boxes fell from the loaded cart. He said later it was all he could think to do at the time but it was very embarrassing.'

'Thank the Lord the lad had the presence of mind to do what he did and to hell with embarrassment!' Unity answered sharply. 'Red cheeks fades easy, broken bones takes an age to mend; so what did the other one do, the one who was going along of the railway station?'

'I looked for him after being helped to my feet but he was not among the people who came to offer assistance, he was nowhere to be seen. I thought it a little strange after his being so helpful—'

A fretful cry emanating from the drawer, Anne broke off and went at once to lift the baby into her arms, crooning gently as she rocked him.

Leaving her seat Unity placed the finished work aside. Anne had thought his disappearance strange; *it felt like I was being pushed*, was what the wench had said. Was that what had caused her to topple into the path of a loaded wagon and not the catching of her foot? She had been eager to believe the word of a man whose fancy clothes and speech marked him a gentleman and therefore would do her no harm, just as her were eager to believe Clara Mather would be satisfied to be left alone with the Glebe Metalworks and so would wreak no mischief . . . but that woman were the soul of malice and her greed would not stop there. But it were not Clara Mather had walked beside Anne Corby along that street.

Lifting the kettle from the bracket above the fire and replacing it with the pot of broth which would be the evening meal, Unity felt the cold touch of foreboding trickle along her spine. What had that gypsy woman said? Steam rising from the kettle spout hovered in a tiny vaporous cloud above the hob and as Unity stared it drew together, moulding and shaping until the heart of it became a face . . . the face of an old woman whose eyes seemed brilliantly alive and whose wrinkled lips made no movement even though words came clear to Unity's mind.

. . . malignance has reached out . . . shipwreck . . . slave . . . they be the workings of the Dark One . . . his hand reached . . . it will reach again . . .

The baby's sharp wail broke the trance which of a sudden had settled on Unity, the illusion fading as she moved to Anne's side.

'He be ready for a feed.' She smiled but the smile hid a shudder as she reached for the warm milk. Did that amulet the girl had carried possess some sort of power, an evil which now threatened her as it seemed it had threatened some Russian?

. . . it will reach again . . .

Pouring milk into the feeding bottle Unity's hand trembled.

12

It had been a wasted journey!

Clara Mather slammed the door of her bedroom angrily. She had lowered herself by going to that house, humbled herself by asking like some paid help if she might speak with Anne Corby . . . like some paid help! Clara's fist struck the top of her night stand sending a glass rattling against the water carafe. She, Clara Mather, having to ask! And that woman, she had the instinct of a vixen.

'*You can come in,*' she had said, '*though I'll not pretend you be welcome.*'

Welcome! Clara snatched off an upswept-brimmed, small-crowned straw hat fashionable a decade ago, jabbing it into the box she had left on the bed. That was the last thing she expected of Unity Hurley . . . of all the women in Darlaston she alone had challenged when the older men had been sacked from the Glebe Metalworks, she alone had made the accusation of families being forced into poverty while Clara reaped the profits made from the work of men little older than boys. Truth it might have been but Unity Hurley's business it definitely was not! Loosing her charcoal frogged coat she hung it in the wardrobe.

It was almost as if the woman had sensed her reason for calling at that house yesterday, her sharp eyes following every movement; and her answers when asked about Jacob's daughter, they had been as sharp. '*Who is living beneath Laban Hurley's roof be naught to do wi' nobody but him,*' she had clipped.

But the evidence had been there. Clara took out the black mourning suit carrying it to the bed, lifting the sheet which protected it. A drawer had sat beside the hearth, a drawer set with a blanket in the manner of families too poor to provide a cot; a bed for an infant new born.

Sliding the bottle from her pocket she stared into its green depths.

An infant new born . . . but one with not long to live! It would have been so easy. Her fingers curled viciously about the hard cold glass. Two drops in the milk jug she had seen covered by a beaded cloth, the extract of wolfsbane was so powerful it would need no more to see that child to its grave. But she had not been given the opportunity, the few seconds it would have taken; had the woman left the room . . . but it had not happened. Unity Hurley had placed herself squarely in front of that drawer and moved not an inch.

She had had no clear view of the inside of the drawer, only the blanket peeping above a corner telling its use; nor had there been a cry from it, no snuffles of a sleeping baby. Had it been there or had Anne Corby already left trailing her bastard with her as Jacob had trailed his child? Unity Hurley would give no answer.

But the threat to Quenton was not gone. A fresh burst of anger clawed deep in Clara's stomach. So long as Anne Corby or her child breathed, Quenton's future – the future she had schemed to provide – would be jeopardised. But fate had not given her the means only to snatch it away after one chance, instinct told her there would be another. Returning the small bottle to the inside of the ruched muff Clara's lips thinned to obscurity. Next time she would not fail.

So Anne Corby had returned to Darlaston. Abel Preston placed the saddle tree, a metal frame which formed the body of any saddle, on the flat surface of the workbench to test it for unevenness. The tree rocking slightly beneath his hand he reached for a rasp and filed the metal sides. But it could not be her own home, Butcroft House, she had returned to otherwise Quenton Mather would not have chosen the street for his dirty work, that would have been done at the house, a place where none would see, none except maybe his mother, and she would turn a blind eye. Clara had never been able to see wrong in her son and her sight wasn't likely to improve now.

The metal frame perfectly level he took the piece of pigskin he had previously prepared by skiving the edges and shaving the thickness with a sharp blade, and he now applied strong adhesive to attach it to the metal.

'You'll need to bone that down well, Abel, lad.'

'I'll do that.' Abel smiled, smoothing the leather with a block of wood, ensuring every part of leather and metal bonded.

'Ar, I knows you will; you be a fine worker, I can trust your pieces to have no faults.'

The older man moved on through the workshop, settling at his place beneath the line of windows. Glancing after him, Abel experienced the sharp stab of pity which often struck as he watched the man who had taught him every step of the leather trade, guiding his hands, training his eye until his skills matched those of his tutor. Laban Hurley had taught his own sons, brought them into the trade almost from the time they could hold a buckle or a mushroom-shaped wooden masher, he had instructed them in every aspect, how to select the finest leather, to prepare and dress it, to cut a shape from it without wasting a scrap, taught them until his sons ranked among the best; and then they had gone to fight the Boers leaving this man to fight his heartbreak and his business to become a shadow of what it had once been.

Satisfied the pigskin was well smoothed and secure enough to protect the webbing from coming into contact with the metal, thus safeguarding against rust, he set it aside, knowing it needed the glue to dry thoroughly before doing any more to it. Glancing once more at Laban, whose head was bent over his work, he selected a stiff paper pattern, placing it expertly on a length of white serge. Yes, the old man's heart was broken but what work he produced was still the finest, constructed with only the very best of materials.

Could the same be said of Jacob Corby's works, of the lorinery produced there? Not every time! Marking round the paper pattern, taking care it did not move beneath his fingers, he frowned. That firm had not followed Laban's style, some of its metal work was rough and poorly made, causing Laban to return it. But what else could you expect of young lads fresh from the schoolroom? Working metal required skill and for that to be acquired took training. Yet Clara Mather provided no apprenticeship, the reverse were her policy: use her workers while they were young enough to sweat for pennies and get rid of them when they asked for pounds.

But now things were no longer completely in that woman's hands. The brother would not return. That much Laban had divulged when told of the happening in the churchyard. But the niece was here in Darlaston . . . that could mean only one thing: Clara and her beloved son were no longer sure of their hold over Glebe Metalworks.

The cutting shears put aside, Abel stared at the white cloth. Had he been wrong in thinking what he had, was Quenton Mather's snatching of that girl from the streets not so he could satisfy some vile craving but to . . . ? Breath leaving his lungs in a long slow stream, Abel felt his insides contract. No, not even Quenton would want to see the girl seriously harmed; but the mother, there was a different fish altogether and what the mother said do . . . ! But would Quenton really go so far? The answer to that was yes, the man would ride on the coat tails of the devil if his mother told him to.

There had been no reason given for his attack. Abel's fingers moved deftly over a task he had done many times, straining the serge over the seat of a saddle webbed and trimmed the night before. He had walked Anne Corby the rest of the way, giving no vent to curiosity as she paused at the Hurleys' house. Was she living there? Had Clara Mather already spewed her venom?

Anne had always been afraid of the woman. His mind flew back over the years, seeing a small girl flinch then drop the posy of mauve and white clover handed to her by a gawky teenaged lad with dark wind-teased hair, her small legs moving as quickly as they could back to the woman who snatched angrily at her hand, almost dragging her away; and all the time Quenton, the sly spiteful Quenton, had smiled.

He had wanted to hit him then. Abel tucked the serge under the head of the saddle, distributing it evenly towards the upward curving cantle, tacking it neatly beneath. He had wanted to smack the grin from his face, punch away the smugness and spite but Quenton had been smart enough to keep his distance; last night, though, the distance had closed . . . and Lord, it had felt good!

The smile rising from deep inside settled on his mouth. Quenton Mather would tread carefully from now on.

She had told Unity the whole of her story . . . all the events which had occurred during her journey to England and then to Darlaston, told of the reason of her going to Bentley Grange and the conversation with Sir Corbett Foley, but she had not told of being attacked by her own cousin.

'We must not add any more,' she murmured softly to the baby nestled in her arms, 'they have been so kind to us it would not be fair . . .'

'What would not be fair?' Work she had completed that morning wrapped now in a piece of cloth to prevent its being soiled by fingermarks, Unity stood framed in the arch that gave on to the scullery. Searching for a quick answer but finding none, Anne dropped her glance. She did not want to lie but neither did she want to cause possible worry to a woman who had already been kind enough to provide her with shelter; Unity Hurley had known Clara Mather for years, she must know she would be capable of visiting her anger on anyone helping Anne Corby, that must not happen to Unity and her husband.

'If leaving this house without the telling of it be what your mind is saying be unfair then it be right.' Unity set the wrapped bundle on the table. 'But it would be just as unfair on my part to let you go thinking you have to remain in it . . . you be free to follow the way of your own choosing. If go you must, then bear in mind what I said to you . . . hand that child to an institution and I will offer a home to it; they won't refuse, for the Parish has many poor little waifs and orphans to keep and so will welcome having one go to a good home, one where he will be loved.'

'My aunt knows I am here, she will—'

'Get her arse kicked if her comes here again!' Unity interrupted, a determined line to her mouth. 'I'll be having no truck with that woman and her knows it, so her'll keep away from Blockall and from this house especially; that being the case it strikes me you'd be better off here than anywhere, besides you'd be doing Laban and me a kindness.'

Burping loudly the baby brought back a little of the milk Anne had just fed him.

'Pardon you.' Anne smiled, dabbing at the tiny mouth with the square of cloth placed beneath his chin, but her smile faded as she caught the silvery gleam of tears before Unity turned away. Laying the child in the drawer that was his bed, covering him with a soft blanket, she moved to where the older woman stood beside her work table beneath the window. Were those tears her fault, had she said or done something so hurtful? That was the last thing she would ever want to do. Distress obvious in her voice, Anne spoke quietly.

'Unity, I . . .'

But it seemed the woman did not hear. Her gaze fixed beyond the window she murmured to herself.

''Twere from that very spot I watched. Tall and straight they walked, side by side as they'd always done. Matthew, the eldest said it were a man's duty to fight for his country, and Luke . . . he never was left behind, "Matt did it so I did it" was ever his saying whether it were jumping over the brook or climbing the tallest tree; so it was that day. Down that street they went, every step they took pulling the heart from my body. My boys, my heart and my soul, walking away from me for ever.'

The photograph stood on the parlour mantel shelf – two young men in soldiers' uniform – they had to be Matthew and Luke, they had to be Unity's sons! Realisation filling her with pity, Anne reached her hand to the woman whose sob beat like a single drum.

'They fought brave so we were told,' the words went on, heartbreak pouring out in a stream, 'did their duty. But what good be that to a mother whose arms ache to hold her sons, whose heart cries in the dark hours when her sees them smile, feels her soul call to them as they turn to wave, feels it wither and die inside her as they fade into the night.'

A terrible shudder shaking her whole body Unity sank to the chair set alongside the work table, covering her face with her apron.

She had made no mention of her sons until now. Sinking

to her knees Anne gently held the sobbing woman. She had listened to the tales of another's sufferings while speaking no word of her own, saying nothing of the terrible pain tearing inside her; Unity Hurley had comforted and cared for a stranger while all the time she must have thought of her own sons lying dead on some foreign battlefield. No one could give Unity back her children but maybe there was a way to ease a little of the pain. Glancing to where the child lay, Anne whispered against the other woman's ear, 'The child which was born in this house let him grow in it. Love him as you loved Matthew and Luke, watch him grow as you watched them, let him be your son.'

Unity had held her in her arms, their tears flowing together. With the bridle wrapped carefully in the piece of cloth Anne walked along Church Street remembering how they had clung together in a kitchen filled with memories for Unity, memories she would never lose and a sorrow that was deep and raw as it had been all those years ago. It was a sorrow Anne had tried to ease the only way she had known, and though the words had stabbed like a knife she had whispered them, *let him be your son*.

She had felt the tremor fly through the woman held in her arms then Unity had put her gently aside, her head shaking, a tremulous smile on her mouth.

'*A child has but one mother,*' she had said quietly, '*they be joined by a thread the strongest of knives can't break, you know for you feel it. I love the child this house seen born but one broken heart be enough, I would not have you suffer the same; but this I will ask, make your home with Laban and me, let it be as though we were truly grandparents to the boy, to share in his love, to share him with his mother.*'

She had agreed with all her heart. Passing St Lawrence church she felt a shiver run along her spine. Would Quenton

Mather try to attack her in the future? Refusing to let apprehension kindle into flame she crossed into King Street, her glance going to the tall chimneys rising to the right. The workhouse! At least that was one worry she would never have again, her child would not endure life there.

Reaching the saddler's shop Anne answered the man's dour remarks on the weather. She had been here several times now, delivering purses and bags stitched by herself and Unity.

'A good bit of work.' Long grey sideburns almost meeting on his chin, the shopkeeper inspected each piece. 'But that's what be ever got from Laban Hurley, don't let no inferior goods get past his nose; a man can rely on Laban . . . and seeing the way the world be going it be likely a lot more than one man going to be relying on the stuff produced along of Regency Leather!'

Asking the meaning of what he had said, Anne felt her chest tighten with the answer. Lifting the flat cap perched on top of iron-grey hair, scratching absently at his scalp, he squinted through eyes screwed from working long hours in the shadowed recess of the small shop.

'Don't you read the newspapers?' He let the cap drop. 'But there you go, young wenches don't have no time for reading of the papers, they be too fond o' gallivanting about; well, the papers be talking of Kaiser Bill and his struttin'; be like his father afore him do that one, a war mongerer, won't be satisfied 'til his country and many another along of it be at war!'

Leaving the shop with its rich smell of leather and polish, Anne breathed deeply, the face of Andrei Yusupov floating in her mind, his words ringing in her brain.

. . . with that package goes the peace of nations . . .

She had thought it a strange thing to say, but strange as it was it could not mean war . . . yet Sir Corbett also had referred to such action. The man's prediction returned, mingling with that already in her brain.

. . . the hounds of war are straining at the leash . . . I fear time is running out for the peace of nations . . .

But war! Anne drew another lung-filling breath, forcing her mind to order. The thought was inconceivable, the whole idea laughable! Countries would not fight each other ever again, too many hard lessons had been learned in the past, no more would young men such as Unity's sons be called upon to give their lives; and as for a piece of jewellery, lifeless metal and stone, having anything to do with it . . . the idea was utterly incongruous!

The money the shopkeeper had paid bit into her hand, her fingers squeezing into her palm at the words crashing into her mind.

Evil finds many ways.

Her father's words pushed their way past the tumult of thoughts.

It twists into the heart, whispers its foulness into minds, pours its poison into souls until they become corrupted with its malignancy.

But evil is the working of the devil, Anne answered in her mind. It is practised through people not through an amulet! A trinket could never carry such power. But even as the thought hurled itself at the others she heard the quiet reply: *Evil finds many ways.*

Abel Preston flicked a sideways nod towards a side room, its door tightly closed. 'Laban is in there. He's talking with Sir Corbett Foley.'

'Has he come to collect his saddle? I saw some of the work Unity did on it, he will be pleased I'm certain.'

'I've no doubt of it, Laban is the finest craftsman in the whole area. And this part of the Black Country produces the best leather products to be found anywhere.'

Abel Preston was proud of Laban's skills and proud of

the trade he himself had been taught. Anne watched him clear a stool of several pieces of dressed hide so she could sit down.

'I think p'raps you should wait here rather than disturb Laban and Sir Corbett.'

He had glanced at her as he spoke but his eyes had lacked . . . what? What had she seen in those eyes whenever they had met during the brief years she had lived in Darlaston? Taking the seat cleared for her, Anne strove to see into the past, smiling to herself as she saw the face of a fourteen-year-old boy laughing up at a small girl caught halfway up a tree too scared to move another inch.

'*What are you doing up there . . . moppets like you shouldn't go climbing trees.*'

The boy had smiled as he said it then with all the agility of a leopard had climbed to the side of the frightened child and with infinite care almost carried her down, standing her on the ground, his eyes twinkling as he wiped her tears on a scrap of dirty rag.

That was what was missing now from his eyes, that was what she had seen in those early years . . . the gleam of laughter! But it was missing now as it had been missing when Quenton had come sauntering up to that tree. Abel had turned on him, his accusation savage.

'*You left her up that tree, didn't you!*'

The words were so clear and sharp in her mind, Anne glanced towards the figure at the workbench. He might almost have spoken them now, but even as her memory gave the words, the enraged face of Quenton Mather joined the scene playing in her mind, his face dark with anger, his words snapping pompously.

'*It has nothing to do with you, nor with any other ragged-arsed factory hand, so clear off before my mother—*'

'*Oh yes, your mother.*'

Anne watched cold contempt harden the young mouth to a granite line.

'It seems she forgot to teach you how unkind it is to treat your cousin as you have, so it is up to a ragged-arsed factory hand to do it for her.'

The picture blurred as Abel's fist swung and the voice of her cousin became a yelp.

Why had Abel Preston taken it upon himself to help her, to beat his warning into her cousin's ear not to harm her ever? But it had been an empty threat so far as Quenton had been concerned.

'Anne, my dear, I didn't know you were here or we would have ended our meeting immediately.'

Glancing at the two men coming from the inner room Anne's throat closed on a gasp. Leaning heavily on the Malacca cane, his face swollen, eyes almost closed beneath purple bruises, Sir Corbett Foley limped towards her.

13

'An accident you say.' Unity shook her grey head as Laban's explanation finished. 'Well, I can't say I be surprised . . . riding about in a tin box! That be all them motor car things be, noisy smelly tin boxes that can only see a man finish up in a wooden box; a man like Sir Corbett Foley should ought to have more sense than go putting himself in such a contraption, it be naught less than inviting trouble. What be wrong with a horse and carriage? It served all these years so why go a changing of it now . . . progress, bah! It's just downright foolishness you ask me!'

'You can't stop change.' Laban moved from the supper table to take his chair at the fireside. 'The world moves on though I admits there be times when I'd have it stand still.'

'Well, that don't never be like to happen, not when you have folk building daft machines and other folk daft enough to buy them!' Unity gathered dishes, clattering them together emphasising her contempt.

'You'll change your way of thinking when you be riding in one of them yourself.'

Her hands coming to a sudden halt Unity glared at her husband. 'Me ride in one of them things! The day won't never dawn, Laban Hurley, don't never set your mind to thinking I would trust myself to step into a contraption such as Corbett Foley has, 'cos you'll die waiting!'

Catching Laban's roguish wink, Anne followed the older

woman into the scullery, hiding her smile at the continued mumbling. But Laban had been correct in saying the world moved on, change must always take place . . . but change did not always prove the better for the people it was aimed at, the preachings of her father had shown that even though he denied it.

Drying each dish Anne let her mind wander through the desert of wasted years.

. . . the gods you worship are nothing but stone idols . . .

The voice of her father drifted over the wilderness of an empty childhood.

. . . there is no god other than the one who sacrificed Himself so you might live . . .

So often had those words been hurled like missiles at people bewildered by their strangeness. Their bewilderment had gradually changed to fear, they were being bullied into giving up something they had known and loved, had lived with for long centuries; then fear had become anger with tribes split as some accepted the new credo whilst others clung to the old and family had fought family, killing in the name of change. But her father had seen no blame in what he did, he had gone blindly on across Africa and into the East, blind to the human damage left in his wake; but then her father had ever been blind to the sufferings of others. Preaching the gospel of Christ had been his all . . . but could Jacob Corby's way of carrying that message, of forcing it down the throats of gentle innocent people, be the way Christ would have wanted it preached?

'Change don't always be for the best!'

Unity's retort seeming to answer her thoughts Anne gathered the finished dishes, carrying them into the kitchen where she set each in its place.

'Did Sir Corbett say how that accident 'appened?' Unity had followed behind, now she settled to the work Laban had brought to be done at home, her fingers moving steadily as she plaited the leather strips Anne had already skived.

'He did, though it seemed a queer account to me.'

'In what way queer?' Unity passed the supple strips one between another, first to the left then forward between the next two strips, crossing them into position with deft, perfectly assured movements years of constructing whips of exactly the same sort had bestowed on her.

Laban took several moments before answering. Blowing a steady stream of tobacco smoke, watching it become swallowed hungrily in the chimney he mulled over the question.

'In what he said about the fog.' His answer was quiet as if spoken only in his mind but Unity's reply was sharp.

'Fog! What fog? There's been none hereabouts for these past months 'cept that given off by them there steel and iron works and that don't be fog but smoke, though I grant sometimes it lays over the town like black fog when there be no wind to carry it away.'

Laban eased the pipe from between his teeth, studying the long white clay stem. ''Tweren't that,' he said, 'Foley knows the difference atween foundry smoke and fog. He knows fog don't come and go in the space it takes to say it.'

Pulling each leather strand tight Unity completed the plait by hammering it square with a wooden mallet.

'So you thinks he were imagining it, daydreaming or some such? Well, that be another thing a man can't go doing in one of them fancy machines, they don't guide themselves same as a horse'll do.'

'I didn't say it were simply a fancy of his mind.' Laban replaced the pipe, drawing deeply on it.

'Then what do you be saying?'

Or rather what was Laban not saying! Anne moved to the rough crib, lifting the child who had begun to whimper. Sir Corbett Foley was too down-to-earth an individual to imagine things. Yet Unity had been correct in saying Darlaston had not yet seen the fogs brought on by winter.

The child in her arms Anne whispered soothingly into the tiny ear but her mind was with Laban. Just what was it the man had been told?

'When I saw the bruising along of his face I thought that horse of his had thrown him, but then he said –'

The explanation spoken so quietly had Anne's nerves taut as bowstrings.

'– he said he had intended going on horseback but the box going along with him were too awkward to hold while in the saddle.'

'So what was wrong with going in a carriage?'

Another stream of tobacco smoke sucked greedily into the wide blackness of the chimney, Laban shook his head.

'The questions you ask, woman! I don't know why he chose not to take a carriage and I didn't ask; 'twere no business of mine his riding to the railroad station in that motor car.'

'Railroad station?' Unity laid the finished whip aside, casting a smile at the now quiet child as she moved to take the pretty flowered teapot from the hob.

'That were the place Foley said he were heading.' Laban heard the note of enquiry in his wife's tone and resigned himself to repeating every last word that had passed between himself and the owner of Bentley Grange. 'He said there were a matter he needed to discuss with somebody, though exactly what that matter were he didn't get round to divulging. All he did tell were that halfway to Darlaston the motor car began to vibrate, jerking and bucking like a horse fresh to the saddle; said he tried to steer the thing to the side of the road but there was no controlling of it, it seemed almost as though it had a mind of its own, then there was the fog.' Laban frowned into the fire. 'He said it seemed to come from inside the motor car itself.'

Anne's nerves jolted, her hold tightening about the small body. Could it have been the amulet . . . was that the matter he needed to discuss?

'Fog came from a motor car!' Unity sniffed her feelings. 'He must have been too familiar with the bottle.'

Laban turned to watch his wife spoon tea from a painted tin caddy. 'Corbett Foley weren't drunk but he were—'

'What?' Unity scalded the tealeaves. 'What were he if not drunk . . . sober folk don't go seeing fog rise from a motor car!'

Turning back to face the fire Laban held the pipe in a slightly shaking hand and let his gaze drive deeply into the glowing depths. 'I've seen men drunk and I've seen men sober.' He paused and it seemed to Anne his bent shoulders shuddered beneath the deep breath he drew in. 'I've also seen men feared. That were the look I saw on that man's face today, Sir Corbett Foley were a man feared.'

'Feared!' Unity's rejection of the notion evident in the scorn-wrapped retort she stirred sugar vigorously into freshly poured tea. 'What's a man like him have to be feared on!'

'The amulet.' Anne's quiet interjection had both faces turn towards her.

'That be nonsense, wench!' Swift precise movement disguising the tremble in her mind, Unity took charge of the baby Anne had bathed and changed an hour before. Settling him once more into the drawer which was his bed she returned to the table, fussing unnecessarily with the teacups. 'Talk like that be naught but nonsense. How could a piece of jewellery, a thing wrought by the hand of man, give rise to fear? I'll tell you how, it be caused by daft folk spreading tales that be no more than superstitious blether . . . feared of a trinket; Lord, whatever will I hear next!'

Swivelling slowly in his chair Laban looked hard at his wife. 'What's this about an amulet?'

'It was something I brought from Russia,' Anne answered quickly. 'I – I asked Unity not to speak of it to you, not because I didn't trust you not to talk of it but because of its power to harm. I should never have mentioned it at all . . . I have opened the way for evil to strike at you both.'

'Evil!' Laban frowned.

'You best tell him everything, wench.' Unity handed her husband a cup of steaming tea before lowering herself into her chair.

Fingers tight about her own cup Anne retold the whole of what had happened since being handed the amulet, finishing with the words spoken to her as Sir Corbett turned from placing the covered trinket in the drawer of the cabinet: 'like a flood, once evil begins it cannot be stopped but must run its course'.

'That was the all of what he said?' Laban broke the silence he had kept during the long explanation.

She had not wanted to repeat those final words . . . did not want to speak them now. Anne stared at the tea which had gone untouched. Was it that she felt them to be too incongruous, too illogical to be believed? But Sir Corbett Foley did believe in what he had said and so had Mikhail Yusupov before him.

'Were that the all of what were said?' Laban repeated his question, his eyes intent as they looked at Anne.

'No.' It was almost a whisper. 'No . . . he – he said almost the same words Andrei Yusupov said to me at our parting . . . "I fear time is running out for the peace of nations."'

'The peace o' nations, now what were that supposed to mean? The things folk do say, an' 'im an educated man an' all; I swear sometimes the smarter a man be supposed to be the dafter he is . . . peace o' nations . . . bah!' Unity shook her head.

Placing the pipe between his teeth Laban removed his

glance from the two women. Gazing deep into the fire he saw not the dancing flames but the spearpoint flash of gunfire and the black pall of smoke lying over fallen bodies.

. . . the hounds of war are straining at the leash . . .

War! Tying the ribbons of her cotton nightgown Anne's fingers trembled. Could there really be any credence to those words? No . . . she stared at her own frightened face reflected in the mahogany-framed mirror set on the wall, no . . . it was as Unity had said as she had set the supper table . . . superstitious senseless prattle which none with the least bit of brain would believe. And Corbett Foley of all folk should know better than to go spouting rubbish which only served to frighten them as brainless as himself.

Sir Corbett was very far from brainless and so was Mikhail Yusupov. They were men of a different world to that of Laban and Unity, they moved in circles whose information was not always given to the ordinary people . . . but war! The country had lived through the horrors of that.

In the quiet of the bedroom that had once been shared by Unity's sons, Anne took her own sleeping child, holding him protectively close to her breast. How many times must Unity have held her children this way, how many times soothed their infant cries and as they grew quieted their fears and sorted their troubles? And what had she truly felt when they had left her to go fighting in a foreign country, in a world so different to their own? Heartbreak? Was that what she herself had felt when it seemed she must part with her son? No, it was not a strong enough word to describe the emotion that had ripped her heart to shreds, and it held only a shadow of the feelings which must have lain beneath the smile forced to Unity's lips, the smile which underlay the pride she had felt in her tall strong sons. No, heartbreak was a poor word. Anne touched her mouth to the soft downy face, feeling the

warmth of smooth velvety skin. It must have been a nightmare
of anguish, a torture more painful than could be described, it
was the death of the soul; but that death had not ended the
woman's pain.

Anne's heart twisted in sympathy. She had seen it on
that kind face, a lost haunted look, a look of searching for
something she would never find; had heard the echoes of it
those first weeks when Unity had come quietly into this room
to give the baby its nightly feed and had known the agony of
it lived on, returning in the silent hours, even the night not
setting her free from the torture of remembering.

'But we will try to help,' Anne whispered against the tiny
cheek. 'We will love her and you will be the grandson that
dreadful war denied her.'

Returning the baby to its own bed Anne tried to settle to
sleep but closing her eyes gave access to the shadows of fear,
to the cries of women robbed of their children. It must not
happen again . . . it must never happen again! But earnest
as her silent prayer was the answer which echoed chilled
her heart.

Evil finds many ways.

She had to be given a second chance. There had to be a
way . . . there *must* be a way.

Heaven helps those who help themselves.

It was an old adage and for many perhaps a true one. Lying
sleepless in her bed Clara Mather stared into the flickering
shadows cast by the oil lamp set close. She could hardly
expect heaven to help with what it was she wanted . . . but
she could help herself.

That first time . . . she had been so close that day. With her
thin lips clamped she let the episode run again in her mind.
If only Unity Hurley had stepped from that poky kitchen,
just a moment was all it would have taken, a moment and

it would have been done, and half of the threat which hung over Quenton would have been wiped away. But it had not happened, Jacob Corby's grandchild still lived and with it the threat to her own son.

Quenton! Clara's fingers gripped the sheet. If just a quarter of his brain was set to thinking of the future! But he was an almost carbon copy of his father . . . leave things to her, Mother would take care of things. It would be the same in this; if Quenton's path was to be swept clear she would have to wield the broom. Well, the broom stood ready. She glanced to where the wardrobe stood wreathed in shadow. All that was needed was the chance to use it.

The chance *would* come. Clara closed her eyes but her fingers retained their hold on the sheet. The problem was when and where would opportunity present itself? That was the crux of everything . . . the second time could well prove the last; if she didn't strike when that moment came she might well never have the chance again.

Prepared! Her eyes slowly opening Clara smiled into the shadows as if welcoming an old and dear friend. That was it, she must be prepared. True, the essence of wolfsbane was ready and more than powerful enough to see a child safely out of this world, but left where it was in the pocket of her mourning coat meant any opportunity she might have to use it would needs be coupled with time, time to take it from that coat and place it in her bag. But chance was not always so favourable.

Throwing off the covers she padded quickly across the room, throwing open the door of the tall wardrobe. Touch born of experience she reached into the dim interior taking out the carefully covered suit. Reaching into the ruched muff she felt the small bottle cold in her hand. This must be always with her. Lifting her bag from its place on the shelf of the wardrobe she slipped the bottle inside. From this moment she would carry it everywhere she went.

Returning bag and suit to their respective places she had half closed the door then paused as light from the lamp caught its mirrored front in a pale gold gleam. A smile cold and venal touched her thin-lipped mouth, her eyes following the shift of the limpid reflection which faded into obscurity as she slowly pushed the door closed.

Light was so easily snuffed out. Slipping into bed she let the smile play. So was the life of a child!

14

'But what if he refuses, what if he says the circumstances of birth forbid it?'

'I doubts he'll do that.' Unity smiled at the girl whose lips trembled on her words. 'Vicar be an understanding man, he won't allow no dictates to prevent a soul being brought to God.'

Fastening the coat which years before had become too small, Anne let her glance wander to the child gurgling happily in his bed, her fingers clumsy as she realised what Unity was asking of her: to tell her son was a bastard, a child born of lust . . . of rape.

'If only I could be sure.' Unaware she had given voice to the thought, Anne was startled by the sharp response.

'There be only one way of knowing that. You go to the vicar and asks; we can give that child of your'n his name, we needs no help in that but only a man of the cloth can enrol him in the community of heaven. He needs be baptised, taken into the church.'

'Are bastards accepted into the church?' Anne's heart tripped on the thought.

Her hands falling to her sides Unity glanced at the photograph adorning the mantel shelf. 'The love of Jesus Christ be given all babes,' she said softly, 'no matter the way of their coming nor of their going. The vicar along of St Lawrence knows that, he be more'n a man in a long frock wi' a book in his hand, he be a man with a soul and I be thinking he won't turn you away.'

. . . he won't turn you away . . .

Her hand on the brightly polished brass knocker set high on the heavy door of the vicarage Anne hesitated. What if Unity's words proved empty, what if this representative of church and faith refused to baptise her son, turned her away with nothing but condemnation? But she had done nothing to be condemned for.

'Oh, I didn't 'ear you knock.'

Anne blinked at the woman who had opened the door.

'I 'pologises if I've kept you standin'. You'll be wantin' to see the reverend; come you in, hisself be in the study.'

Why had she come here, why had she listened to Unity? Every sense telling her to turn and run from this house, Anne followed in the woman's wake.

Middle-aged, silver at the temples, eyes a faded blue beneath sensitive brows, the white collar a shriek against the dark grey-black of his cassock, a man looked up smiling as his housekeeper ushered Anne into the pristinely neat yet small room.

'Welcome,' his smile deepened as he rose to his feet. 'What can I do for you?'

Would his smile be so warm, his welcome as genuine once he heard? Anne perched unhappily on the edge of the chair he pointed to.

'My name is John,' he smiled again, showing strong, well-cared-for teeth, 'Father John Pickard.'

Almost too quiet to be audible Anne answered, 'Anne – Anne Corby. I – I want to ask will you baptise my child?'

Blue eyes regaining a little of their lost radiance the man resumed his seat, drawing to him a sheet of paper then dipping the nib of a pen into the well of a glass inkstand.

'Baptism, is it? Bringing a soul into the family of God is a service which never fails to fill my heart with gratitude and pleasure. Now, if we can take a few details, Mrs Corby . . .'

'Miss.' Anne swallowed hard. 'I am Miss Corby, I am not married.'

A slight frown drawing the sensitive brows closer together, the pen hovered over the empty page.

'But you said the infant was *your* child.'

Clutching her fingers together, her breath catching in her throat, Anne nodded.

'And the father . . . is there a reason why he should not marry you?'

Silence following the question seemed to press in upon Anne, a weight threatening to push her into the ground. This was the moment she had known would come, he would no doubt express a sorrow at having to refuse her request yet still he would turn her away; bastards were not welcome into the fold of the faithful.

'There is every reason.' She forced the words to come. 'He is not in this country.'

Was it a sigh of relief she had heard? Anne raised her head at the soft sound, meeting the return of a smile.

'Does he – the father – know of his child?' A shake of her head answering him the vicar went on. 'Then you must write to him, a letter will surely bring him home—'

'That will not be possible.' The interruption was filled with a quiet assertion that had the frown return to the man's face. 'You see I do not know the name of the father of my son.'

The chink of pen being returned to the glass inkstand the only sound disturbing the oppressive stillness, Anne rose to her feet. She would not embarrass the priest by staying longer. Thanking him briefly for seeing her she turned for the door, but before she had taken a step the man spoke quietly.

'We do not have the confessional in this church, Miss Corby, and the forgiveness of any sin we view as being the prerogative of our Lord and no other; however we as His ministers are ever ready, and I hope willing, to listen and if possible to offer help.'

'It was no fault of my child . . . the church is wrong to allow the sins of the father to fall upon the child!' Words ripping from her in a vehement mixture of defence and admonition, Anne whirled to face the priest. 'He deserves the right to be counted amongst the children of God, to be baptised into the love and faith of Christ. Who are you to deny any child that, regardless of his begetting!'

'Who indeed!' Clean, long-fingered hands spread wide on the gleaming desk. 'And who am I to say where any fault may lie? But again I say as a man of God I am willing to listen if my doing so might bring any sort of solace.'

Solace! Anne dropped heavily to the chair she had just vacated. What comfort could anyone give a girl who had pushed a man to his death, a spike through his throat, who had watched a mother she loved dragged from a sleigh and torn to pieces by ravening wolves then days later had been raped by a laughing beast of a man: what words could anyone use which would erase the horrors she had endured? Yet even as the thoughts raged in her mind Anne began to speak, telling the priest the tale of abuse which had led to the birth of a child, the finish of which was a further imploring.

'God knows he is innocent of any blame, a perfectly innocent child who must carry the stigma of his birth all the days of his life. Can the church add to that by denying him baptism?'

His kind eyes relaying his sympathy, Father John Pickard reached again for the pen. 'No, my dear,' his finely marked mouth smiled with the reply, 'the church will not add to that, your son will receive baptism, he will be welcomed into the body of Christ.'

Joshua Laban! Unity smiled through a mist of tears. The child were to be named for her Laban. The vicar had agreed to the baptism and Anne had chosen the names. Laban. She sniffed loudly. Anne Corby had given both herself and Laban something they had never dreamed to have . . . a child to carry his name.

'And a proud one you'll make it, you see if I don't be right.' Lifting the gurgling infant she lay him in the old-fashioned, deep-bodied perambulator Laban had bought from the pawnshop. She had pushed this so many times, Luke laid snug beneath its covers while Matthew perched on its end, his legs dangling beneath the handle, his heels drumming against its wicker frame.

Glancing at the photograph which was a copy of that kept in the parlour and lovingly dusted each day she smiled. 'You would have loved her and the child, loved them as we do.'

'I have the purses wrapped –'

Anne entered the kitchen, interrupting the whisper.

'– is there anything you want me to bring from the town?'

'No.' Unity blinked her eyes clear. 'No doubt, you'll have enough to carry home with what Laban will have waiting, seems there be more work every day, 'sides I've the intention of going into Darlaston meself and this here young man be going to escort me.'

'I see!' Anne pretended offence as she looked at her son, his dark eyes wide and alert watching every movement. 'So you prefer another woman's company, do you! Well, listen to me, my lad, misbehave and you are in serious trouble.'

A gurgle her answer Anne laughed. 'A fat lot of notice he takes. Seriously though, you don't have to be burdened with him, I can just as easily take him with me.'

'He be no burden.' Unity buttoned her coat determinedly. 'And you and me can walk together as far as the leather works then him and me will carry on. You need have no fears for this lad, I've got a feed all wrapped and keeping warm 'neath the blanket should he need it.'

'I will never fear for him so long as he is with you.' Anne kissed the lined cheek, aware of the stifled sob greeting her words. These two people, Unity and her husband, she would trust them with her life, no – she smiled, following after the older woman as she left the house – she would trust either of them with far more than that, she would trust them with her son's life.

'Now you make sure Laban don't go piling too much on you.' Unity had chatted all the way from Blockall, now nearing the middle of Church Street she glanced at Anne when there was no reply.

'You mark what I says . . .'

But Anne was not marking what she said, instead she was staring towards the grounds of St Lawrence churchyard, the look on her face one of horror. But what was there in the churchyard that could possibly frighten the wench? Unity's frown deepened as Anne drew closer to her side, the girl's glance still resting on something she alone could see. Was it something yet in those grounds or something which had been there before . . . something which had happened, and had put the fear of the devil into Anne Corby? Whatever it was the wench had kept it to herself.

'This be where we leaves you.' Unity halted. 'There be no sense in you passing the Regency works when it's that place you were meant to visit.'

'What?' Her voice shaking slightly Anne blinked the vision of Quenton from her mind. 'Oh yes . . . well, I will see you two at home.'

Watching the slight figure pass through the tall gates marked Regency Leather, Unity walked slowly towards King Street, whose small, closely huddled shops proved the town centre. Fear of the devil . . . She rounded a corner into Cock

Street, bringing the perambulator to a halt outside Thomas Cooper's pawnbroker shop. Her gaze on the dusty window she saw nothing of the goods displayed for sale, only the frightened face of a girl staring towards a churchyard.

'Thinkin' to buy yourself a new outfit, Unity?'

Startled by the thin voice, Unity forced a quick smile. 'I heard the King was having a do along of the palace so I thought to get meself a frock.'

'You've 'ad your invite then?'

'Of course, postman brought it this morning, special delivery. Have you had yours?'

Hustling a small enamelled box from a pocket hidden somewhere amid the volumes of black skirt, the sallow-faced woman tapped the lid with a forefinger before opening it and offering its contents to Unity.

''Ad it yesterday.' Nodding at Unity's refusal of snuff she sprinkled a little of the tobacco-coloured powder onto the back of one hand then with two quick breaths drew it into each nostril.

Unity smiled a little more readily. 'It be no use my going into Thomas Cooper's then Ginny, for you'll have had the pick of his stock.'

'Oh ar,' the other woman laughed raucously, 'an' a tiararra to go wi' it.'

Coming to the doorway of the grocer's shop on the opposite side of the street a figure dressed in the ever-present black, which was the badge of the poorer women of the town, stepped sharply back inside but a keen glance remained with the women laughing together a little along the street.

'Be there summat as you've forgot?'

Not removing her glance Clara Mather nodded, asking a quarter pound of tea be mixed for her, adding sharply she wanted 'all leaves and no sweepings'.

Ignoring the grocer's offended mumblings she watched the

sallow-faced woman walk away towards the junction with
New Street. The one who was left . . . it *was* Unity Hurley,
and with a perambulator! That could only hold Anne Corby's
child! Blood quickening in her veins she handed the grocer
the five pence he asked, then, as Unity disappeared into the
pawnbroker's, went quickly into the street. It was empty. Clara
drew a rapid breath. She had known there would be a second
chance, one like this wouldn't be offered again.

Conscious the grocer might just possibly be glancing
through his window she made the pretence of settling her
purse deep into the bottom of her bag while in reality she
released the stopper from the small glass bottle that she now
carried everywhere with her.

She had to do it now, she had to take the chance! With
one hand holding the bottle she tipped it, smearing some of
its contents over the gloved little finger of the other.

Now . . . she must do it now!

Jabbing the cork back in place, every pulse pounding, she
walked steadily the several yards to where the perambulator
stood. The street was still empty. Reaching her goal she
glanced at the child, its dark eyes wide, a rosebud mouth
open in a smile.

Now, before the Hurley woman came out!

Quick as the thought itself she thrust her hand towards the
gurgling infant, pushing her finger into the tiny mouth.

It was done! An old-fashioned black bonnet bobbing on her
head, Clara walked away. She must not hurry, must not draw
the attention of anyone who might suddenly appear.

Reaching the corner with King Street she risked a glance
behind her. The way she had come was still deserted. Tension replaced by a soaring jubilation she took care not to
appear any different from the other women going about
the business of buying their evening meal. It had been a
good decision of hers to wear black, this way, the bonnet

veil flopping low over her brow, she was faceless among the rest.

Faceless! She smiled inwardly. And very soon now her brother's daughter would be childless!

'You knows I'm right, you shouldn't go there by yourself, the track along through them fields don't be the safest of places come nightfall.' Laban Hurley looked at the slight figure facing him, a determined line to the well-shaped mouth.

'There is nothing to fear, I have walked that way many times before.'

'Ar, no doubt you have!' Laban was curt. 'But how many of them times alone? You be a young woman—'

'Laban, it is sweet of you to worry for me but really there is no need.'

Setting aside the semi-circular-bladed round knife he was using to thin the edges of a piece of leather, Laban's jaw set in the no-nonsense mode Anne had seen him use when speaking of any tradesman who had dared suggest a less-than-top-quality product could easily pass as the best and bring the same money. Now that look was directed at her.

Laban's hands came up to his chest, the thumbs hooking into the straps of the hide apron reaching past his knees. 'No need, is it! Then there be the same need of you going to Bentley Grange!'

'But Sir Corbett—'

'Be shaken but not badly injured!'

Laban was not going to be moved. Glancing to where Abel Preston was working on a saddle, Anne caught the slight essence of a smile accompanied by the merest lift of powerful shoulders. She would get no support from that quarter. But she could not leave it at that, Sir Corbett Foley had been too kind in the past for her to simply ignore him now.

'I'm sorry.' Anne's answer was firm, matching that of Laban

in its determination. 'Sir Corbett is an old and much-respected friend of my family and I see it as a duty to call on him to ask after his health.'

'And I see it as my duty to go along with you!'

Anne's eyes softened. Laban was concerned for her safety but walking all the way to Bentley and back after a long day's work was too much to ask; though he would rather die than admit it, Laban sometimes showed his years and she could not ask him to tire himself even more on her account.

'No,' she shook her head, 'I can't ask—'

'Laban!' The quietly spoken interruption brought two pairs of eyes to rest on the man now openly watching from the long sunlit workbench. 'If it isn't too forward a suggestion on my part, perhaps I could accompany Miss Corby to Bentley?'

'But—'

'There is nothing else to do with the evening,' Abel swiftly cut Anne's objection. 'If it is alright with both of you then I would quite enjoy a walk to Bentley.'

'Alright!' Laban beamed. 'It be more'n alright, it be the perfect answer, don't it, Anne?'

'Thank you, Abel.' Beneath Anne's smile rested the unsaid finish to her sentence: that would be the perfect answer.

15

Laban had insisted they leave for Bentley Grange as soon as Abel had washed his hands and face in the rain barrel kept in the yard at the rear of the building. 'No sense in going home to change your clothes, lad,' he had said, 'it be close on evenin' now and it'll be quite dark by the time you've done that; it's my guess you'll not be wanting to do other than wait in that kitchen so changing of your clothes be naught but a wastin' of time . . . an' I'll have enough explaining to do to Unity, her'll be worrying as it is when her hears, without adding to the time it'll tek to get that visit over and this wench back home in Blockall.'

Walking beside the tall, broad-shouldered figure Anne hid a smile. Of all the reasons in the world Unity might think of to fear for her well-being, Abel Preston was not one of them.

'Laban says you are thinking of having your son christened.'

He said it easily, no note of censure in his tone but that did not necessarily mean he held her free of blame. 'It takes two to play that particular game' was a phrase often murmured in Darlaston when a girl fell pregnant the wrong side of marriage, and she was not married nor never had been so why should he think differently of her? After all, he knew of the child, why should he not know he was illegitimate?

'Unity thought it time.'

'And you?' He answered the flat tone, not looking at the girl who barely reached his shoulder.

She did not have to answer, she was under no commitment

to tell him anything; yet deep inside Anne knew she wanted to, felt some strange urge to confide in the man who had so often as a lad taken her side against Quenton and his mother.

'I – I wasn't sure,' hot blood surged to her cheeks, 'I wasn't sure the church would baptise . . .' Anne felt her throat close.

She had done many things that she regretted, ending a man's life by pushing him backwards onto a spike, not checking for a rifle beneath her mother's rug before setting off from that inn in Radiyeska, then later stopping at that house for a drink of water . . . but she would not be adding Abel Preston to that list.

Waiting a moment, wanting yet not wanting to answer Anne swallowed hard against the conflict of emotions blocking her throat.

'I . . .' her voice trembled, 'I thought that seeing he . . . seeing he has no father—'

'Your husband—'

'I have no husband!' Shooting from her in a force that shook her to the core, the words dropped into silence, then as he made no reply added whisperingly, 'I have no husband.'

Beside her Abel Preston's sympathy welled like a tide. Anne Corby's life seemed to have had more than its share of ups and downs and now to be left widowed and with a child to care for.

'Did it happen while you were abroad . . . did your husband die before your return to England?'

He did not know, Laban had not told Abel Preston of her disgrace. Suddenly Anne felt a wild desire to laugh, to let go the rein, release that tight hold she struggled with day after day, the self-condemnation, the blame for her own stupidity. Instead she turned her face away, answering quietly.

'Yes, it happened whilst I was abroad, but no, my husband did not die . . . you see I was not married.'

Now Abel Preston would walk away from her, think of her as no better than a slut, a common whore; from this moment any trace of their old friendship would be gone.

'Did the man know you carried his child?'

The quietness of it shook her. If he had accused her, reproached her as a wanton she could maybe have handled it better. Teeth clenched, Anne felt the tears spill silently onto her cheeks.

'No.' She shook her head. Then, unable to contain it any longer whispered the whole terrifying ordeal.

Hands tightening at his sides, Abel fought cold anger which minutes before had been laughter. What kind of man was it could do that to a girl, agree to her taking a drink of water from a well then knocking her to the ground and raping her? What sort of sly, worthless . . . ? Quenton! The swine had tried it in that churchyard! For a moment rage overcame common sense and Abel let it flow. Had it been in Mather's mind to shame his cousin in this despicable way, burdening her with his child, letting her face the world alone and leaving it to the spiteful tongues of Darlaston to drive her from the town? No. He breathed deeply, grasping his thoughts back into his own control. She had said it had happened in Russia, the man responsible was a Russian; Quenton Mather had never been absent from Darlaston for more than a couple of weeks at a time.

Anne forced herself to go on, aware of Abel's silence, aware of what he must be thinking, that a man didn't do such a thing unless a girl had first led him on. 'That was why I thought the church . . . with there being no father with me, with not being able to tell his name or show a marriage certificate . . . I thought baptism might be refused a – a bastard.'

There she had said it! She had said aloud what others probably whispered behind her back; but Abel Preston would always know he had heard it from her lips, that she had made no pretence, no effort to hide the truth of her child.

He could hear it in the tremble of her voice, see it in the shaking of her clasped hands, the pain coursing through Anne Corby at thought of the life facing her son.

'You must not blame yourself, and the child once he is old enough to reason for himself will not blame you . . .'

Soft as the evening breeze fanning her blazing cheeks Abel's words bore no sign of contempt, no essence of disgust but only the gentle tenderness one might use to an unhappy child.

'You were innocent. Truth be you were probably never told of such things by your parents, never warned to be wary or given to dream there were such men as would take advantage of and abuse a young girl.'

Only half of that was true! The pang of guilt she had so often felt during that long traumatic journey across Europe at last found the basis of its existence in Anne's mind. Her parents had never spoken to her on any subject to do with the side of life involving relations between a man and a woman. It would have been totally unacceptable to her Bible-spouting father, whilst her gentle, so-caring mother maybe had thought a girl of so few years to be too young to be introduced to a topic of such intimate nature. Whichever the cause, she herself had been given a glimpse of the lust felt by some men, that alone should have been her warning. She ought to have realised following that encounter in the inn at Radiyeska, those men sitting around the stove, the landlord, his vile intention . . . she should have known! But she had not and now an innocent child must suffer her naivety, her carelessness, must bear the brunt of that for all of his life, live with the heritage she bequeathed him, a heritage of shame.

'You are not to blame, you have to believe that, Anne. If you and your son are to have any kind of life you have to believe in your own innocence . . . I do.' Taking her arm,

Abel turned her gently to face him, his chest tightening at the tears glinting on flushed cheeks. 'I always believed you, Anne,' he repeated quietly, 'and I always will.'

Shown into the dimly lit bedroom, lamp-thrown shadows flickering over heavy, ornate furniture, Anne felt the needle-point of alarm prick at her nerves. Sir Corbett had been bruised that day she had seen him at the leather works, bruised and leaning a little more heavily on his stick, but she had thought it no more than a stiffness of the joints caused by his motor carriage accident; it was, after all, only to be expected that he be not quite his old self, but to find him taken to his bed!

Seeing the anxiety mirrored on her face a hand flapped limply before dropping back onto the exquisitely embroidered bedcover.

'No need to look like that, girl, I'm not about to depart for the hereafter just yet; be the idea of that doctor fellah, insists on a few weeks' rest in bed . . . huh! The man's a fool! I told him I'd tek a few weeks of rest only after they dresses me in a shroud and sets me in me box . . . and that ain't going to be for a long time yet.'

Glancing at the manservant who had accompanied her to the room he ordered another lamp to be lit and then, when the offer of refreshment was refused, demanded he himself be brought a glass of brandy after which the servant was dismissed, leaving them alone.

Swallowing first a mouthful of brandy he laid the glass aside.

'I'm glad you came, Anne,' he beckoned her to a chair drawn beside the bed, 'I intended sending you a note asking you come to see me; there – there are things I wish to talk to you about.'

The doctor had been right to insist on bed rest. Anne caught the shadow of weariness flick across the bruised face as his head relaxed back into the huge, white, frilled pillows.

'Not now,' she answered gently, 'whatever it is it will keep until you are up and about.'

'Up and about!' He snorted. 'I'll have to shoot that damned doctor first, he's like an old hen . . . fuss, fuss! I tell you it's enough to drive a man mad.'

'He wants only what is best for you.'

'And who is to know what be better forra man than the man himself!'

Truculent as she remembered he could be, Sir Corbett Foley frowned back at her, causing Anne to smile.

'Viola,' his gaze drifted so he smiled at a different face in a different time, 'you were the prettiest girl this town ever saw and I loved . . .'

It tailed away and Anne watched the mists of sadness form a silver veil over eyes heavy with unhappiness.

. . . *and I loved* . . .

The words echoed and re-echoed. Had Sir Corbett Foley been in love with her mother . . . could that have been the real reason for her father having dragged them half across the world . . . had his proselytising been for true love of God or a jealous regard of his wife's love?

'I'm sorry, girl, I drifted off for a moment . . . an old man's habit, I'm afraid.'

With the mist blinked away the usual brightness lit the man's eyes but the unhappiness remained etched in lines not so easily disguised. He had lived with pain, Anne realised with shock, not in the limbs, not pain which a doctor could cure but the pain of a broken heart. Sir Corbett Foley had loved deeply but that love had been lost to him.

'I wanted to see you –'

He was speaking again. Anne pushed her thoughts away.

'– there is something I wish to tell you.'

Not of his love for her mother. Sir Corbett was a gentleman of his time, he was of an era the world would not see again, and what lay hidden beneath the cloud of unhappiness evident now on his fine features would go with him to his grave.

'You were no more than a child when your parents left this town and not old enough to know what your mother planned for you. Your father left everything in his sister's hands, he trusted her but your mother did not, Viola could be wise in some things but blind to others, she did not see—'

His love . . . was that what her mother had not seen? Watching the shadow of sadness deepen on his face Anne felt a wave of pity wash over her. A lifetime of plenty, that had been Sir Corbett Foley's life, years of wanting for nothing . . . except for the love of a woman he could never have.

'Viola,' taking a deep breath he went on, 'Viola did not see the sort of life Jacob Corby was condemning her to – yes, girl, I say condemning for he knew the dangers that lay ahead, the jungle fevers and river sickness that had destroyed stronger men than him, yet still he ruled that she and you go with him. Oh Lord . . . oh Lord, why did I not tell her!'

Eyes closed, mouth firmed against a sudden trembling he turned his face away. But sorrow was not hidden by the move only echoed by the shudder of his body. He was suffering almost as she had suffered seeing that wolf snatch her mother from the sledge, he too had lost for ever that which he loved most. Sitting in silence Anne waited.

'Forgive me.' Snuffling into a large cambric handkerchief he avoided the need to look directly at her. 'Damned head cold . . . comes of lying in that ditch . . . damned motor carriage . . . should 'ave known better than to take it! There,' he sniffed, reaching for the glass of brandy and swallowing a little, 'that's better. Now for what I was saying . . . your mother had no trust in Jacob's sister and for that reason asked me to take various things into my possession to hold in trust for you should it be she did not return to England. I said she was wise in some things and this, I think, was one of them. Had Clara Mather got her hands on what were left with me it would have been fed into the fire long since.'

Replacing the glass on the night table he pointed to the opposite side of the spacious room.

'There,' he said easing himself higher on the pillows, 'there in that escritoire, top drawer on the left, you'll find a box.'

'Not tonight.' Despite the pallid lighting, Anne saw the bright spots of colour high on cheeks which in just a few days had become sunken. 'Whatever it is will keep until—'

'No!' Catching her hand he shook it once, the quick gesture one of command, then his voice lowered taking on a gentler tone. 'No, Anne, I made that mistake once long ago, I waited and waited until it became too late, the one thing which I truly loved was taken by another and only then . . . when she . . . only when the chance was gone did I realise what I had allowed to happen. They have a saying for that sort of thing, don't they? I shut the door after the horse had bolted. Well, I won't be caught that way again so bring that box to me.'

A box! Her legs threatening to give way beneath her, Anne crossed to the elegant writing desk, its delicate structure seeming strangely out of place among the heavier, more masculine furniture. Was this where Sir Corbett had kept the amulet? Was it in the box he had asked she bring to him?

. . . only when the chance was gone did I realise what I had allowed to happen . . .

The words filtered from the shadowed corners of the room.

. . . I had allowed to happen . . .

Hands shaking as they rested on the drawer Anne felt a frisson of apprehension travel through her. Did that mean Sir

Corbett felt there to be some threat in keeping that trinket in this house, was he about to ask her to take it away, perhaps keep it herself?

Slowly pulling open the drawer she stared into the indistinct interior, her vision taking moments to adjust, to mark the outline of a box.

'Take it out, Anne, bring it over here.'

To refuse would be an admittance of distrust, an accusal; but why would a man who had always shown her only kindness try to . . . ? He wouldn't! Thrusting her hands into the drawer she lifted out the box. Sir Corbett Foley would never deliberately place her in the way of harm.

'These were your mother's.' The box set beside him on the bed Corbett Foley took out a sheaf of papers. 'She honoured me with her trust and now I am fulfilling it.'

Papers! The box held only papers! Guilt and relief rolling into one, Anne's fingers twined in her lap. How could she have ever let herself imagine what she had?

'These,' he held the folded papers out for her to take, 'among these are deeds given to your mother on her marriage. Your father allowed them to remain in her name and for that I respect him, not many men would forgo the proceeds brought to them by marriage. But when it came to his own property, his house and iron works, Jacob Corby had no such fore-sight, his sister would run them both, she would look to things until his return. Your mother, though, she had no faith in that woman and for that reason left those papers with me. Take them with you, girl, and, if you will, a word of advice to go with them. Wait until the time is right before letting Jacob's sister know what it is you have for her claws are sharp and they will strike deep if she feels herself and that son of hers threatened.'

'Papers, just papers!'

Hearing the relief in her voice the greying brows drew

together. 'Yes, girl, papers . . . what did you think was in that box?'

Colour warming her face, Anne looked into eyes which minutes before had been misted by memories. 'I . . .' she hesitated. 'I thought perhaps the amulet.'

'No.' He shook his head. 'That thing had worked too much harm already. I destroyed it, threw the pieces into the fire and buried the ashes where no one will find them. Let them lie in darkness like the creature whose work it did. Forget it, child, forget you ever heard of it; you are safe now, be sure it cannot strike at you or at anyone again.'

'It tried to strike at you . . . it did, didn't it? The fog you spoke of to Laban, that which you thought came from a box you had with you, it held the amulet?'

Nodding slowly he leaned deeper into the pillows. 'Yes,' he breathed, 'yes, it was the amulet. I was taking it to Lichfield, to the Bishop there. I'd talked to the local man along of Bentley Church but he seemed to think I was either a crank or losing my mind; anyway he said it was beyond his jurisdiction to deal with anything of that nature and said it would have to be handled by the Bishop. That being so I shoved it into the motor carriage and set off for the railroad station.

'I was halfway when a mist struck up. At first it didn't register with me that it was not widespread, then I noticed the fields to either side were clear, the sun shining on the stubble left from the harvesting. That was when I looked at the seat beside me. At first I thought I was dreaming, then that p'raps that priest fellah was right and my mind was going . . . but it was neither of those things; I *was* seeing a mist and it *was* coming from that box. The road was too narrow to stop . . . feared a bump with a wagon, you know . . . so I drove on. I swear,' he looked at Anne, his eyes darkening with something she could not understand, 'the power contained in that amulet knew what I was going to do, for even as I looked at it the car began to vibrate and that mist thickened; it swirled in grey whorls, twisting and turning, wrapping about my face, filling my nostrils, squeezing between my lips, clogging my throat until I could not breathe. It was a foulness I could taste, could feel.' He paused, obviously still feeling the effects of the moment. 'It coiled about my neck like a living thing, tightening and choking, and I knew it was intent upon killing me. I tried to control the car, to bring it to a halt but try as I might I had no strength against what was in that carriage. Then I felt a blow to my head and knew no more until I woke up here.'

'And the box?' Anne could not hide the shiver that ran along her spine as she asked.

'It were brought here with me and as I told you I broke the amulet into pieces, hammered the stones until they were no more than shards then put the whole lot to the fire. Rest easy, child, it can do no more harm.'

His face stark and grey against the pillow, Sir Corbett Foley closed his eyes wearily. She had tired him. Anne rose and, kissing the man's brow, turned to leave. 'I will call again when you are feeling stronger.'

Forcing his eyes to open he watched the slender figure move into the shadows. He had lied to the girl, lied . . . but only to set her mind at rest. That box which held the amulet had not been brought to Bentley Grange and no search of the motor carriage or of the ground where it had collided with the hedge had revealed any trace of it. It was gone but not destroyed! He had felt its evil touch him a little more each day since that accident, felt its malignance draining the strength from his body. What would the people of today's world say if they knew a perfectly sane, responsible man believed in witchcraft and curses? He smiled weakly. The modern world did not know as much as it gave itself credit for!

At the base of the curved staircase of the graceful old house,

Anne smiled her goodnight to the manservant waiting to see her and Abel out.

'How is he?'

Abel's question met no answer for Anne heard only the words repeating in her mind.

. . . it can do no more harm . . .

The box with her mother's papers clutched tightly in her hands she heard the echo and re-echo.

Rest easy, child, it can do no more harm.

Why did those words bring no comfort to her heart?

16

They had talked of little after leaving Bentley Grange. Abel walked beside Anne trying to avoid looking at the moonlight dancing in her hair. He had thought often of her since that night in the church grounds, felt a pleasure in seeing and speaking with her on the days she came to Regency Leather bringing the goods she and Unity had worked on, but he had not expected that pleasure to develop into this. Stealing a glance at the figure keeping pace with him he felt a quick sharp jerk in his chest, the same catch of breath in his throat as happened whenever he caught sight of her or heard the sound of her voice. Little Anne Corby . . . the child he had often fought over, often shielded from her snotty-nosed cousin and tyrant of an aunt . . . she had been no more than six years to his grown-up fourteen . . . no more than a babe.

But Anne Corby was no longer a babe. Moving only his eyes he glanced again. Anne Corby was a woman and beneath a wan shadow which still showed in her face she was a beautiful woman. Beautiful and the inheritor of Butcroft House and Glebe Metalworks. In a few weeks she could take that inheritance into her own hands; Anne Corby would be a wealthy woman while Abel Preston would never be anything other than a saddle-maker; yes, she would have money, wealth he could never match, but she would not know of an even greater wealth . . . the wealth of his love for her.

When had he realised it? Hands deep in his pockets Abel let his thoughts ramble in the soft silence which had settled over the newly mown fields and which was drawing them both into itself until to break it would feel akin to committing a crime. When had he realised he was in love with Anne Corby? The question was not new to him, he had asked it of himself many times when night brought no peace from the thought of her, no rest to a body aching to hold her close; but the answer . . . the answer when it finally came had been a shock, he could not remember a time he had *not* loved her. Truth was he had always been in love with Anne Corby!

Immersed within that same world of silvery silence Anne wrestled with the problem of whether or not to divulge what the older man had disclosed concerning the cause of his accident. She did not want to keep anything from Abel but would Sir Corbett wish her to speak of it to someone else? After all, he had said the vicar of Bentley Church had looked on his story of the amulet with clearly discernible disparagement and, visiting him after his accident, had spoken of that fog as a figment of an overwrought mind, an illusion born of shock and injury. Would Abel think along the same lines, would he think the owner of Bentley Grange a man with problems of the mind? And what of her own involvement with the pendant worn by a Russian monk whom Mikhail Yusupov had termed 'mad'? Would Abel believe her? He would not have to answer, for she would observe the advice Sir Corbett had given and forget about the thing she had carried from Russia, forget it had ever existed.

'What name have you chosen for your son?' Abel had to break the chains circling his mind, to gain some respite from the emotion grasping his heart.

'What?' Anne had to push her way up from the soft depths.

'I asked what name you were giving your son?'

'Joshua,' Anne smiled in the shadowed moonlight, 'Joshua Laban.'

Beside her Abel nodded. 'He will be so proud of that, will Laban, and Unity too; it's a thousand pities they had only two children, one more would have taken away the pain of losing Matthew and Luke.'

Nothing would ever take away the pain of losing a child. Anne's heart twisted at the thought of just how close she had come to parting with her own son. Unity's pain had softened to an ache bearable by day, but in the solitude of the long night hours she knew it returned to rend the woman apart, breaking her heart as it had when first hearing both of her sons were dead. How had Unity survived such a blow? Anne felt the catch of breath in her throat. It was a strength she herself would never have, she could not go on living now without Joshua.

'Did you know Matthew and Luke?' She asked the question out of need to break the silence, a silence which would provide a breeding ground for thoughts which brought no happiness.

'Yes.' Abel's voice seemed to hold a smile. 'They were both some years older than me but they never treated me as a kid, not the way some lads get treated when they first start to earn their living, being sent to fetch sky hooks or a rubber hammer. Some men think that to be funny but the Hurleys were not like that, they treated a young lad with the same respect they showed to visitors come to order a saddle or harness, the good manners some only show to a man of property: but not Laban and his sons, money and position meant nothing to them, they lived by the teaching which said all men are created equal therefore they should be treated with equal respect.'

As Unity and Laban had treated a stranger, a young woman heavy with child. There had been no condemnation on seeing a hand which wore no ring, no closing the door in her face; they had not acted as Clara Mather had acted, turning her from her own home. Pressing her fingers hard about the box she carried, Anne glanced away into the darkness, a darkness that covered Butcroft House . . . her house! But it would never be hers, she had no proof of inheritance, just as it was certain her father's sister would have proof the Glebe Works along with everything else he had owned had been deeded to her possession. Not that she minded, let Clara and her son take it all. But what of Joshua when he was grown . . . would he so easily forego what should rightfully have been his?

'It almost destroyed Laban when his boys were killed.' Abel talked on quietly. 'He lost the joy he had once had in the leather he worked, but never the pride; what he produced was ever of the same quality, one which could not be surpassed by any other in the trade; but now I see that joy returning . . . you have given him that, you and little Joshua, I saw it when he told me he and Unity were to stand as godparents.'

They had both beamed with pleasure when she had asked them to fulfil that office. 'It is kind of them,' she answered, remembering their wide smiles and Unity's rocking the child in her arms, singing to him that he would be 'baptised along o' the best'.

'Anne.' Abel interrupted the memory. 'A male child needs two godfathers, will the second one be your cousin, will you give Quenton Mather that honour?'

Passing at that moment the lych gate of St Lawrence church, Anne looked at the silhouette of the old sandstone building but the beauty of it was lost among the shadows of horror . . . the horror of being dragged into the darkness enveloping the grounds, the threat of Quenton!

'No.' Clogged by the emotion she had to struggle to contain the reply was little more than a whisper.

Their footsteps lost amid the rumble of a carter's wagon passing on its way from King Street, Abel returned the driver's jovial greeting, then, as the cart drew away, said quietly, 'Anne, if you have no one better suited in mind, then might I stand as your son's second godfather?'

For a moment no words would come. Abel Preston, the boy who so often had been there to champion a little girl, to fight off a spiteful cousin, to answer back the aunt who terrified her so much she had never spoken of her unkindness to her mother; the boy who had taken the trouble to spend time with a six-year-old!

Her face tilting upwards, moonlight a liquid silver in her eyes as she turned to him, Anne knew her whole heart lay in her answer. 'There could never be anyone better,' she murmured, 'my son could have no finer godparent than Abel Preston.'

She had pushed the tip of her finger deep into the child's mouth, held it there a few seconds, felt the tongue pull greedily on it, heard the small gulping sounds of swallowing. It had swallowed the poison! Clara Mather stared at the leather gloves lying where she had put them on her bed. She had been determined to burn them once her cleaning woman had left the house but then instinct had warned she might need them again. There had been no time to recoat her fingertip, no time to administer a second dose of wolfsbane, it had been difficult enough to use the first time while keeping it hidden in her bag; she could not have taken the risk of repeating the process when any second Unity Hurley might have emerged from that pawnshop. But would what she had done serve the purpose intended, had there been sufficient extract on the glove to achieve her aim . . . would it eliminate the problem of Anne Corby's by-blow?

Her hair braided and hanging over her shoulder, lamplight casting a yellow hue over a plain white cotton nightgown, Clara stared at her own reflection in the mirror of her heavy mahogany dressing table.

If not, she would try again and keep on until she was successful. It would be doing her brother a kindness, honour the memory of a man who was respected in this town, take away a stigma he did not deserve, the stigma of a bastard grandchild. Jacob had been a God-fearing man and she, his loving sister . . . yes, she was doing this for him.

Smiling in the contentment of finding justification in other than committing murder simply to further her own ends, Clara picked up the gloves carrying them to the wardrobe, hiding them behind a large hatbox. The cleaning woman was never allowed to set foot in this room but then Clara Mather was not always in the house and when the cat was away . . . a little care was preferable to a lot of regret! About to close the wardrobe she hesitated. How much was left in that bottle? She had put it away so hurriedly she had not checked. What if opportunity came and there was insufficient of the extract to take advantage of it?

Reaching her bag and carrying it to the bed, she stared at it for several moments. The blackness of it was stark as the shadow of death against the bed cover. The shadow of death! Tracing a finger along the intricate braiding of the bag she smiled at the simile. It was an apt one.

Taking the tiny bottle, still wrapped carefully within the folds of a handkerchief so no drop which might possibly have trailed from its lip that afternoon could have touched her skin, she held it to the lamp letting the light reflect in its glass body. Green and shiny as an emerald it glowed between her fingers. She had always had a fondness for the colour. Twisting it now she watched the deeper hue of the liquid move against its sides, sliding like the shadow of a serpent. The shadow of death! She smiled again. It was a shadow would play over any who posed a threat to Clara Mather or to the inheritance intended for her son!

★   ★   ★

He had wanted . . . what? What had he wanted? Abel Preston watched the girl turn along the narrow passage which gave entry to the row of houses, each joined like a Siamese twin to its neighbour. Anne Corby, the girl he had known all of his life yet hardly knew at all. She awakened feelings in him he had never experienced before. True, as a lad he had felt protective. Turning back along Church Street he smiled to himself. Had it been that he enjoyed playing Sir Lancelot or was it the fact that being in Anne Corby's corner afforded him the satisfaction of giving that toad of a cousin of hers a hiding?

That was certainly something he had never regretted and he definitely did not regret punching him in the mouth the night he had caught him manhandling the girl in the churchyard. Reaching the corner of Bilston Street he followed its course, crossing the Leys to Alma Street. Pausing at the one narrow entry which gave access to the rear of a string of tiny terraced houses he thought again of that evening he had heard a cry come from St Lawrence churchyard and a frown settled heavily between his brows. Quenton Mather had been no friend to his small cousin and he was no friend to her now she was grown. Quenton Mather was a coward and a bully but his was not the real threat to Anne Corby, that took the shape of a woman and that woman was his mother.

Walking past the back of the houses, shared privies casting small islands of shadow onto the moonlit communal yard, the frown deepened.

Clara Mather had played God in that metal works. Her word was not to be questioned, her way to be followed in the smelting of ore even though she knew precious little of the process. Clara was a woman determined her word should become law and to be sure it did any attempt to change it resulted in even the most experienced of workmen being sacked.

Lighting the candle kept on a saucer on the narrow ledge beneath the sash window of the scullery, Abel stood a moment watching the pale gleam stab defiant fingers at the encircling shadows.

Her word . . . her way! Clara Mather ruled Glebe Metalworks. She would not relinquish that power . . . nor would she let her brother's daughter stand in her way!

Removing his jacket and hanging it on a peg set in the wall he poured water from an enamelled jug into a matching bowl, the coldness of it stinging his skin as he washed.

Anne Corby might have rejected her father's legacy, turned her back on it as Laban had confided, handed it lock, stock and barrel to her aunt, but that agreement had been simply a verbal one, one which, should she wish, Anne Corby could renounce at any time, deny any such agreement. Maybe at the time she had meant all she had said, perhaps she still did . . . but what of the child? What of Joshua?

His face and arms dried and the water emptied into the one drain serving the yard, Abel settled before the fire kept burning in the tiny living room.

The boy would grow and, given the tongues ever ready to wag in Darlaston, he would come to know his heritage, come to know what was rightfully his. Would he take the same attitude shown by his mother? The answer to that was a highly probable 'no'. If the lad grew with any desire to take what had been denied him, to claim his own, then chances were he would fight for it. Clara Mather understood that only too well.

Coals settling into the bed of the fire sent a flurry of sparks dancing, their vivid twinkling life snatched from them in the black void of the chimney.

Snuffed out . . . destroyed! Abel stared at the dark emptiness which seconds ago had held dazzling pinpricks of vibrant light. Now they were gone, lost to the world for ever, their challenge to the blackness no longer existing.

Clara Mather understood only too well!

The thought returned, chilling in its implication. Would she act in the same way, strike at Anne Corby and her son thereby removing the challenge for ever?

His fingers tightening about the arms of his chair, Abel watched colourful flames twine together, seeking each other's comfort before entering the black void.

It was not any probable 'no' which answered the question in his mind, it was a very definite 'yes'.

17

He was such an ordinary man! Anne stared at the figure standing in the centre of Unity's living room, his shoulders stooped, his grey hair yellowed by the light of an oil lamp placed on the table beside him. He wore no flowing white robe, no great feathered wings spread from his back and no glittering circle of light played about his head as she had always been taught. Had her father not instilled into her the appearance of those heavenly beings, those great Messengers of the Lord; had he not said they were glorious in their holiness, transcendent in their majesty, that even the least of God's angels was sublime in his beauty; how much more then the Archangels, the greatest of those beings?

But he showed none of that glory, the one come to take her child, none of the infinite grace and splendour afforded him by custom of the church, yet was he not of the highest, one bidden from the Throne of God, the great Angel of Death?

But he was so ordinary!

Anne met the faded eyes behind heavy owl-like spectacles, watched the thin lips move, a long, clean-fingered hand dip into a black Gladstone bag.

So ordinary!

The hand emerged from the bag, the lips moving again as the head turned towards Unity. Such an unremarkable head, so grey, so plain! Where was the shimmering aura which blinded in its brilliance? Where the countenance whose beauty was such that man could not comprehend? Was it that this was a lesser being . . . was the sin of her child's begetting so black the great Archangel would not himself come for the tiny soul? But that sin was not Joshua's!

The last of her thoughts cried aloud, Laban stepped quickly to her side. 'Come, wench,' he whispered, 'let me tek you upstairs.'

The softly spoken words hovering on the edge of her mind Anne turned her gaze towards the sound. 'Why?' It was a question dredged from a vacuum, an emptiness of heart and soul. 'Why could he not come himself . . . why blame an innocent child?'

'Let me take her.' Unity reached both arms to the girl held by her husband, but lost in her bewildered world Anne felt nothing as she was taken gently and led from the living room.

How could heaven be so cruel, how could the God her father had loved, had sacrificed everything to follow, turn His wrath upon a tiny child?

'C'mon, wench, drink this down.'

Uncomprehending of the liquid spooned into her mouth, of the tear-marked face bent above her own, Anne swallowed.

She would speak to the lesser being. She swallowed a second spoonful, no taste of the potion registering on her senses. She would speak to that so-ordinary-looking spirit, explain Joshua's innocence, tell him it was she, she who had sinned.

In the dim light of a candle Unity watched the eyelids flicker, heard the faint words.

'I'll tell him he is mistaken. I am the one he came for. I am the one guilty of sin. I am the one the Great Angel of Death has sent him to take . . .'

The spoon held in her hand, tears running unchecked down her lined cheeks, Unity listened to the words trailing off into drugged sleep, words addressed to a higher power.

'Lord forgive mine offences . . .'

Turned into the pillow the lips moved, the almost silent words coming now on a last wakeful breath.

'. . . take me, please . . . take me in place of my child.'

'But how – how did it happen?' Abel Preston looked up from the girth strap whose one end he had skived, shaving the thick leather to half its thickness.

'That be the selfsame question I asked o' that doctor.' Laban Hurley's head moved slowly, its side to side motion that of a man still bewildered by what had so suddenly happened to his world. He had been given the message by a neighbour's lad, a boy breathless with the urgency laid upon him.

'*You be having to go home, Mister 'Urley,*' the youngster had gasped, holding a spot beneath his ribs which ached with the effort of running. '*Missis 'Urley, her said to tell you that you have to come now, right away.*'

He had given the lad a penny and watched the simple gift breathe fresh life into winded limbs, hurtling him towards the nearest sweetshop. Matthew and Luke had raced like that when given a penny to spend on bull's eyes or treacle toffee.

'I mean if the child had been poorly then Unity would have known.'

'Ar, Abel lad, her would have known.' Laban let go the memories. 'Her would have had that little 'un to the doctor afore you could bat your eyes, but there weren't nothing wrong with him, not when her took him to the town.'

But when she got home . . . ! What illness could strike so quickly and with such dire results? Taking up a number four pricking iron Abel marked the end of the bridle to be stitched.

His own work lying idle in his hands Laban watched the younger man cut a length of six-cord, hand-made waxed thread, inserting it into a single needle before knotting one end.

'Unity were beside herself when I got home.' He talked on quietly, even now unbelievingly. 'I couldn't get no sense out of her, then the woman from next door took me to that carriage . . .'

Laban had told him of the perambulator, of how he had spotted it outside Thomas Cooper's pawnshop in King Street and paid half a crown for it, then wheeled it all the way to Blockall despite the jokes of men he met on the way.

'At first I thought the child asleep . . .' Laban's eyes followed the movement of the needle back-stitching the straps on to the webs at the places Abel had marked, but his inner eyes looked at something else, at a small child lying motionless, his tiny face showing the first hint of marble. 'I couldn't tell what the fuss were about, then I touched a little hand . . . it were cold, cold as ice. I wanted to pick him up, to warm him with my own body, to hold him 'til he woke up, but the woman stopped me, her said it were best the doctor see him first. That were when I went to sit with Unity, and while we waited together for the neighbour to bring the doctor her told me of what her knew.'

Working in silence Abel listened, hearing the heartbreak in the old man's voice, hearing the pain that had struck once before, that agony of having beloved sons ripped from his life.

'The little 'un had cooed and gurgled when her set him in that carriage, seeming to answer as her talked to him, kicking at the covers when her tried to tuck him in but by the time her got to Cock Street he were asleep, the same as when her come out of Tom Cooper's shop; he were fast asleep but her couldn't resist touching a finger to that little face. My Unity loved that babby –' his breath catching in his throat Laban blinked at the tears filling his tired eyes '– her loved that babby as her had loved her own.'

And now the child was dead! Abel kept his glance on the

strap he was stitching to the saddle, allowing the other man to keep his dignity; Laban Hurley was not one for public display, he would not want his tears witnessed by another.

'I asked the doctor the same question you yourself asked.' Laban cleared his throat but his hands remained unaccustomedly idle. 'I asked him how could it have happened, what could have took a child's life when he had no sickness, when he smiled and cooed? He answered me that no doctor knowed the cause, that many a babe were laid to sleep in perfect health yet never woke again. Unity must not blame herself, it was no fault on her part, it had happened many times afore this and no cause or reason to say why, seemed the poor little mite just died in his sleep.'

'And Anne?' Abel asked when it seemed the other man had done speaking. 'How is she taking it?'

Glancing down at the leather in his own hands Laban appeared to weigh the question, to search in his mind for the appropriate answer.

'Like somebody in a dream,' he said after a moment, 'her hears naught of what be said to her and sees only what no other eyes see. We thought the sleeping draught that doctor took from his bag would help, that when the girl woke her would be in a proper sense o' mind but it's like Anne don't want to wake.'

She did not want to wake! Abel sent the needle expertly through the holes he had pricked with the iron, stitching the leather strap grain side down. Did she blame herself, hold herself responsible for something the cause of which not even doctors understood?

'When her does speak it be something or someone neither me nor Unity can see, her begs to be taken in place of the child, saying over and over hers be the sin, hers be the offence, it be her life should be forfeit; but that wench be innocent as her own child be innocent, so why should the Lord take one simply to punish the other, why make her suffer what Unity and me suffered all them years ago?'

Pain they both suffered still. The stitching finished, Abel laid the work aside, going to that corner of the room set aside for brewing tea. A mug would probably be of some benefit to Laban. Should he ask to see Anne, would it help or would his presence at the house be an imposition? Spooning tea into the enamelled creamware teapot pock-marked with chips which attested to its age and use he covered it with water from the kettle always kept boiling on the iron stove. He wanted to see her, to comfort her, to hold her in his arms and whisper it wasn't her fault. One hand clenched about the teapot handle, the fingers of the other gripping the small rounded knob of the lid, Abel felt the rush of feeling which attacked his chest each time he thought of Anne Corby. Yes, he wanted to hold her . . . Lord, how he wanted to hold her! To tell her she was not to blame; but that was not all he wanted to say, he wanted to tell of his love, the feelings which had always been there deep in his heart, tell of a friendship with a little girl which had awakened into love for a woman; he wanted to tell Anne Corby all of this, but those were words which must never leave his tongue.

'I heard it twice, once in King Street and again in Pinfold Street.' Clara Mather hid the triumph that had sat warmly inside her all day.

'Women's talk!' Quenton studied his third brandy, holding the Stuart crystal goblet at eye level, watching the facets of light dance through it.

'It's more than that!' Clara snapped, irritation swamping triumph. 'One woman said the doctor was along of Blockall in the early evening.'

Quenton lowered the glass but did not look at his mother. She got on his nerves with her constant harping about Anne and the brat she'd given birth to; if there had been the least chance of Jacob's daughter claiming anything at all she would have done it by now, instead she was lodging in some poky house, what sense did that make?

'There's no surprise in the doctor being in Blockall,' he answered, disinterest plain in every syllable, 'the place is a warren; there is always some outbreak there, if it's not measles then it's chicken pox and if it's not that then it's something else, so where is the strangeness in a doctor visiting?'

What he meant was he had no interest. Clara's irritation grew. No interest when his every comfort, his very future depended upon what she had heard gossiped over in the town being fact. With that child gone half of the battle was won and the other half would be won as easily.

'There is no chicken pox in Blockall nor any other child-hood ailment.' She forced a calmness she did not feel.

'Yet the doctor was called,' Quenton yawned rudely, 'and to where . . . let me guess . . . ah yes, to the Hurley house, now who is living there who could be sick?'

Why did she put up with this, why tolerate indifference bordering on insolence, why not turn him out of the house, let him fend for himself for a month or two? That would bring reality home sharp enough; her son had led too pampered a life to exchange it for work . . . any kind of work. But then prevention often worked effectively as any cure!

'It seems that, like your father, words and warnings have no effect upon you.' Clara watched the brandy goblet rise, the golden amber liquid significantly reducing as he swallowed. Wait for him to lower the glass because her next words might very well – no, definitely would – cause him to choke. 'That having been so often proved, I have arranged for you to take a lesson of a different kind, in fact several lessons. You are to start at Glebe Metalworks at five o'clock tomorrow morning as a labourer. Depending upon how you succeed at that you will move on to other work, let us say feeding the furnaces, they tell me that is very good for burning starch out of a man.'

'The Glebe!' The glass banged onto a side table and Quenton shot upright in his chair. 'Me work in a bloody metalworks, that'll be the day!'

As she rose slowly, taking time in smoothing her skirts, Clara's thin mouth etched her returning triumph, but her eyes were hard and cold as she looked at him. 'Yes, that day will be tomorrow, and just in case you should think of not turning up then think a little more carefully on this. The doors of this house will be closed to you, every account you so liberally use will be closed and not so much as a halfpenny will you get from me.' Lifting her hand as his mouth opened, she went on. 'This is no idle talk, Quenton, if you doubt my word then do not go to the works in the morning; but I warn you, it can be harder for some to make a living than by shovelling coke!'

He needed to be shown, needed to realise *she* was mistress of Butcroft House, *she* ran Glebe Metalworks and *she* held the purse strings; Quenton must be taught which side his bread was buttered! In the privacy of her bedroom Clara Mather gave rein to the anger bubbling inside her. Quenton was a fool. Sufficient unto the day . . . let tomorrow look to itself . . . that was his motto. Well, tomorrow was going to be a hard one for him, tomorrow he would begin to appreciate just where he stood, whether in or out of Butcroft! She had been too lenient with him, even as a child he had been allowed his own way, and from his being thirteen years old that way had been one of avoiding any physical labour and, no more than two years later, of ignoring any effort made to get him to listen to advice. But he would listen from now on, either that or . . .

Or what? Sinking to the bed she sat staring at her hands clutched together in her lap. Everything she had ever done had been for him. Buttering up to her brother, upholding his religious fervour until it became a mania, agreeing he should follow the path set out for him by the Lord and of course he must take his wife and child with him, the last being urged without a care of where that path might lead, her one desire being that all his worldly goods be signed into her care. And she had taken good care, making as much profit as she knew how and paying most of it into an account bearing her name, sacking men to employ school leavers at a fraction of the pay . . . yes she had taken too good a care of the business to see Quenton fritter it away. But Clara Mather could not live for ever, should Quenton not alter his ways who then would this house and ironworks go to?

But he would alter . . . he had to! Today had been a turning point in more ways than one and soon there would be another, soon there would be no obstacle in Clara Mather's path.

It had been so easy. Fingers losing their tension Clara stared at shadows sliding furtively close as if testing the efficacy of the bedside lamp. She had smeared the poison on the tip of her gloved finger, put it in the child's mouth and it had sucked as if at its mother's nipple.

'*Next door sent her lad to fetch Laban from his work, and that afore it were finishing time.*'

Clara listened to the conversation again in her mind.

'*Her said Unity 'Urley were beside herself, crying summat bitter that the babby were dead.*'

'*But that babby don't be Unity 'Urley's so where was its mother?*'

'*Seems her were off somewhere.*'

Off somewhere! Clara's mouth thinned with satisfaction at the remembered criticism in the voice. Her niece would not be well thought of by the women of Darlaston, they would have no sympathies for a woman who left her child to be minded by another while she followed her own interest, and that in turn would mean neither sympathy nor interest when Anne Corby went the way of her son!

But just what had her niece's interest been? Clara thought for a moment, then dismissed it. Not that it mattered, the girl would not be alive long enough to develop any long-term interest.

One was gone, one to follow!

Rising to her feet Clara slipped out of skirts and blouse, folding each with the meticulous care she had practised from being a girl. *Care in all things* had been her mother's creed and it was one she herself had adopted almost religiously. And it had paid off. She slid her nightgown over her head and unpinned her hair, watching it fall like wispy grey ribbons over her bony shoulders. It had not always looked like this. Once it had been thick and gleaming as dark honey and her eyes had been the colour of a dove's wing . . . so what had taken it all away?

Jealousy.

The word came from the inner reaches of her mind, breaking through the barrier she had so long ago placed around it.

Jealousy . . .

Robert Mather's dying words had been meant as sympathy but they had proved too near the truth, a truth she refused to recognise yet which nevertheless had stayed with her through the years.

'Jealousy has stripped everything which might have been beautiful about you.'

He had looked at her through sad pitying eyes marbled with the violet shadows of death.

'Jealousy of a brother who was given what you were not, of his property, of his wife whose looks were pretty and nature-gentle as a spring dawn when yours were not . . . of a life you can never have; jealousy is a canker within you, Clara, a cancer of the mind.'

But what had he known! The voice fading, she drew a brush savagely through hair devoid of shine, an angry glance meeting iron-hard eyes reflected back from the dressing mirror. Robert Mather who hadn't enough go in him to meet life let alone tackle it head on. No, that had been her job, the only legacy he had left her. Well, it would not be the same for Quenton! She would see to it he faced the realities of life . . . she would see him ready to accept the legacy left him by his mother.

One was gone, one to follow!

The thought returned and Clara met it with a smile.

She had killed one Corby . . . she would kill the other.

18

He had received no baptism in the church. The priest had not held him over the beautiful stone font at St Lawrence, there had been no service.

Unity Hurley stared at the black of mourning, the clothes she had bought fourteen years ago when one brief official letter had informed her of the death of her beloved sons. So many years, so much pain! She had thought nothing could ever equal the grief that letter had brought, that never again would her heart know that agony. But she had been wrong. That child lying downstairs, the tiny scrap which had brought joy again to her soul, the babe who had kindled joy afresh, now lay dead.

Why? Why him? That had been the question his mother had asked, moaning it from the depths of a misery Unity understood only too well, crying it from a terrible despair. But tears and lamentations could not undo what was done; the child was at rest in blessed peace . . . only the living must suffer.

But would the child she had loved, the one she would grieve for as even now she grieved for her own sons, be resting in blessed peace?

Hair half-braided, her fingers became still but blood coursing in her veins seemed to crash against her ears.

The priest had come to the house, brought silk stola and holy water. He had spoken words of repentance asking the soul of the child be forgiven and accepted into heaven, then with the water had made the sign of the cross on the tiny forehead.

But the child had not been named!

The eyes reflecting back at her were filled with a fear she would not allow to show when with Anne Corby, but it was constant in her heart.

The child had not received the sacrament of baptism! Unity stared into her own fear.

Words of repentance, of asking forgiveness for a wrong the child was not responsible for, were they words sanctioned by the priest's office or by the compassion of a man's heart? Were they words which would admit a nameless child, one unsanctified by holy baptism, into paradise or were they just an empty salve?

'The lad did all he could.' Laban spoke gently, guessing the thoughts plaguing her mind. ''Twill do no good you worrying, best you take your rest for that wench will need your strength tomorrow.'

And not only the girl. Unity sighed as she tied the ribbon at the neck of her cotton nightgown. He too would need her strength as he had needed it before. She had never said it but she had known that, without her, Laban would have given up after hearing of his sons dying in that terrible foreign land, he would have let his life fade from him as theirs had faded; but she had urged him quietly to work . . . to live.

'I'll come to bed in a while.' She smiled at him, at the tired face she loved so well. 'I'll just peep in at the girl first, make sure her be sleeping.'

Drawing a shawl about her shoulders she went to the room they had given to Anne. Opening the door just wide enough to see inside, Unity frowned. The candle burned in its pottery holder but the bed was empty.

'It was my fault.'

Coming to the last narrow stair Unity paused at the door

which gave on to the living room, a door which now stood open.

'It was my fault.'

Every word was an agonised sob pulling at Unity's heart-strings.

'When you were born I would not take you in my arms, I did not look at you, I left it to Unity to care for you.'

The murmuring ceased on a long-drawn sob and Unity caught her breath at what she saw by the light of candles. Anne Corby, hair loose over her nightgown, was knelt beside the tiny white coffin, her dead baby clutched in her arms as she rocked slowly back and forth.

Tears filling her eyes Unity shivered, the blood running cold in her veins, but she did not move as the broken murmurings began again.

'I refused to hold you, to touch you for I knew I could not keep you; but it was not because I felt nothing . . . I soon realised in my heart I loved you but fear of love kept me from lifting you to my breast, fear of losing you as I had lost the one person I had truly loved in my life, my mother. It is for that reason, my own blind selfishness, my wanting to keep myself from hurting any more, that heaven punishes me by taking you away for ever . . . but I loved you, my darling, I loved you.'

In the flickering, uncertain light of the cold room Unity saw the darker head press close to the tiny unmoving one, heard the heartbreak in every sobbing cry, her own heart feeling echoes of pain the years had only dulled. Let the wench cry, let her be with her son as she herself would have given her very life to have been with her own sons, to have held them in her arms, whispered her love as she whispered goodbye. But that had not been given her. She had not washed and dressed them for burial as she had dressed this child, not placed a penny in their mouth as she had done for him, nor would she see the place where they lay with no headstone to mark their bed. But she knew where their souls were; like everyone baptised into the faith of the Lord they were with Him now. But this child . . . what of his immortal soul?

Standing on the lowest step, tears streaming over drawn cheeks, Unity spoke deep inside. Take him in your arms, Matthew and Luke, take him as you would a brother for that was how your mother loved him; bring him to the Mother of Christ, tell her of how he was not baptised, show him to her . . . ask her mercy. She was a woman whose son was taken from her, she will not refuse this little one the love of heaven.

A sound from the room above breaking her silent prayer Unity wiped a hand across her cheeks. It would do no good for the wench to see yet more misery. Her limbs stiff from the cold of rooms that could see no fire and whose closed curtains could allow no light or warmth of day to banish their gloom until the funeral was done, Unity crossed to the kneeling girl.

'Give him to me, wench –' she spoke quietly, afraid that one more straw would have Anne collapse completely '– let me have him.'

'No . . . please . . .'

It was a strangled cry, its desolation vibrating among the shadows.

'You have to be strong, girl, strong enough to let him go.' Unity reached for the tiny body, easing Anne's desperate fingers gently but firmly until they released their hold, then, resisting the urge to hold him against her one last time, placed the little corpse back in its coffin.

'I can't leave him.' The breath of Anne's sobs caught the pale flame of the candles placed beside the coffin and set their light flickering in a wild dance about the cold walls. 'I can't leave him here alone.'

Had she done this each of the five nights the dead child had lain in the house, come down to sit beside him through the hours of darkness . . . sat here unheard, drowned in her misery, in the agony of her baby's death?

Reaching through the gloom to where familiarity told her a shawl hung from a peg on the stairs door she draped it about the girl's heaving shoulders.

'Then you shan't leave him,' she answered, some inner strength masking her own heartache. 'We'll sit with him together.'

What would the folk of Darlaston think if she did not go to that house, to at least pretend to a show of sympathy? But that was all it would be, a pretence. She felt no sympathy and certainly no sorrow, that child's death had been a relief to her, an obstacle cleared from her path.

Setting her black bonnet on her head, Clara Mather lowered the tulle veil over her face, arranging the folds neatly, meticulously, where they touched her chin.

What did it matter what folk thought! She would go to the Hurley house, she had to be certain that the talk she heard in the town was true, she had to see for herself this bastard grandchild of her brother was truly dead. But would Unity Hurley let her in or would she slam the door in her face? That would make a more convincing picture in the eyes of people who always gathered to watch a corpse taken from the house, she would be the grieving aunt denied a last goodbye.

Drawing on black leather gloves Clara held up the little finger of her left hand. It had been an act of genius smearing the tip with wolfsbane and inserting it in the child's mouth, an idea only a shrewd brain would think up . . . and Clara Mather was nothing if not shrewd.

'The flowers be in the brewhouse, mum; it be cooler in

there, keep 'em fresh like.' The daily woman looked up as Clara entered the kitchen.

Clara glanced towards the cheap enamel clock, there were ten minutes to the woman's finishing time but she wanted no paid help in the house when it was uncertain how long she herself would be absent, noses grew long and fingers itchy when there was no one about to slap them back into place.

'There's no need for you to stay,' she snapped, 'I'll lock the door myself.'

The woman had scurried off like a rabbit with a fox on its tail. Clara collected the bunch of pale blue pansies she had given old Zeb Davies of Dangerfield Lane sixpence for. She had only bought them for appearances' sake and sixpence had been enough to waste, she wouldn't throw that much away when it was the turn of Jacob's daughter to go under the sod.

The clock of St Lawrence church rang the half hour. Clara quickened her steps. Her daily woman had said the service was scheduled for eleven o'clock, that left her thirty minutes . . . more than enough time to reach Blockall.

'It be time, Unity.'

Unity nodded to the neighbour who, as was usual in such circumstances, had taken a couple of hours from his work to help out. It had been a battle to get Anne to leave the room long enough to wash and dress in the dark skirt and coat a second trip to Darlaston had procured. But it was no pawnshop had supplied that mourning outfit as it had supplied the silver christening cup she had bought that day; those clothes, together with a high-necked white lawn blouse, had come from Sophie Hartshorne's dressmaking shop in Walsall Street and the veiled bonnet from Lucy Corbett's millinery. In fact everything the girl now wore was new, her heart might be in tatters but she would not see her son into his grave dressed the same way.

Bending over the kneeling figure Unity whispered, 'You have to come away now.' Then, seeing the hand closed over a tiny marble-cold one, added gently, 'Joseph Bishop be waiting, we mustn't keep him from his work.' Glancing towards Laban stood at the empty fireplace her look said for him to take Anne into the scullery. It would be too much for her to watch the nails being driven into the lid of that sad little box, to see her child closed away from her for ever.

As Unity's hand touched her shoulder Anne felt a cry rise in her throat, the wild cry of heartbreak and anguish that weighed like lead inside her. But she must not release it. Rising to her feet she gazed at the tiny form dressed in the white, figured-silk christening robe Unity had made and dressed her own children in for their baptism. He was to have worn it for that same ceremony but instead he was wearing it as his shroud . . . her baby would never bear a name.

'But to me you will always be Joshua, my son . . . my son whom I love with all my heart, whom I will always love.'

It was only a breath but each word was heard by Unity and despite her resolve to be strong for them all a sob rose to her lips.

Standing beside the little coffin as Laban led the girl away, Unity draped a soft white woollen shawl over the still form, a shawl she had crocheted so many years ago. Matthew had been carried to church in that shawl and so had Luke, now it covered another child she loved, but this one it would cover only in death.

'Be you ready, Unity?'

Tucking a corner of the shawl over the silver cup she had lain beside the child, Unity kissed the little face for the last time. 'You don't be alone,' she whispered, 'I know you don't be alone; my Matthew and my Luke be there taking care of you. They will love you as we all loved you, they will keep you 'til I come.'

In the scullery, light from its window dulled by a closed curtain, Laban's arms supporting her, Anne felt every sound of the hammer drive through her like a knife, felt the cry rise again to her throat. But she must not let it free, to cry out now would be to shatter her soul, scatter its fragments over a thousand different dimensions. Turning her face into Laban's shoulder, her hands clenched against his chest, she hid the scream of a broken heart.

'I just called in to offer these. I don't want to impose . . . it's just I wanted to show my sympathy . . . if Anne would have no objection.'

'It be right kind of you, lad, I be sure the girl will hold no objection.' Laban nodded his appreciation, taking the bunch of cream carnations and green ferns that were Abel's tribute and passing them to be placed alongside the wreath which a few pence collected from every house in the street had provided.

'I – I'll get back to the works then.'

The deep rich tone cutting through the sadness blanking her mind, Anne turned her head. 'Please,' she said, 'you were to stand at my son's baptism, will you . . . will you stand instead at his funeral?'

He would stand in the flames of hell if she asked it. Abel's throat tightened as he met eyes swamped with tears. Why had this happened to her, hadn't fate tormented her enough without taking her child! Holding his arms stiffly at his sides, the only way he could prevent them reaching out for her, he nodded.

'I wish to see the child!'

Strident and demanding the voice floated into the living

room which was gloomier still now the candles beside the coffin were extinguished.

'I am its great aunt come to pay my respects . . . I *will* see the child.'

Glancing quickly at Laban, Abel stepped past Joseph Bishop standing hesitantly at the open door. Clara Mather, breathing heavily, glared from behind the wispy veil.

'The coffin has been closed, the lid is already fastened down.' Abel kept his answer discreetly low.

'Then open it!'

The demand was directed at Unity, completely ignoring the fact it was Abel who had spoken to her.

'I'm sorry, Mrs Mather, that can't be done but if you wish your flowers to be placed in the hearse—'

'My flowers will be placed on the coffin . . . that is where they belong!' Clara's reply hurled itself now at Abel, her anger at being confronted by a workman, his trousers and jacket obviously worn from labour, was clear on her features despite the veil.

'Anne, dear child—'

'I told you,' Unity stepped forward, blocking Clara's way, 'I told you there were no welcome for you in this house that day you called and there be no welcome now; you'll please me by leaving.'

'Don't you dare speak to me like that—'

'Please, Mrs Mather, I'm sure a scene is the last thing you would want with so many people listening.' Quiet and diplomatic, Abel smiled at the woman whose gloved fingers moved constantly, gripping and releasing the stalks of the pansies. 'Perhaps you would care to follow along with me.'

'Follow with you, follow with a common work hand. Get out of my way!'

'This be the funeral of a child!' White with anger, Unity hissed her words between clenched teeth. 'And unless you wants it to be your'n as well you'll leave my house; for if not, though I be called to answer before the Throne this very day, I swear I'll wring your scraggy neck!'

The very tenor of it halted Clara in her tracks. Unity Hurley was not a woman to push too far. But the purpose was served, the group stood out in the street had heard the exchange, they would be the judge of who was right and who in the wrong.

'There'll be a reckoning,' she murmured too low to be heard by any ears cocked from outside, 'and you, Unity Hurley, will foot the bill!' Then, raising her voice so it reached her avid listeners, each word deliberately broken, she said, 'You, Anne, the child of my brother, my own kin, turned your back on me, refused to live beneath your own father's roof, turned instead to strangers; now – now you refuse to allow me to say good-bye to his grandchild. But one day –' she turned a loathing glance to the girl standing dumbfounded by the outburst '– one day Anne Corby will find the truth of what her's done!'

Stepping onto the footpath running flush with the front of the house Clara paused, dramatically kissing the flowers she held, then, handing them to a watching neighbour, stalked away, the dark veil hiding her smile.

Clara Mather had no more wanted to pay her respects than her wanted to try flying off the church steeple. Her nerves quivering Unity nodded to Joseph Bishop, waiting for her cue.

'Come on.' She took Anne's hand in hers. 'It has to be done but have no fears, I'll not leave your side.'

She wanted to hide, to hide where no one would ever find her again. Where was the darkness, the black void which had sucked her down, carried her into oblivion when the wolves dragged her mother from that sleigh? Why did it not come, why did it not release her from this torment?

But the darkness did not come, there was no relief for Anne Corby, for the girl who had turned from her own child.

It was her fault, hers the crime but his the punishment; he and not she had been taken from the earth.

Thoughts like razors slashed at her heart as Anne watched Laban take up the small white box adorned now with a wreath of white rosebuds, then slowly followed behind as Joseph Bishop, flat cap held across his chest, led them from the house.

Daylight harsh after days and nights of candlelit rooms, Anne blinked confusedly. Why were women grouped on the footpath, shawls pulled low over their faces, sobs following the movement of hands tracing the cross on brow and chest? And four young girls, each in white dress and ribbons, a purple sash tied about the waist, why were they stood a few feet from the door? She had only seen one funeral, one conducted rapidly and grudgingly in a freezing Russian graveyard. There had been no flowers then, no one had paid respects to a man shoved hurriedly into a rough box and even more hurriedly laid in the ground; there had been no group of sobbing shrouded women and bare-headed men following Jacob Corby to his final rest.

Drawing level with the children Laban gently set the tiny coffin in their hands and, with head bowed, followed the several yards to where a handcart stood waiting, garlanded with posies of buttercups, clover and blue forget-me-not which each child in the street had gathered and woven.

Reaching it, Laban again took the tiny box reverently, setting it like a beautiful white pearl on its blue and gold bed, then, the girls taking their places two on each side of the cart, stepped to Anne's side as Joseph Bishop took up the handles, and to the tearful whispered blessings of the onlookers led the pitiful little group down the street.

19

He had been unable to hold her.

Abel Preston stared at silver-etched patterns of moon drops filter like pale gold rain through the leafy branches of sycamore trees dotting the waste ground of the Leys bordering Alma Street.

He had stood in that churchyard longing to go to her side, to put his arms about her, be with her in her grief. But that right had not been his. He was not family nor did he stand in that special place Unity and Laban shared in her affections; to Anne Corby he was no more than an acquaintance and as such he had stayed in the background, stood apart from the three grouped together beside the dark opening in the earth. But his heart had not stayed apart, it had gone out to the weeping girl, and the love contained within it willed to comfort her even though she had no knowledge of its existence.

'*Ashes to ashes, dust to dust . . .*'

Bathed in the golden aura of moon-filled sky Abel's heart twisted as in his mind he heard the words followed by a cry of torment, saw the girl he knew he loved drop to the ground, reaching down into the dark opening, reaching for her child.

That moment had taken every vestige of his willpower, each atom of strength to remain where he was while every fibre strained to go to her. Then the sad little ceremony had ended. He had taken her hand, held it for a brief moment between his own and she had smiled her thanks for his being there; but her eyes had held only emptiness, a vacuum of loneliness where life and love should have sparkled, an emptiness echoed in his own heart. His loneliness was from a different cause but it cut as deep; he had found his love but it was one he could not have, Anne Corby was of a different world to his. True, she had not yet redeemed her place in it but sooner or later she would and there would be no room in it for Abel Preston.

Unity had been in to say goodnight and now the house, warmed again by fire in the grate, lay wrapped in silence, but Anne lay wide-eyed, staring at the pictures in her mind. The priest had met them at the lych gate. Dressed in a long cassock, a white cambric surplice deeply edged with lace reaching three-quarters its length, he had waited, Bible in hand, whilst Laban again lifted the tiny white coffin and handed it to the children who, following behind the priest, carried it to the door of the church to be taken once more by Laban.

So much kindness. Every child in Church Street had picked a posy helping to create a bed of flowers for her son to rest in, and every woman had stood at her door to say goodbye. While men the little procession had passed on its way to the church had removed their hats and bowed their heads, women shoppers crossed foreheads and breasts in tribute to the tiny corpse. Kindness! Anne felt her heart swell under the pressure of grief. There had been that in plenty but it had not touched the icy emptiness which still lay inside her.

Life would be hard, Unity had told her after they had returned from that heartbreaking little grave. It would have to be lived from day to day but they would live it together, one helping the other until with God's mercy the pain would begin to lessen.

But the pain would never lessen . . . and why should it? Pressing knuckles hard against her mouth she held back the cry brought by a remembered touch of a tiny hand clasped about her finger, eyes the colour of deep oceans smiling up into her face. Why should this torment ever leave her . . . a mother who had refused—

'But it was not because I didn't love him,' despite the pressure of her hands the words sobbed their way into the shadowed room, 'not because I did not want him. I wanted him to be safe, to be where he would be cared for.'

Yet you were prepared to put him to the workhouse even after Unity had asked he be entrusted to herself and Laban!

It came like an accusation, the stark truth of it snatching at her in the darkness, a cold condemning truth she could not deny.

'I cannot alter what I did.' Her broken whisper brushed the silence. 'I was too full of self-pity. Forgive me, my little one, forgive me and believe I did come to love you, to love you with all my heart. And that love will never die, you will for ever be a part of me.'

Beyond the window a great golden moon sailed in a sea of its own brilliance, reflections of silver bathing the small bedroom in glittering light, but Anne saw none of the beauty. Swimming with hot tears her eyes saw only the dresser at the foot of the bed . . . a dresser with all of its drawers in place.

This was what Mikhail Mikhailovitch Yusupov and others had feared.

Sir Corbett Foley's fingers tightened about the newspaper.

This was what they had dreaded, the evil of that madman Rasputin. They had heard his boasting, his drunken raving when he claimed his powers could set the world aflame. Was this somehow an attestation of that power?

'We are united in the opinion that the one we speak of was the motivating force behind that assassination in Sarajevo.'

Corbett Foley's mind recalled an earlier letter of Yusupov's. If it was as they thought, that Rasputin's evil was behind the murder of the Archduke Ferdinand, then could it be he was also the architect of this disaster? But that was impossible, no man alone could have that power.

. . . with that package goes the peace of nations . . .

He remembered the phrase Anne Corby had repeated; the phrase spoken by Mikhail's son when giving that amulet into her keeping. But this . . . ! Lifting the newspaper he read again the headline printed in heavy black letters: 'Britain at war with Germany'.

But no man . . .

The thought only halfway repeated was checked by another.

. . . no man . . . but the evil of Satan!

Was this the work of the devil, a war that would spread from nation to nation?

The newspaper falling to the bed, Sir Corbett Foley's eyes closed against the horror of such thinking.

. . . the peace of nations . . .

Would heaven allow that to happen? Could evil be so strong, could men be given such power . . . and was Rasputin among those possibly so chosen?

The Tsarina's closest friend Anya Vyrubora's recovery from certain death indicated he was. Eyes still closed, Corbett's mind recalled the details of the terrible derailment of a train returning to St Petersburg from Tsarskoe Selo, the Tsar's country home. Although pulled from the wreckage alive, the woman's body was so crushed and mangled she was beyond the help of doctors. Rasputin had gone to her bedside and, focusing so hard upon that broken body his own had dripped with perspiration, he had taken her hand saying, '*Annushka, Annushka . . . rise!*' The woman had immediately awoken from her coma and risen, though true to the monk's prophecy she lived the rest of her days a cripple.

The power of life over death? Only heaven or hell held that and heaven would not plunge mankind into war; but if only a little of so tremendous a power had been given to Rasputin, a man besotted by evil, would he not use it in other ways? Ways which would harm individuals . . . such as cursing a pendant, endowing a piece of jewellery with the power to harm any who touched it – as he was certain it had tried to cause his death in that motor carriage?

Anne Corby had touched it! Eyes which grew more and more weary with the days opened slowly. She had not looked upon the piece, he believed her in that, but nevertheless even though protected by cloth her hands had touched it. A coldness creeping over him, Corbett Foley rested his hands on the newspaper. Shipwreck, abduction, an accident with a cart! All potentially fatal . . . were they the product of a curse placed on that pendant . . . would it strike again?

It must not happen. He must ensure the daughter of the woman he had lost, the woman he had never ceased to love, be protected.

'I lied to her, Viola,' he whispered into the quietness of his room. 'I lied, my love, so she would have no fears, now I must make certain no harm shall touch the girl again.'

Leaving the newspaper to lie on the bed, Corbett Foley threw back the covers. It must be now or it might never be done at all, his strength would not last much longer. Crossing to the ornate fireplace he pressed the centre of an expertly carved Tudor rose, watching a panel slide silently open. It had guarded many secrets in its three hundred years but none more closely than that which must now be revealed.

'*Trust no one*,' his grandmother had commanded. '*What folk are not told cannot be repeated.*' He had followed that order until she had died.

Reaching his hand into the small cavity he drew out a neatly folded parchment, holding it while memories flooded his mind.

Viola had married. She was lost to him and his pain had turned to madness, madness which had left a servant girl with child. His grandmother had been furious but as always had taken matters into her own hands.

Only at her deathbed many years afterwards had he learned of the girl's fate. She had been confined in a mental institution, dying there five years later; but her child had been taken by his grandmother to be reared by a couple who had her absolute trust. But he had not been given that information freely . . . he had been forced to pay for it with a promise, the promise he would never bring disgrace upon the Foley name by admitting he was the father of a bastard.

He had not reneged on his word, never *spoken* of that girl or her child, but here on this parchment the *written* word told it all.

Carrying it nearer the lamp he read the document through carefully, checking all details were as he wanted, that every fact as he knew it was recorded in absolute truth and the signatures of both witnesses were plain and legible, before re-folding it. This could not erase the wrongs he had done, it could not absolve him of blame for a young girl's misery, but pray God her child might in time forgive a father it had never known.

Leaving the envelope with its contents on his night table he drew his dressing robe tighter about him, then, the malady which had steadily robbed him of strength slowing his steps, he walked to the bedroom which had remained unaltered since his grandmother's time.

Entering the room he lit a lamp then locking the door, listened for a sound which said he had been heard.

Elizabeth Foley had been a powerful woman in many ways. It would have been easy for her to have cleansed that servant girl's womb of the child he had set within it. Money and influence were not the only avenues open to her, Elizabeth Foley's powers went far beyond those boundaries. Yet she had not used them; for reasons never told to him she had allowed the child to be born, allowed it and its mother to live. Though the girl's life had not been a long one, the child lived yet and in all those years Elizabeth Foley had remained silent, only the touch of death releasing the words from her lips . . . words he had followed with a promise. Now that promise must be broken. His child – Corbett Foley stared into the yellowy light of the oil lamp – *his* child! It was the first time he had thought that way. He had fathered it but never owned it, never held it as an infant, never walked with it as it grew . . . if only it had been Viola's child, a child begotten of love between them . . .

From the distance a church bell pealed but though the sound was faint it dispelled the trance beginning to trap Corbett's mind and he shook his head to clear the dream.

Viola had had her own child, one now threatened with a danger more grave than she could possibly conceive, one which might possibly claim his own life should he intervene, but that was the only gift he could now offer the woman of his heart.

Carrying the lamp to where a tall cupboard stood against one wall he opened both doors, using the light to see the contents neatly stacked on shelves. Yes, Elizabeth Foley had been a powerful woman and these were her tools.

In his earliest years he had stood at her knee, listening to words he had not understood. Then with the death of his parents at sea she had brought him from boarding school to be educated at home in Bentley Grange and alongside that more formal tuition had come her own teachings; to him she had imparted greater knowledge, a wisdom ancient as man himself; a secret-whispered lore passed through the ages, an intimate sharing of the powers of magic. Now he must call upon that power, use the teachings of his grandmother . . . but would they prevail against the dark malevolence incorporated into that pendant? Only the Lord who held knowledge of all things had the answer.

Once more the bell of the distant church sounded faint in the silence of the old house. There was little time before the moon would hide her image in the dawn. What was to be done must be done quickly.

Setting the lamp where its light still fell across the shelves he gathered various implements and ingredients upon a large round table placed beneath tall, arched windows.

Had he remembered all that was needed? And the words . . . would memory fail him, play him false? His blood quickening, he whispered the request for blessing his grandmother had him repeat whenever he was present in this room.

> I call upon the powers of right,
> I speak to that which was old
> When time was born.
> I stand before you in humility,
> Bless and consecrate me in courage and in strength,
> Give power to my words,
> Lend wisdom to my mind.

With the final word it seemed the shadows rustled against the walls, darkness moving beyond the reach of the lamp. Would the powers he called upon answer him as they had answered his grandmother, or would they strike him down? Questions could be asked for ever . . . only actions determined results. Glancing once into the thick gloom circling the edge of the lamp glow he breathed deeply then, his movements slow, began the task no other he knew of could perform.

Taking a slip of paper on which he had written Anne's name he placed it in the centre of the table. Something the girl had owned or even touched would have been more powerful but he had nothing of that. Rapidly as shaking hands permitted he took the seven white candles selected from the cupboard, setting them in a circle about the slip of paper. Pausing a moment he stared at the rest of what he had brought to the table and in that moment the darkness seemed to live, to move towards him. Corbett Foley's spine tingled; there was more in this room than shadows! The challenge had been sensed, the pendant was lost but the evil of it was here all around him.

The request for blessing running silent in his mind he lit each candle and as the flame of the seventh one flared into life he extinguished the lamp then drew back the windows' heavy velvet drapes.

Glorious in its fullness the moon filled the room with an ethereal beauty, spilling light over the table, etching the candles' golden flames with an aura of shimmering silver, bathing the table and its contents in liquid light. Around the room the glistening purity of moonlight fought shadows which retreated at its touch and Corbett smiled. The ancient powers were with him, yet still he must work against time.

Taking up a small, silver-hafted knife he held it first to the beam of light streaming in the window then sliced a small piece from a sprig of oak, placing it in a shallow pottery bowl, repeating the process with a twig of hawthorn. That done, he lifted both hands to the moonlight and whispered softly.

> Thy strength to my strength,
> Thy powers to my power, I call upon thee.
> Spirit of Oak thy strength impart,
> Spirit of Hawthorn protection lend,
> Sandalwood, Myrrh and Cinnamon oil
> Join thy powers to evil despoil.

Lifting the bowl he held it towards the window. Around him darkness muttered its threat and he knew he must be quick. Taking a breath to steady his nerves he went on.

> Spirit of light I call thee,
> Spirit of air I call thee.

Above the bowl a cloud of crystal light hovered then, soundless and breathless in its beauty, fractured into a myriad dancing rainbows. Glancing at the slip of paper at the heart of the ring of lighted candles he took a spill and held it to each flame before dropping it into the bowl.

Waiting while the contents burned he dipped a finger into the ash, drawing a ring around the candles, then, standing with palms uplifted towards the silvered windows, intoned quietly.

> Light which banishes darkness
> Circle without end and with no beginning,
> Fuse thy powers, bind thy protection
> About Anne Corby, banish all evil from her.

For several seconds all was as it was and then as his ears filled with silent music he watched the moonbeams draw together into a brilliant shaft, falling in a silver column over the ring of candles.

It was his answer. Anne Corby would be protected. A sigh of gratitude rising to his lips, Sir Corbett Foley turned to leave and as he did so a cloud across the moon stole the silver light and the shadows strengthened. From each corner a rustling murmured its breath, playing over the spearpoints of candle flames and Corbett froze into stillness. He had made one mistake. He had asked protection for Anne Corby while requesting none for himself. Stingingly aware of his own danger he turned back to the table and in that moment saw the cloud of dark shadow leap to the table, felt the fingers of blackness close about his throat, the breath of death fan his face.

The sigh still on his lips, Corbett Foley fell across the burning candles.

20

It had been nigh on a year since they had laid that tiny body to rest, months in which Anne Corby had spoken barely a word. Her stitching of a girth strap finished, Unity laid it aside, stretching her back as she got stiffly to her feet. The girl did all that was asked of her, skiving leather to the exact thickness wanted, stitching neat and even any piece given her to work; she learned quickly, giving no cause for complaint but her heart was not with her hands, that was ever beside that tiny grave. It was to be expected that a mother grieve for her child, she had done it herself, but it could not be allowed to exclude all else. Anne Corby had to live life not whisper at its side like a shadow. The healing must start but it would not begin until the wound of sorrow was opened.

Smoothing her apron in an automatic gesture Unity drew in a determined breath. No one would do it if she didn't. Her boots sounding on the well-scrubbed wooden stairs she pushed away the fears of rebuff. The girl might well choose to throw her concerns back in her face but at least that would be a change from silence.

The door to the room that had once been shared by her own sons stood open. Pausing at the threshold Unity's determination faltered at sight of a thin, black-clad figure standing beside the chest, one hand caressing a partly opened drawer.

Was she doing the right thing? Unity heard the stifled sob. Would what she hoped be what was achieved or would Anne

Corby refuse the hand held out to her . . . could she, Unity Hurley, risk losing yet one more of the folk she loved? But Unity Hurley was not the only one she must think of.

'Anne,' she spoke, giving her mind no time to change itself, 'there's something needs to be said and none as'll do the saying of it but me. The child be gone and though it be right you should mourn, it don't be right you should shut yourself off from everything excepting your work; you have to live, wench.'

Anne turned. Eyes glistening with tears fastened on Unity. 'Why . . . why should I be allowed life when it was my failing to love my son brought him to his grave? It should be me lies in that churchyard.'

The words caught at Unity's heart but she thrust the pain of them aside. She had to be strong.

'Stop that!' she snapped. 'You've wallowed in the bath of self-pity long enough and now it's time to climb out. You don't be the only mother to lose a son. Just look around you as you walks to and from the leather works, see the women with heads bowed, see the tears which streak their faces, hear the sobs they can't hold back! Theirs be a grief equal to your own and one to equal mine, for like me they bear the sorrow brought of not knowing where their sons lie. War be a terrible thing, it snatches the lives of men and leaves women to cry. But though they cries they have the courage to live for the sake of others, a courage Jacob Corby's daughter should have.'

Pausing for breath she watched the pale face crumple, hands lift to hide tears. It was cruel to speak to the wench like this but cruelty must sometimes be the tool of kindness.

'It be time to lay aside selfishness,' she went on, her voice hard, 'consider others and not just yourself! This war we was told would last no more than a couple of months, be nowhere near its ending and there'll be more mothers and wives yet to add to the river of tears flooding this land. Be you satisfied to

watch that happen while you shirks your responsibilities? Be
that all folk means to you!'

Anger at herself for speaking to Anne as she had rippled afresh
in Unity as she entered the living room but this time it was
anger born of a different cause. It was anger born of fear,
a fear so awful it had left her trembling. Laban had held the
newspaper for her to see a banner of a headline pronouncing
'Britain at War with Germany'. She had felt the world, her
world, tremble around her; once again young men would be
called upon to give their lives . . . but it wasn't only the fighting
which killed, long hours of endless labour killed men too. But
what did the Kaiser care about that? What did any of them
leaders care, they slept easy in their beds at night while men
like her sons and husband . . .

   Choking on that memory of a year ago she glanced at
Laban. He had worked a full twelve hours at the leather
works and now sat working still by the light of the lamp,
the strain of the long hours showing on his tired face; and
now there was this to add to his burden, Abel's leaving the
firm! Was it because of Anne Corby he was going? She had
seen the feelings in the lad's face, feelings he carried for that
wench, asking after her when in those early days following the
burying of the child she, Unity, had taken and fetched leather
work; she had seen his eyes cloud over at hearing the wench
were no better.

   Turning to the fire she busied herself with the kettle, hiding
concern she could not altogether dismiss. Abel Preston had
always had a soft spot for the little wench along of Butcroft
House, playing with her on them outings took by the Sunday
school. The kettle held in her hands Unity allowed her mind
to travel back to days long gone. Matthew and Luke had
declared themselves 'too old now for babbies' trips' but she
had gone along, enjoying the ride on farm wagons, joining in

the children's songs. It was on those outings she had watched young Abel point out flowers to a wench who stood no higher than his waist, heard his patient answers to a thousand and one questions, never being too 'grown up' to spend time with her. But now they were both grown up and the look which sprang to his face whenever he talked of her could not be labelled childish interest. Abel Preston felt deeply for the daughter of Jacob Corby but they were feelings it would do no good to hold, ones which boded naught but heartbreak. Despite all the wench had said, the property of her father still belonged to her and a woman of property didn't go weddin' herself to a saddle-maker.

'Be the wench alright?'

Laban's words winging her back to the present, Unity scalded water over tea leaves ready in the pot, her sharp answer the result of worry.

'It be yeself you should be asking that of! How long will you be alright when left to work the leather on your own, how do you expect to manage if Abel goes?'

'That don't mean we have the right to ask him to change his mind; the lad must follow after what his heart tells him be the thing to do.'

'We said that once afore!' Unity's answer burst out. 'We said that when Matthew and Luke told they wanted to join up . . . they fought for Queen and country and what did it get them? Six feet of earth in a land we'll never see! And that's what it'll get Abel Preston.'

'Maybe it will.' Laban nodded, marking out a piece of pigskin for tomorrow's cutting. 'But that be his choosing. He's a man full grown and his own master, t'ain't like he had kin to worry over.'

'No, he has no kin but that ain't to say he don't have them that love him . . . the lad has been like a son to both of us ever since his coming into the leather.'

Abel Preston had been like a son. Laban laid the pigskin aside, taking another of the carefully selected pieces and beginning to mark the outlines of a saddle seat. He had been given all the skills taught to Matthew and to Luke, now he must be afforded that same freedom and no ties of friendship must be called upon to bind him.

'There be plenty others have gone.' Unity banged cups on the table, distress and anxiety jerking her movements. 'You need only look at the streets, there don't be hardly a face over fifteen or under fifty.'

It was an exaggeration. Laban continued marking the pattern. But the absence of young men was obvious, leaving not only the streets but the town's workplaces almost empty. They had answered Lord Kitchener's appeal for his 'New Armies', volunteered in their hundreds to fight this war with Germany, but how many of those hundreds would live to see their homes again?

'And who be going to make the things them lads be needing to fight with?' Cup in hand, Unity glanced again at her husband. 'Who be going to make guns and the bullets needed to go with them . . . who will mek the saddles and harness you y'self says the army have ordered by the thousands, and that without all the other necessaries! I says them government ministers should ought to think straight, but then that be like asking for the moon . . . it ain't never like to happen!'

'I shall make the guns and the bullets.'

Surprised by the quietness of the words Unity and Laban glanced to where Anne stood framed in the doorway which gave on to the stairs. She never should have done it . . . should never have spoken so harsh. Unity's worry for Anne returned. It had done naught for the wench but unbalance her further.

'Anne, wench,' she spoke gently, 'I be sorry I spoke to you as I did—'

'But I am not!' Anne's voice was steady. 'It was what was needed, the time for selfishness is, as you rightly said, ended, as is the time for evasions. Tomorrow I take on my responsibilities. Here –' she held out the papers given her by Sir Corbett Foley '– is all I need to claim what is mine; that is what I shall do.'

'You mean you'll take—'

'I mean I shall claim all that was my father's, it will be put to the fighting of this war. Were Sir Corbett still living I would ask his help and advice but since that is not possible . . .' She tailed off, leaving the thought. Were he still living! Horrors which had plagued her mind since the announcement of the man's passing rushed in on Anne. Was it that thing she had carried to Bentley Grange had somehow caused the death of her parents' friend? Was it responsible too for the war the country was now bound up in?

. . . with that package goes the peace of nations . . .

It rang like a bell in her brain. First Russia and Germany, now France and Britain, how many more nations before the evil of it was played out? How many more lives would it claim?

'Take care, wench,' Laban said quietly, 'Clara Mather be a force to be reckoned with, her'll not loose the reins willingly.'

'Then her fingers will be rapped and so will those of any other who stands in my way.'

'Words be all well and good but that woman be sharp as a blade and can stab as deep.' Unity glanced to Laban letting anxiety show in her eyes. 'A young wench be no match for her.'

'Unity is right in her words.' Laban spoke again. 'If it be you means as you says, Anne, and your eyes tell me that be so, then I'll go along at your side.'

Stepping further into the sitting room Anne shook her head.

'Not to Butcroft House, that I must do alone, but I will need you both by my side in all I do next; I shall need the skills of your hands and the love of your hearts. Will you give me that, will you help me rebuild my life?'

Unity swallowed the lump risen in her throat. 'You have no need of asking that, wench, Laban and me look on you as our own and won't never see you struggle so long as it be in our power to help.'

'Then help me now.' Anne spread the papers on the table. 'Show me how best to use what my mother left to me.'

She had been refused. Clara Mather read again the letter with its official heading. 'It is regretted,' the words screamed up at her from the page, 'but given the severity of the present situation every able-bodied man is required to serve in the armed forces. No exception can be made.'

No exception can be made! Clara stared at the cold black print. She had written to the War Office stating that Quenton was needed to run the ironworks, that without him to supervise the making of iron and steel the works would close and the war effort be deprived of a much-needed asset, and this . . . this had been her answer. Quenton had been conscripted, taken into the army despite her threat.

No exception can be made . . . she read the words again, letting her eyes follow the rest: 'In the event of possible closure of Glebe Metalworks a replacement manager will be appointed.'

A replacement manager! Clara threw the letter to the floor. Not while she held those works. A month ago she had received that notification, a month in which she had shut down that factory, sacking every man left to work in it; and it would remain shut, no more metal would be produced there no matter should the government send a hundred replacement managers! And men like Laban Hurley . . . he had come protesting that without lorinery he could not complete orders for harness, that without strap buckles, snaffle bits, spurs, stirrups and the many other pieces of metal furniture the leather industry called for he would go out of business. So let him! Clara's thin mouth clamped. Without business he would be unable to give Jacob Corby's daughter lodging, and no other home in Darlaston could carry a mouth which couldn't feed itself. Maybe then the girl would leave . . . there may yet be no need for the wolfsbane hidden in her bag.

'Letter for ya, mum.'

Clara snatched at the envelope, not looking at it until the daily woman was gone from the room.

The handwriting was precise and neat but it was the cipher in one corner held her gaze. The War Office. Clara's fingers tightened. The War Office . . . was this a letter to say they had appointed their replacement manager?

Tearing open the heavy cream parchment envelope and extracting the single sheet of paper her eyes glued themselves to the imprint of a badge at its head . . . the military insignia of the King's Royal Rifle Corps. Quenton's regiment. A coldness creeping into her stomach she scanned the same neat hand, then, unbelieving, scanned it through again.

'Dear Madam,' she read, 'It is with regret I must inform you of the injury sustained by your son, private Quenton Mather, during action on the Somme. Private Mather will shortly be repatriated for recuperation in Britain.'

It was signed with a scrawl almost impossible to read but that was of no consequence. Quenton, her son, was injured . . . her son was probably crippled for life! His application for exemption from compulsory military service on the grounds of essential war work had been rejected whilst the likes of Abel Preston had been deemed as engaged in too vital a production. Leather, pah! Anger clawed again. How could saddles be more important . . . why her son and not Preston!

It is with regret . . .

She read the line again. Was this letter the crab to catch an apple? Did those people at the War Office think that by returning Quenton home she would start up production at the Glebe? Well, let them think! As a cold smile touched her tight mouth she folded the paper, setting it back into the envelope. Let them all think; but they would see it snow in hell before they saw the gates of that ironworks open again!

He had explained to Laban. Abel Preston walked around each room of the tiny two-bedroomed house that was his home. Somehow they still seemed to hold the essence of the grandparents who had raised him.

'I won't be gone long, Gran.' He touched a finger to a white Wedgwood jug given her on her wedding day. It had been the pride of her life and even now he seemed to hear her saying anxiously, 'Now don't you be a touching that!'

She would have cried at his going but Grandad would have understood.

He glanced at the clay pipe still in its place on the mantel above the fireplace. He had watched his grandfather make that pipe, fashioning it from clay dug from the garden, shaping bowl and stem with quick assured fingers, then letting an excited boy walk with him all the way to Wednesbury where for a penny it would be fired in the kilns of Potters Lane. Yes, his grandfather would have understood the need now in his grandson as he had always done; he would have known why, even though exempted from military service, he must join up; understood the feeling which had coursed inside him from the moment this war had been declared, a feeling which said he should be side by side with the men of Darlaston, fighting alongside men he had grown up with.

Laban, too, had understood. Staring into the cold empty grate he saw again the old man's face, the gentle nod of his grey head. There had been love in those tired eyes, the same love he had seen in Unity's after she had recovered from the shock of his decision . . . but in Anne Corby's eyes there had been nothing.

''*Ave a meal wi' us lad afore you goes, I know Unity would like that.*' Laban's invitation to the house in Blockall had seemed the answer to a prayer, a request made to the Almighty that he be given one moment with Anne Corby, not a moment alone with her, that had been too much to ask – yet that too had been given. She had said virtually no word during the hour the meal had taken nor in the next after it, sitting with her eyes lowered. She was in pain, he had known that, but he was in pain too. He had longed for the touch of her hand, for one sweet taste of her lips but she had seen nothing of the torment inside him.

'*I'll leave Anne to walk with you to the corner, her legs be younger'n mine.*'

Had Unity guessed the longing inside him, had one unguarded second given him away? He had glanced at her but she had already moved towards a table holding a number of leather belts and pouches ordered by the military. How would they manage, swamped with so much work and him leaving them? A flush of guilt had surged along his veins but that surge was little against the flood which had built higher each time he saw another of the men who were his friends go to fight while he remained behind. Enlisting was a remedy which would cure that particular malady but what of the other ailment? That which had him lie wakeful in the night? What would cure him of loving Anne Corby?

She had walked with him to the corner of the street. He breathed deeply, memory painting her portrait on the canvas of his mind. Without a shawl to drape her head the breeze of evening had played with tendrils of hair, lifting and tossing chestnut strands, teasing them like silken veils across a pale, heart-shaped face. She had looked so vulnerable it had been a test of strength not to take her in his arms, but as she had wished him goodbye her eyes had been like green oceans, empty and desolate. There had been nothing there for him.

He had thought once . . . hoped – that evening they had walked home from Bentley Grange – hoped an old friendship re-lit might flare into something warmer; but with the death of her son Anne Corby had drawn deep into herself, shut herself behind a barrier of sorrow where he had no right to intrude. But he had no such barrier behind which to shelter, no invisible wall to keep the pain from his heart, the ache of loving Anne Corby; his only relief might lie on the battlefields of France.

'It's better this way, Gran –' again he touched the elegant jug with the tip of one finger '– a bullet can't hurt more than this.'

Behind him the sound of a footstep caught his ear. One more moment and he would be gone. Smiling sadly at the clay pipe he whispered, 'You should understand, Grandad, you always understood.'

Still not turning towards that footstep he straightened the bag slung from his shoulder then laid it aside. The army would give him all he needed.

'Would you put these things away for me, Mrs Davies?' He had asked his next-door neighbour to care for the house during his absence; she was a kindly body and would keep it spick and span as his grandmother always had.

'I would be glad to, Abel.'

Across the morning the clock of St Lawrence church chimed, its call spreading faintly to the tiny house. It was time to go. With one last look at the clay pipe he turned towards the door.

21

She had woken from that familiar nightmare. Anne walked briskly along Church Street, her black coat brushed, her boots polished bright, the papers given her by Sir Corbett Foley carried in Unity's leather bag. She had woken suddenly, her body bathed in the perspiration of fear. It had been the same dream, the same in which a man reached for her, a man with a bloodstained spike protruding from his throat. She had fled from him, urging a terrified horse across an endless white desert while foam flecks of the animal's terror whipped her face like flakes of snow and she had called to her mother, called as grey slavering jaws snapped, closing over a gloved hand. Then she had been standing in a churchyard staring at a tiny coffin glistening white as a pearl. A black-robed priest with orthodox Russian hat had raised one hand whilst Laban held a box of soil towards her. 'Ashes to ashes,' the words of the priest had stabbed at her as she had walked to the edge of that dark hole, but the soil she sprinkled fell not on a white coffin but on a plain deal one . . . plain except for a brass plate which read Abel Preston.

The nightmare had held the torment which so often plagued her sleep, but last night it had contained a new element, a disturbing addition which at first she could not fathom; but as she had lain staring into the paling dawn the answer had come, the cause of the tearing pain splitting her heart was made plain: the reason was Abel Preston!

He had come to the Hurley house last night, come to say

a last goodbye before leaving to join his regiment. She had walked with him the few yards to the corner of the street then turned from him, locked in the blindness of her own selfish world, a world it had taken a nightmare to breach. It had shocked her as much as Unity's angry words had shocked before, but the truth of it had come like sun after a storm. Abel Preston, the friend of her childhood, a dear friend, but he was more than that – she blinked hard against rising tears – Abel Preston was the man she loved . . . and now he was gone!

'I will write to let you know where I'll be, Mrs Davies, supposing I'm allowed . . .'

Abel's words trailed into nothingness as he turned to face the figure stood in the doorway. Sunlight dancing on rich chestnut hair made it glimmer like dark fire around a face which could have been carved from ivory except that the mouth moved in a smile which snatched the breath from his lungs.

'Anne!' He stepped forward, his hands stretched towards her, then stopped. He must not give way now; the pain of holding those hands in his, of touching her only to be repulsed was one he could not bear. Scarcely controlling the tremor in his voice he forced a smile. 'What brings you here . . . is something wrong . . . Unity, Laban?'

Anne swallowed, nervous now she was here. What could she say to him, would he laugh at her, telling her not to harbour foolish notions come to her in the night? Maybe – maybe he loved some girl . . . was promised . . .

'Anne, you have to tell me, is something wrong?'

The force of the realisation which had followed her nightmare bringing a flush to her cheeks, she lowered her gaze. She could not tell him the truth; it was enough that he was going into this dreadful war, she must not add any more to the worry of that, and Abel was a man who would feel that way by having to tell her he could not return her love.

'There is nothing wrong, Abel.' She raised her eyes, hoping desperately the emotion churning inside her did not reflect in them. 'I only came to apologise—'

'Apologise,' he frowned, 'for what?'

'For my rudeness, not only last evening but for months past. I have ignored your kindness, your friendship. I ask you to forgive me and – and know my prayers are with you wherever you go.'

'There's nothing to forgive,' the frown melted, 'you were in pain, I understood that; the loss of your son can't have been easy to bear.'

It had been hard, the hurt of it constant and deep . . . and should this war claim Abel! The quick slicing agony which had felt all too real in that nightmare struck her now, leaving her trembling. She could not live through that a second time.

Make her go! Abel's hands curled into tight defensive balls, his stomach was taut against the fierceness of his own emotions. Don't let her stand there looking at him like that, the glitter of hidden tears silvering the deep green of her lovely eyes, that sweet mouth trembling. Oh Lord, let her leave now while he still had his senses!

'Abel, I—'

No, no he couldn't listen any more! Turning away as she spoke his name he said abruptly, 'I have to leave now. Please tell Laban and Unity I appreciate their friendship.'

Unity and Laban! Anne's insides shrank. He had no word for her.

'Stay safe, Abel.' She smiled at the strong back turned to her, adding the soft whisper, 'Stay safe . . . for me.'

Everything was in order. Her mother's Will leaving her property to her daughter had been duly attested. The old solicitor had spoken kindly, saying he remembered the wife of Jacob Corby, though he did not mention her choice of refusing to leave everything with him, choosing instead to take certain documents away with her. Anne, he hoped, would not follow the same practice.

And she had not. That part of her business over, Anne walked quickly across the open square of the Bull Stake towards Butcroft.

. . . look around you as you walks to and from the leather works, see the women with heads bowed, see the tears which streak their faces, hear the sobs they can't hold back . . .

Unity's angry words rang in her mind as women, shrouded in dark shawls, walked past, their heads bowed beneath the weight of grief or fear. She had felt that same fear on leaving Abel, the fear of never seeing him again. He had not turned to her when she left that house but she had not needed to see his face, that was printed on her heart; Abel Preston would always be with her. The thought a measure of comfort against the ache of parting she entered the gates of the home which had once been her parents', her knock no longer timid on the heavy door.

A flush of indignity at having to open her own door rising to her sallow cheeks, Clara Mather silently cursed her departed cleaning woman. Helping the war effort, she was going to serve as a conductress on the trams. Conductress, pah! Going to become a whore more like; with a husband away with the forces the slut was making the most of her chances.

'I want no . . .' Snatching the door open, Clara paused in mid-sentence, then recovering quickly she snapped, 'I have no time to talk with you!'

A hand halting the already-closing door, Anne's stare was hard.

'Then you had better find time for I have a deal to say to you.'

There had been no 'aunt', no sign of the deference she was

used to. Clara felt a faint frisson of alarm run along her spine. What had brought Jacob's daughter to her door?

'I don't want to hear—'

'I am sure you don't,' Anne cut her short, 'but you are going to listen nonetheless.'

'Not in here, there be no invit—'

Hesitating just long enough to cast a withering glance over the hard face, Anne pushed the door wide.

'I need no invitation to enter my own house.'

There was no mistaking the tone in that voice or the implication in those words. Letting the door swing shut, Clara followed the black-clad figure to the sitting room.

'Like you, I have little time and even less wish to talk with yourself so I will make this brief . . .' The girl had not taken a seat nor was there any hint of uncertainty in her stance. The frisson increased along Clara's spine. Whatever had gone on in Anne Corby's life since the death of her bastard did not bode good for Clara Mather. Why had she let it go this long? Irritation burned, devouring Clara's alarm with its flame. Why had she not dealt the same with the mother as with the child?

'Today I have taken steps to claim the inheritance my father left to me.' Anne saw the shock rise to the hard eyes, the tautness of surprise draw the thin mouth into obscurity. 'You may continue to live here in this house but from this moment I and I alone will administer the Glebe Metalworks. Neither you nor your son will set foot inside its doors, you will have no say in its running and no jurisdiction over its employees. I have arranged for a sum large enough to account for your personal needs –' Anne's head lifted in anticipation of the reaction to her next words '– as for Quenton, your son has lived on my father's charity long enough, he will find no more with me.'

'Charity!' Clara exploded. 'Charity! I've worked hard these fifteen years.'

'In recognition of which you will be paid an annual sum,'

Anne answered calmly. 'Quenton on the other hand has, so far as I can ascertain, done little at the Glebe except cause mischief.'

'He kept the books!'

'Ah yes, the books.' Anne nodded, not missing the look which clearly said Clara regretted her outburst. 'Book-keeping was the one thing my father did teach me, and though I have given those at the works only a cursory inspection I could already detect discrepancies. It would appear my cousin kept not only the books but a considerable amount of the profits, of which, hopefully, there is sufficient left to provide himself with a home, for there will be no place for him at Butcroft House.'

'You can't deny him . . .' Fury lighting flares in her usually cold eyes Clara stuttered her protest. 'You can't—'

Meeting the red-hot anger with the cool determination so suddenly found, Anne interrupted. 'I can and I have. Choose now, abide by my decision and stay away from the Glebe or leave Butcroft House today.'

'The Glebe is closed!' Clara's thin mouth sang its triumph. 'It were closed the day my son were taken by the army and it will remain that way. Its workers, what were left after the conscription, have been sacked and, clever as you might think yourself, you can't make iron without men.'

'You did!' Anne's contempt was obvious in the retort. 'You managed with boys fresh out of the classroom, paying them in pennies when you would have had to pay skilled men in pounds; tell me, was that your idea or Quenton's? Did the money sweated from those boys also find its way into his pocket? You don't need to answer for it shows in your face. But that too is ended.'

'You still won't have the running of that works, the government be going to appoint a manager!'

Hearing the spite in the reply, Anne was suddenly a six-year-old child again having a favoured toy snatched from her grasp. Her aunt had always disliked her, snapping and hurting on every possible occasion, lying to her mother as to the cause of a little girl's tears, but Anne Corby was no longer that frightened child nor would there be any more tears. Holding the final dredges of that old unhappiness tight within herself Anne looked into the cold eyes that so many times had haunted childhood dreams, and this time she did not quiver.

'In that case,' she returned evenly, 'I need have no worries as to making iron. I trust you will inform your son of my decision.'

Where had she found the nerve? Walking away from Butcroft House, Anne could hardly still the tremble in her body. She would never have thought to have the courage to speak to her aunt as she had, to deliver ultimatums; but now that courage had been found and she was going to need it. So far only one aspect of her recent resolve had been dealt with . . . her father's sister was one thing, running an iron and steel works was something altogether different.

'*You be tekin' a lot on.*' Laban Hurley had looked up from the soft pigskin he was stretching over a half-worked saddle. '*Metal foundries be no place for a wench, God knows they be no place for men neither, the bowels of hell be the only true description for such places.*'

They had argued this with Unity in complete accord with her husband. '*Whoever heard the like!*' she had said tartly on hearing Anne's decision. '*A young woman running a metal works, it be preposterous!*'

It was also preposterous that half the world could be at war, men dying like leaves in winter, but it was happening. Unity's face had changed with that answer. She had recognised that the world was suddenly a different place to the one she was used to, that now for the first time women must be called upon to do many of the jobs formerly believed to be beyond their skills and capabilities. A half-stitched rein in her hands she had looked from Anne to Laban but said no more.

'*You don't have no idea what metal-working be about.*' Laban had returned to the work in hand.

'*I had no idea what leather-working was all about until you taught me.*'

'*There be a difference, a saddle or any leather article don't go involving the tipping of crucibles filled with molten metal; you don't know the danger—*'

'*But I know the* need,' Anne had interrupted with quiet determination. '*I know our forces need the arms and equipment to fight this war, that we must not sit back and say we cannot supply them no matter what the cause. You are right, Laban, I don't have the knowledge or the experience to run a foundry, so help me, please . . . tell me what to do.*'

He had seen determination before, seen it in Matthew's eyes when faced with a job a man twice his age would have balked at, seen it in Luke's young face when told he could not yet be given the task of single-handedly making a saddle; seen it on both of those beloved faces when they had said they were going to fight for their country! Now he was looking at it again on the face of a young woman.

'*Most of the lads working the Glebe be already gone into the army.*' Laban had set his work aside. '*But that don't go to say there be no metalworkers left in the town. There be men Clara Mather tossed out so as to take on kids straight from the schoolroom; they don't be lads no more, in fact most of them be too old for conscription but given the chance they'll come back to the foundry, they'll teach the young and run the place for you, ar and keep it a deal safer than Clara Mather ever did. Get you along to King Street, ask for Aaron Butler and tell him it be Laban Hurley sent you. He's the best hand ever worked in the Glebe and what he don't know about puddling iron don't be worth the knowing. Tell him what it be you holds in mind and he'll steer you right . . . and mind –'* Laban's glance had held the trace of a warning '– *remember what you yourself said but a minute since, you have no knowledge of metal-working, so you be guided by them that does!'*

She had followed that advice. Aaron Butler had listened, puffing all the while on a yellowed clay pipe. '*Be you certain it don't be no concern of Clara Mather no more? I'd sooner work for the devil hisself than I would that woman, but if I have your word . . .'* He had squinted at her through a haze of grey smoke. '*Jacob Corby's daughter, who'd have thought . . .'* He had puffed again then nodded. '*I worked for your father and I'll work for you, leave it to me and I'll have your foundry smelting iron, an' this time it won't be the rubbish Clara Mather was turning out.'*

Good as his word, he had opened up the works her aunt had closed months before, setting the iron ore the foundry produced to the making of steel, while moving the making of lorinery to the further side of the yard, opening buildings long left empty.

How had he managed it! Removing her clothes, slipping a cotton nightgown over her head, Anne thought over the events of the last two weeks. Aaron Butler had found a work force among the former workers laid off by her aunt, they were not young men any more but dedication made up for years, and experience was more valuable now than youth. But Aaron had not rested there, he had recruited from the schools lads in their final year, but where Clara had pushed boys in at the deep end Aaron kept them strictly from furnace and crucible, teaching them each skill slowly and with infinite care.

But that had not meant she herself had been entirely free of responsibility. Time and again she had argued with men her father's age, men who clearly saw her as a silly young woman playing at being a man. But she had soon shown those who prevaricated over deliveries of iron ore or said they could not supply her with coke to feed the furnaces that it was no game she was playing, that either they filled her orders willingly or the government would do it for them.

Drawing a brush through her hair Anne smiled at the memory of raised eyebrows and stuttered replies. Like Unity's, the world of those men had changed and the fact that they disliked the new mattered not at all; they had not deterred her and neither would the next task she must face.

Laying the brush aside she began automatically to braid her hair, an earlier conversation with Unity and Laban repeating itself in her mind.

'*It be impossible!*' Unity had exclaimed on hearing what her husband told them. '*There don't be no way folk can make that number of saddles and equipment; I reckons you must have heard cock-eyed.*'

'*There were nowt cock-eyed in what I heard nor in what that there War Office man said,*' Laban had answered. '*He told it straight; it were foreseen that many, many thousands of military saddles, together with harness and infantry equipment, would be necessary to see this struggle to a conclusion and it were to the like of us and the men of Walsall they looked to supply them.*'

'*It be one thing to look, it be another to do!*' Unity had been scathing. '*Did that fancy London man tell you how that were to be managed or did he think you just have to wave your magic wand and there they be all finished and polished? They comes along of here, all lardy-da with their boots blacked and whiskers waxed, and not an idea in their heads as to what be entailed in saddlery; they think it be no more than ask and have! You should have told him . . . told him that even if you could produce more there was not the space to work in, you've already brought the Regency up to what it were afore—*'

She had broken off, not wanting to speak what remained in her mind, unwilling to remind her husband of the loss of their sons, but Anne had seen the quick flicker of Laban's eyes and knew he needed no reminding, that memory was with him always as were her own, her fast-held memories of a baby boy she would love for ever. She had listened for a while, then when Laban could see no solution had voiced her own proposal.

Fastening off each thick plait with ribbons, she rinsed her hands and face in water poured from a fat-bellied jug into a blue-and-white china bowl. This time it had been Laban's turn to look askance whilst Unity had supported the plan. Now it was settled.

Turning back the bedclothes Anne climbed into the narrow, iron-framed bed, drawing the covers up to her throat.

Tomorrow she would set the whole thing in motion. The home her mother had willed to her at Fallings Heath had several large outbuildings, and using the money which came with it these could easily be fitted with workbenches for the marking out of patterns and the cutting of leather shapes, while others could be used for the setting up of machines which would replace much of the more straightforward hand-stitching. Laban had gaped at that.

'*Machines . . . d'you know the cost of one of them?*'

She had known and she had her reply all ready. Thirty pounds was the cost of one machine but it would do the same work in a day a dozen stitchers could do in a week; besides, what better use could her mother's legacy be put to? Half a million horses and mules held by the army, Laban had been told, and every one of them needing draught harness, riding harness and pack saddles. Put with these the thousands of belts, knapsacks, kit bags, courier bags and personal items carried by officers . . . the list was unending; if it was to be done then machines must be used.

But Laban had not capitulated quite that quickly. Supposing she bought them there new fangled machines who would there be to work them? Where was the labour to be got from? Again she had been prepared for the question. The firm supplying the machines would give instruction to herself but it would be better if someone with a deeper knowledge of the demands of the leather trade could be taught first. That person would know if the claims made were in fact feasible.

It had taken Unity no more than the blink of an eye to volunteer but Laban had still remained unconvinced, saying even so clever a machine needed folk to work it and where was they to be found!

Aaron had shown her the answer to that and she repeated it. '*We will go to the schools. There are girls in every one coming up to twelve years old. They will need employment and this way it can be given to them; and before you say factories be no place for wenches think of the sisters and mothers already working in the munition works, on buses and in the fields, women doing the jobs the war has taken men from; as for these girls there is no mother in Darlaston would not trust her daughter to work under the eye of Unity Hurley.*'

So it had been settled. Turning off the lamp she stared at the shadows rushing in around her. Her life was becoming fuller by the day . . . so why did it still feel so empty? As she closed her eyes her mind was filled with a vision of a strong handsome face, one in which a mouth lacked a smile, and beneath darkly winged eyebrows midnight-blue eyes held doubt, doubt and a question. Abel Preston's face. With her eyelids pressed harder down Anne tried to clear her mind but the face still watched. He had not smiled at her that morning on leaving his grandmother's house, but she had seen the same unspoken question in his eyes. She too had had a question, but like Abel she would not voice it, would never ask could he love a girl who had given birth to a bastard.

22

. . . There will be no place for him at Butcroft House . . .

Clara Mather swiped a hand at the Staffordshire figurine with an intensity which sent it tumbling from the mantel.

How dare a strumpet – for that was what she was or else how would she have come back to Darlaston with her belly filled and her hand empty of a wedding ring – how dare she say who could and could not live in this house! But she had. Clara kicked savagely at the broken pieces of porcelain. She had papers, she said, papers proving her identity and confirming her right to everything. She had already taken the Glebe, got it up and running while in the town was talk of a saddlery opened at Fallings Heath and proving a godsend to many women as well as girls just leaving school.

Godsend! Fury surging hot in her throat Clara stamped her boot hard on the china fragments, grinding them into a spreading white powder on the red Turkish carpet. Anne Corby had proved no godsend to her. Charity, she had called it, charity Quenton had lived on! It was no charity had kept that works going when her father had swanned off to preach to the world, no charity had kept this house in good order, that had been the work of Clara Mather; without her there would be nothing but a heap of rusting metal and a house falling to pieces. And in payment of those years of dedication she was given a pension . . . a pension! And her son . . . ?

Clenching her fingers painfully into her palms Clara stared unseeingly into the heavily furnished sitting room.

Quenton was to be robbed not only of an inheritance she had laboured for but also of a home. Oh there had been that note the day after his return; briefly written, it had expressed the wish for a speedy recovery from his wound but contained no withdrawal of Anne Corby's previous ultimatum; it had expressed no wish that Quenton continue to live at Butcroft House.

But he had the right to a place here, more right than she despite her mother's papers. Clara's fingers bit deeply but she felt none of the pain. Viola Bedworth! She hadn't been such a milk sop after all. She had guessed the plan in her sister-in-law's mind, guessed it and countermeasured it. But the prize was not all claimed yet and when it was Anne Corby would not be the victor!

Calmed by the thought Clara cleaned away the evidence of her anger then preparing a supper tray carried it upstairs to her son's bedroom.

She had not said where she was going. Relaxed against his pillows Quenton smiled as he heard the front door close behind his mother. Not that he had any interest in what she did or where. Pushing the tray aside he reached for a cigarette. This was another of his habits his mother frowned upon, but let the hag frown it would make no difference, this was his life and nobody was going to direct it for him. The army had thought they could. Pursing his lips he blew a series of smoke rings, watching them rise through the pool of light cast by the bedside lamp to lose themselves in the canopy of shadow spread over the ceiling.

That lieutenant had taken a shine to him. He needed a batman who knew a good piece of cloth when he saw it, not some factory wallah who'd never seen a decent pair of trousers let alone a pair with a neatly pressed crease. But it had been no batman the lieutenant had wanted. Trickling smoke through his lips, Quenton let the memories ride. Just four weeks, that was all the time it had taken to get his batch of conscripts to France, just four weeks to take them all to hell.

And that was what it was. Every step of the way to the front line had been a march through ankle-high mud, rain lashing like knives against the face and at every stopping place had been the wounded; grown men moaning with pain, some no more than lads of seventeen and eighteen screaming with agony while others, half hidden by bandages red with blood, lay silent, already in the grip of death.

That had been the fate awaiting all of them. Staring into semi-darkness which seemed to hold living pictures, he watched bedraggled figures drop wearily into trenches half filled with water. The tents, what there was of them, overflowed with men blown apart by bullets and shells, and the next day it would be his turn. But that moment fate had smiled on Quenton Mather. He had dragged himself from that trench, and finding a bucket of clean water had carried it to the rear of one of the tents and there he had stripped, using the water to wash his body free of mud and grime.

Among the shadows he saw the bucket rise, its remaining contents catching the afternoon light, shimmering like a transparent veil as they fell over sand-coloured hair to trickle in glistening rivulets over a strong body. Then with a shake of the head, whisking the pale hair back from the forehead, the eyes opened.

Opened in more ways than one. Quenton smiled again. The officer had stood there watching, making no attempt to reprimand or order, clearly enjoying what he saw. And himself? He had seen opportunity. Turning full on to the lieutenant whose gaze could not lift from that smaller thatch of sand-coloured hair he had stared back. Wordless, with no movement other than the slow raising of a steadily thickening organ, he had made his offer. That same evening he had been

appointed batman. Taking care of the officer's equipment and
needs by day and his very different equipment and needs at
night had been the price paid to get himself freed of what
would almost certainly be a painful death, nearly every man
going over the top met a bullet and Quenton Mather would
be like to be among them.

He had wondered if he would match up to requirements.
Women, yes, he'd had plenty of them and enjoyed them all,
willing or not; but a man, that was a new game entirely.
But not an unsatisfactory one. Extinguishing the last of the
cigarette in a thickly cut ashtray he lay back, the trace of a
former smile hovering about his lips. That first night he had
filled a tin bath with hot water, lathering perfumed soap into
it until it boasted a thin covering of foam. Officers and other
ranks . . . a world of difference lay between them but it was
one he had crossed.

The lieutenant had entered the tiny bedroom of his billet,
his grey eyes smiling as he slipped elegantly from his clothes.
Almost like a woman. Quenton remembered the thought
which had struck him. Then with the same graceful, almost
feminine movements he had stepped into the bath.

'*Why don't you join with me?*'

Beneath the covering of sheets Quenton's body stirred as
the soft words whispered again in his head. At first he had
hesitated but with the urging of his brain that it was this man
or the trenches he had shed his own clothes. It had been so
easy, and so damned pleasurable.

Closing his eyes he let the memory wash over him. He
had stepped close to the bath, the man sitting in it raising
a soap-lathered finger, tracing it slowly from navel to sand-
coloured bush.

'*You will like this . . .*'

The smile had parted well-shaped lips, showing the tip
of a tongue resting on the edge of teeth which might have

been manicured; a tongue which had not remained long in its nest.

'. . . *and this* . . .'

He had leaned his head a little over the edge of the tin bath touching his tongue to the column of flesh standing erect among its pale soft shroud. The soft, kitten-like lick had acted like a tornado on his senses. Quenton gave himself completely to the sensual reverie. Hands had cupped his testicles, squeezing lightly, stroking, caressing; then the lips had parted widely and he had been in the man's mouth, the warm moistness having him gasp and thrust. It had been a pleasure that had grown to an addiction. In the weeks which followed they had lain together, each night given to making love, each day bringing thoughts of new delights. Why had he ever bothered with women when all they thought about was what they could get in return for their favours, why had it taken until then to find the perfect answer?

At least, it had been perfect until word came that they were required at the front line. It would not affect them, the lieutenant had said, an officer had been wounded and he was ordered to stand in until a replacement could be sent from Blighty. But that had not calmed the fear which struck. One officer had been wounded, this one might be killed and what would become of Quenton Mather then? The army was not going to use him as cannon fodder. That was when he had begun to make his plans. They had been less than a week in that hell hole which was the Somme. The officers had been given a billet, a half-demolished house only yards from the trenches at Vlamertinghe. He remembered the sun, it rarely broke through the pall of gun smoke lying low over everything, but that day a few apologetic rays fingered their way to rest on thick, deep mud and glisten on rat-infested trenches. He had carried the lieutenant's midday meal into the billet when the sounds of distant shots were joined by shouts of ''*Ere they come*.' Drawing his side arm the lieutenant had made for the door but a shell chose that moment to explode just beyond it and the man had died with a splinter through the brain.

It had been as though it were a play on some theatre stage and himself an actor in it. Quenton watched the images move through his mind. For half a moment he had stared at the bloodied face turned sideways in the figure's fall then he had grabbed the side arm from the dead hand and shot himself in the thigh. The sudden stab of pain had brought a scream to his lips but that had been lost among the madness outside. Knowing he had to set the scene if what he had done was to be accepted as an accident he had replaced the revolver in the dead man's hand then had lain in the wreckage a little in front of him. It had to work, it had to look as if in the sudden mêlée the lieutenant had fired, inadvertently wounding his own batman in the process. And it had! He had lain through the night and into the next day until reinforcements had broken through; from there it had been a field hospital then home to England for recuperation.

It had been as if the fates had read his mind for he had planned and hoped for just such an opportunity. An accident, bad luck, old chap. Luck! His smile deepened. Quenton Mather could always make his own luck!

The memory vivid and alive in his mind was reinforced by the stab of pain shooting now through his thigh. A shot of brandy would help but there was none in the house, that much he had found out during his mother's shopping trips. He had gone through each room of this dreary place but was careful to be back in his bed before she returned. Lord! He winced again, a fresh spasm catching the breath between his teeth. It was worse here now than before he was called up, something to do with Anne Corby taking over Glebe Metalworks: but whoever heard of a woman running an iron foundry? Frowning, he touched a hand to his throbbing leg. Once he deemed it near enough the finish of this war and himself safe from recall to the regiment he would see to his cousin; there wouldn't be a manufacturer or iron ore supplier anywhere in the country would deal with her. She would have to return management of the place to him or go under.

Pain like the swift thrust of a blade bringing a film of sweat to his brow, he threw off the bedcovers. There had to be some sort of relief in the house, an Aspro tablet or a Beecham's Powder, anything which would dull this blasted pain; he might have thought twice before using that revolver had he realised this was the result. But no, he wouldn't have done – clutching at the bedside table he waited for the sharpness of the pain to subside – what would have been his chances of finding another nancy boy officer? None as high as the chance of being sent over the top, and that was a chance too many.

Moving gingerly, avoiding putting his full weight on his injured leg, he walked slowly from the room. If he used his head, let no one see him walk, he could make this injury see out the rest of this bloody war with him in no danger of taking any more part in it.

There was no medicine in any downstairs room, his earlier searches for brandy had already shown that. The bathroom? It was his best bet. But the spartan little room which had been his mother's pride since it was converted to hold a cast-iron bath and indoor privy boasted no more than the essentials of soap, towels, flannel and paper. Christ! Did his mother think an Aspro tablet would sabotage her household budget!

Irritation heightened by a short flare of pain he slammed a fist against the well-polished door. Polish . . . Oh, his mother made sure the house carried a good supply of that, but a bloody painkiller!

From the hall below the chime of a long-case clock brought his brain under control. Wherever he was to look he must do it quickly, his mother had never been a woman who spent two minutes getting a job done when one minute did well enough.

His mother . . . of course! He turned towards the room she had moved into the moment her brother had vacated the house. If Clara Mather had anything she wanted nobody else to have benefit of it would be somewhere in her own bedroom.

Moving as quickly as the stiffness in his thigh permitted he entered his mother's room, his eye moving rapidly over the meticulous neatness of dressing table and mantel. Nothing! The word hissed in his brain. But then had he really expected there to be anything which might possibly hint at her having a weakness of any sort, even a bloody headache!

He had half turned when a stray beam of light from the landing darted across the bed, glinting on something standing on the night table, something which gleamed with an interesting brilliance.

A bauble? Gem he had not known about? Something saleable?

Curiosity heavily tinged with greed temporarily relieving the ache of his thigh, he moved to the table.

'A bottle!' He spat the word aloud. He should have known his mother would not leave anything worth a farthing lying where another might see it. Tight fisted . . . ! Clara Mather's grip on anything was tighter than a Jew's arse in a market, too mean to fart 'cos it brought no profit. So what was this?

Taking the small, reeded, green glass bottle in his hand he uncorked it. Smelled of nothing he recognised. He sniffed again. Nothing . . . but that was not surprising seeing his mother had never believed in dosing him with medicines. So what was it for? He held the bottle to the light. Whatever its use there wasn't a great deal of it left. It could only be a curative for pain of some sort his mother did not speak of . . .

women's pains . . . of course, that was it. Clara might act like some female gorilla but the fact remained she was a woman with the same monthly course as all the rest, and that was likely to be a source of discomfort. Touching the bottle to his lips he took a tentative sip. Honey, he traced his tongue over where the bottle had touched. Quite a pleasant taste compared to some of the stuff shoved at him in that field hospital, and if it would stop this damned ache . . . !

Holding the bottle over his open mouth he tipped the contents, shaking the last dregs onto his tongue before swallowing. Should he search the drawers and wardrobe, make certain there was nothing hidden which he could turn to his own use, maybe sell once he was out and about? He might not get so favourable a chance again. Taking a step towards the tall chest of drawers he paused. Lord, that women's cure was strong stuff! Glancing towards the light filtering in from the landing he blinked as it danced. P'raps he should forget a search, p'raps he should . . . he should . . . The thought slipped away into oblivion, the light swayed and danced, his wide-open eyes following . . . following into blackness.

'I thinks you should come home along of me.' Unity Hurley threw the woollen shawl about her shoulders tying the corners together in a knot beneath her breasts.

'I have to look in on Mr Butler, I know he was worried the consignment of iron ore for next week's smelting would not come in time.'

'Then let him go chase after it, you already be half the size you was six months gone and Lord knows you was no thicker through than a kipper between the eyes. I tells you, wench, you has to let up or you'll be along of St Lawrence pushing up the daisies!'

'I'm well enough.' Anne smiled. 'You fuss too much.'

'Ar, and you work too much!' Unity's answer was sharp

as she reached for a bundle of leather strips cut for military satchel straps.

Anne eyed the leather strips skived and thinned that day by girls closely supervised by Unity. 'I'm not alone in that,' she observed, 'how many of those will find their way into Unity Hurley's house tonight, I wonder?'

'Nobbut a couple, I like my fingers busy after supper.' Turning quickly from Anne's knowing smile she called to the last of the girls giggling and chattering as they wrapped themselves in shawls.

'Now you wenches be sure and keep together, you knows what them there Zeppelins be capable of for you've all seen in the newspapers the damage done by their wicked bombs along o' Wednesbury an' Walsall, and God knows they could come again at any time.'

'But Mrs Hurley, I was going to go to the Picturedrome, it be showing a Mary Pickford and Douglas Fairbanks picture—'

'I don't care if it be showin' pictures of King George and Queen Mary theirselves!' Unity snapped. 'You get yourself home to your mother, Polly Gibbons, and that goes for the rest of you. If I finds either one of you have been anywhere near Crescent Road or any other road your house don't be in then it's Unity Hurley you'll be answering to, and just to make sure I'll be calling in on Sarah Gibbons and one or two others afore I goes home.'

Hands on hips she stared at the crestfallen Polly and the girl did not dare press her desires further but muttered beneath her breath as she left with the others.

'Picture palace indeed!' Unity sniffed. 'What be young wenches coming to!'

Maybe one day a girl might be able to visit the new picture houses without first asking permission of her parents. It was a risqué thought and one Anne kept to herself.

'They are young—'

'Exactly!' Unity rounded. 'Too young to be going visitin' places like picture palaces, and on their own . . . ! I never heard the like.'

Picking up her own bundle of strips already skived and ready for making into straps for back packs, holsters, cross belts for officers or the thousand and one other uses they were put to and the stitching of which could be put to outworkers, women unable for whatever reason to take up employment at Fallings Heath, Anne watched the older woman extinguish the lamps.

'I will deliver these to the women and bring the finished ones home for Laban to take on to the Regency works in the morning.'

She waited while Unity locked the door behind them. The girls had already disappeared but in the darkness ahead their peals of laughter echoed.

'I'd still be happier should you stay alongside of me,' Unity said as they emerged from Cook Street, turning left at Walsall Road.

Anne knew it was consideration for her welfare had Unity apprehensive but what could possibly happen? Yes, alright the Zeppelins might well return with more bombs, but they could not live their lives afraid to go anywhere because of that; this war could not be fought hiding away at home, the men at the front needed all the equipment that could be made and it would not be much if folk were frightened of their own shadows. Now were it not that Sir Corbett had destroyed that amulet, hidden even the ashes it left where they would never be found, maybe Unity may have had cause for unease; but it was gone for ever, it could never harm herself or anyone ever again.

Poor Sir Corbett! Anne walked on in silence. Who would have guessed? True, he had looked unwell the night he had given her those papers but he had assured her his doctor had said he was on the mend. But he had not been on the mend, instead he had suffered a major heart attack, dying immediately. '*Doctors!*' Unity had scorned when they had heard the news. '*They think they knows it all but summat like this proves they don't.*'

'Well, if you be adamant you wants to go along of that foundry then this be where we parts company.' Unity halted but her quick glance moved busily over the scene around her. The Bull Stake was almost in darkness, its tall gas lamps unlit, shop windows shaded to a dim pinprick of light. Bloody Zeppelins, she thought bitterly, take the light from folks' lives every which way you looks; and them folk mostly women and girls, hardly a man left to be seen. Lord, what would be the true cost of this war!

'Give them strips here to me.' She reached for Anne's bundle of leather strips, taking them from her arms without waiting for an answer. 'I have to pass them houses to get to me own, it'll do me no hurt to drop these in on the way.'

And give you the perfect opportunity to check the girls have arrived home safely. It was no wonder women called at Fallings Heath almost daily, wanting employment for their daughters. She heard again the phrase she so often heard those mothers speak: *Unity Hurley takes the same care of wenches as does their own kin.* And it was true. Anne hid her smile. Not one girl was allowed to walk home alone.

'Now you remember and ask Aaron Butler to walk with you once your business be finished, Blockall don't be a hundred miles from where he lives.'

It had taken more than one assurance before Unity had been satisfied, but the concern for her well-being was genuine. Yes, Unity and Laban both loved her . . . but Abel Preston, there was no love in him for Anne Corby. What had driven her to go to his home that morning? She had thought he would already have left so where was her reason? Anne walked on towards Butcroft, oblivious of the darkness and its quietly moving shadows. What had she told herself? Not the truth; not that she had gone to that house hoping to find some intrinsic echo, some intangible essence of him, something she could hold deep in her soul. She had found that, but also she had found a cool unsmiling man, a man with doubt and question in his eyes . . . a man with no feeling of love for Anne Corby.

23

Clara Mather let herself into the house then stood listening at the foot of the stairs. All was quiet. Was Quenton asleep? She would make him cocoa anyway, take it up to him and if he were sleeping she would drink it herself.

Hanging her everyday coat and bonnet in the ornate oak hall cupboard she went briskly to the kitchen warmed by a fire still bright from the stoking of half a bucket of coal thrown on before she had left a couple of hours before. She had not intended to take so long, after all Quenton was still tied to his bed, but it had proved a fruitful two hours.

Reaching the tin of Bournville Cocoa from the pantry she spooned rich-smelling powder into a large cup and, together with two heaped spoons of sugar and a little milk, mixed it to a creamy brown paste. She had gone to the Glebe Works. Pouring a cupful of milk into a small, cast-iron pan she set it to boil over the fire. Aaron Butler had been cagey, evading wherever possible giving a direct answer to her questions, but then she had said it was Quenton wished to speak with his cousin, Quenton who could not move from his bed from the wound he had sustained fighting for his country and Aaron Butler had wavered. He could make no appointments nor no promises on behalf of Miss Corby, but *''Erself alliz calls in afore the works closes for the night; I'll tell 'er of this visit but that be all I can do.'*

The milk having come to the boil Clara stirred it into the cup. She had found out what she wanted to know. With the

Glebe closed for the night, there would be no one there except perhaps for a watchman who no doubt would be too sleepy or too drunk to see what went on around him. *I will run the Glebe.* Clara set the cup on a tray. *I alone will be responsible.* A smile disturbing the tight line of her thin mouth Clara mounted the stairs. Her niece, Jacob's daughter, had taken over management of the iron works; but now that management was about to end!

Clara watched the cocoa stain spread across the carpet, reaching like some dark unearthly finger towards the figure sprawled face down just beyond the bed.

'Quenton!' It was a half scream as she dropped to his side, a half scream that became a howl as the figure lay unmoving beneath her hands.

Quenton. Crouched over the still form she cried his name again and again until at last reality forced its way into her brain. Quenton, her son; the only person in the world she had ever cared for, the one she had worked and schemed for, her son was dead. But how . . . and why had he dragged himself to her bedroom? Had he called to her and received no answer, had that brought him crawling to this room seeking help?

'I didn't mean to stay away so long,' she whispered against pale, sand-coloured hair, 'I only went for your sake, everything I do is for your sake . . . the Glebe was yours, she had no right to take it, I killed her child so it could never come to stand in your path and tonight I found a way to kill her; tonight every obstacle would have been removed . . . Quenton,' it came wrapped in a series of sobs, 'Quenton, my love, my son.'

How long she crouched there Clara did not know but, her joints stiff, she sat up on her haunches then rolled the cold body onto its back, lifting the shoulders and head, rocking him as she might a fretful child. It was the movement that sent the arm falling from her lap; the movement which showed the right hand with fingers clenched about some object almost hidden in the broad palm: an object which glittered green in the light from the hall.

The bottle! Clara stared at the phial she had forced the cold hand to release. How . . .! Then she remembered. She had taken it from the bag to see how much of the wolfsbane remained, then left it beside her bed. There had been no call to replace it in its hiding place since there was no longer any cleaning woman to go peering where she wasn't wanted. But Quenton had found it and drunk it. Had he thought it to be some sort of medicine, a sedative prescribed by a doctor or chemist which might dull his pain long enough for him to fall asleep? He could not have known the true contents, that they would bring the sleep from which there was no awakening.

Letting the lifeless figure rest again on the floor she stared at the pale face. This was the fault of that slut, that whore, the child of her oh-so-righteous brother, him spouting the Bible at all and sundry while his own daughter played her dirty little games with any passing man. 'It was her killed you,' Clara touched the cold face. 'It was her, if she hadn't come back . . . if she had died like the other two . . . But she will . . .' Her head lifting, eyes blazing a maniacal glint matching the gleam of reeded glass held in her hand, she laughed, a short, almost howling laugh which echoed in the silent house. 'You won't be alone, my son, the trollop will go with you. You must have a companion, you must have your cousin; you won't be the only one the Angel of Death comes for this night. Anne Corby too will look into his face, feel his icy touch; she too will ride in his shadow.'

'*Erself alliz calls in afore the works closes for the night . . .*

Aaron Butler's words rose like a hymn in her brain. Her head jerking upwards she laughed again, a high-pitched, demented screech of a laugh. It was her killed Quenton!

Clara's mouth worked spasmodically. Her . . . Jacob's whore of a daughter! But Quenton must not go lonely into the grave.

Suddenly calm, the lunatic gleam fading to leave her eyes cold and hard, Clara glanced at the face of the figure lying on the floor at her knees. 'Rest easy, my son,' she whispered, 'Anne Corby will never have this house nor will she be mistress of the Glebe after this night. Your mother will see to that as she has always seen to everything.' Stroking the dead face once she leaned to kiss the marbling lips then climbed stiffly to her feet. First she must get rid of that bottle. Taking the cork from the table she went from the room.

He had not asked would she write to him. Head bent against rain beginning to fall in large splattering drops, Anne waited for the tram to rattle past then hurried across the Bull Stake, following in the vehicle's wake until turning right into Mill Street. The Glebe Works was the sprawling building a little over halfway along. '*You should write the lad a line.*' Unity had said those words several times since Abel Preston's leaving, but how could she? How could a girl write to a man who had not asked she do so? It – it was too forward. Abel would think her cheap, a girl with no morals, the type to conceive a bastard child!

She had thought . . . hoped . . . he would write her a note, just a few brief lines to say he was well but that he missed . . . Her? Brushing a hand over her cheeks she wiped away raindrops mixed with tears. That had been like wishing for the moon, and just as useless. Abel Preston would miss his home, he would miss the quiet company of Laban, there were many things he might miss but Anne Corby was not among them. She prayed for his safety. Stood whenever she could beside the tiny grave which held her child she prayed for them both. Joshua and Abel, two loves of her life and both of them gone.

But Abel Preston is not dead! Sniffing back the tears she chided her self-pity. He would not die, the amulet would not strike . . . Almost as quickly as the thought arose she checked it. That thing was destroyed, any power it might have been imbued with was destroyed along with it; she must not allow any trace to linger by attributing to it any other happening, there could be no more place in her mind for what Unity called 'superstitious claptrap'. There had been enough of that, it had been stupid to allow herself to be carried along by it, they were tales for children.

But Sir Corbett Foley had not been a child and neither was Mikhail Mikhailovitch Yusupov or his son. They had all been clearly afraid and so had the gypsies she had travelled with; they had not seen so much as the cloth the amulet had been wrapped in yet somehow they sensed its presence. And its evil . . . ? A shiver ran through Anne. Why else would they have kept so wide a distance from her?

'There you be, miss, I'd just about give you up.'

Aaron Butler's gravelly voice breaking in on her thoughts, Anne's smile was almost grateful. The acrid taste of iron dust and red-hot metal finding her throat she coughed as she followed him into the cloying atmosphere of the foundry, its heat overpowering after the cool of night. From one end the furnace, stoked to hold its heat overnight, spilled an eerie red glow from around its door. The gateway to hell men called it, while women gave this war the same name. Following Aaron, hearing his repeated warning to 'mind wheer yoh steps,' Anne wondered just how many gates did that region boast?

'That iron ore come in late this afternoon, be well it did for we couldn't have smelted another day without it and letting the furnaces out be a bad job forrit takes a deal of time to bring 'em up to heat again.'

'But we will have produced enough to fill our quota,' Anne

answered, glad her mind was drawn from thoughts of that amulet.

'Reckons the govermint don't never see enough as plenty, they seems to want more every week but they'll have to look elsewhere from now on for we be driving flat out; what with lads of just fifteen year old having to register for conscription and liable to call up—'

'They won't ever be called upon.'

'We all hopes on that but already there be young men of eighteen years who got no choice . . . I tell you, miss, we was all sadly deluded when we thought this lot would be over in less than a six month and I reckons there'll be many more yet to grieve over the dying of a loved one.'

. . . dying of a loved one . . .

Standing in silence while Aaron lit a lantern, Anne could not force those words from her mind. Abel was with those fighting men . . . he had not written . . . could it be he was already dead?

'Will you want to go through the books?'

'No!' The strangled cry was an answer to her own thoughts, she must not think Abel was dead, she must never think that! 'No –' she turned the cry into a cough '– I – I called only to see if everything was all right.' She coughed again hoping it would fool the man she had appointed foreman.

Fooled or otherwise Aaron Butler kept his counsel, simply nodding as Anne turned to leave. 'Old Zeck be set for the night.' He glanced at the wooden hut outside of which a brazier glowed.

Following the line of Aaron's glance Anne smiled at sight of the old man, his flat cap pulled low, his chin resting on his chest. 'Let's not disturb him, he looks so comfortable.'

Drawn back into the corner of the wooden hut, beyond the reach of the flickering light of the brazier, Clara Mather smiled. The watchman of the Glebe was comfortable . . . in fact he would never feel discomfort . . . he would never feel anything again.

He had seen her come through the gate in spite of her keeping to the shadows. Clara watched the couple walking away. An old man ought never to have had such keen vision! Well, his eyes would see no more. It had been so simple. Anne Corby had not arrived yet but he could take her into the foundry to where Aaron Butler could deal with her queries. She had protested that the air in the works was too acrid for her health, instead accepting the old man's offer that she wait in the hut. That had been her chance. Coming up behind the old armchair he always sat in she had slipped the long-bladed knife from her sleeve. It had passed easily through the worn fabric and only a slight grunt had told the blade had found his back. So easy! But that knife had been meant for a different target. Clara's teeth clamped hard. She had meant to use it on that trollop, meant to slip into the works' office and wait for her there. But Aaron Butler had not come out, Jacob's daughter had arrived and now they had left together. The slut couldn't leave, she must go with Quenton, the promise had been made . . . his mother had told him he would not go lonely to his grave and his mother loved him, she always kept her promise . . .

A sudden spurt of flame from the brazier lit the immediate darkness, showing Clara's face as she stepped from the shadows, playing over tight-screwed lips, reflecting on the insane gleam of her eyes. 'Wait,' she whispered, grasping the haft of the knife, pulling it from the dead watchman's back, 'wait, my son . . . I will send her to you, you shan't go alone.'

Making to leave the hut, knife clutched in her hand, Clara froze. Footsteps, someone was coming into the yard. Returning to the shelter of the shadows she waited. It was not the shuffling gait of Aaron Butler. Holding her breath, the knife ready for any who might come into the hut, she listened. The steps were quick now, quick and light, the steps of a woman . . . Anne Corby?

Was it her returned for some reason? Returned alone! Silent as a wraith, one with the darkness, Clara slipped from the hut. Overhead a truculent moon drew the blanket of rain-soaked cloud about itself. That figure . . . she could not be sure! Clara's fingers clenched, driving the knife handle into her palm. But who else would come to the Glebe at this time of night? An iron foundry was hardly the place for a love tryst. It had— The thought halted as if quenched by the sudden shaft of light as the moon shunned its cover. The whole yard was bathed in a fresh-washed brilliance and only yards away Anne Corby stood perfectly highlighted.

Now, it had to be now! She had never disappointed her son, never let Quenton down . . . she would not fail him now. Moving like a phantom, the hand holding the knife raised above her head, Clara covered the distance between them, a screech of pure pleasure escaping her lips as she lunged driving the knife deep into flesh.

'I told you,' she babbled triumphantly, 'I told you you couldn't have the Glebe . . . I told you it belonged to Quenton . . . you should have gone while you had the chance, left Darlaston for good, but you didn't, so I took that chance away from you.'

The peal of the bell of All Saints Church ringing from the other side of Walsall Street cut into the madness that was Clara's brain, leaving the one thought: she must hide the body, but where?

Again the peevish moon chose to display her charm, spreading a curtain of silver over the silent yard, over the girl fallen half into an empty crucible. A laugh bubbled from Clara's mouth. Even the moon was showing approval, showing she had done right, why else would it show the way?

Drawing out the knife, she let it clatter to the rough setts paving the yard, then with abnormal strength caught Anne's legs, tipping her completely into the crucible. But what when the workers came to fill the container with ore? They would see the body! With a swiftness that spoke of the Clara of yesterday, the manic laughter ceased. They must not find it, Anne Corby must disappear completely . . . and what better way? Clara smiled into the darkness. There was no better way!

'Who the bloody hell were crackpotical enough to fill a crucible with ore afore lifting it onto the rollers!' Aaron Butler glanced irately at the faces of the young lads stood in the yard. Nobody had owned to the error but then he couldn't blame them, he would have done the same himself as a lad just starting in the iron.

'Don't be too bad, Aaron.'

Aaron glanced at the man addressing him. An armband circled his left arm showing he had attested for military service but had not been called away from the vital work of producing iron and steel, an armband which saved him the humiliation of receiving the white feather of cowardice. There were no more than six of these men to bear the brunt of the work and they kept the younger lads from as many of the dangerous jobs as they could, but soon enough those lads would be called upon to shovel coke into the furnace and in some cases even tip the red-hot metal. This bloody war had a lot to answer for!

'If you takes the other side, Jack, I reckon we can lift this lot onto the truck.'

'You pair minds what you be at!' Aaron raised a refusing hand but the crucible filled with iron ore was already lifted.

'That don't be heavy as I'd have thought.' The one called Jack frowned.

'How can you tell that?' his friend grinned. 'You don't exactly go shovelling of ore all day.'

'No,' Jack turned away from the truck, a low wooden platform set on wheels, 'but all the same I would have taken 'em to be heavier than that, they certainly feels it when we lifts 'em from the truck onto the bed.'

'Then p'raps I should ask Aaron there to let you off the lifting seeing you be getting old.'

One laughing, one mumbling, the two men walked together into the foundry.

'Well, c'mon lads,' Aaron returned to the task in hand, 'them furnaces'll be gone out afore you gets this ore to 'em. And you others get them wheelbarrers filled with coke. At this rate we'll all be bowin' to Kaiser Bill!'

Following after the two pushing the truck he dismissed them back to the yard as the loaded crucible, taken by a pair older by a couple of years, was lifted onto the bed of steel rollers which would take it to the mouth of the furnace. Another couple of months would see several of these lads reach their eighteenth birthday, how soon following that might they find themselves at the front . . . how many of them would be dead long before ever they saw nineteen? But he could not afford to dwell on that, none of them could.

Across from near the furnace the cry came, 'Lift 'er skirts,' and with it Aaron raised a hand to shade his eyes, protecting them from the heat and brilliant glare as a chain was hauled on, lifting the door of the furnace and revealing its white-hot maw.

'Right,' he nodded briefly, confirming the temperature to be correct, 'get that load in.'

'The first smelt always goes in at six thirty, see the clock, it's almost that now.' Sitting beside her son's body, Clara glanced at the clock stood on the mantel in her room. 'I put her in that crucible,' she smirked, 'I thought that appropriate . . .

she couldn't have it all 'cos it's yours, isn't it, Quenton? All yours. They won't find her –' hysteria sharpened a laugh to a shriek '– nobody will know she's in that crucible, I covered her with lumps of iron stone, it will go into the furnace and . . . what did you say . . . the watchman? Shhh!' Touching a finger to her mouth she bent over the still form, a giggling whisper squeezing past her thin lips. 'Shhh, it's a secret, I didn't tell him and you must not . . . I didn't tell him I had the kitchen knife up my sleeve; he doesn't know –' the whisper broke to a cackle, her normally cold eyes glowing with a crazed frenetic gleam '– he doesn't know . . . I pushed it into his back; he didn't see me.' She laughed again, a high-pitched screech which rang back from the silent room. 'Nor did she, she didn't see the knife but it saw her . . . it found the whore who wanted to rob you. But she won't now, she's gone – gone into the fire.'

From beyond the open door the night lamp left burning on the landing flickered then went out leaving the room caught in thick clustering shadows, heavy curtains she had drawn hours before forbidding the new light of morning.

She must make breakfast, Quenton would be hungry. Rising to her feet, her step sure despite the gloom, she left the room, picking up the lamp from its customary place on a heavily ornate stand as she passed along the corridor. At the head of the stairs she halted. Eyes blazing hatred she stared into the black well of the hall.

'No!' Lips curled back she snarled, 'No, you can't come back, you can't take it, it's Quenton's . . . you shan't have the Glebe, Jacob . . . you shan't!'

With the lamp lifted to hurl she stepped forward, a long scream echoing behind as her foot missed the first step, pitching her headlong down the stairs.

The creak of metal accompanied the turning of the handle

which set the bed of metal rollers in motion to carry the crucible towards the searing heat of the furnace. So near to the scorching mouth that the hair on their arms fizzled, two well-muscled men, a rag tied about their brow to soak up sweat threatening to blind them, stood ready with bars equipped with flat, spade-like metal plates with which to push the container deep into the glowing furnace.

'Stand away!' Aaron's warning topped the serpent hiss of the cavernous maw, then, 'What the hell!' He cursed as a shout rang above the clang of rollers. Ready to push the crucible onto the lip of the furnace one of the men caught his foot and stumbled, throwing his full weight against it. More aware than the younger men of the danger threatened he barked, 'Get them skirts down . . . you men, stand back!'

It took only a minute for the furnace door to lower, cutting off the terrible blasting heat, but to Aaron the minute was eternity.

'Be you alright?' Whipping the soiled neckcloth from about his throat he wiped it across his streaming face. 'Be you all right, lad?'

But the man did not answer he could only point to the spilled lumps of ore and the arm which lay across them.

'God Almighty!' Aaron breathed, disbelieving his own eyes.

'It – it be a body!' The man who had stumbled glanced at the others before drawing back. 'It – it be a body!'

It was a body all right and unless he was very much mistaken it was a body covered in a fair amount of blood. Again Aaron's mind was quicker than the rest. 'You, lad,' he nodded towards a young man, his face white as milk, 'there be a blanket in that there watchman's hut, go spread it on the floor, an' you, Jack, you give me a hand to carry this poor sod.'

24

'I knew it, I knew it all along. I said there were summat wrong when her didn't come home but you wouldn't have it, you would insist her had gone to Bentley Grange to help out with them wounded soldiers . . . you would have it!'

He had been wrong. Laban Hurley put his arms about his wife as she threw her apron over her face. He ought to have gone to Bentley Grange and checked on the wench. He had been wrong but there was nothing to be done about that now, best let Unity cry, she had held too many tears too long, these were best left to spill.

He had known Unity was worried when the girl had not shown by supper time but Anne Corby was a woman grown, they could not expect no more than her sometimes do a thing without consulting them first. Unity's tears spent he moved to his chair beside the fire. Taking his clay pipe from the mantel he packed the brown stained bowl with delicate shavings of Shag tobacco. The girl had often gone from the Glebe to the house of Sir Corbett Foley since it had been given over as a temporary hospital for troops brought back from France, why would he think last night to be different? Holding a spill to the fire he watched it catch the flames. Hadn't she stopped there nights afore when the place had been pushed for hands . . . hadn't they always found her a bed so she didn't have the walk back to Blockall in the early hours? It were only common sense to think the same had gone on this time. But it hadn't!

Fingers tightening on the slender clay stem he let the

thoughts flow in waves through his mind, fresh ones rushing in, washing others away.

Aaron Butler had sent a young lad to fetch him to the Glebe. The doctor had already been there and was still tending to a figure laid on a table in the tiny office. The other man had held him back, the look on his sweat-marked face saying he should wait until the doctor had finished his work.

Laban drew smoke into his mouth, expelling it in short puffs which the chimney sucked hungrily into its dark throat.

'*Be you ready forra shock?*' Aaron Butler's voice had held a quiet warning but it had not been enough to prepare him for what he saw. Her face leached of any colour other than dark purple circling both eyes Anne Corby, her clothing stained with blood, had lain as if dead. '*She has lost a lot of blood,*' the doctor had warned as he had turned to close the bag he always carried, '*but the wound though deep is not lethal; given care and nursing she should make a satisfactory recovery.*'

It was the only time Laban had been guilty of quietly thanking God the Sister Dora Hospital and every other place for miles around was filled to bursting with injured men. The girl could be nursed at home, the doctor had agreed, though he would need to call every day. He had brushed aside the constable desperately trying to make notes in a small notebook, telling him peremptorily, '*All questions will have to wait.*'

But his own questions could not wait. Laban watched pipe smoke swirl a lavender trail into the chimney.

Who . . . why . . . ? Aaron had done his best to answer but all he knew was the girl had been shoved into that crucible and it was only the fault of its uneven loading, the fact it was top heavy, had caused it to topple, otherwise . . .

Otherwise the wench would have gone into the furnace. Whoever had put her in that crucible had intended just that. Laban felt the same cold shiver he had felt that morning.

'*An' old Zeck an' all*,' Aaron had gone on. '*The doctor reckons it was most probably the same knife killed him, it were found out in the yard; poor old bugger never hurt a soul, why the hell should somebody want to kill him?*'

'I'll just go take a peek upstairs, see her be all right.'

Laban made no demur at his wife's quiet words. Unity's heart had near broke when the men had carried the girl into this house, seeing her every few minutes helped ease her own pain.

Who would want to kill either of them? His thoughts returned as his wife tiptoed quietly up the stairs. Old Zeck Carter hadn't never had a misword with nobody, there weren't a soul in the town would wish the fellah harm. But Anne Corby . . . he took the pipe from his mouth, holding it forgotten on his knee . . . the same could not be said of her.

A sharp rap to the door interrupting the rest, Laban rose from his seat, glancing at Unity coming back into the room.

Tapping out his pipe into the ash of the fire before replacing it on the mantel he watched Unity open the door to the street.

'You have my apologies for this, but the inspector wouldn't have it lay over until mornin' . . . says we have to clear this lot up quick as we can, so if you don't mind there be a few questions you might be able to answer.'

Nodding assent to the man he had known from boyhood, Laban pointed to a chair. 'Anythin' I can do . . . you knows you needs only to ask.'

Glad of the opportunity to busy her hands Unity turned at once to the business of making tea, adding a comment to her husband's answers only when called upon to do so by the apologetic constable.

'It all ties in together with what Aaron Butler says.' Smiling his thanks the policeman accepted the tea. 'Says the reason they didn't know about old Zeck was due to them never bothering him 'til after the first loading of the furnace . . . they made a practice of letting him sleep until the rest of 'em knocked off for breakfast then they took across a mug of tea. It shocked the lad who found him . . . had to send him home, they did.'

It had shocked everybody. Laban took his cup, noting his wife's shaking hand. It had shocked Unity most of all.

'Do there be any idea who done it?'

'That knife be the only thing we have to go by so far. The station be organising an appeal . . . somebody might recognise it, though the inspector thinks it be a bit of a far-fetched hope – a knife be a knife after all, he says. Shows he ain't a "leatherman", eh Laban?'

'Not a one wouldn't know 'is own tools,' Laban agreed.

'Nor a woman neither.' Unity looked up from the military satchel she had brought home to stitch. 'Whether her be in the workshop or the kitchen any woman knows her own utensils. If that knife be from Darlaston then somebody will recognise it. One place you could start—' She broke off, aware of Laban's glance.

'You asked was there anybody held a grudge against Jacob Corby's daughter?' It had to be brought into the open. Laban watched his old friend set his empty cup on the table. To come out later in the investigation would make it look as if he and Unity had wanted to hide something. 'Her along of Butcroft House, Jacob's sister, there were no love in her for the wench. Her saw her own hand being taken from the Glebe, hers and her son's, that wouldn't suit Clara Mather. I don't be saying her would turn to murder—'

'Her won't be turning to nothing any more.' The constable's face took on a grim look. 'Nor can we question her. Truth be, Laban, her were found this afternoon lying at the foot of the stairs with her neck broke; seems her fell while bringing the lamp down to refill it.'

'Oh my Lord!' Unity's hand dropped the needle. 'Oh my good Lord.'

'I were told to tell you so you can inform the girl, prepare her for what will be in the papers soon enough. But I ain't said the all of it; the son were found upstairs dead as a doornail in the room we think were his mother's, judging by the clothes in the wardrobe. He must have heard her cry out and thought it to come from the bedroom so struggled in there, but it proved too much, him being weak from that bullet wound . . . seems his heart just give out.'

Clara and her son dead! An old man dead and Anne Corby almost the same! As she washed cups in the scullery, Unity's nerves danced. Could it be the work of that thing the wench had carried from Russia . . . could it truly be a thing of evil? She had told the girl such talk was naught but superstition, believed only by the gullible, but deep inside she believed otherwise. Had its potency somehow remained even though the bauble was destroyed? No. She loosed the lip caught between her teeth. Should what had happened be the work of that trinket then Jacob Corby's daughter would be dead as his sister. The only evil had been that nursed in Clara Mather's heart and now that was stilled for all time; the only real threat to Anne Corby's safety was gone for ever.

'I have to attend for the sake of my father, I know he would wish me to.'

'After all that woman tried to do to you . . . doing her utmost to rob you of what were rightfully your'n?' Unity Hurley watched the young woman she had nursed for a week ease a painful shoulder into the black coat she had worn at that first funeral. Now there was an account for heaven to take note of, a tiny babby teken from the earth afore ever having the chance to do a mischief and the like of Clara Mather given a whole lifetime in which to do nothin' but!

'It is all in the past now.' Anne drew a glove slowly over her left hand, hoping the wince of pain the movement caused did not show on her face. She had been fortunate the blow had caught her shoulder . . . it had not caused the damage it would have had it been a few inches more towards the heart.

Lowering the veil of her bonnet Anne hid the smile fleeting across her eyes as Unity's reply to the doctor crept into her mind. '*Fortunate!*' she had said tartly. '*You counts it fortunate to have a knife stuck in a shoulder, then what would you count unfortunate!*'

The doctor had closed his Gladstone bag before turning to the indignant woman, then said quietly, '*A knife in the heart, Unity . . . now* that *I would count unfortunate.*'

'I still thinks you shouldn't be up yet, it be too soon, and as for going to a burying . . .'

Expecting Unity not to give ground easily, Anne's answer was quick. 'I feel much better, and I need to be up some time so it might as well be now.'

'Then I be coming with you—'

Interrupted by a knock to the door Unity broke off. Going into the scullery to collect the flowers she had asked be brought to the house Anne caught the voices, Unity's asking, 'Can't one of the others see to it?'

'Sarah and Rachael Giles both said as 'tis you should have the deciding.'

The second voice sounded young and not a little nervous. Anne's smile hovered. Unity could be a mite disconcerting to the newer employees.

'There be a to-do over at Fallings Heath —' Unity glanced as Anne re-entered the cosy living room '– seems a special order's been sent through, some out of the ordinary sort of courier bags needing turnover edges, as well as collapsible kit bags . . . officer stuff, so Rachael thinks. Any road up, her can't be saying who be best to set to the job.'

'There is only one woman fitted for that task, you. But you can't do them all yourself. You need the help of a couple of the others, but the naming of them has to be done by you if there is to be no disagreement.'

'You be right.' Unity nodded resignedly. 'But—'

'No buts. You have my promise I will come home as soon as the service at the church is ended.'

The walk had tired her. Alone apart from the priest, Anne stood at the open graveside. She had not stood alone at the grave of her son nor passed along streets where no woman had wept and no man removed his cap. But not one soul had afforded Clara and her son that mark of respect, no one had any liking for the Mathers.

The Lord had taken His justice.

Unity's remark rang in her mind. But with justice must surely go mercy; God would forgive and she must too.

At the head of the grave the priest raised his hand, the sleeve of his robe dark against a patch of heavy rain-threatened sky and suddenly her mind was back in Russia at the makeshift graveside of her father. The sky had been heavy there, the clouds dark with snow. That priest too had raised his hand in blessing but though most of the hurried mumbled words had been unintelligible to her she had heard the false, hollow ring of them. There had been no heartfelt blessing of church accompanied Jacob Corby's passing into his place of rest and none but herself to ease her mother's sorrow. Her mother. Anne's eyes shifted to the trees bordering the churchyard, seeming again to see those grey, silently loping bodies, the slavering jaws and long yellow teeth – teeth which had dragged her mother from that sleigh – where was heaven's justice in that?

'Will you be needing a few moments, Miss Corby?'

Chased by the man's words the mental images drew back into the deep hollows of memory but Anne knew they would return as they often did to haunt her nights. Shaking her head she set the wreath of white lilies beside the heaped-up earth which would cover the last of her relatives, then, thanking the priest, turned back along the path.

'There was no one to pray for them, they were not loved as you were, my darling.' The black veil hiding tears gathered on her lashes she looked at the tiny patch of earth with its marble headstone. 'There was no Unity and Laban to grieve for them,' she whispered, 'no Abel to show his respect but then they had not deserved it, and I did not deserve . . .' Emotion choking her, she sank to her knees on the moist grass below the stone engraved 'Joshua Laban Corby, asleep in the arms of Jesus'. 'I did not deserve you . . .' The sob resounded on the quiet afternoon. 'I refused to let myself love you . . . I thought I could not support . . . Oh, my love, my little love, there is not a day I do not think of you, not a night I do not hold you to my breast, kiss your sweet little face . . . I love you, Joshua . . . you will always live in my heart.'

The effort of speaking too much, she kissed the bunch of purple-headed violets nestling in deep-green waxy leaves and laid them against the stone.

They had found no lead to the knife. The police inspector had been polite, apologetic almost. Anne moved between the rows of women and girls each busy at the workbenches and sewing machines, watching the quality-checking of each finished piece. No one had recognised the weapon used to wound her and kill the old nightwatchman. A thief, the police had assumed, a thief she had disturbed, but what would a man steal from the Glebe . . . a pocketful of crude iron? Even the lorinery, crucial as bits, spurs, stirrups and every other piece of harness furniture might be to the war, it would be difficult to sell for a few pence in the whole of an area where so many workshops produced the like. So who . . . and why? The answer might never be found.

'The wench says as they were nailing it up when her went past to take them finished bridles along for Laban's approving, says there was a list long as your arm . . .'

The woman talking with Unity glanced up from her stitching as Anne joined them but did not pause in her account of the posting of the latest bulletin naming the men returned for convalescence.

'. . . poor souls all of 'em, gassed or crippled, I tell you when they gets that Kaiser they should gas and shoot *him* then hang the wicked bugger where everybody can see.'

Another list of repatriates. Anne's thoughts of the knife and her own brush with death evaporated like mist in the sun. Maybe this time . . . ! She could go now, she could leave the works, go to the town hall and read the list of names, she could . . . But what of those other women sat on the benches? Each of them had husband, father, son or sweetheart away at the fighting, and though it was obvious they too had heard of the posting of yet another list, not one of them had left the work they knew was vital. Neither must she. Avoiding Unity's eye she continued on along the line of benches, speaking quietly to a young girl struggling to learn a complicated technique, to another anxious her stitching prove unsatisfactory. Any one of these had more right than she to leave what they were doing, to go read those names; she had none at all.

Settling herself to work as best she could with a shoulder still stiff, she tried to clear her mind but thoughts drifted in and out; there and then not there, petals in the wind.

. . . I will write to let you know where I'll be, Mrs Davies . . .

Those were the words he had spoken in his grandmother's house when he had mistaken her steps for those of his next-door neighbour; but when he had turned and seen her standing in the doorway he had not added to them. The realisation which had come as those last precious minutes had ticked away cut keenly now as they had then. He had not added that he would write to her. Was that not proof? Proof he had no feelings at all for Anne Corby.

Selecting a pricker punch with ten teeth, Anne ran it over a piece of firm hide intended for an officer's kit bag, taking care not to drive so deeply as to weaken the leather but exerting just enough pressure on the hand tool to mark the spot where the needle would carry the thread.

He had not offered to write to her nor had he asked she write to him. Setting the leather aside she proceeded to mark the next piece before taking them to the more experienced stitchers. Would the Abel Preston of her childhood, the Abel who always tried to heal her hurts, heal the pain she felt now if he knew of it? But then he would never know. Returning to the bench, she reached for leather she could not see through the haze of tears touching her eyes. Abel Preston would never know what lay hidden in her heart.

The funeral of Clara Mather and her son had been over this past fortnight. Unity added salt to the pan of potatoes suspended from a bracket over the fire. How long would it be before Anne Corby moved to her own house, how long before Laban and herself were left once more with only memories of someone they loved? The wench 'adn't spoke of such intention but it took no genius of mind to know it would be soon.

'I – I read the list of repatriates posted today.' Anne's shyness showed in the tiny falter. 'Abel was not among them.'

Brushing the few clinging grains of salt from her palm, Unity nodded. 'I checked the list meself same as always and like you says young Abel's name weren't on it; that could be a blessing, it could mean he's safe and unhurt; or else it could be he were sent to one of them there other hospitals, him having no family to care for him.'

Or it could mean he was missing, even lying dead, in some godforsaken spot! She had heard men she helped nurse at Bentley Grange, men out of their senses with sickness, babble about bodies so blown apart by gunfire as to be unrecognisable, of others lying unconscious or dead in trenches half filled with water, rats nibbling at their limbs.

Not that . . . dear God, not that! Hands trembling, she dropped the cutlery she had taken from a drawer.

Unity ignored the clatter of knives and forks. Anne Corby thought her feelings hid from the world but they were not hid from Unity Hurley; the wench had feelings for Abel Preston . . . feelings which showed in her eyes when off her guard, them special feelings a woman carries for only one man.

'I told him,' she went on, 'told him the night afore he left to write mine and Laban's name as next of kin so there would be a home to return him to, but he said that would be writing a lie for he had no kin; the lad could be stubborn that way.'

Perhaps if she wrote to those hospitals, asked if they had a patient by the name of Abel Preston . . . but those hospitals would be as busy as the ones close by, every one of their staff would be run off their feet, she could not expect them to check through endless lists of names. Thoughts crowding into her brain, Anne retrieved the fallen cutlery, taking it into the scullery to wash. He had no kin . . . neither did she. That at least she could share with Abel Preston.

'What I want to know is where they'm going to put all them wounded?' Unity reached the lamb chops from the oven where they had cooked until tender, then set the roasting pan on the hob, not glancing at Anne as she returned to the room . . . give the wench a minute to get herself together, to continue to hide her true feelings. 'The Sister Dora and West Bromwich District Hospital be filled and according to what a body read from the newspaper, so do Dudley Guest and the Corbett along of Amblecote; seems every hospital for miles around be bursting of its doors, to say nothin' of the likes of Bentley Grange. It be right good of that new owner to open the place to the nursing of wounded but I doubts it'll hold many more.'

Placing the third plate in its accustomed spot on the table, Anne forced her attention to the words. 'I doubt that, too,' she said, holding the older woman's glance as she turned from tending the meat, 'which is why I have offered Butcroft House for the same purpose.'

'Butcroft!' Unity's mouth gaped. 'You've give that house to be a hospital? But I thought . . . Laban an' me we both of us thought . . . with it bein' your home . . .'

Light from the solitary lamp mixing with the glow of the fire danced auburn glints in chestnut hair as Anne shook her head. 'My home is here,' she said softly, 'please, don't turn me from it.'

25

Taking the crumpled sheet of paper from the pocket of his tunic, Abel read it through with the aid of a lantern shining weakly from a broken beam in the roof of a house reduced almost to a shell by constant pounding of German guns. The poor light did not really matter, he had read it so many times he could 'quote it verbatim' as his officer had once said of his own letters. He wasn't a bad chap, that lieutenant, one you would be pleased to call a friend . . . but it made no sense to want to call any man friend when death waited over the next rise. There had been so many of them. He rested the hand holding the letter against the shattered wall. Men he had known from home, others from areas he did not know at all, men whose life had been snatched from them.

It was mind-numbing watching so many casualties, some already dead as medical orderlies carried them off the field, others crying with the agony of gunshot or shrapnel wounds, but, worst of all, what destroyed the soul was the sight of lads just eighteen years old . . . lads less than a month after being sent to fight and already lying dead. Where in God's name was the sense of it all . . . what prevented the ones still alive from going mad? The answer was there in his hand. Letters from home kept men from sinking into madness, letters from loved ones, letters from friends and even ones like this . . . brushing dried mud from his eyelashes he glanced again at the paper, a letter from a next-door neighbour.

It had come weeks ago and been read daily since his

receiving it. It was his one contact with a world which, in the hell he was in now, seemed only a remembered dream, its smiling faces, warm homes and freshly cooked meals a fantasy of imagination. Had he truly once lived in the sanity of a world at peace, a world where men did not live with that one thought, kill before you are killed?

From each side the snores of men defeated by weariness rose and fell in concerted rhythm. Despite his own bone tiredness, Abel smiled. It was so well regulated the sleeping men might well be dreaming themselves under the all-seeing eye of the regimental sergeant major. Now there was a man to be reckoned with! Folding the sheet of paper he replaced it in his pocket. Half a dozen like Sergeant Major Potts advancing with stick under his arm would see every man jack of the Kaiser's legions running full pelt back to the Fatherland. But those men were no different to the British soldiers; they too were men dragged from their homes to fight their master's war. Lord! He sighed loudly. What wouldn't he give to have the Kaiser and his Crown Prince, Lloyd George, Herbert Asquith, Horatio Bottomley and all the other war mongers sitting in a dugout half filled with rainwater, their slimy legs in mud to the tops of their puttees, most of them bleeding, all of them numb from shell-shock; this war would not last another hour. But that sort did not know the horrors of the trenches, they only sent others to endure that.

'You should get some sleep, Preston.'

Squinting into shadows only deepened by the narrow reach of the anaemic lantern glow, Abel made to salute the officer.

'No need for that.' The quiet voice was heavy with the man's own weariness. 'Find yourself a place and sleep while you can.'

In this chaos of fear there was still humanity. Abel watched the tall figure melt into the shadows. That man had no need to check positions, to squelch through trenches or dodge shells whistling down on buildings to come to speak to the troops huddled there; as an officer he could send others to do that . . . but not this one. Since being posted to this command he had taken part in each battle, whether a skirmish or a full onslaught, and after it had made the rounds, a quiet 'well done' for every survivor, words of encouragement and reassurance for the injured. And for the dead? Wedging himself between slabs of fallen masonry, Abel closed his eyes. Not even Lieutenant Harold Allen could give reassurance to them.

Glancing through a gaping hole in what had once been the roof of someone's home he saw the first pink tinge of dawn. The only normal thing in this mad abnormal world. Outside, the quiet crunch of the officer's boots halted. Was that man too watching the sunrise, was he too wondering how man could destroy man as both sides were doing, taking lives in great swathes with neither thought nor reason, just a blind obedience.

Beyond the nearest ridge the sound of heavy guns ripped apart the blessed minutes of silence, adding their flashes of brilliant crimson to the gentle dawn. A new day? Or his last day? It was not an idea fresh born in his mind, it was there every moment, with him, part of him, as it was part of every man caught in this devil's trap of war.

Around him the choir of snores sang undisturbed, gunfire making no impression on bodies weary almost to unconsciousness. There had been rumours of a big push, an attempt to throw the enemy back at Ypres; were those guns the overture to the symphony of death, the music which would accompany so many into their graves?

Was today to be his turn . . . would he be one of the many? Taking out the letter he read it again, searching between the lines as he had a hundred times. But he would not find what was not there. Mrs Davies had written that all was

well with his home, but it was not that which he yearned
to hear of.

He had thought that maybe, with his being so far from
England, she might write to him. But he could not expect
that. He returned the envelope to his pocket. Anne Corby
was not a girl to write uninvited and he had not asked she
should.

Why hadn't he? It was a silent query, a cry rising from his
soul. They had been friends in childhood, friends since her
returning to Darlaston. Dropping his head onto his knees,
Abel heard the reason in his heart. He had not asked she write
to him in friendship for it was not Anne Corby's friendship he
wanted, it was her love.

'Christ, don't they ever stop!'

'Now c'mon, Dusty, you knows you'd miss it if they did.'

From several corners his companions began to wake,
immediately indulging in banter he knew kept each man
sane, kept him from thinking of what lay ahead.

'Think I'll tell old Pottsy I needs to see the MO.'

'You do that, Nutty me old mate, an' you'll be seein' the
devil long afore the Hun sends ya to 'ell with 'alf a shell up
ya arse!'

The answer swallowed in laughter, Abel lifted his head.
The last of the men were awake, some enquiring about 'tea
in a china cup with cream and extra sugar, my man', others
coughing and shivering with the first signs of swamp fever.

'Anybody got a fake 'til I gets a parcel from 'ome?'

'Get lost, Baker, ya scroungin' git!' Amid the mounds of
rubble an arm raised. Instinctively Abel ducked, the air from
a flying boot fanning his face.

'One fake won't hurt ya.' Baker returned the boot the same
way it had come.

'And it won't hurt you neither, 'cos you ain't getting one!'

'I thought you was my mate,' Baker tried again.

'Yoh think any bloke be your mate if'n he's got a packet of fakes in his pocket. Well, that be where mine be stoppin' . . . in me pocket!'

His fingers brushing the letter, Abel fished his own packet of Woodbine cigarettes from his pocket, handing them to Baker.

The envelope touched his fingers as they returned the cigarettes. It could soon be too late, the chance might be gone for ever. In the near distance a gun boomed, the shell it delivered shaking the earth beneath him. The last chance!

Reaching the backpack set on the ground beside him he took out the notepaper he had carried halfway across France. This was not the right thing to do. He paused. Had Anne Corby wished to hear from him she would have told him so. Beyond the shattered building a bugle blared sharply. Shoving the notepaper back, Abel climbed wearily to his feet.

'What's this world coming to!' Unity tutted her disgust as she read the newspaper. 'Them there Bolsheviks should be horse whipped; I've never 'eard the like, it's the same as putting the man in gaol along with his whole family!'

'People behave as they don't mean when they're hungry.'

'Hungry!' Unity glared at her husband over the top of the newspaper. 'The folk of this country have gone hungry many times but they haven't never laid hands on their king!'

'P'raps it be more than just hunger, though heaven knows that can rip away a man's senses, especially when he sees his little 'uns suffering, newspapers don't always print the truth.' Taking a handmade, six-cord, waxed thread, Laban fed the purposely constructed pointed end through the eye of a three-inch quilting needle.

'Well, maybe we don't get to read the all of things but I can't see any newspaper being so daft as to print a story like this if it don't be the truth.'

Pulling the thread tight after each stitch Laban began to attach the girth strap to the saddle flap. 'You know the old saying,' he smiled, 'there be naught so queer as folk.'

Folding the newspaper Unity nodded as she set it aside. 'Ar, I know it, but they have to be mighty queer to go telling the world such a thing as is printed there if it be naught but a lie. Still, we have more to worry about than what them Bolsheviks be doing.'

Laban glanced across to his wife settling herself beside the clamp she insisted on keeping. She worked hard as any man and stitched better than many and every evening stitched yet more pieces, but every day orders came from the War Office requesting still more. Saddles, bridles, harness, satchels and a host of other things beside streamed from the saddlers of Walsall, yet the demands of the army went on. But how long could the supply go on, how long before women like Unity, ar and men like himself, working longer and longer hours, gave way under the strain? How long could men not yet fully recovered from wounds received on the battlefield, and already at work in the leather or anywhere else, be of assistance? God damn men like the Kaiser, men blinded by ambition! Cursing beneath his breath he stabbed the needle into the leather.

'How much longer do you reckon this war to go on?'

It was softly asked but Laban heard the heartache inherent in the question, a question which really asked how many mothers must suffer as I suffered, how many must lose their sons as I lost mine?

'There be no telling,' he answered, 'but it must be over soon now.'

Why must it? The clamp between her knees, Unity bent to her stitching. It had already lasted years while the country had been led to believe it would be over in six months, so why should it be soon now? Lads were still being taken in their thousands; every day more women could be seen with tears on their faces, men with black armbands announcing yet one more of the family dead in war. Would the nightmare only stop when no more men were left to sacrifice?

But death in battle was not enough. Her lips tight as the thread drawn behind the needle, Unity stitched on in silence. Men breathing their last in a bed of mud or cut to pieces by shell fire was not sufficient, women and children too had to die. The Zeppelin, that brainchild of some deranged lunatic, had brought the horror of that nightmare to the Midlands. It had flown over the Black Country loosing its bombs on Tipton and Bradley. But that had not been enough for the devils flying in it; they had brought it on to Wednesbury where a bomb had wiped out an entire family with a direct hit, and them doing no more than sitting peaceful in their own home; and then it had moved on across to Walsall. Fingers moving in steady rhythm, Unity's thoughts ran on. A bomb had dropped onto the centre of the town, right onto Bradford Place, shrapnel splintering from it striking a passing train; many passengers had been cut by shards of flying metal, Mrs Slater, the mayoress, being injured so bad she had died of wounds to her chest and stomach. How could acts such as that be justified? Reaching for a sharp-bladed knife with which to cut the thread, Unity stared at the blade gleaming in the yellowy light of the lamp. If only she could meet up with the man who had flown that Zeppelin, he would be wearing his gizzard for a necklace!

I ain't heard no word from him.

The words rang in Anne's mind. They were the same words she heard every week when she called to enquire of Abel's next-door neighbour if she had had news.

No word! She crossed the Bull Stake passing in front of a tram, its bell indignantly demanding she hurry. The woman said she had replied to Abel but that had been months ago. There had been no more since unless letters had gone astray . . . maybe been wrongly addressed? No, Mrs Davies might not be exactly a young woman but she had all of her senses, she would have made no mistake. So why had Abel not written again? She could go on asking that question and each time find a possible answer, yet never know the truth.

Reaching the gates of Butcroft House she stood still. There were many truths might never be known, truths such as why was her cousin found in his mother's room, surely he would have heard the crash of that falling lamp, the scream of a woman hurtling down the stairs . . . would he not have come to the head of those stairs instead of to her aunt's bedroom? Then there was the death of the nightwatchman and her own assault . . . was the conclusion reached by the police the correct one or was it, as Unity declared, '*summat as they've come up with 'cos they have no idea what they be about; as for that there inspector, he's no more sense than a sucking duck!*'

At the end of the short drive, window lights subdued in accord with the Defence of the Realm Act, Butcroft House stood tall against the night sky. This house had been her home, a place she should be happy to return to; instead it seemed to hold an aura of threat, a shadow of menace. She could go back, send someone in her stead. The idea tempting, she stood for a moment, the sound of a tram reaching faintly across night-still streets, its bell evoking memories of a different sound, a different time: the soft swish of runners over snow, the tinkling of bells on horse harness, the vast silent spread of the Russian steppe. There had been fear there, too, and death . . .

To her side a shadow moved in the darkness bringing a scream to her lips, startling a cat emerging from the bushes.

She was behaving like a child. There was nothing here to be afraid of, she was simply letting imagination run away with her. Now, if she didn't hurry she really would have something to be wary of . . . the sharp end of Unity's tongue for getting home late yet again.

'It is so kind of you to think of our patients, Miss Corby, especially when you have so much else to do.' White cap flaring stiffly to her shoulders, matching cuffs on each wrist, a silver buckle gleaming on the scarlet belt circling her waist, the matron led the way to the study, boots clicking on floors cleared of carpet.

Much as she would have enjoyed a cup of tea, Anne refused the invitation knowing it would take someone from her duties. 'I was thinking earlier of what you said regarding the men who are recovering well, of their having to occupy their time.'

'One of the drawbacks of convalescence, I'm afraid.' The starched cap barely moved as the woman's head shook briefly. 'They are each of them thankful to be back here in England and grateful, as we all are, for your generosity in loaning this house for a medical unit, but a man can only play so many games of cards, darts or dominoes before boredom removes his appetite for them; boredom is a dangerous thing, Miss Corby, it can lead to apathy, and once that sets in it makes the task of healing so much more difficult. What they really need is to feel useful again, to feel they are still helping those remaining at the front. These men cannot . . . will not . . . rid themselves of the thought that this is still everyone's war, injured or not, and they must help win it.'

'Which is why I brought these along.' Opening the bag she had brought with her, Anne laid the contents on the desk, quick to explain as a frown settled between the woman's neat brows.

'Those patients without injury to the upper body could help a great deal. Leather goes through many processes before becoming a finished article; it can need to be skived to reduce its thickness; sometimes a piece has to be bevelled, thin shavings removed from its edges before burnishing with a smooth piece of boxwood; there is channelling using a race . . . a tool shaped like a V or U which marks a groove that facilitates the bending of the leather; then there is buffing, this is eliminating scars or surface scratches with the use of an abrasive—'

'This is all very well,' the matron lifted the palm of one hand resting on the desk, 'but what you describe is surely skilled work, and though the military are ever at pains to return men to their own areas of the country not all of our patients may have been formerly employed in the leather industry.'

'Every aspect of leather-work is skilled, some obviously only a craftsman can perform, but those I have mentioned can be quickly learned given careful tuition and this would release experienced workers to the more complicated tasks.'

'That I can understand.' The starched cap resisted the nod. 'But you also should understand that space here is at a premium. Did I wish to, I could not sanction a square foot of it as a workshop; also, the risk of infection . . . fibres floating on the air are not advisable where open wounds must be dressed. You do see that, my dear?'

It was a perfectly feasible refusal but one Anne was not prepared to take. 'I do see,' she answered, 'but the space I was thinking of is not part of this building . . . it is the garden house. It was built for my mother. She would often sit there away from my—' She paused abruptly, the word 'aunt' swallowed back into her throat. The garden house had been her mother's retreat from her sister-in-law's sharp, ever-critical tongue, a place to hide away.

'Do you mean the long greenhouse set beyond the trees! I'm afraid that place would be too damp for my patients to sit in.'

The finality embodied in that clipped tone struck a chord in Anne. That was the tone adopted by Clara Mather whenever she spoke to a small, frightened little girl. But Anne Corby was no longer that little girl and she was no longer to be easily defeated by a tone of voice.

'You are mistaken.' She lifted a cool glance to the woman facing her across the desk. 'The garden house was not built, or ever used, for the cultivation of plants. My father had it designed as a retreat, a place my mother could sit and read or do her needlework free from the bustle of a busy household. It boasts several stoves which provide more than adequate heating, its roof resists the heaviest of rain, while its floors are not concrete but wood, raised from the ground on low stilts. I think, should you inspect it, you would find it more than suitable for the purpose I have proposed.'

It had not ended there. The matron had placed several more obstacles in her path. The sound of her steps echoing from the setts, Anne retraced her way across the Bull Stake, continuing into King Street. St Lawrence church had already chimed nine but the shaded light of shops not yet closed and the few women still marketing gave a reassurance she found comforting.

Where is the coal for the stoves to come from? Who will attend when nurses could not be spared to carry meals to the workroom? Who will teach the patients to work the leather? The questions had been answered one by one until, at last, there was agreement to put the final and most vital question of all to the men: were they willing to take part? It had been promised that a reply would be sent tomorrow. But there was another hurdle to cross – Unity and Laban. They were of the opinion she already did too much and Unity voiced that opinion regularly. It was true she did not have much time to relax, but to relax was to have freedom to think, to remember.

The empty bag clutched close to her middle she glanced to her right, a tremble flickering in her veins as the low-squat huddle of the workhouse materialised dark and threatening against the shadows, and with it the horror of what she had so nearly done. Her baby, her sweet innocent child, she had thought to leave him there, give him into a life that would most probably have been one of hardship and misery. Bastard . . . the word edged into her mind. Joshua would never have been allowed to forget he had no father, forget his heritage of shame. But would the workhouse have proved worse than where he was now? Would he have died if she had taken him there? Would they have loved him more than she had? Had her selfishness stolen her baby's life, snatched it from him, throwing it away before he had the chance to live it?

'Watch where you be going . . . almost had a body off her feet . . . some folk have no thought 'cept for theirself!'

'I'm sorry, I'm so sorry.'

Anne's apology followed after the grumbling figure, but it was more than an apology to the living . . . she spoke to her son.

26

Puffing on his clay pipe and nodding intermittently, Laban listened to Anne's outline of what she had proposed to the matron.

'It be a good idea,' he said when she was done. 'Keeping a man's hands busy leaves his mind no chance to wander.'

Sitting at her clamp beneath the window, Unity had continued to stitch a section of military pack saddle, leather hockles protecting her fingers. A man's mind might not wander with his 'ands busy but that couldn't be said of everybody; 'adn't she watched this wench move about the workshop at Fallings Heath, seen her 'ands work confident and sure while her eyes spoke of a mind far away?

'There be one thing, though,' Laban continued, 'there be men as don't take kind to women telling 'em what to do nor how to do it. Mayhap there'll be a few of that kind up at Butcroft.'

'I – I had not thought of that.'

Neither had that matron for all her buts! Unity smiled grimly to herself.

'Might do well to give some thought to it afore you sets yourself to deciding to go on with this venture—' Laban began.

'And it might be well to forget it altogether!' Unity let her needles drop. 'You be doing too much as it is; first it was helping out at the Regency works, then comes the taking over of the Glebe and as if that don't be enough you opens up them buildings along of Fallings Heath, putting them to the leather; but that ain't enough, you have to help out at Bentley Grange and at Butcroft, fetching and carrying hours you should ought to be resting . . . and now this, setting up a workshop for patients. I tells you, wench, you be going to work y'self out and that'll get nobody nothin'!'

'The wench were only thinking of others—'

'Be that as it might!' Unity interrupted sharply. 'But too much thinking of others and not enough of one's own self brings no good in the end. I says this be naught but a hare-brained idea. Being in two places at the same time be summat the best of folk can't master and that is what her'll try to do, be at Fallings Heath and at Butcroft both; well, I says no, it be too much for one wench, you tell me if that don't be the way of it . . . go on, you tell me!'

'It do be the way of it.' Laban met Unity's challenge, a smile directed at Anne just a gentle curve of the mouth. 'Unity be sharp in her telling but be right nonetheless. What you be suggesting, though good in itself, needs a more careful thinking.'

'But it would work, I know it would.' Anne looked from one to the other, seeing concern on Unity's face, sympathetic agreement on Laban's.

'I be of the same mind,' he nodded, 'but I agree also with Unity; it's too much for you to take on along with what you already does.'

She had wanted so much to give those men an answer to what she saw so often in bleak eyes, heard in flat hopeless tones as she talked with them: a chance to fulfil a need, the need to feel useful, in some small way to stand alongside their friends in the field, to go on fighting the only way they could.

Seeing disappointment mirrored on the small face Laban glanced at his wife, looking for the support she had never once failed to give. It was there now, smiling back at him from blue eyes age was fading to grey.

'That don't mean to say as you shouldn't see it done, wench,' he said quietly, 'just to shape it different like.'

How could she shape it differently? A frown drawing her brows together Anne looked at the man she knew loved her as he would a daughter of his own.

'I said as men don't take kind to women being placed above them in the workplace,' Laban answered the query born in that frown. 'It's summat they don't be comfortable with, p'raps the world will change one day but today ain't one day, it's now; that being the way of it, set them to work with a man to do the supervising, that way they'll be content and you won't have an extra burden on your shoulders.'

Nodding agreement Unity took up her needles. 'Laban be right, a man ain't comfortable in his work then he don't give of his best.'

'I understand that.' Anne's hands rose and fell. 'And of course a man would be best . . . but where do we find one, every man left to the town is already in employment.'

His pipe finished, Laban tapped the bowl gently against the chimney breast, blowing several times down the slender stem before laying it aside. Smoothing a piece of soft pigskin previously laid across the table he spread a paper pattern on it, marking its shape carefully.

'Not every man,' he said, head bent, 'I hears as how Bert Jeavons be sent back with a bullet wound to the hip, no bones broke but painful. Bert were always good with the leather and mild tempered with lads—'

'That don't be the way his Sarah be telling, her says he be like a bear with a sore –' Unity paused then went on '– well, never mind what be sore but her reckons he don't be easy to live with.'

'Nor would any man be with Sarah Jeavons on his back all

day, reckon that were Bert's chief reason for enlisting as soon as he did.'

Catching Laban's wink, Anne hid her own smile, hoping it did not show in her voice as she asked could a man with a hip injury, albeit not too serious, manage to work?

Keeping his eyes on his marking, Laban avoided Unity's. 'If it means keeping out of Sarah's way then I reckons Bert Jeavons could manage to fly, any road you let me go talk with him, I think you'll find him saying yes.'

Cutting her thread with a sharp bladed cap knife, light catching its pointed end gleaming like a tiny star, Unity released the clamp, putting the finished section of pack saddle aside.

'And you must content y'self with that,' she looked at Anne, 'it's a strong back you've proved to have, wench, one them parents of your'n would be proud of, God rest 'em, but the strongest of backs break when too great a load be put on it.'

'I only wish to help.'

A smile greeting the reply Unity watched the girl settle to stitching a belt. It wasn't Anne Corby's only wish, but heaven alone could grant what her heart cried for. 'They knows that along at Butcroft and at Bentley Grange,' she said as she selected another section and set it in the clamp, 'and so does everybody in Darlaston, there ain't a family as don't regard you with respect. You've come home, wench.'

Anne watched the line of stitches grow. The hardship Clara Mather had brought to many seemed forgiven if not forgotten, Anne Corby had gained people's respect, she had Abel Preston's respect . . . that would have to be enough for he would never give her his love.

Her hands trembling in her lap, teeth clenched against the fear beating in her throat, Anne stared unseeing into the mirror above the washstand in her room.

Tsar interned at Tsarskoe Selo.

It rang over and over in her brain, beating like a hammer on an anvil.

Tsar and royal family arrested.

It was still happening . . . Sir Corbett had destroyed the amulet but the evil of it was alive, breathing, moving, wreaking its havoc. Abduction in Istanbul, shipwreck, almost run down by a cart in Dover, she had allowed herself to be persuaded each of these incidents was no more than coincidence, things which could happen any time to anyone, tricks of fate. But the woman Beshlie, the old gypsy who had come to sit at her fire that one evening in France, she had felt that same evil.

A jewelled piece . . . given by a Rai, a great lord who fears for one greater still . . .

As though rehearsed the words came back, stabbing themselves into her brain.

. . . but it be too late, the great one be already marked for death . . . his juval and his chavvies . . . they have looked on the devil's trinket . . . though they be innocent of guilt they will be sucked into his maw . . .

Mikhail Mikhailovitch Yusupov was a great Russian lord but the Tsar was greater still. Was he the one the gypsy meant? Juval and chavvies . . . they were Romany words for woman and children, and the newspaper report stated all of the royal family were being held at Tsarskoe Selo, one of the Tsar's country homes.

But the amulet, the thing given to Rasputin, worn by him despite its reputation, Sir Corbett had said it was destroyed, even the ash of its remains buried in some secret place. It was gone so its powers, imagined or otherwise, could not be responsible for what had happened in Russia. The whims of fate? Anne's fingernails pressed into her palms but she felt no bite. The gypsy woman had not believed so; the workings of the Dark One, she had called the shipwreck and abduction; but she had not stopped there.

. . . it was his hand reached to you and it will reach again . . .

The tricks of fate had not ceased with her returning to Darlaston. With her stare locked on the mirror she saw the shadows behind her head gather themselves together, draw into filmy features, a mouth smiling with contempt as it stared back at her, Quenton's mouth! Even as she gasped it was gone, the misty greyness of it fading and reforming until the steely eyes and tight face of Clara Mather glared from the mirror's depths.

. . . treachery and malevolence . . .

The gypsy's words had proved themselves true, Quenton had threatened and his mother had tried to take her inheritance: that had been their treachery.

Within the depths of the mirror the hard eyes seemed suddenly to gleam, the mouth to curve with a smile so vicious Anne caught her breath, then a tendril of mist broke away to form itself into a separate figure, the tiny figure of a child, its eyes closed in death. Joshua! The scream she had held back so long now a clawing choking hand at her throat, she watched the vicious mouth open in a laugh, a filmy finger touch the infant's lips.

The very movement spoke of evil and with it came a terrible thought. Had her aunt been responsible for her baby's death, was this the malevolence spoken of?

Evil knows many ways.

How many times had her father said those words? But this . . . her son's death . . . !

Blackness swirling in her head Anne felt herself drawn down, ever down into a dark pit, and as she fell she heard a voice following, a voice repeating over and over . . .

. . . it will reach again . . . reach again . . . reach again . . .

*   *   *

She had dreamed it all, the horror of the night before was a figment of her imagination, the result of overwork to which Unity equated her pallor. Glad of the chance to breathe the outdoor air Anne walked more slowly than usual. A dream, yet it had stamped its mark, a deep sleep leaving her tired and drained of energy. She had risen this morning at her regular time, talked over tea and toast with Unity and Laban but all the while that terrible scene played in her mind . . . the image of a vicious grinning face . . . a finger touching her baby's lips. It was all too wicked yet it seemed all too real. Clara Mather had vowed that the house and the foundry would never be returned, that they were the true inheritance of her son, that she had worked so they could be his . . . had she also killed so they could be his?

She could not believe that. It was a dreadful thing to think! Her aunt had been a spiteful woman but she would not take a child's life. Nightmares such as she had had last night were just that, nightmares. They were unreal fantasies of the mind and to think of them any other way, to allow them to dwell was foolish as it was foolish to believe a lifeless object, a thing crafted of metal and stone could hold any kind of power. Good or evil was of man's making.

But Mikhail Yusupov and Sir Corbett, both logical sensible men, why would they speak as they had? Unless . . . yes, that had been their reason: make believe a piece of jewellery carried ill luck and it would not be stolen. But that did not explain the gypsy woman's . . .

No! She pushed the rest away. Whatever Sir Corbett had done with the trinket, sold it or destroyed it, the thing was gone from her life; she would not think of it again.

'I were told as I might catch you here –'

A figure huddled in dark clothing stepped in front of Anne.

'– so I waited. It be a fair step to Blockall.'

Shawl drawn low obscured the features, but the voice? Anne hesitated, she had heard it before.

'Mebbe's you'll be thinkin' it be wrong of me to wait for you in the street like this but, as I says, Blockall be a bit far for old legs so I asks you don't take what I done unkindly.'

'Of course not, Mrs Davies.' Recognition dawning, Anne smiled. 'But what brings you here?'

'This.' A hand emerged from beneath her shawl and the woman held out a letter.

Even in the fading light of evening Anne could read the words stamped heavily across the envelope.

H M War Office.

Abel . . . Abel was dead! Too stunned to answer she stared at the envelope in her hand. He was gone from her life, there was no more chance of writing to him, no way of telling him of her true feelings . . . it was too late!

'I'll be leaving that there with you and getting away 'ome afore it be dark. Goodnight to you, wench.'

Her mind blanked with dry tears, Anne stood unaware of the woman drawing her shawl sheath-like about her spindly frame and hobbling away, unaware of the slow fall of night, of people making their separate ways home or to shops now cautiously lit with a candle; she knew only the pain binding her chest.

Abel . . . she had wanted to say so much to him . . . needed him to know . . . but he would never know, for Abel Preston was dead!

'C'mon, wench, come you home.'

Somewhere in the emptiness a voice reached to her, an arm passed about her shoulder.

'Abel,' she whispered, 'Abel he—'

'I know, wench, I know, but this don't be the place.'

Memories of an earlier letter, of a different woman stunned with grief flooded Laban's mind. Yes, that was of another time but the anguish and heartbreak would be the same. This girl was not mourning two sons as he and Unity had; but the loss of a friend you cared for was bitter enough. He had seen the friendship grow, watched it over the months. But the lad had not spoken of what lay hidden inside him, he had loved this daughter of Jacob Corby and it was surely because she was that man's daughter he had held his silence. Now he would never break it.

His arm supporting her he nodded, acknowledging the quiet murmurs of sympathy as they walked. Darlaston had become a town of tears where no one asked why.

A young child had come to the Regency works, sent by his mother to tell of Anne Corby stood like a statue of stone along of the gate of Butcroft House and answering nobody as spoke to her. He had rewarded the lad with a penny and seen his eyes light up like torches and sparks fly from metal-rimmed clogs as he raced for Charles Cadby's sweetshop. The woman had seen the sense of sending for him rather than for Unity with Regency Leather being sooner to reach than Fallings Heath, nevertheless her would need be called, a woman were ever best at a time like this.

'Old Mrs Davies give it to her?' Unity came downstairs from putting Anne to bed. 'I would have thought her to have had more thought than to push a letter like that into a wench's hand, why not bring it here to the house?'

'The woman be near enough seventy, and not so sturdy on her feet as her once was, it be too much of a trek from her place to this.'

Unity nodded. 'The woman be a kindly soul and done what her seen to be right, it's me who be wrong to go talking against her.'

''Twere a shock to you as well as to her upstairs.' Laban reached for his wife's hand, patting it consolingly. 'We all say things we don't mean when we be upset.'

'Some of we says nothin' at all.'

'Her's still not spoke?'

Withdrawing her hand Unity reached for the teapot warming on the hob. 'Naught but that one word over and over: Abel. It . . . it's almost like her feels guilty, guilty for—'

'Guilt!' Laban looked up from the tobacco he was shaving into paper-thin slivers. 'What mean you by that?'

Having spooned tea into the pot Unity hesitated. Laban did not like a prying woman . . . but she had not pried, she had asked no question, but she could not avoid words the eyes gave voice to. She had seen what had not been said, caught the quick flush of colour to the girl's cheek whenever Abel Preston had called, the note of eagerness which was more than enthusiasm for the walk whenever she had been called upon to take finished work to the Regency. It was not only Abel had feelings, Anne Corby had the same.

'Before I tells what I think let me say this, Laban Hurley. I've asked nothing and been told nothing, I keeps my counsel . . .'

'But?' Pressing tobacco into the bowl of his pipe Laban knew better than to show the smile hovering behind his lips.

A sharp, almost angry thump placing the teapot on an intricately cast trivet, Unity stared defiantly at the bent head.

'But nothing! I sees what I sees and there be no blame in that!'

Holding a spill to the fire then to the pipe, Laban sucked on the long stem, his smile still hidden. He knew his wife well, she would need no more prompting . . . he had only to wait.

'I wonders you haven't seen it for yourself . . . but then a man don't see nothing as don't be served on a plate or in a tankard.' Quick hands matched by a now edged voice Unity covered a pinprick of irritation.

'Nobody would say there was.' Laban puffed several times before tapping out the lighted spill.

Nerves as yet not completely free of the emotion of the past couple of hours, Unity sniffed tartly. 'So long as it be understood! I seen what neither that wench upstairs nor Abel Preston thought to be seen, I seen they had feelings one for the other even though it could be as they didn't realise as much theirselves. You might argue it don't be so but I guesses her feels guilt for never speaking of them feelings afore the lad went away and yet a bit more for never writing even a line to him.'

Taking the mug handed to him, Laban set it in the spot the teapot had occupied on the hob and where it was easily reached from his chair. 'Mebbe's the lad didn't ask her to.'

'Ask!' Unity snapped like a bull terrier. 'If'n a wench waits to be asked all the time then there be a lot of things her won't get!'

'But you can't hardly expect a young woman to go writing letters to a man if he didn't ask.'

Unity's hands rose slowly to her hips, the firelight catching the glint in her eyes. 'Have years taught you nothing? A war with the Boers and now this one with Germany and you still haven't learned! The world be different to the one we was born to, it be a place where you needs grab opportunity, for life might be taken away afore there be the chance to live it. What be a letter after all? Pen strokes on paper . . . a word of friendship from a home left behind ain't exactly like a wench offering to . . . to—'

The irate words ended as swiftly as they began, a flush suffusing Unity's face as she turned away. Behind the veil of tobacco smoke Laban set free his tortured smile. The world had changed but not so much his wife could finish that sentence.

'I know you've asked no question.' Vindication of his belief in her diplomatically asserted, Laban went on, 'but what be in that letter the wench were given?'

Lowering her hands to her sides Unity shrugged. 'You might ask what be on the other side of the moon for I could answer that with equal truth. I don't know what be written in that letter for it still be sealed.'

'Sealed . . . you mean her 'asn't opened it?'

Unity's head shook briefly. 'I means just that. Her hand be clutching it as if it were beaten gold but the strength to open it, to read what it says, don't be in her. Yet, until it be read, the knife Anne Corby feels in her chest won't never be drawn.'

27

The house lay in silence but the sound of it throbbed in Anne's ears. Unity and Laban had been so thoughtful, asking no questions of her though both must want to know the circumstances of Abel's death, what it was had claimed the life of a man they looked upon almost as a son. But she could not tell them, could not read the words which would finally take him away from her, nor could she give the letter to be read by them. While it remained unopened, unread, Abel was still alive, she had only to wait for his return.

The letter was a mistake, to have gone to Mrs Davies proved it was a mistake; all letters from servicemen were checked by the censor and somehow this had been replaced in the wrong envelope, going to the wrong person. Abel would write to her here, he would . . . he would . . .

Across the uncertain light of morning the sound of St Lawrence church clock drifted across the roof tops.

But Abel would not write . . . she had received no word in all the months he had been away. There had been no mistake. She turned her face into the pillow. Whatever lay inside that envelope had not been intended for her; Mrs Davies had simply brought it out of kindness because of her weekly enquiry after Abel's well-being.

Footsteps on the stairs followed by a lighter quicker tread told of Laban and Unity up and readying the house prior to leaving for work. Her body heavy, Anne lay still. There was no sense in any of it . . . the leather, the Glebe, Butcroft

House, Bentley Grange . . . what good did any of them do? The war went on in spite of them; men got injured, they came home to recuperate only to be thrown back into the hell they had left: the factories and foundries turned out implements by the thousands but they had no effect, the fighting went on and men continued to die, men who were loved . . . men like Abel.

'I've fetched you up a cup of tea.' Quietly, as if not wanting to find her awake, Unity stayed a few seconds in the doorway then came to the bedside and set the cup on the tiny table. 'Laban has banked the fire and there be a slice of bacon in the oven when you be ready forrit.'

Eyes closed, Anne made no reply.

'I be sorry, wench . . . sorry for you both but that be the way of it, the lad be gone and we be left to get on with things.'

Get on with things! Something inside Anne sparked into life, flaming in every vein. That was the motto everywhere she went, in every shop, every workplace; we must get on with things.

'Why?' Her eyes springing open she stared up at the woman stood beside her bed. 'Why must we get on with things? No matter what we do or how hard we strive to do it, it makes no difference . . . men die and it makes no difference!'

'I know you be hurting—'

'Hurting!' Anne's laugh was half anger, half heartbreak. 'Why should I be hurting, it's only lives we are wasting.'

'Wasting, is it!' Unity's voice rang in the quiet house, her own anger vibrant and sudden. 'Then mebbe we should send the Kaiser one of them fancy telegrams apologising for opposing him, telling him we be sorry for not wanting him on the throne of England and please to come straightaway for we all be wanting nothing more than to be his rubbing rags! Lie you there nursing whatever be inside you . . . me? I'll get me shawl on and go tell every woman in Darlaston who's lost a man or lad that their death makes no difference, that like Anne Corby they should down tools, do no more to end a war we didn't start, see whether it makes any difference to them!'

The slam of the door a testimony to her feelings, Unity swept out of the room.

. . . see the women with heads bowed, see the tears which streak their faces . . .

Anne stared at the closed door.

. . . you don't be the only mother to lose a son . . .

Those had been Unity's words. She had been angry then as she was angry now, condemning then as she was condemning now.

. . . theirs be a grief equal to your own . . .

Memory rolled the words through her head and instantly she challenged them. Mothers and sweethearts could grieve for lost love, Anne Corby could only grieve for a love never spoken of.

. . . though they cries they have the courage to live for the sake of others . . .

Like some terrible game of to and fro the words hurled themselves back from the past. She had done that. Anne's fingers clutched the bedcovers. She had gone on after the loss of her son, living for others, believing, though her heart seemed dead, the work of her hands gave them the chance to live . . . but Abel had not lived, he too was lost to her, taking with him her strength, her will.

. . . there'll be more mothers and wives yet to add to the river of tears . . .

She could not help that she was empty, she had given all she could, Unity could not expect more.

Silent as the house was the answer slamming into her brain seemed to fill it with the scream of its own fury.

Be you satisfied to watch that happen while you shirks your responsibilities? Be that all folk means to you!

Unity had been right that first time, it was time to lay aside her selfishness. She must go on otherwise Abel's death and the death of every other man would be a farce, a worthless sacrifice. Throwing aside the covers her hand brushed the envelope she had clutched through the torment of the night hours. She would do what she had to do . . . she would do it for Abel.

Washed and dressed she turned to tidying her bed, her glance deliberately avoiding the letter lying beside the pillow. She would do what she had to, she would share the grief of so many other women . . . but first she must share their courage, she must face what was written in that letter.

There had been a hint of tears, a choking in the voice quietly saying her apology for the words which had gone between them an hour or so since, but the wench bore a look which said more; it said that though unhappiness were not gone it could be borne. Unity fetched a mug of tea from the table around which the women and girls sat to eat their midday meal. Placing it beside Anne she took her own seat at the workbench. The wench had courage . . . it would 'ave been easy for her to stay in the house, no excuse was needed on her part to take time off from the job . . . but Anne Corby were made of better stuff. The true privilege of being the gaffer of any works was the setting of a good example; that were this wench's creed and it were one would stand her in good stead.

'I think you should read this.'

Glancing up from the clamp holding part of an unfinished courier bag in its jaws, Unity watched an envelope being drawn from Anne's pocket, saw the broken seal beneath the boldly stamped 'Censored' and heaved an inward sigh. The wench had opened it, had accepted what had happened . . . that was the first step to healing, the days to come would each bring their own burden but each day that burden would be less heavy.

'It don't be for me to read.' Unity gently pushed away the hand holding the letter, her own eyes glistening with compassion.

Taking the hand touching her own, Anne closed the fingers over the letter. 'Abel was more than a friend to you and to Laban,' she smiled, 'he loved you as he might love a mother and a father . . . you more than I have the right to read what is in that envelope.'

It had been so many years, so long since that first letter, just a few handwritten sentences but they had brought her world crashing down, had stolen joy from her life. The years had told her it could never happen again, the pain would never be relived, yet now as she withdrew the paper from the envelope her hands shook and her heart cried with a sorrow too deep to speak of. A film deforming the uncertain scrawl still further she blinked rapidly, leaving the dislodged tear to lie on her cheeks as she read.

Dear Missis,

I calls you that though I have no knowing to weather you be a married wumun or no but only as you be friend to Abel I be sending this as wos asked by him afor he went over the top but he give me no saying of weer it wos to come so I found the adresing of it in his kit bag hoping it finds you as it leaves me.

Respectful
Alfred Bunn

Alfred Bunn? This be for somebody else!

Reading the unspoken message in the look lifting to her,

Anne shook her head while pointing to the second sheet of paper as yet unfolded.

A quizzical frown not clearing from her brows Unity spread the single sheet, her glance lifting after she read the first words.

'This be written to you,' she said, handing the whole back to Anne. 'It be your name is written on it so it be for you alone to see. I thanks you for the offer to share in the reading of it but a private letter be private; I needs only to know do it tell Abel be safe.'

Returning the envelope and its contents to her pocket Anne took the mug of tea, holding its warmth with both hands. 'No,' she answered quietly, 'it says a heavy bombardment had begun and he had no time to write more.'

Over the top! It meant they had gone into battle. Her tears spilling fresh, Unity took up her needles and pushed them through the strong leather. God keep them, God keep them all.

'There's been no delivering for nigh on a week . . . goes on much longer and we'll have to close the lorinery down.'

'Close!' Anne turned to the man at her side. 'But without those pieces nothing can be made up, not saddles not harness, nothing!'

'I knows that same as you does.' Aaron Butler fingered his scalp beneath his flat cap. 'But without the stuff to work with my hands be tied.'

First it had been the brass. Not enough copper had been the first excuse, that had been followed by there not being enough zinc. *'Everyone wants the same thing.'* The reason given rang in Anne's mind. *'You understand, Miss Corby, much as we would like we cannot supply every foundry.'* So the making of horse brasses had ceased. Not that the loss of brass had been a hardship, the war had seen little call for non-essentials; but spurs, bits, stirrups, buckles, harness rings and cart furniture were not non-essentials, without them the army could not operate, guns and materials could not be transported, food and medical equipment could not reach men who needed it.

'What exactly was the reason given this time?' Anger holding her mouth tight, Anne glanced at the man she had placed in charge of the Glebe Works.

'There be no one reason.' Aaron Butler pulled the cap into its usual place low on his forehead. 'If it don't be one it be another. Somebody don't have the nickel or the chromium, and steel don't have the right degree of hardness we needs without it, then if it don't be a shortage of alloys it be a shortage of coal and coke. I tells you, Miss Anne, it feels like a man be being strangled.'

Not a man. Anne smiled grimly to herself. But a woman! And she was not being strangled but starved out of existence. A woman in the iron and steel business had not been met with any enthusiasm by men with feet stuck firmly in a man's world and now some of them, it seemed, intended to be rid of that unwanted nuisance.

'Thank you, Mr Butler.' She rose, nodding briefly as he opened the door of the small office. 'I know you are doing your best as are the rest of the men. Please give them my thanks.'

It were a shame. Aaron Butler watched the slight figure walk across the yard and out through the gateway. The wench had tried making a go of things, her had not turned her back on the foundry as her father had nor run it into the ground like Clara Mather. Her had showed a courage many a man wouldn't have showed, standing up to the big nobs, the coal-mine owners and their like, but now they had beaten her. The Glebe would soon belong to one or another of 'em and they would all delight in slapping the wench back into her place.

★   ★   ★

'But you can't go in there, such a thing be unheard of!'

'Unheard of no doubt, but not impossible.' Anne set the small round hat firmly on her head, its narrow brim devoid of veil sitting square on her brow.

'Of course it be impossible, no decent woman would dream of settin' foot in that place!' Unity was not to be deterred.

Taking up soft calf gloves Laban had made as a gift for her, matching the colour of the leather to the soft cream of the cuffs and collar of the russet suit she had bought herself the year before, Anne smiled, but it was a smile which in no way conceded defeat, then said firmly, 'Then it will have to be an indecent woman.'

'Of all the hare-brained ideas this be the best!' Unity exploded. 'A young wench . . . no husband at her side . . . you'll be the talk of the town!'

'I doubt it will be the first time for that.' Anne smoothed the gloves over each finger.

'And I don't doubt it'll be the last time folk'll have respect for you. Can't you see by going into that – that place you be leaving yourself with not a shred of reputation barring the sort any wench be better without!'

Unity's concern was well founded. Anne smoothed the belted jacket of her velour suit. Maybe no decent woman would speak to her after news of what she was about to do reached their ears, but right now that was the least of her worries. It was one thing turning up on that doorstep, getting into its hallowed halls was quite another.

'If you must go then at least wait for Laban, let him go along of you.'

'No.' A quick shake of the head added emphasis to Anne's answer. 'This is something I wish to do alone. I understand your fretting and I love you for it but I cannot let that alter what has to be done; all I care about is your respect, yours and Laban's, I pray that will not be taken from me.'

'Oh my little wench!' Gathering the slight figure into her arms, Unity held it close to her breast, her words a whisper. 'That'll never be took from you nor will the love we holds for you. Matthew and Luke were the breath of my body, the blood in my veins, but what the Lord took with one hand He replaced with the other; He took my sons but sent me a frightened lonely girl, He sent me you . . . you to become the beat of my heart, the light which lifts the darkness from my soul.'

Would what she planned reflect upon the couple she had grown to love so much . . . would people refuse to associate with them as they would with her? Clasped in Unity's arms Anne felt her resolve waver. They had done so much for her . . . but then so had all those men like Abel, they had done so much for everyone and she could not ignore that.

It would have been so easy to have changed her mind and stayed in the house, Unity would have seen that as the sensible thing to do and maybe it would have been so, but what would it have achieved? Questions running in her brain every bit as rapidly as the tap of boots on the setts she hurried along Church Street. She would go by way of Waverley Road; with so few houses there would be less chance of being seen to turn into Slater Street whose only building was the locally known 'Temple'. It was a strange name to give to an establishment gossip said practised more than gambling behind its doors.

The carefully shrouded windows of houses afforded little comfort as she hurried past them but the sudden wide emptiness and the spacious grounds of Templeton House were positively forbidding. She could run past the old square building set back among its screen of trees, run on to the end of the street and turn the corner into Victoria Road; there would be people there, folk hurrying about their business.

But what of her business, the matter which had brought

her here tonight, was that to be forgotten . . . was she to turn her back on Darlaston as her father had done?

To her left the pillars of the old house, each topped with a stone phoenix, rose black against the night sky. Out of the ashes of the old a new life arose. For this once-graceful home its new life was not one of pride; bought by a group of industrialists for the purpose of combined business meetings it was thought by many to serve for meetings of a very different nature.

A glorified whorehouse! Unity had spat her own description. Decent folk don't even have the hearse go past that place! And she must not go past . . . she must go in.

'You sure you're in the right place?' Heavily rouged beneath a coating of face powder, her lips an unnatural shade of red, a woman raised a pencilled eyebrow.

Blinking in light strong after the unlit road, Anne nodded. 'If Mr Thomas Bradley is here then I am in the right place.'

'Hmmm, Thomas Bradley, you say?' The woman cast a long disparaging glance. 'Not his usual choice but then he does like variety. You will find him in there.' Pointing with a fan, an amused smile on her painted mouth, she swept away in a rustle of perfumed taffeta.

Getting in had not been difficult after all. Anne breathed deeply, gathering courage. Would getting out be as simple?

The room to which she had been directed was large and square, a many-crystalled chandelier hanging from an intricately designed stucco ceiling throwing glittering shafts of light over gilt-framed portraits, the eyes of their long-gone subjects seeming to rest on Anne stood in the doorway.

During her childhood and often in her teens, while constantly following behind her father, she had asked her mother to describe the home they had left behind, but though the descriptions of Butcroft House had made it sound so grand

and conjured many dreams, none of them could match the tasteful splendour of what she looked at now.

Momentarily overcome Anne stared. Around the perimeter of a beautifully patterned blue carpet, a polished parquet floor gleamed beneath caressingly subdued crystal wall lamps while delicate porcelain figurines posed on elegant side tables.

'That is Mr Thomas Bradley.'

The perfumed woman who had swept away now stood at her elbow. Having almost forgotten the reason for being here Anne brought her gaze reluctantly to the table where another woman whispered close to the ear of a heavy-set man, a thick, gold watch chain draped across a dark green waistcoat.

'Who?' he asked, irritated at being interrupted. 'Who d'you say?'

The whisper having been repeated, eyes enrolled in fat looked directly at Anne and when he spoke it was with dismissive sarcasm.

'I don't remember invitin' you here.' The jowled face, with its elaborate adornment of side whiskers, turned back to the game of cards.

'There are quite a few things you do not remember, one of them seemingly being your wife.' Anne faced the man flanked on both sides by young women, their giggles suddenly stilled.

A bomb exploding in the centre of the room could not have had a more profound effect. Each of the several tables fell silent, all heads turning to watch in disbelief.

'What the bloody hell did you say?' His eyes almost out of their sockets, the heavy frame half rising from his chair, the man flung the hand of cards across the table.

Fighting the turbulence in her veins Anne forced herself to answer calmly. 'I think you heard what I said but should I be mistaken then I will repeat it more loudly. I said one of the things you have seemingly forgotten is your wife.'

Colour riding above a white winged collar painted his heavy face with fury as Bradley rose, kicking the delicate spindle-legged chair backwards. 'D'you know who you be talkin' to?' he snarled. 'I'll wring your bloody neck!'

'We all know who she is talking to.' An amused voice called over the startled hush. 'But what we are interested in is what she is here for . . . she's not exactly dressed for entertainment.'

'I don't care what her be here for—'

'Oh come on now, Bradley,' the voice intervened again, 'let the wench say her piece, we could all do with a diversion . . . then you can wring her bloody neck.'

Above a chorus of laughter coupled with assenting shouts the voice called again. 'Speak up, wench, let's all hear what you have to say, but first tell us your name.'

'The name be Corby.' Bradley's snarl was vicious. 'This be Jacob Corby's spawn, the wench who thinks to be in the business of iron and steel.'

'Not thinks.' Anne's gaze travelled over each table, its steady assuredness stilling the laughter of each man in turn. 'I am in that business and have every intention of remaining so and should the manufacturer of iron ore whose works are situated at Darlaston Green have the slightest sense at all he will recognise that fact.'

Thomas Bradley's splutter rose above the quick, amazed gasps of the daringly gowned and painted women and the half-amused laughs of their gambling companions. His clenched fist striking the table, sending coins jumping in the air, he glared at the girl daring to speak to him as no man in the town would. 'Be you –' lips drew back emphasising his fury '– be you threatening me?'

He could strike her where she stood, one blow of that hammer fist would probably save him the trouble of wringing her neck.

'Not only you.' Her answer sounding calm though every nerve jangled, Anne looked from the suffused face to others now watching with new interest. 'It is not a threat but a message and it is for every man like you, those who scheme to take every delivery of ore for himself, those who withhold materials simply to prevent a woman using them.'

'So how d'you propose to alter what we do? Invade us with the British army!'

'Not quite.' Anne ignored the sniggers. 'The one I will bring will prove far more formidable.'

Thomas Bradley's laugh bounced over the tables, the confident roar of it finding several echoes in the throats of the assembled works and mine owners. To be threatened by a slip of a girl . . . this was amusement of a different kind.

Standing the fallen chair back on its legs the portly figure sat down, podgy hands reaching for the scattered cards. 'You have we all trembling in we boots, so what is this army you be threatening to bring?'

Had she really made a mistake, would her words make any difference . . . what would Unity say? As if given by the woman herself the answer rang clear: *words only make a difference if they be said.* Drawing a deep breath, Anne said hers.

'It is an army of women. There are hundreds in Darlaston, women with husbands, sons, fathers and brothers fighting a war so you and they can live in safety, every day risking their lives to keep this country free. Imagine what those women will do when they hear of vital supplies being kept from their men because you and others in this room resent a woman being part of what you see as a man's business, you whose petty ignorance enhances the odds of their loved ones being killed through not having that with which to fight. Those hundreds will become thousands as every town within miles learns of what you are doing; they will sweep over you in a great tide which will not recede until every stick and stone of your little empire is destroyed.'

Taking a five-pound note from the table, Thomas Bradley folded it into a slim strip, his fingers following its path as he pushed it into the low décolletage neckline of his giggling friend for the night. 'And who be going to tell this army?' Fat fingers stroked the half-exposed breasts. 'Or do that also be a part of your fantasy?'

It was sickening to watch the flabby lips close wetly over the heavily carmined mouth. Gossip was not unfounded in what it said about the 'Temple'. There was nothing to prevent his doing the same to her. Anne's nerves flicked disturbingly, yet somehow her reply sounded unafraid. 'It is a part of no fantasy but it is a part of fact; that fact being Jacob Corby's spawn will tell them.'

'You!' Bradley roared loud as before. 'And how do you propose to do that?'

Quiet as he was loud Anne gave her answer. 'Through the newspapers. This may come as a surprise to you, Mr Bradley, but women can read and they will certainly read what I have to tell them and, make no mistake about it, they will act . . .' Pausing enough to let her gaze touch each astonished face she went on, 'This war has taught women many things and if you are wise, gentlemen, you will allow it to teach you one also. Women are here to stay!'

28

'You went to the "Temple" . . . you mean you actually went inside!' Laban shook his head in disbelief.

'Not only that but her told Thomas Bradley good an' proper, her said—'

Laban raised a hand, halting Unity in mid-sentence. 'I think it best her tells it herself.'

She must have repeated the whole event at least half a dozen times, each telling continuously interrupted by Unity whose questions grew in number with every one. Patiently Anne began all over, glad of Laban's quick frown or tiny negative shake of the head which prevented Unity's repeating her own performance.

'Eeh, wench,' he said when she finished, 'Thomas Bradley meks a bad enemy.'

Halfway through cutting a slice of bread from the loaf, Unity snorted. 'Hmmph, he don't make a good friend neither judgin' by what a body hears in the town! Seems it ain't only the Glebe he be snatchin' iron ore from, there be cries of shortage from them as works at the Vulcan foundry and John Tolley's place along of the Green, add that to the talk coming from the Nut and Bolt, the Albion Screw and Rivet and two or three others who all says the same thing . . . they gets to make less each week as goes by. I reckons that them men hearing what Anne had to say will be already puttin' two and two together and Thomas Bradley knows they won't come up with three, they'll see him as he really is, so crooked he couldn't lie straight in a bed! They'll soon realise who be drinkin' from their pot and be like to break it over his head, and if they don't then the women of this town will.'

'It be all well and good to talk,' Laban answered, 'but Thomas Bradley be slippery as fish in the Tame . . .'

'Ar . . . and tastes just as bad!'

'That be my Unity,' Laban grinned at Anne, 'got a plaster for every sore.'

It was true, Unity was ever ready with an answer; hopefully the one she had just given would prove true. But if it did not, if Thomas Bradley continued to snatch each consignment of iron ore, would she carry out her own threat? Holding the supper plates in her hand Anne stared at the cloth-covered table, the pretty pattern of scarlet poppies at its corners suddenly becoming patches of blood, the blood of men injured . . . of men killed . . . and she knew. Yes, she would carry out her threat if need dictated; she would reach out to every woman in the country, and they would not let her down.

She had not told Unity everything despite the questions. She had not spoken of the painted women, of the gowns which her friend would have said 'showed more flesh than you sees in a butcher's window', or of the five-pound note tucked where a man's fingers ought not to be. The whole room with its gambling cards, its glasses of brandy and giggling, fawning women, had reeked of more than perfume and cigar smoke; it had held an aroma of something else, of something she never wanted to remember yet never quite forgot; it held the memory of the inn at Radiyeska. True, the room in the old Templeton House had not the stench of dirt and grease as had the inn in that Russian village, nor had the people in it been dressed in foul, evil-smelling furs and unwashed linen, yet their finery had not hidden the looks she had been given, the mocking smiles of the women, the lustful stares of their companions. That was what had unnerved her most, the looks she had seen as some of those men had watched her; they were the eyes which stared in her nightmares.

Not wanting to be caught in the mesh of dreams, even waking ones, Anne reached for her nightgown, slipping it over her head before going to the drawer which held the letter. Forgetting the braiding of hair which fell in rippling folds about her shoulders, she took the envelope, holding it to her breast. This was what had given her the courage to go to that place, to face Thomas Bradley.

Carrying the envelope to the bed she sat. Unity and Laban had asked so many questions, going over every detail of that visit and she had answered, yet deep inside she had wanted to be alone, to read again the letter from a soldier, a man she could not thank, for the only address given was the solitary word, France.

Who was the man who had taken the trouble to write? Was it a man or, as the composition of his letter suggested, a lad for whom schooling had been as brief as for some of those she knew were already working in the munitions factories and foundries? A lad who had lied about his age in order to join the army? Slipping the sheets of paper free she opened the first, her gaze scanning the uncertain script. Unity had read this and her look too had shown gratitude as she finished, but she had barely glanced at the second sheet, the one which bore the name Anne.

Holding it now closer to the lamp beside her bed she read slowly, absorbing every line of the clear strong hand, anxious not to miss even a comma.

My dear Anne,

Forgive my writing, I know it is a liberty I should not take but in a few moments our unit will be part of a special offensive and it could be I will not have another chance. I want only to

say how much I valued our friendship . . . how I value it still;
that ever since we were children you have held a special place
in my heart, and it is thought of you keeps that heart alive in
these regions of hell. I thank you for that friendship as I thank
Unity and Laban for theirs.
   God keep you, Anne.
   Abel

. . . it is thought of you keeps that heart alive . . .

The music of those few words played like an anthem in her
mind as she touched the paper to her lips.

She had been special to him – she looked again at the letter
– special only in friendship it was true but she would carry
those words in her heart for ever.

Returning the pages to the envelope she slipped it under
her pillow, then, putting out the lamp, crossed the room to sit
beneath the moon-dappled window. Was it night where Abel
was, was the moon as bright? Did it bathe those awful trenches
she had heard wounded men talk of in the same liquid silver
light? Did Abel think of her when he looked at it?

Touching her fingers to the glass she traced the pale
feathery streaks. 'God keep you too, Abel,' she whispered,
'God keep you, my love.'

. . . part of a special offensive . . .

Anne thought of the words contained in the letter old Mrs
Davies had brought to her all those weeks ago, weeks in which
she had hoped another might follow if only in the same way,
weeks in which, like so many other women, she had poured
her prayers into the ears of God, prayers asking Abel be kept
alive. But there had been no more letters, no word from him
or his unknown friend.

'Be this all right, Miss Anne?'

Caught by the question she glanced at the girl watching

her with wine-dark eyes, her pert nose covered with freckles. Taking the proffered strap she examined it closely, the only way she had learned satisfied the hard-working girl.

'It's very neat, Amy,' she smiled handing back the finished strap, 'keep that up and the saddlers will find themselves with a competitor.'

The girl grinned, pleased at the compliment, but her answer came with a shake of her head. 'That don't never be like to happen, the leather 'aves jobs as be only done by men an' no matter how clever a wench's hands they won't never do no cutting out nor no assembling of the pieces together. We can do the stitching but when it comes to the meking of a saddle and the likes of special work like that it needs skills a woman won't never be learned.'

Anne moved on, an encouraging smile given to each girl working the sewing machines, to each woman at her clamp. What Amy had said was true enough three years ago but with this war things had changed. Before that women had never been taught or even thought to serve as conductresses on trams, as railway clerks, ticket collectors or porters; they had not dreamed of becoming 'munitionettes', filling shells with explosives which turned their skin and hair yellow, or of replacing their menfolk in the making of chains and bricks: there had been many changes in many walks of life so who was to say a woman could never become a saddle-maker?

Setting work aside as Unity rang a brass bell announcing midday break, the women and girls brought out their respective packages of sandwiches while Anne turned to the kettle simmering on a round, cast-iron stove.

'Well, that were how I 'eard it!'

A plaintive voice rose on a note of pique while a chorus of quieter ones murmured anxiously.

'I tells you, I heard plain as I hears you now. It were in Billingsley's tobacco shop in Victoria Road. Dick Billingsley were serving a man and they was talking about the numbers of casualties, said as there was hundreds . . . nobody knowed truly how many.'

'Might not have been our lads, could have been the other side, you might not have heard the all of it.'

'Hmmph.' Indignation undisguised the first woman rallied her defence. 'I don't be deaf Maudie Sinkins, and I don't be daft neither. I was left to stand 'til that man were served and I heard every word was said.'

'We can be sure of that, Maudie.'

A chorus of laughter circled the table where the women sat to eat bread and cheese each had wrapped in a piece of cloth. Brewing tea in a large enamelled pot, Anne was only half listening.

'Can't but hear in that shop,' Maudie snapped, 'the place be no bigger than a pocket handkerchief.'

'So what *did* you hear?'

Her audience fully attentive at last Maudie glanced at their faces. 'I heard as how our troops had made this big push in France, gone right over the line and that hundreds was dead and injured in a place called Wipers.'

'Oh my God!' A woman crossed herself while Anne mentally corrected the mispronounced Ypres.

'According to what Billingsley said there was so many hurt and dead the authorities couldn't never bring 'em all home, hundreds he said there was an' that not accounting for them as be missing.'

In the silence Maudie's words brought, the woman who moments before had crossed herself piously now brought an angry fist to the table. 'It be his fault,' she hissed, 'how many more poor souls be going to give life or limb afore the swine of a Kaiser be knocked back? Lord, what wouldn't I give to get my hands round the throat of the wicked bugger!'

Used to the chatter of women lightening the long hours of

the day with conversation, Anne's mind remained with her own thoughts. Abel had written her once, why did he not do so again? Was it because she had sent no reply . . . did he think her affronted, annoyed by his forwardness? But surely he must realise he had put no address . . .

'France!'

The half-scream startling her, Anne set the heavy teapot down with a thud. At the further end of the table a young woman, markedly pregnant, was staring at her with eyes ablaze with fear.

'Millie!' Anne's feet seemed not to touch the floor as she ran to the girl.

'France,' the girl sobbed in Anne's arms, 'my Bill be gone to France, last week they took him . . . he be dead . . . he be dead . . .'

'No – no he is not dead,' Anne soothed the sobbing girl. 'Your husband is safe . . .'

'Give her to me.' Calm yet sympathetic, Unity took the distraught figure, talking softly as she helped the girl to her feet, holding her as she led her from the room. 'Nobody has said your Bill be dead but I be saying this . . . he won't be too pleased should all this crying and carrying on harm that babby you have inside you.'

Watching Unity and her charge pass from the room, another of the women shook her head. 'I wonder do that there Kaiser see the horrors of this war, do he place a care on the suffering of men or the tears of women . . . do he not realise the wickedness of his actions?'

Sat on a stool the oldest among them, a grey-haired woman, her shoulders stooped from years of labour, raised her head. Eyes clear despite her years commanded silence as they passed from face to face before she spoke.

'Don't mek no difference what the Kaiser says nor what he feels nor don't feel. This war be not his doin' nor do the horrors of it be in his keeping to end when he sees fit.' The woman's look came to rest on Anne, a look filled with deep and ancient knowledge. 'It be evil stalks the world, evil which sets man against man . . . the evil of Satan hisself. 'Tis that Dark One had the mekings of this war, one we thinks so vile it won't never come again, but Satan don't never be satisfied and evil always will find a way.'

Evil will find a way.

The words of her father! The woman's look had dropped away and the others were once more talking among themselves but Anne was suddenly in a world of her own, a world where Jacob Corby stood with Bible in one hand, his thin wasted frame almost lost among swirling, wind-driven flakes of snow as he raised the other towards a gathering of muttering people, their bodies swathed in thick furs. But it seemed his glittering, fever-filled eyes looked only at a young, pale-faced girl shivering with cold as he uttered the well-known words. *Evil . . . evil will find a way.*

Had it found a way . . . found it through her? Had the pendant once worn by the monk Rasputin truly been endowed with the evil of Satan . . . was she responsible for . . . ?

Pressing her fingers into her sides to hide their trembling, Anne forced her legs to carry her from the room.

'That woman has a mouth as big as a parish oven!' Unity threw the potato she had peeled into the pot. 'And her mind be like rich folk, wanders all over the place while learning nothin' . . . all her talks be a load o' mullock!'

But it was not rubbish Maudie had talked. Anne peeled another sprout, cutting an X in the base before putting it with those ready for cooking. The newspaper stands she had passed coming through the town had all carried headlines, some saying 'Forward Offensive at Ypres', others declaring 'Heavy Losses at Passchendaele'. Was that the special offensive Abel had mentioned in his letter, was he among the injured . . . among the dead?

Catching the quiet sob, Unity laid her knife aside. 'What be it, wench?' she asked gently. 'And don't go telling me it be nothin' 'cos I knows better. I watched you all through the eating o' dinner, you spoke hardly a word to anybody; you was as near breaking point as were young Millie . . . that were why I asked you to take her home.'

Unable to hold the tears any longer Anne covered her face with her hands. 'That – that offensive—'

'That bloody Maudie!' Unity pushed away from the table. 'Her mouth be open so often I wonders her tongue don't get sunburnt!'

'It – it isn't what Maudie said,' Anne sobbed behind her fingers, 'it's – it's Abel.'

Stopped in her tracks Unity stared at the bent head. 'Abel? What be the lad to do with you crying? Do his name be on the list posted on the Town Hall board?'

Lowering her fingers and wiping her eyes on the apron covering her skirts Anne shook her head. 'No – no his name is not on the list.'

'There you be then, all this blartin' be for no need.'

Tears were not always controlled by need. Anne dabbed her eyes again. Taking out the letter she had read on coming home then placed in her pocket, she held it towards Unity. 'It is what Abel said, what he put in his letter. Read it, please, I – I want you to.'

From the mantel shelf above the fireplace the tick of the tin clock filled the silent minute it took for the brief letter to be read then, understanding reflecting in her own moist eyes, Unity nodded.

'Could the offensive Abel speaks of be the same as that Maudie spoke of, the one the newspaper says took place in Passchendaele?'

Handing back the letter, her own voice edged with anxiety she could not completely erase, Unity answered quietly, 'I don't know, wench, and that be the truth of it, we can only wait and pray . . . put our trust in the Lord.'

'Isn't that what we have done these three years!' Flung like an accusation, Anne's words rang with a sharp bitterness. 'And what good has it done? What good can it do against the evil I brought—' It ended with the suddenness with which it had poured out. Anne's glance dropped to the vegetables she had been preparing. She had not intended to speak of the fears still inside her.

'The evil you brought . . . what evil do that be?' Unity let the clock tick the seconds away but her gaze did not move from the girl sat at her table.

'It – it was what my father often said.' In no more than a whisper Anne began the explanation she knew Unity would have before the topic was allowed to rest. 'The same thing was said today by Mary Haddon.'

Without interruption Unity listened to all that had been said during her absence from the workshop, listened to the growing quiver in the voice, watching the mounting tremble of fingers which jerked despite being clasped together.

'Mary 'Addon be an old woman,' she said when Anne finished speaking, 'one who lived too many years in the shadow of her father. He spent more of his time preaching an' spouting the Bible along of Darlaston Green than ever he spent a minding of his wife and family. Always a threatening folk with the devil, forever going on about the ways of evil, but folk d'ain't never take notice, they knowed he was a Roarin' Ranter.'

'A lay preacher too zealous in his own beliefs.' Anne smiled thinly. 'So was my own father.'

'Mebbe yes, mebbe no; what showed in Jacob Corby after his leaving Darlaston I can't be saying. But you never spent the years along of your father Mary 'Addon spent along of hers, your brain don't be completely drubbed clear of common sense like that woman's. Huh . . . evil will find a way, what will her talk of next?'

'But does the church not teach that Satan at his fall was given charge over the earth? If so, does he not have power—'

'Yes, he has power!' Unity snatched the pan of sprouts, setting it above the fire. 'That be the crux of the matter, it be *him*, an' not some pendant, for that be what them tears you've shed be about and not just fears for Abel Preston, though they be for him an' all. You still fears that trinket, that which you carried from Russia, the same thing you took to Bentley Grange, held the power to take life, to create war . . . well, that don't be so. The devil be jealous of what were allowed him by the Lord, and he guards it well, too well to set the smallest part of it in any pendant or anything else a man might use for his own workings. The tales told you be no more than the chains set to bind that fear, to hold you and others as easy influenced tight in its coils. Oh wench . . . wench —' staring at Anne over the top of the salt box now in her hands, Unity's head swung slowly side to side '— you knows yourself it all be foolish superstition, and all the things you puts to it be no more than coincidence.'

Superstition and coincidence! Hours later, lying in her bed, Anne stared into the darkness. Shipwreck, abduction, an accident with a cart . . . all of those things had happened whilst that pendant had been in her possession; and when it was given to Sir Corbett, a car accident followed by his unexpected death . . . could they all be coincident?

Falling into sleep Anne stared into a nut-brown face enlivened by brilliant blackberry eyes, a wrinkled mouth repeating softly, *it will reach again . . . reach again.*

29

There had been many names listed on bulletins since the announcement of the battle at Ypres which Maudie had talked of, but the one she looked for was never among them. Nor had there been any word at the Davies' house. Worry, which was her constant companion, felt sickeningly heavy in Anne's stomach. The woman had welcomed her as always, offering tea, asking would she like to 'pop in next door, see everythin' be all right?' But she had refused, saying she had come simply to enquire of a friend. The old eyes had looked keenly at her then and she had turned quickly away, not wanting to admit to what she saw in them and what she realised could not be hidden from her own . . . the deep look which said it was more than friendship brought her to this house every week.

If only she knew, if there was someone she could ask, someone who would tell her whether Abel were dead or alive. But, as Laban had pointed out, she had no number or regiment, only a name to go on, and in the chaos of war . . . He had not needed to say more, that if Abel were among those 'missing in action' the authorities would be unable to answer. Unity's advice had been more precise: '*You must wait and pray.*' Turning left into Pinfold Alley, Anne admitted Unity was right. All she could do was pray.

'There you be, miss; two packets of Shag, two of Erinmore and four packets of Woodbines. I'm sorry it couldn't be more but baccy isn't easy got these days.'

'It is very kind of you, Mr Watts.' Anne counted coins into

the hand of the smiling tobacconist. 'I'm certain the men in the convalescent unit will bless your name.'

'Well, you tell 'em I be wishing them all a speedy return to 'ealth. Now you tek care going back, the Alley be dark most nights, but when there be no moon . . . Well, like I says, you tek care.'

Pushing purse, tobacco and cigarettes into the bag Unity had half filled with provisions from her own pantry in answer to the regular appeals by newspapers that anyone who could spare an item of food donate it to the hospitals, Anne smiled at a man holding the door of the small, dimly lit shop touching his flat cap with a 'G' night, miss' as she passed.

Mr Watts had not exaggerated when saying the Alley was dark. Anne walked quickly from the isolated shop making sure her feet lifted well clear of the uneven setts. Once in the broader Pinfold Street the dull gleam afforded by the carefully shaded windows of a condensed line of shops would alleviate the darkness.

Hearing the sound of wheels coming from behind, she stepped closer in against the wall of a house. Carriages did not often drive through the Alley. Glancing up to the driving seat as the vehicle halted alongside she saw the hand raised above a head, the whip it held beginning a downward journey, heard a voice grate, harsh and angry.

'You think your threats worry me, that I'll dance to your tune . . .'

With the last word the thick handle struck hard across her neck, sending Anne twisting against the wall.

'. . . women be here to stay, you says . . .'

The whip struck again, knocking her head-first against the rough brick, and the darkness of the Alley became a living, suffocating blackness wrapping itself around her.

'. . . well, Thomas Bradley be telling this . . . you won't be one of 'em!'

Words and blows became a blur following after her into the void.

'I knows what you says and I knows what I think and the two don't be the same thing.' Unity sponged the darkening bruise on Anne's forehead. 'A trip over the setts could set you stumblin' into a wall, givin' you a nasty knock to the head, but it don't set weals across your neck nor shoulders neither, so how do you explain the ones you 'ave?'

'I can't,' Anne answered through a throbbing headache.

'That be my backside of a tale, what you means is you won't!' Unity's tongue was sharp but the hand applying cooling Witch Hazel was gentle.

'I – I tripped and fell.'

'You fell right enough but it were no trip of the foot sent you head-first into that wall, it were a blow, in fact I thinks it were several blows and ain't nothing you say will alter my mind to that.' Unity set the bottle of Witch Hazel on the small bedside table then, using the corner of a scrap of clean white rag, smoothed a little Germolene ointment over Anne's broken skin.

'There, that be what the doctor advised afore he was rushed away to see to an accident. Now get you into bed and I'll fetch you up a cup of tea, but nothing for that headache, doctor says there could be risk of concussion.' Gathering up her utensils Unity ignored the question 'What accident?'

Had someone else been injured . . . had Thomas Bradley used that whip handle on another person? Every movement painful Anne removed the towel draped about her breasts, following it with skirt and underclothing. Nausea sweeping over her, she let the nightgown drop over her head, ignoring her uncombed hair, grateful to climb into bed.

She could understand Thomas Bradley striking herself but why another? And who was his other victim?

'There you be.' Unity bustled back into the room, a mug in her hand. 'You drink this while it be hot then get you off to sleep.'

Heaving herself up against the pillows Anne took the tea, sipping first then asking, 'What was the accident the doctor was called to?'

'It were lucky for you a man come out of that baccy shop when he did, he got Mr Watts—'

'Unity, did Thom— was anyone else hurt beside myself?'

Sighing heavily, her hands crossing over her middle, Unity Hurley shook her head. 'I see you'll get no rest until you knows . . . and neither will I. The man who brought you 'ome said he'd seen you in the tobacconist shop, he wanted naught but a box of matches so was out almost as quick as yourself. Said he seen a carriage, he thought it stood still but couldn't be sure, for at that moment one of them train engines blasted its steam whistle and the horse took off as if a torch were held to his rear. Then at the corner with Pinfold Street the wheel of the carriage struck the footpath and it bounced, pitching the driver into the road. The man said the driver were dead, his neck broken when folk picked him up. I suppose it were the constable sent for the doctor, he'd need official certification of death. Anyway the doctor give instruction as to what was to be done for you. Then Mr Watts, knowing where you lived, set you in a hansom and asked the man with the matches to stay long of you 'til you got here.'

Dead! Anne stared at the mug in her hands. Tipped from the carriage! His neck broken!

'The driver,' she whispered, 'who was he?'

A louder sigh emphasising impatience with questions when Anne should be sleeping, Unity replied, 'I thinks you know well who it be but I'll tell you anyway. It were Thomas Bradley, and afore you says anything more you might as well know I don't be sorry! I knows it were him and that he tried to kill you tonight so don't go expectin' no tears from me.'

Left alone Anne drank the tea but when sleep finally came it brought a gypsy's face, its wrinkled mouth repeating . . . *it will reach . . . reach . . .*

It had been ten days since the occurrence in Pinfold Alley and most of the marks were faded almost completely. Anne looked at the sheaf of flowers, their stalks stood in a bucket of water beneath the scullery sink, white carnations with a delicate frill of yellow edging each petal.

There had been a wreath of the same flower, white edged with the mourning colour of purple which, despite Unity's arguments it should not, had been sent to the funeral of Thomas Bradley. It had been a tussle of wills but Unity had eventually agreed the widow would not have known of her husband's intent or of his attack, that the stress and possible heartbreak of losing him was enough for the woman to bear and a little kindness would be appreciated. So the wreath had been delivered.

Now it was time to forget. Laban had been in agreement with her decision, pointing out to his wife there was no proof of what had happened having been more than the result of a fall. Yes, a carriage had been seen, but whose carriage and had it come to a halt? The alley had been pitch dark, the man was not certain . . . Unity had not been pleased but in the end she had recognised it would gain nothing to accuse a dead man.

'Couldn't you wait until tomorrow? It still be a bit soon for you to be out and about.'

Anne smiled at the woman who had come into the scullery. The hair was a little greyer than it had been when she had first taken a pregnant girl into her home, a few more lines etched the eyes, but the heart was the same; kind, compassionate and loving: the same heart which had cared for and loved a tiny baby and had not once turned away from the mother who had rejected him. Looking now at the face shadowed with concern, Anne felt a rush of warmth. Putting both arms about the slightly stooped shoulders she hugged her. 'I love you, Unity Hurley,' she murmured, 'I love you.'

The cemetery was deserted. Anne glanced about the quiet grounds. Few people visited in mid week unless it was for a funeral. Kneeling beside a small patch of earth she did not hear the grass-muffled tread behind her as she pulled the sprouting weeds.

'There is still no more news of Abel . . .'

She spoke quietly and as she leaned to lay the bunch of carnations against the polished headstone the silent tread came closer.

'. . . there has been no other letter . . .'

Anne talked on, unaware of being watched, of being heard.

'. . . I had hoped after that battle at Ypres . . . but there is no use in hoping . . .'

A little way from her a figure waited and listened, the low sunset casting no shadow of the tall presence.

'. . . I wish you could have known him, Joshua . . .'

Anne's fingers caressed the name carved in the stone.

'. . . Abel Preston was a fine man, he would have been your friend as he was mine, you would have loved him as I loved him, as I will always love him.'

A short, stifled catch of breath betraying she was not alone Anne turned quickly, a scream rising to her throat as hands reached for her.

She was on her feet, her hands held tightly in stronger ones, a deep voice making no impression above the fear so suddenly gripping her.

'Anne.' The strong hands shook her once. 'Anne, it's me,

it's me. I'm sorry, I didn't mean to frighten you . . . Anne, it's me!'

The revolving carousel of trees and shapes, that moments before had been St Lawrence churchyard, slowed and the voice began to penetrate.

'I shouldn't have come up behind you like that, I should have waited but when Unity said where you were—'

'Abel!' Held in his, Anne's hands trembled, her eyes opening wide in disbelief. 'Abel, oh Abel! I thought . . . I thought . . .'

'Not that I was some freak out for a good time?'

That smile . . . how she had missed that smile. She freed her hands, afraid somehow her true feelings would show in their shaking.

Watching the sharp turn of the head, the glow of sunset adorning chestnut hair with the glint of rubies, quick tears glistening like the first dew of morning in the soft hazel eyes, Abel's insides lurched with an old familiar stab. This was what had kept him alive day after endless, shell-pounded day, what had kept him going through long sleepless nights; the thought, the hope of seeing this beloved face again.

'When did you arrive? Where have you been staying? How long have you been home?' Knowing she must speak yet knowing also she could not speak what was in her heart Anne let the questions tumble one after the other.

'Which one would you like answered first?'

He was smiling again. Didn't he know what that smile did to her, didn't he know? But of course he did not know, he must never know. Anne pulled her thoughts together but as she turned to leave the churchyard she could not entirely hide the yearning as she asked, 'Why did you write only once?'

'The letter, Alfred Bunn sent my letter? I should not have written it, not have asked him to send it, what good could it do!'

'Did you mean what you wrote, that I held a special place in your heart?'

Christ, don't let her look at him like that. How much was a man expected to take before breaking! His body tense against the strain of his feelings, lips tightly drawn, Abel tried to hold back the words but they pushed free in an almost angry demand.

'Did you mean what I heard you say a few minutes ago, the words you spoke over Joshua's grave? Did you, Anne?'

He was so tall, this man she loved. For long seconds Anne stared into the navy eyes and for the first time read the truth of what lay in their depths. 'Yes,' she answered softly, 'yes, Abel, I meant what I said.'

It wasn't a whoop, it wasn't a grunt, it was a deep sob which rose from his very depths and she was in his arms, held close, his mouth seeking her own.

'I did not mean to eavesdrop,' he said a thousand kisses later, 'but I had so long wanted just to be near you, to hear your voice again, I could not force myself to leave, then, when you said those last words, I knew I could not go without speaking to you. Oh my dearest, if you only knew my heart . . . if you knew how much I love you.'

Her heart throbbing with joy Anne lifted her mouth again. 'Tell me, spend the rest of your life telling me . . .' The whisper ceased as his lips closed over her own.

The porch of the ancient church looked out over silent stones bathed now in the scarlet-gold of the lowering sun. Sitting in its shadowed privacy, Abel's arms still reluctant to release her, Anne rested her head against his shoulder.

'I love you so much, Abel,' she said quietly, 'I knew I loved you before you went away.'

Abel's arms tightened. 'And I loved you, my darling, so much I thought it would kill me.'

'I'm so happy it did not.' She smiled against the jacket of his khaki uniform. 'But why did you not speak of your feelings before enlisting?'

His gaze travelling over her head Abel watched the gleaming beauty of sunset painting the church grounds.

'How could I?' he replied. 'You were the daughter of Jacob Corby. You had not only his name but his property; the Glebe Works, Butcroft House and possibly more beside, and I knew that even though you had not yet claimed them the day would come when you would. You would be a wealthy woman while I – I was Abel Preston . . . a saddle-maker with a cottage and a few pounds of savings.'

Pushing a little away from him though not clear of his arms, Anne looked at the face half lost amid the lengthening shadows.

'That would have made no difference then, it makes none now . . . I love you, Abel. I may have been late in realising it but I have always loved you, even from being a child. I don't care about money or property, it is you I care about: I love Abel Preston and I want to spend the rest of my life with him.'

Abel's smile was gentle, his eyes finding hers darker than the evening shadows which played over them. 'As he does with you,' he said, 'but you can never become Mrs Abel Preston.'

It was sharper than a slap, more cruel than the blows rained on her with that whip. A gasp tearing from her, Anne drew back, staring in disbelief.

'But . . . but you said you love me.'

'I do, more than life itself.'

'Then why?' she asked, trembling. 'Why can I never become Mrs Abel Preston?'

'Because of this.' Taking a paper from the pocket of his jacket he handed it to Anne.

A frown coming to her brows she glanced at it. Was it a marriage certificate? Was the reason she could never become Mrs Abel Preston because the name was already held by some other woman?

'Read it, Anne.'

The words reaching quietly she unfolded the paper, holding it to where the remaining daylight revealed the words.

My son,

Apart from the biological truth of those words I have no right to address you so, but in all the years since begetting you my heart has loved you. That cannot be an excuse for my never owning you nor is it offered as one, it is simply a statement of fact.

I was a lad of twenty-seven when you were conceived, your mother a girl of sixteen. My grandmother would not countenance marriage, of her grandson to a chambermaid, it would bring disgrace to her house and dishonour to the family name. Bound also by the terms of my late father's Will, I had not a penny of my own until my thirtieth birthday, so agreed to my grandmother taking matters into her own hands. To her dying day I did not know how. Your mother was entered into a private hospital where she died giving birth, you following an hour later. That was the story given me and only after my grandmother's passing did I find out you still lived.

By that time you were past your twenty-third year . . . already a man. So why did I not come to you then? The answer is I could not bear the hate and resentment I would see in your eyes. You were happy with Mrs Davies and I could not take that happiness from you, yet neither could I justify keeping your true heritage from you.

I was allowed to make registration of your birth due to the auspices of the Registrar General who declared himself satisfied with the evidence laid before him and with the affidavit I signed before Magistrates. Those documents, together with this letter, I leave to be forwarded after my death.

I pray one day you might come to think kindly of me.

Corbett Foley, Kg.

Abel took the paper, slipping it back into his pocket. 'You see,' he smiled, 'you see why you cannot become Mrs Abel Preston.'

Still shocked by what she had read Anne could only whisper, 'You – you are Sir Corbett's son!'

'Yes, and as my father's son I ask you to take his name, I ask you to become Mrs Abel Foley.'

Reaching her once more into his arms he looked deeply into shining eyes. 'Will you, my darling?' he whispered. 'Will you marry me?'

His mouth on hers, her heart bursting with love, Anne heard an echo of words drifting back from the past.

. . . you are home . . .

Yes, she was home. Nestled in the arms of the man she loved with all her heart she let the words sing. The unhappiness which had dogged her life was over. The imagined powers invested in a pendant, those silly tales and superstitions, misfortune or coincidence, which she had allowed to fill her mind with shadows of fear were over; the nightmare was ended. Abel loved her and soon this terrible war must end.

Across the quiet churchyard the shimmering red-gold of the sun's departing bathed the earth with beauty.

With a smile in her heart, Anne turned to meet Abel's kiss. There would be no more shadows of fear.